THE DEVIL'S STAR

"*The Devil's Star* is a big, ambitious, wildly readable story. . . . It's compelling. Harry Hole . . . can be compared to the early, hard-drinking, rebellious Harry Bosch of Michael Connelly's series. . . . But Nesbø's novels are . . . more expansive than Connelly's; he's willing to slow the crime-solving process to introduce strange characters and odd corners of Oslo. In this he sometimes recalls Ian Rankin's John Rebus novels with their rich, far-flung portrait of Edinburgh. . . . It's a novel worth reading, for its characters, for the quality of its writing, and for its wealth of detail."
—*Washington Post*

"It's fascinating to watch this Norwegian author adapt our homegrown monster [the serial killer] to a foreign culture. . . . Harry Hole . . . brilliant . . . no one is better. . . . A plot that speeds along like a bullet train."
—*New York Times Book Review*

"There's Nordic noir, and then there's Nesbø noir. Jo Nesbø's reputation as the reigning bad boy of Norwegian crime fiction has grown steadily in the USA with the critically acclaimed novels *The Redbreast* and *Nemesis* and now *The Devil's Star*. . . . Hole and the killer eventually converge in this sordid, suspenseful tale that veritably drips with blood and angst."
—*USA Today*

"The most brilliant detective on the Oslo force. . . . Hole and *The Wire*'s Jimmy McNulty were separated at birth. . . . A gritty, gripping thriller."
—*Entertainment Weekly*

"The plot lines begin an intricate, inventive intersection. Hole reminds me of Michael Connelly's Harry Bosch, an all-too-human tough guy who is absolutely committed to doing the right thing by any means necessary and damn the consequences. Nesbø winds in strands from previous Harry Hole novels (which have won all sorts of international awards) as he keeps the surprises coming and the suspense high."
—*Times-Picayune* (New Orleans)

"A tight, suspenseful mystery. . . . [Nesbø's] narrative is swift and suspenseful. His characters have more depth and ambiguity than those in most thrillers. His plotting is so clever that it begs to be read as self-parody."
—*Pittsburgh Post-Gazette*

© Peter Knutson

About the Author

Jo NESBØ is a musician, songwriter, economist, and one of Europe's most critically acclaimed and successful crime writers. His first novel featuring Police Detective Harry Hole was an instant hit in Norway, winning the Glass Key for Best Nordic Crime Novel of the Year— the most prestigious crime-writing award in Northern Europe. Nesbø lives in Oslo.

Jo Nesbø

The Devil's Star

TRANSLATED
FROM THE NORWEGIAN
BY

Don Bartlett

HARPER PERENNIAL

NEW YORK • LONDON • TORONTO • SYDNEY • NEW DELHI • AUCKLAND

A hardcover edition of this book was published in 2010 by HarperCollins Publishers.

THE DEVIL'S STAR. Copyright © 2003 by Jo Nesbø. English-language translation copyright © 2005 by Don Bartlett. All rights reserved. Printed in the United States of America. No part of this book may be used or reproduced in any manner whatsoever without written permission except in the case of brief quotations embodied in critical articles and reviews. For information, address HarperCollins Publishers, 195 Broadway, New York, NY 10007.

HarperCollins books may be purchased for educational, business, or sales promotional use. For information, please e-mail the Special Markets Department at SPsales@harpercollins.com.

Grateful acknowledgement is made for permission to reprint from the following: Lyrics from 'I Got a War' by Gluecifer; reprinted by permission of Universal Music Publishing, AB, Sweden. Lyrics from 'Noen Å Hate'; music and lyrics: Michael Krohn © Air Chrysalis Norway AS, printed by permission.

First published in Norway as *Marekors* in 2003 by H. Aschehoug & Co. (W. Nygaard), Oslo.

Published in Great Britain in 2004 by Harvill Secker, an imprint of Random House.

FIRST HARPER PAPERBACK PUBLISHED 2011.
REISSUED IN HARPER PERENNIAL 2017.

Map by Reginald Piggott

Library of Congress Cataloging-in-Publication Data is available upon request.

ISBN 978-0-06-113398-5 (pbk.)

17 18 19 20 21 LSC 20 19 18 17 16

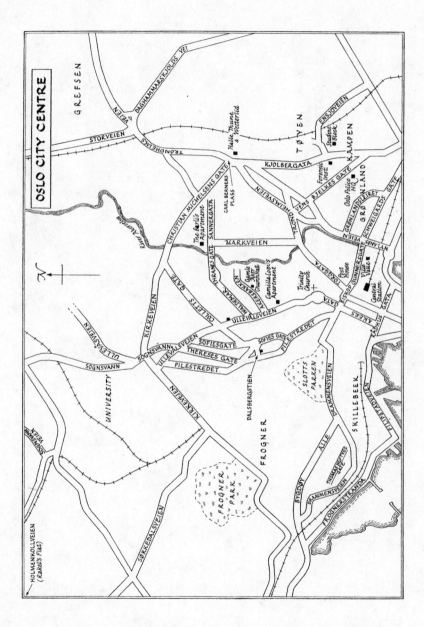

OSLO CITY CENTRE

Part One

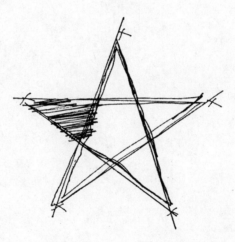

1

Friday. Egg.

THE HOUSE WAS BUILT IN 1898 ON A CLAY BASE THAT HAD SINCE sunk a tiny bit on the west-facing side, causing water to cross the wooden threshold where the door was hung. It ran across the bedroom floor and left a wet streak over the oak parquet, moving west. The flow rested for a second in a dip before more water nudged it from behind and it scurried like a nervous rat towards the skirting board. There the water went in both directions; it searched and somehow sneaked under the skirting until it found a gap between the end of the wooden flooring and the wall. In the gap lay a five-kroner coin bearing a profile of King Olav's head and the date: 1987, the year before it had fallen out of the carpenter's pocket. But these were the boom years; a great many attic flats had needed to be built at the drop of a hat and the carpenter had not bothered to look for it.

It did not take the water much time to find a way through the floor under the parquet. Apart from when there was a leak in 1968 – the same year a new roof was built on the house – the wooden floorboards had lain there undisturbed, drying and contracting so that the crack between the two innermost pine floorboards was now almost half a centimetre. The water dripped onto the beam beneath the crack and continued westwards and into the exterior wall. There it seeped into the plaster and the mortar that had been mixed one hundred years before, also in midsummer, by Jacob Andersen, a master bricklayer and father of five. Andersen, like all bricklayers in Oslo at that time, mixed his own mortar and wall plaster. Not only did he have his own unique blend of lime, sand and water, he also had his own special ingredients: horsehair and pig's blood. Jacob Andersen was of the opinion that the hair and the blood held the plaster together and gave it extra strength. It was not his idea, he told his head-shaking colleagues at the time, his Scottish father and grandfather had used the same ingredients from sheep. Even though he had renounced his Scottish surname and taken on a trade name he saw no reason to turn his back on six hundred years of heritage. Some of the bricklayers considered it immoral, some thought he was in league with the Devil, but most just laughed at him. Perhaps it was one of the latter who spread the story that was to take hold in the burgeoning town of Kristania.

A coachman from Grünerløkka had married his cousin from Värmland and together they moved into a one-room flat plus kitchen in one of the apartment blocks in Seilduksgata that Andersen had helped to build. The couple's first child was unlucky enough to be born with dark, curly hair and brown eyes, and since the couple were blond with blue eyes – and the man was jealous by nature as well – late one night he tied his wife's hands behind her, took her down to the cellar and bricked her in. Her screams were effectively muffled by the thick walls where she stood bound and squeezed between the two brick surfaces. The husband had perhaps thought that she would suffo-cate from lack of oxygen, but bricklayers do allow for ventilation. In the end, the poor woman attacked the wall with her bare teeth. And that might well have worked because as the Scottish bricklayer used blood and hair, thinking that he could save on the expensive lime in the cement mix, the result was a porous wall that crumbled under the attack from strong Värmland teeth. However, her hunger for life sadly led to her taking excessively large mouthfuls of mortar and brick. Ultimately she was unable to chew, swallow or spit and the sand, pebbles and chunks of clay blocked her windpipe. Her face turned blue, her heartbeat slowed and then she stopped breathing.

She was what most people would call dead.

According to the myth, however, the taste of pig's blood had the effect of making the unfortunate woman believe she was still alive. And with that she immediately broke free of the ropes that bound her, passed through the wall and began to walk again. A few old people from Grünerløkka still remember the story from their childhood, about the woman with the pig's head, walking around with a knife to cut off the heads of small children who were out late. She had to have the taste of blood in her mouth so that she didn't vanish into thin air. At the time very few people knew the name of the bricklayer and Andersen worked tirelessly at making his special blend of mortar. Three years later, while working on the building where the water was now leaking he fell from the scaffolding – leaving only two hundred kroner and a guitar – and so it was to be another hundred years before brick-layers began to use artificial hair-like fibres in their cement mixes and before technicians at a laboratory in Milan discovered that the walls of Jericho had been strengthened with blood and camel hair.

Most of the water, however, did not run into the wall, but down it, because water, like cowardice and lust, always finds the lowest level. At first the water was absorbed by the lumpy, granular insulation between the joists, but more followed and soon the insulation was saturated. The water went right through it and soaked up a newspaper dated July 11, 1898, in which it said the building industry's boom time had probably reached its peak and the unscrupulous property specu-lators were sure to have harder times ahead. On page three it said that the police still had no leads regarding the murder of a young nurse who had been found dead from stab wounds in a bathroom the previous week. In May, a girl mutilated and killed in a similar way was found near the River Akerselva, but the police would not say whether the two cases could be connected.

The water ran off the newspaper, between the wooden boards underneath and along the inside of the painted ceiling fabric of the room below. Since this had been damaged during the repair of the leak in 1968, the water seeped through the holes, forming drops that hung on until they became heavy enough for gravity to defy the surface tension; they let go and fell three metres and eight centimetres. There the water landed and terminated its trajectory. Into water.

Vibeke Knutsen sucked hard on her cigarette and blew smoke out of the open window on the fourth floor of the apartment building. It was a warm afternoon and the air rose from the sun-baked asphalt in the back yard, taking the smoke up the light blue house front until it dispersed. On the other side of the roof you could hear the sound of a car in the usually busy Ullevålsveien. But now everyone was on holiday and the town was almost deserted. A fly lay on its back on the windowsill with its six feet in the air. It hadn't had the sense to get out of the heat. It was cooler at the other end of the flat facing Ullevålsveien, but Vibeke didn't like the view from there. Our Saviour's Cemetery. Crowded with famous people. Famous dead people. On the ground floor there was a shop selling 'monuments', as the sign said, in other words, head-stones. What one might call 'staying close to the market'.

Vibeke rested her forehead against the cool glass of the window.

She had been happy when the warm weather came, but her happiness had soon worn off. Even now she was longing for cooler nights and people in the streets. Today there had been five customers in the gallery before lunch and three after. She had smoked one and a half packets of cigarettes out of sheer boredom. Her heart was pounding and she had a sore throat; in fact, she could hardly speak when the boss rang and asked how things were going. All the same, no sooner had she arrived home and put the potatoes on than she felt the craving in the pit of her stomach again.

Vibeke had stopped smoking when she met Anders two years before. He hadn't asked her to. Quite the contrary. When they met on Gran Canaria he had even bummed a cigarette off her. Just for a laugh. When they moved in together, just one month after getting back to Oslo, one of the first things he had said was that their relationship would probably be able to stand a little passive smoking, and that cancer researchers were undoubtedly exaggerating. With a little time he would probably get used to the smell of cigarettes on their clothes. The next morning she made up her mind. When, some days later, he mentioned over lunch that it was a long time since he had seen her with a cigarette in her hand, she answered that she had never really been much of a smoker. Anders smiled, leaned over the table and stroked her cheek.

'Do you know what, Vibeke? That's what I always thought.'

She could hear the pan bubbling behind her and looked at the cigarette. Three more drags. She took the first. It didn't taste of anything.

She could barely remember when it was that she had started smoking again. Perhaps it was last year, around the time he had started staying away for long periods on business trips. Or was it over New Year when she had begun working overtime almost every evening? Was that because she was unhappy? Was she unhappy? They never rowed. They almost never made love either, but that was because Anders worked so hard, he had said, putting an end to any discussion. Not that she missed it particularly. When, once in a blue moon, they did make a half-hearted attempt at love-making it was as if he wasn't really there. So she realised she didn't really need to be there, either.

But they didn't actually row. Anders didn't like raised voices.

Vibeke looked at the clock: 5.15. What had happened to him? Generally he told her if he was going to be late. She stubbed out the cigarette, dropped it into the back yard and turned towards the stove to check the potatoes. She put a fork into the biggest one. Almost done. Some small black lumps bobbled up and down on the surface of the boiling water. Funny. Were they from the potatoes or the pan?

She was just trying to remember what she had last used the pan for when she heard the front door being opened. From the corridor she could hear someone gasping for breath and shoes being kicked off. Anders came into the kitchen and opened the fridge.

'Well?' he asked.

'Rissoles.'

'OK . . . ?' His intonation rose at the end and formed a question mark. She knew roughly what it meant. Meat again? Shouldn't we eat fish a little more often?

'Fine,' he said with flat intonation, leaning over the pan.

'What have you been doing? You're absolutely soaked with sweat.'

'I didn't do any training this evening, so I cycled up to Sognsvann and back again. What are the lumps in the water?'

'I don't know,' Vibeke said. 'I just noticed them.'

'You don't know? Didn't you work as a sort of cook once upon a time?'

In one deft movement he took one of the lumps between his index finger and his thumb and put it in his mouth. She stared at the back of his head. At his thin brown hair that she had once thought was so attractive. Well groomed and just the right length. With a side parting. He had looked so smart. Like a man with a future. Enough future for two.

'What does it taste of?' she asked.

'Nothing,' he said, still bent over the cooker. 'Egg.'

'Egg? But I washed the pan . . .'

She suddenly paused.

He turned round. 'What's the matter?'

'There's . . . a drip.' She pointed to his head.

He frowned and touched the back of his head. Then, in one movement, they both leaned backwards and stared up at the ceiling. There were two droplets hanging from the white ceiling fabric. Vibeke, who was a little short-sighted, wouldn't have seen the drops if they had glistened. But they did not.

'Looks like Camilla's got a flood,' Anders said. 'If you go up and ring her bell, I'll get hold of the caretaker.'

Vibeke peered up at the ceiling. And down at the lumps in the pan.

'My God,' she whispered and could feel her heart pounding again.

'What's the matter now?' Anders asked.

'Go and get the caretaker. Then go with him and ring Camilla's doorbell. I'll call the police.'

2

Friday. Staff Leave.

OSLO POLICE HEADQUARTERS IN GRØNLAND WAS SITUATED AT the top of the ridge between Grønland and Tøyen, and looked over the eastern part of the city centre. It was constructed of glass and steel and had been completed in 1978. There were no sloping surfaces; it stood in perfect symmetry and the architects Telje, Torp & Aasen had received an award for it. The electrician who installed the cables in the two long office wings on the seventh and ninth floors received social benefits and a good bollocking from his father when he fell from the scaffolding and broke his back.

'For seven generations we were bricklayers, balancing between heaven and earth, before gravity brought us down. My grandfather tried to flee from the curse, but it followed him right across the North Sea. So the day you were born I swore to myself that you would not have to suffer the same fate. And I thought I had succeeded. An electrician . . . What the hell is an electrician doing six metres off the ground?'

The signal from the central control room ran through the copper in the exact same cables the son had laid, through the partition between the floors moulded with a factory-made cement mix, up to Crime Squad Chief Inspector Bjarne Møller's office on the sixth floor. At this moment Møller was sitting and wondering whether he was looking forward to or dreading his impending family holiday in a mountain cabin in Os, outside Bergen. In all probability, Os in July meant dire weather. Now, Bjarne Møller had nothing against exchanging the heat-wave that had been forecast for Oslo with a little drizzle, but to keep two highly energetic young boys busy with no resources other than a pack of cards minus its jack of hearts would be a challenge.

Bjarne Møller stretched his long legs and scratched behind his ear as he listened to the message.

'How did they discover it?' he asked.

'There was a leak down to the flat below,' the voice from the control room answered. 'The caretaker and the man from downstairs rang the bell but no-one answered. The door wasn't locked, so they went in.'

'OK. I'll send two of our people up.'

Møller put down the receiver, sighed and ran his finger down the plasticated duty roster which was on his desk. Half the division was on leave. That was the way it was at this time every year. Not that it meant that the population of Oslo was in any particular danger since the villains in the town also seemed to appreciate a little holiday in July. It was definitely low season as far as the law-breaking that fell to the Crime Squad was concerned.

Møller's finger stopped by the name of Beate Lønn. He dialled the number for *Krimteknisk*, the forensics department in Kjølberggata. No answer. He waited for his call to go through the central switchboard.

'Beate Lønn is in the lab,' a bright voice said.

'It's Møller, Crime Squad. Could you get hold of her?'

He waited. It was Karl Weber, the recently retired head of *Krimteknisk*, who had recruited Beate Lønn from the Crime Squad. Møller saw this as further proof of the neo-Darwinist theory that man's sole drive was to perpetuate his own genes. Weber clearly thought that

Beate Lønn shared quite a few genes with him. At first sight, Karl Weber and Beate Lønn would probably have seemed quite different. Weber was grumpy and irascible; Lønn was a small, quiet grey mouse, who, after graduating from Police College, would blush every time you talked to her. But their police genes were identical. They were the passionate type who, when they smelled their prey, had the ability to exclude everything else and simply concentrate on a forensic lead, circumstantial evidence, a video recording, a vague description, until ultimately it began to make some kind of sense. Malicious tongues wagged that Weber and Lønn belonged in the laboratory and not in the community where an investigator's knowledge of human behaviour was still more important than a footprint or a loose thread from a jacket.

Weber and Lønn would agree with what they said about the laboratory, but not about the footprints or the loose threads.

'Lønn speaking.'

'Hello, Beate. Bjarne Møller here. Am I disturbing you?'

'Of course. What's up?'

Møller explained briefly and gave her the address.

'I'll send a couple of my lads up with you,' he said.

'Which ones?'

'I'll have to have a look to see who I can find. Summer break, you know.'

Møller put down the phone and ran his finger further down the list. It stopped at Tom Waaler.

The box for holiday dates was blank. That did not surprise Bjarne Møller. Now and then he wondered whether Inspector Tom Waaler took off any time at all or if he even had time to sleep. As a detective he was one of the department's two star players. Always there, always on the ball and nearly always successful. In contrast with the other top-notch detective, Tom Waaler was reliable, had an unblemished record and was respected by everyone. In short, a dream subordinate. With the indisputable leadership skills that Tom had, it was on the cards that he would take over Møller's job as Chief Inspector when the time came.

Møller's call crackled through the flimsy partitions.

'Waaler here,' a sonorous voice replied.

'Møller. We –'

'Just a moment, Bjarne. I'm on another call.'

Bjarne Møller drummed on the table while he was waiting. Tom Waaler could become the youngest ever Chief Inspector in the Crime Squad. Was it his age that made Bjarne Møller occasionally feel somewhat uneasy at the thought that he would be handing over his responsibilities to Tom? Or perhaps it was the two shooting incidents? The inspector had drawn his gun twice during arrests and, as one of the best marksmen in the police corps, he had hit the target both times with lethal results. Paradoxically enough, Møller also knew that one of the two episodes could ultimately push the appointment of the new Chief in Waaler's favour. SEFO, the independent police investigation authority, had not uncovered anything to suggest that Tom had not fired in self-defence. In fact, it had concluded that in both cases he had shown good judgment and quick reactions in a tight situation. What better credentials could a candidate for the Chief's job have?

'Sorry, Bjarne. Call on the mobile. How can I help you?'

'We've got a job.'

'At last.'

The conversation was over in ten seconds. Now he just needed one more person.

Møller had thought of Halvorsen, but according to the list he was taking his leave at home in Steinkjer. His finger continued down the column. Leave, leave, sick leave. The Chief Inspector sighed when his finger stopped against the name he had been hoping to avoid.

Harry Hole.

The lone wolf, the drunk, the department's enfant terrible and, apart from Tom Waaler, the best detective on the sixth floor. But for that and the fact that Bjarne Møller had over the years developed a sort of perverse penchant for putting his head on the block for this policeman with the serious drinking problem, Harry Hole would have been out years ago. Ordinarily Harry was the first person he would have rung and given the assignment to, but things were not ordinary.

Or to put it another way: they were more extraordinary than usual.

It had all come to a head the month before, after Hole had spent the winter reworking an old case, the murder of his closest colleague, Ellen Gjelten, who was killed close to the River Akerselva. During that time he lost all interest in any other cases. The Ellen Gjelten case had been cleared up a long time ago, but Harry had become more and more obsessed and quite frankly Møller was beginning to worry about his mental state. The crunch came when Harry appeared in his office four weeks ago and presented his hair-raising conspiracy theories. Basically, without any proof he was making fanciful charges against Tom Waaler.

Then Harry simply disappeared. Some days later Møller rang Restaurant Schrøder and learned what he had feared: that Harry had gone on another drinking binge. To cover his absence, Møller put Harry down as on leave. Once again. Harry generally put in an appearance after a week, but now four weeks had passed. His leave was over.

Møller eyed the receiver, stood up and went to the window. It was 5.30 and yet the park in front of the police station was almost deserted. There was just the odd sun worshipper braving the heat. In Grønlandsleiret a couple of shop owners were sitting under an awning next to their vegetables. Even the cars – despite zilch rush-hour traffic – were moving more slowly. Møller brushed back his hair with his hands, a lifetime's habit which his wife said he should give a rest now as people might suspect him of trying to cover his bald patch. Was there really no-one else except Harry? Møller watched a drunk staggering down Grønlandsleiret. He guessed he was heading for the Raven, but he wouldn't get a drink there. He'd probably end up at the Boxer. The place where the Ellen Gjelten case was emphatically brought to a close. Perhaps Harry Hole's career in the police force, too. Møller was being put under pressure; he would soon have to make up his mind what to do about the Harry problem. But that was long term; what was important now was this case.

Møller lifted the receiver and considered for a moment what he was about to do: put Harry Hole and Tom Waaler on the same case. These holiday periods were such a pain. The electrical impulse started on its journey from Telje, Torp & Aasen's monument to an ordered society and began to ring in a place where chaos reigned, a flat in Sofies gate.

3

Friday. The Awakening.

SHE SCREAMED AGAIN AND HARRY HOLE OPENED HIS EYES.

The sun gleamed through the idly shifting curtains as the grating sound of the tram slowing down in Pilestredet faded away. Harry tried to find his bearings. He lay on the floor of his own sitting room. Dressed, though not well dressed. In the land of the living, though not really alive.

Sweat lay like a clammy film of make-up on his face, and his heart felt light, but stressed, like a ping-pong ball on a concrete floor. His head felt worse.

Harry hesitated for a moment before making up his mind to continue breathing. The ceiling and the walls were spinning around, and there was not a picture or a ceiling light in the flat his gaze could cling to. Whirling on the periphery of his vision was an IKEA bookcase, the back of a chair and a green coffee table from Elevator. At least he had escaped any more dreams.

It had been the same old nightmare. Rooted to the spot, unable to move, in vain he had tried closing his eyes to avoid seeing her mouth, distorted and opened in a silent scream. The large, blankly staring eyes with the mute accusation. When he was young, it had been his little sister, Sis. Now it was Ellen Gjelten. At first the screams had been silent, now they sounded like squealing steel brakes. He didn't know which was worse.

Harry lay there quite still, staring out between the curtains, up at the shimmering sun over the streets and back yards of Bislett. Only the tram broke the summer stillness. He didn't even blink. He stared at the sun until it became a leaping golden heart, beating against a thin, milky-blue membrane and pumping out heat. When he was young, his mother told him that if children looked straight into the sun it would burn away their eyesight and that they would have sunlight inside their heads all day long and for all their lives. Sunlight in their heads consuming everything else. Like the image of Ellen's smashed skull in the snow by the Akerselva with the shadow hanging over it. For three years he had tried to catch that shadow. But he hadn't managed it.

Rakel . . .

Harry raised his head cautiously and gazed at the lifeless, black eye of the telephone answer machine. There had been no life in it for however many weeks had passed since his meeting with the head of *Kripos*, the Norwegian CID, at the Boxer. Presumably burned up by the sun as well.

Shit, it was hot in here!

Rakel . . .

He remembered now. At one point in the dream the face had changed and it became Rakel's. Sis, Ellen, Mum, Rakel. Women's faces. As if in one constantly pumping, pulsating movement they could change and merge again.

Harry groaned and let his head sink back down on the floor. He caught a glimpse of the bottle balancing on the edge of the table above him. Jim Beam from Clermont, Kentucky. The contents were gone. Evaporated, vaporised. Rakel. He closed his eyes. There was nothing left.

He had no idea what the time was, he just knew that it was late. Or early. Whatever it was, it was the wrong moment to wake up. Or to be precise, to be asleep. You should do something else at this time of day. Such as drink.

Harry got up onto his knees.

There was something vibrating in his trousers. That, he now realised, was what had woken him. A moth trapped and desperately flapping its wings. He shoved his hand into his pocket and pulled out his mobile phone.

Harry walked slowly towards St Hanshaugen. His headache throbbed behind his eyeballs. The address Møller had given him was within walking distance. He had splashed a little water over his face, found a drop of whisky in the cupboard under the sink and set off hoping that a walk would clear his head. Harry passed Underwater: 4 p.m. till 3 a.m., 4 p.m. till 1 a.m. on Mondays, closed Sundays. This was not one of his more frequent watering holes since his local, Schrøder, was in the parallel street, but like most serious drinkers Harry always had a place in his brain where the opening hours of taprooms were stored automatically.

He smiled at his reflection in the grimy windows. Another time.

At the corner he turned right, down Ullevålsveien. Harry didn't like walking in Ullevålsveien. It was a street for cars, not for pedestrians. The best thing he could say about Ullevålsveien was that the pavement on the right afforded some shade on days like this.

Harry stopped in front of the house bearing the number he had been given. He gave it a quick once-over.

On the ground floor was a launderette with red washing machines. The note on the window gave the opening times as 8.00 till 21.00 every day and offered a 20-minute dry for the reduced price of 30 kroner. A dark-skinned woman in a shawl sat beside a rotating drum, staring out into the air. Next to the launderette was a shop window with head-stones in, and further down, a green neon sign displaying KEBAB HOUSE above a snack-bar-cum-grocer's. Harry's eyes wandered over the filthy house front. The paint on the old window frames had cracked, but the dormer windows on the roof suggested there were new attic conversions on top of the original four floors. A camera was placed over the newly installed intercom system by the rusty iron gate. Money from Oslo's West End was flowing slowly but surely into the East End. He rang the top bell next to the name of Camilla Loen.

'Yes,' the loudspeaker replied.

Møller had warned him, but nevertheless he was taken aback when he heard Tom Waaler's voice.

Harry tried to answer, but could not force a sound from his vocal cords. He coughed and made a fresh attempt.

'Hole. Open up.'

There was a buzzing sound and he grasped the cold, rough door handle of black iron.

'Hi.'

Harry turned round.

'Hi, Beate.'

Beate Lønn was just under average height, with dark blond hair and blue eyes, neither good-looking nor unattractive. In short, there was nothing particularly striking about Beate Lønn, apart from her clothes. She was wearing a white boiler suit that looked a bit like an astronaut's outfit.

Harry held open the gate while she carried in two large metal containers.

'Have you just arrived?'

He tried not to breathe on her as she passed.

'No. I had to come back down to the car for the rest of my stuff. We've been here for half an hour. Hit yourself?'

Harry ran a finger over the scab on his nose.

'Apparently.'

He followed her through the next door leading into the stairwell.

'What's it like up there?'

Beate put the boxes in front of a green lift door, still looking up at him.

'I thought it was one of your principles to look first and ask questions later,' she said, pressing the lift button.

Harry nodded. Beate Lønn belonged to that section of the human race who remembered everything. She could recite details from criminal cases he had long forgotten and from before she began Police College. In addition, she had an unusually well-developed fusiform gyrus – the part of the brain that remembers faces. She had had it tested and the psychologists were amazed. Just his luck that she remembered the little he had managed to teach her when they worked together on the spate of bank robberies that swept Oslo the previous year.

'I like to be as open as possible to my impressions the first time I am at the scene of a crime, yes,' Harry said and gave a start when the lift sprang into action. He began to go through his pockets looking for cigarettes. 'But I doubt that I'm going to be working on this particular case.'

'Why not?'

Harry didn't answer. He pulled out a crumpled pack of Camels from his left-hand trouser pocket and extracted a crushed cigarette.

'Oh yes, now I remember,' Beate smiled. 'You said this spring that you were going to go on holiday. To Normandy, wasn't it? You lucky thing . . .'

Harry put the cigarette between his lips. It tasted dreadful. And it would hardly do anything for his headache, either. There was only one thing that helped. He took a look at his watch. Mondays, 4 p.m. to 1 a.m.

'There won't be any Normandy,' he said.

'Oh?'

'No, so that's not the reason. It's because *he's* running this case.'

Harry took a long drag on his cigarette and nodded upwards.

She gave him a long, hard look. 'Watch out that he doesn't become an obsession. Move on.'

'Move on?' Harry blew out smoke. 'He hurts people, Beate. You should know that.'

She blushed. 'Tom and I had a brief fling, that's all, Harry.'

'Wasn't that the time you were going round with a bruised neck?'

'Harry! Tom never . . .'

Beate stopped when she realised that she was raising her voice. The echo resounded upwards in the stairwell, but was drowned out by the lift coming to a halt in front of them with a brief dull thud.

'You don't like him,' she said. 'So you imagine things. In fact, Tom has a number of good sides you know nothing about.'

'Mm.'

Harry stubbed his cigarette out on the wall while Beate pulled open the door to the lift and went in.

'Aren't you coming up?' she asked, looking at Harry who was still outside intently staring at something. The lift. There was a sliding gate inside the door, a simple iron grille that you push open and close behind you so that the lift can operate. There was the scream again. The soundless scream. He could feel sweat breaking out all over his body. The nip of whisky had not been enough. Nowhere near enough.

'Something the matter?' Beate asked.

'Not at all,' Harry answered in a thick voice. 'I just don't like these old-fashioned lifts. I'll take the stairs.'

4

Friday. Statistics

THE HOUSE DID HAVE ATTIC FLATS, TWO OF THEM. THE DOOR TO ONE
stood open, but some orange police tape placed it off-limits. Harry
stooped to get his full height of 192 centimetres under the tape and
quickly took another step to steady his balance when he emerged on
the other side. He was standing in the middle of a room with an oak
parquet floor, a slanting ceiling and dormer windows. It was warm,
much like a bathroom. The flat was small and furnished in a minimalist style, as his own was, but that was where the similarity ended.
This flat had the latest sofa from Hilmers Hus, a coffee table from
r.o.o.m. and a small 15-inch Philips TV in ice-blue translucent plastic
to match the stereo system. Harry looked through doorways to a
kitchen and a bedroom. That was all there was. And it was strangely
still. A policeman in uniform with his arms folded was standing by
the kitchen door rocking on his heels. He was sweating and watching
Harry from under raised eyebrows. He shook his head and smirked
when Harry went to show his ID card.

Everyone knows the monkey, Harry thought. The monkey doesn't know anyone. He wiped his face with his hand.

'Where is the Crime Scene Unit?'

'In the bathroom,' the police officer said, nodding towards the bedroom. 'Lønn and Weber.'

'Weber? Have they started calling in pensioners now as well?'

The officer shrugged his shoulders. 'Holiday period.'

Harry had a look around.

'OK, well, close off the entrance and the door. People wander in and out of this building quite freely.'

'But –'

'Listen. That's all part of the scene of the crime. Alright?'

'I understand,' the officer said with an edge to his voice, and Harry knew that in two sentences he had managed to find himself another enemy on the force. The queue stretched for miles.

'But I was given clear instructions to . . .' the officer went on.

'. . . to keep an eye on things here,' said a voice from inside the bedroom.

Tom Waaler appeared in the doorway.

Despite the dark suit he was wearing, there was not so much as a bead of sweat under his dark, thick hairline. Tom Waaler was a good-looking man. Not a charmer perhaps, but he had uniform, symmetrical features. He was not as tall as Harry, but many would have perceived him to be. Perhaps because of Waaler's upright bearing. Or the effortless self-confidence he exuded. Most people working around him were not only impressed, they also felt that his composure rubbed off on them, so they relaxed and found their natural place. The impression of good looks could also emanate from his physical presence – no suit could hide five workouts a week doing karate and weights.

'And he should continue to keep an eye on things here,' Waaler said. 'I've just sent someone down in the lift to close off whatever is needed. Everything in order, Hole.'

The last was delivered with such flat intonation that it was unclear whether it was to be taken as a statement or a question. Harry cleared his throat.

'Where is she?'

'In here.'

Waaler's face feigned a look of concern as he moved aside to let Harry pass.

'Hit yourself, did you, Hole?'

The bedroom was simply furnished, but with taste and a touch of romance. A bed made for one – but with room for two – gave on to a supporting beam carved with something that looked like a heart with a triangle inside it. Perhaps a lover's mark, Harry thought. On the wall over her bed hung three framed pictures of naked men, erotically PC, lying somewhere between soft porn and intimate art. No personal pictures or objects, as far as he could see.

The bathroom an en suite. It was no bigger than the room needed to accommodate a sink, a lavatory, a shower without a curtain and Camilla Loen. She lay on the tiled floor with her face twisted towards the door, but she was looking upwards, at the shower, as if waiting for more water.

She was naked under the sopping wet, white bathrobe which lay open and covered the drain. Beate was standing in the doorway taking photographs.

'Anyone checked how long she's been dead?'

'Pathologist's on his way,' Beate said. 'But rigor mortis hasn't set in and she's still not completely cold. I'd guess a couple of hours at most.'

'Wasn't the shower on when the neighbour and the caretaker found her?'

'Yes.'

'The hot water could have maintained her body temperature and delayed the onset of stiffening.'

Harry looked down at his watch: 6.15.

'Let's say she died at about five o'clock.'

It was Waaler's voice.

'Why?' Harry asked, without turning round.

'There's nothing to suggest that the body has been moved, so we can assume that she was killed while she was in the shower. As you can see, her body and her bathrobe are blocking the drain. That's what caused the flooding. The caretaker who turned off the shower said that it was on full, and I checked the water pressure. Pretty good for an attic flat. With it being such a small bathroom it can't have taken many minutes before the water spilled over the threshold and out into the bedroom. And then not much longer before the water found a way down to the flat underneath. The woman downstairs says that it was exactly twenty minutes past five when she discovered the leak.'

'That's just an hour ago,' Harry said. 'And you've been here half an hour. Seems as if everyone here has reacted unusually quickly.'

'Well, not everyone,' Waaler said.

Harry didn't answer.

'I'm thinking of the pathologist.' Waaler smiled. 'He should have been here by now.'

Beate finished taking photos and exchanged glances with Harry.

Waaler touched her arm.

'Call me if there *is* anything. I'm going to the second floor to talk to the caretaker.'

'OK.'

Harry waited until Waaler had left the room.

'Can I . . . ?' he asked.

Beate nodded and moved.

Harry's shoes squelched on the wet floor. There was condensation on all the surfaces in the room from the steam and it ran down in stripes. The mirror looked as if it had been weeping. Harry went into a squat, but had to hold onto the wall not to lose balance. He breathed in through his nostrils, but could detect only the smell of soap, none of the other smells he knew had to be there. Dysosmia it was called, according to the book Harry had borrowed from Aune, the Crime

Squad's resident psychologist. A condition of the brain when it refused to recognise some smells, it said; often the result of emotional trauma. Harry wasn't so sure about that. He just knew that he couldn't smell a dead body.

Camilla Loen was young. Somewhere between 27 and 30, he guessed. Good-looking. Full figure. Her skin was smooth and tanned, but with the pallor that dead bodies quickly acquire underneath. She had dark hair, which would certainly grow lighter in colour as it dried, and a small hole in her forehead that would soon disappear once the undertaker had done his job. There was not much else for him to do, just put some make-up over what seemed like a swelling in her right eye.

Harry concentrated on the black, circular hole in her forehead. It was hardly bigger than the hole in a one-krone coin. He was always surprised how small holes could be and still take a human life. Occasionally they were deceptive because skin grew over the entry wound. Harry assumed that the bullet in this case had been larger than the hole it left behind.

'Shame she's been lying in water,' Beate said. 'Otherwise we might have found the killer's fingerprints, some threads or DNA on her.'

'Mm. At any rate her forehead was above water. And it didn't get too much water on it from the shower, either.'

'Oh?'

'There is black, congealed blood round where the bullet entered. And there are burn marks on the skin from the shot. Perhaps this little hole can tell us one or two things right now. Magnifying glass?'

Without taking his eyes off Camilla Loen, Harry reached out, felt the solid weight of a German optical instrument in his hand and began to study the area around the bullet wound.

'What can you see?'

Beate's low voice was right down by his ear. She was always keen to learn more. Harry knew it would not be long before there was nothing left to teach her.

'The grey colouring of the burn marks suggests that the shot was fired from close range, but not point-blank,' he said. 'I would guess the shot was fired from about half a metre.'

'Right.'

'The lack of symmetry of the burn marks indicates that the person who fired the gun was taller than her and shot downwards at an angle.'

Harry carefully turned the dead girl's head. Her forehead was not yet completely cold.

'No exit wound,' he said. 'That supports the theory that the shot was fired down at an angle. Perhaps she was kneeling in front of the person who fired it.'

'Can you tell what kind of weapon was used?'

Harry shook his head. 'The pathologist will know all that, as well as the ballistics guys. But there are graduated burn marks and that would suggest a short-barrelled weapon such as a handgun.'

Harry systematically scanned the whole body; he tried to take note of everything, but he could feel that the residual alcoholic stupor was filtering away details that he could have used. No, *they* could have used. This was not his case. When he came to the hand, he saw that something was missing.

'Donald Duck,' he muttered, bending closer.

Beate looked at him quizzically.

'They draw them like this in comics,' Harry said. 'With four fingers.'

'I don't read comics.'

The index finger had been removed. All that remained were black threads of coagulated blood and glistening tendon ends. The cut itself appeared to be even and clean. Harry placed a fingertip cautiously on the white shiny area in the pink flesh. The surface of the severed bone felt smooth and straight.

'Pincers,' he said. 'Or an extremely sharp knife. Has the finger been found?'

'Nope.'

Harry felt suddenly nauseous and closed his eyes. He took a few deep breaths. Then he opened his eyes again. There could be many reasons for nipping off the finger of a victim. There was no reason to think along the lines he already had.

'Could be an extortioner,' Beate said. 'They like pincers.'

'Yes, could be,' Harry mumbled, getting up and discovering the white spaces under his shoes on what he had thought were pink tiles. Beate bent down and took a close-up of the dead girl's face.

'She certainly bled a lot.'

'That's because her hand was in the water,' Harry said. 'Water stops blood clotting.'

'All that blood just from one severed finger?'

'Yes. And do you know what that indicates?'

'No, but I have a feeling I'm soon going to find out.'

'It means that Camilla Loen probably had her finger cut off while her heart was still beating. In other words, before she was shot.'

Beate grimaced.

'I'm going to have a chat with the people downstairs,' Harry said.

'Camilla was living here when we first moved in,' Vibeke Knutsen said, quickly looking at her partner. 'We didn't have much to do with her.'

They were with Harry in their sitting room on the fourth floor, directly beneath the attic flat. It looked for all the world as though it was Harry who lived there. The couple sat up straight on the edge of the sofa while Harry had slumped deep down into one of the armchairs.

They struck Harry as an odd couple. Both were somewhere in their thirties, but Anders Nygård was thin and wiry like a marathon runner. His light-blue shirt was freshly ironed and his hair short, for work. His lips were thin, his body language restless. Although his face was open and boyish, almost innocent, he exuded asceticism and austerity. The red-haired Vibeke Knutsen had deep dimples and a physical voluptuousness that was emphasised by a tight-fitting leopard-pattern top. She gave the impression that she had lived a little. The wrinkles over her lips suggested a lot of cigarettes and the wrinkles around her eyes a lot of fun.

'What did she do?' Harry asked.

Vibeke cast a glance at her partner, but when he didn't answer, she replied:

'So far as I know she was working in an advertising bureau. Design. Or something like that.'

'Or something like that,' Harry said, half-heartedly making notes on the pad in front of him.

It was a trick he used when he was questioning people. If you didn't look at them, they relaxed more. If you gave the impression that what they said was not very interesting, they automatically made an effort to say something that would grab his attention. He should have been a journalist. He felt that there was more sympathy on offer for journalists who turned up drunk for work.

'Boyfriends?'

Vibeke shook her head.

'Lovers?'

Vibeke gave a nervous laugh and looked away from her partner.

'We don't spend our time eavesdropping,' Anders Nygård said. 'Do you think it was a lover who did this?'

'I don't know,' Harry said.

'I can see that you don't *know*.'

Harry noticed the irritation in his voice.

'But those of us who live here would like to know if this looks like a personal matter or if we may have an insane killer running round the neighbourhood.'

'You may have an insane killer running round the neighbourhood,' Harry said, putting down his pen and waiting.

He saw Vibeke Knutsen's startled reaction, but concentrated on Anders Nygård.

When people are frightened they lose their temper more easily. This was a lesson he had learned during his first year at Police College. As recruits they had been told not to excite frightened people unnecessarily, but Harry had discovered that the opposite was much more useful. Excite them. Angry people often said things they didn't mean, or more to the point, things they didn't mean to say.

Anders Nygård eyed him impassively.

'But it's more likely that the person who did this is a lover,' Harry said. 'A lover or someone she had a relationship with or someone she rejected.'

'Why?' Anders Nygård put his arm round Vibeke's shoulders.

It was an amusing pose because his arm was so short and her shoulders were so broad.

Harry leaned back in his chair.

'Statistics. Can I smoke in here?'

'We're trying to keep this a smoke-free zone,' Anders Nygård said with a thin smile.

Harry noticed that Vibeke lowered her eyes as he stuffed the cigarette pack back in his trouser pocket.

'What do you mean by statistics?' the man asked. 'What makes you think they're valid in a case like this?'

'Well, before I answer your two questions, do you know much about statistics, Mr Nygård? Gausian distribution, significance, standard deviation?'

'No, but I –'

'Fine,' Harry interrupted. 'Because in this case you don't need to. Hundreds of years of crime statistics from all over the world have taught us one simple, basic thing. That she's the typical victim. Or if she's not typical, he's the type to think she was. That's the answer to your first question. And the second.'

Anders Nygård snorted and let go of Vibeke.

'That's completely unscientific. You know nothing about Camilla Loen.'

'Right,' Harry said.

'So why did you say what you said?'

'Because you asked. And if you're finished with your questions, perhaps I can continue with mine?'

Nygård seemed to be on the point of saying something, but then changed his mind and glowered at the table. Harry could have been mistaken, but he thought he spotted a tiny smile form between Vibeke's dimples.

'Do you think Camilla Loen was taking drugs?' Harry asked.

Nygård's head shot up. 'Why should we think that?'

Harry closed his eyes and waited.

'No,' Vibeke said. Her voice was soft and low. 'We don't think so.'

Harry opened his eyes and smiled at her gratefully. Anders Nygård sent her a somewhat surprised look.

'Her door wasn't locked, was it?'

Anders Nygård nodded.

'Don't you think that was strange?' Harry asked.

'Not particularly. She was at home after all.'

'Mm. You have a simple lock on your door and I noticed that you . . .' he nodded towards Vibeke, '. . . locked up when I came in.'

'She's a bit anxious now,' Nygård said, patting his partner's knee.

'Oslo isn't what it was,' Vibeke said.

Her eyes met Harry's for a brief moment.

'You're right,' Harry said. 'And it seems as if Camilla Loen shared your opinion. Her flat has a double lock and security chains on the inside. She doesn't strike me as a woman who would have a shower with the door unlocked.'

Nygård shrugged his shoulders. 'Whoever did it could have picked the lock.'

Harry shook his head. 'People only pick locks in films.'

'Someone might already have been in the flat with her,' Vibeke said.

'Who?'

Harry waited in silence. When he considered that no-one was going to break the silence, he got up.

'Someone will call you in for questioning. For the moment, thank you.'

In the hallway, he turned round.

'By the way, who called the police?'

'It was me,' Vibeke said. 'I rang while Anders went to fetch the caretaker.'

'Before you'd found her? How did you know . . . ?'

'There was blood dripping into the pan.'

'Oh? How did you know that?'

Anders Nygård gave a loud, exaggerated sigh and rested a hand on Vibeke's neck: 'It was red, wasn't it.'

'Well,' Harry said, 'there are other things than blood which are red.'

'That's right,' Vibeke said. 'It wasn't just the colour though.'

Anders Nygård threw her a look of astonishment. She smiled, but Harry noticed that she moved away from her partner's hand.

'I used to live with a chef and we ran a little eating house together. That's when I learned a few things about food. One of which was that blood contains albumin, and if you pour blood into a pan of water over sixty-five degrees, the blood coagulates and becomes lumpy. Just like when an egg cracks in boiling water. When Anders tasted the lumps in the water and said that they tasted of egg, I knew it was blood. And that something terrible had happened.'

Anders Nygård's mouth fell open. He went suddenly very pale under his tan.

'Bon appetit,' Harry mumbled and left.

5

Friday. Underwater.

HARRY HATED THEME PUBS: IRISH PUBS, TOPLESS PUBS, NOVELTY PUBS or, worst of all, celebrity pubs where the walls were lined with portraits of regular customers of some notoriety. The theme of Underwater was a vaguely nautical mix of diving and the romanticism of old wooden ships. But at some point, well into his fourth beer, Harry couldn't care less about gurgling aquariums of green water, diving helmets and the rustic interiors of creaking wood. It could have been worse. The last time he had been here people had suddenly burst into a round of operatic favourites; for a moment he had the feeling that the musical had finally caught up with reality. He took stock and confirmed with some relief that none of the four guests in the pub looked as though they were considering breaking into song for the time being.

'Everyone on holiday?' he asked the girl behind the bar as she put his beer in front of him.

'It's seven o'clock.' She gave him change for a hundred-kroner note although he had given her two hundred.

He would have gone to Schrøder if he could, but he had a hazy recollection that he was banned there and he didn't have the nerve to go and find out. Not today. He remembered fragments of some scene there on Tuesday. Or was it Wednesday? Someone had dragged up the time when he had been on TV and had been referred to as the 'Norwegian Police Hero' because he had shot a gunman in Sydney. Some guy had made a few remarks and called him names. Some of what he said had been spot on. Did they end up coming to blows? It was not impossible, but of course the injuries to his knuckles and nose that he woke up with could just as easily have been caused by a fall on the cobblestones in Dovregata.

Harry's mobile phone rang. He stared at the number and saw that it wasn't Rakel this time, either.

'Hello, boss.'

'Harry? Where are you?' Bjarne Møller sounded concerned.

'Underwater. What's up?'

'Water?'

'Water. Fresh water. Salt water. Tonic water. You sound . . . What's the word? Frazzled.'

'Are you drunk?'

'Not drunk enough.'

'What?'

'Nothing. The battery keeps going, boss.'

'One of the officers at the crime scene threatened to write a report on you. He says you were visibly intoxicated when you arrived.'

'Why "threatened" and not "is threatening"?'

'I persuaded him not to. Were you intoxicated, Harry?'

'Of course I wasn't, boss.'

'Are you absolutely positive that you are telling me the truth now, Harry?'

'Are you absolutely positive that you want to know?'

Harry heard Møller's groan at the other end.

'This cannot go on, Harry. I'll be forced to put a stop to it.'

'OK. Begin by taking me off this case.'

'What?'

'You heard me. I don't want to work with that bastard. Put someone else on the case.'

'We haven't got the personnel to . . .'

'Then give me the boot. I don't give a monkey's.'

Harry put his phone back in his inside pocket. He could hear Møller's voice gently vibrating against his nipple. Actually it was quite a pleasant feeling. He drained the rest of his glass, stood up and staggered out into the warm summer evening. The third taxi he hailed in Ullevålsveien stopped and picked him up.

'Holmenkollveien,' he said, settling his sweaty neck back against the cool leather of the back seat. As they went along he gazed out of the window at the swallows as they dissected the pale blue sky in their search for food. The insects had come out now. This was the swallows' window of opportunity, their chance to live. From now until the sun went down.

The taxi pulled up below a large, dark timber-clad house.

'Shall I drive up?' the taxi driver asked.

'No, we'll just wait here for a bit,' Harry said.

He stared up at the house. He thought he caught a glimpse of Rakel in the window. Oleg would probably be going to bed soon. He was probably making a fuss right now to stay up longer because it was . . .

'It is Friday today, isn't it?'

The taxi driver took a cautious look in his mirror and gave a slight nod.

The days. The weeks. My God, how quickly young lads grew up. Harry rubbed his face, tried to massage a bit of life into the wan death mask he walked around with. Last winter hadn't been so bad. He had solved a couple of biggish cases, he had appeared as a witness in the Ellen Gjelten case, he was on the wagon, and he and Rakel had gone from being just a couple of new loves to doing family things together.

And he had liked it; he liked the weekend trips and the company of children. Harry did the barbecuing. He liked having his father and Sis over for a Sunday meal, and seeing his sister, who had Down's syndrome, and nine-year-old Oleg playing together. And best of all: they were very much in love. Rakel had even begun to throw out hints that it might be an idea if Harry moved in. She had used the argument that the house was too big for her and Oleg. Harry had not gone to any great pains to find counter-arguments.

'We'll see when I've done with the Ellen Gjelten case,' he had said. The trip to Normandy that they had booked – three weeks on an old farm and a week on a riverboat – would be a kind of test to see if they were ready for it.

Then things started happening.

He had spent the whole winter working on the Ellen Gjelten case. It was intensive, too intensive, but that was the only way Harry knew how to work. Ellen Gjelten was not just a colleague; she was his closest friend and kindred spirit. Three years had gone by since the two of them had been on the heels of an arms smuggler going by the code name of Prince and since the day a baseball bat had knocked the living daylights out of her. The evidence at the scene of the crime by the Akerselva pointed to Sverre Olsen, an old neo-Nazi the police knew well. Unfortunately they never got to hear his explanation as he was shot through the head when he was alleged to have fired at Tom Waaler during his arrest. Regardless of this, Harry was convinced that the real man behind the murder was Prince, and he had persuaded Møller to let him conduct his own investigation. It was personal, so it went against all the principles they worked by in Crime Squad, but Møller had given him permission, short-term, as a kind of reward for the results that Harry had achieved on other cases. The breakthrough had finally come last winter. Someone had seen Sverre Olsen sitting in a red car in Grünerløkka with another person on the night of the murder, just a few hundred metres away from the scene of the crime. The witness was a Roy Kvinsvik, a convicted former neo-Nazi, now a recent

Pentecostal convert to the Philadelphian sect. Kvinsvik was not exactly what you would call a model witness, but he had taken a long, hard look at the photograph Harry had shown him and said, Yes, this was the person he had seen in the car with Sverre. The man in the photograph was Tom Waaler.

Even though he had suspected Waaler for a long time, it came as a shock to receive confirmation. Not least because it meant that there had to be more moles working with him in the department. Prince could not have operated with such a wide network as he had done without help. That in turn meant that Harry could not trust anyone. So he kept his mouth shut about what Roy Kvinsvik had told him because he knew he would only get one chance, and the whole sordid truth would have to come out in one go. And he would have to be absolutely sure that the root came with it; if it didn't he was done for.

That was why Harry had secretly begun to work on assembling a watertight case against Waaler. However, since he didn't know who it was safe to talk to, this turned out to be more difficult than he had imagined. He began to trawl through the archives after the others had gone home for the day, to tap into the internal computer network, to print out e-mails and lists of incoming and outgoing telephone calls from people he knew Waaler associated with. In the afternoons he sat in a car near Youngstorget and kept an eye on Herbert's Pizza. Harry's theory was that the neo-Nazis frequenting the pizzeria were also smuggling arms. When this theory did not produce any leads he began to shadow Waaler and a number of his colleagues. He concentrated on those he knew spent a lot of time with guns at the firing range in Økern. He followed them from a safe distance, sat outside their homes, shivering in his car while they slept indoors, and returned home to Rakel early in the morning, totally exhausted. He slept for a couple of hours and then went to work again. After a while she asked him to sleep in his own flat on the nights when he had double shifts. He hadn't told her that his night work was off the record, off the time sheets, off the awareness of his superiors, off almost everything.

Then he started doing a turn off Broadway too.

First of all, he dropped by Herbert's Pizza one evening, then another, chatting with the guys, buying rounds of beer. Of course they knew who he was, but free beer was free beer and they drank it, grinned and kept their mouths shut. He gradually realised that they didn't know anything, but he still continued to go there, he wasn't quite sure why, perhaps because it gave him the feeling that he was close to something, the dragon's lair. All he had to do was be patient, he only had to wait and the dragon would emerge. But neither Waaler nor any of his acquaintances ever turned up. So he went back to watching the block where Waaler lived.

One night, at 20 degrees below freezing point, the streets completely deserted, a man wearing a short, thin jacket came walking towards his car with the rolling gait that characterises junkies. He stopped outside the entrance leading to Waaler's block, looked right then left and attacked the lock with a crowbar. Harry sat and watched, fully aware that he risked being exposed if he intervened. The man was presumably too stoned to attach the crowbar properly and as he yanked it down, a large chunk of wood detached itself from the door with a splintering sound. As he did it, he fell backwards and landed in a pile of snow at the front of the block. And that was where he stayed. Lights came on in a couple of windows. The curtains in Waaler's flat moved. Harry waited. Nothing happened. Twenty degrees below zero. The light was still on in Waaler's window. The junkie didn't stir. Afterwards, Harry often wondered what the hell he should have done. The battery on his mobile had gone flat because of the cold, so he couldn't have rung casualty. He waited. The minutes ticked by. Bloody junkie. Twenty-one below. Sodding junkie. Of course he could have driven away, gone to casualty and told them about him. Something moved by the entrance. It was Waaler. He looked comical in dressing gown, boots, cap and mittens. He was carrying two woollen blankets. Harry could not believe his eyes as Waaler checked the junkie's pulse and pupils before wrapping him in the blankets. Waaler just stood there flapping his arms around to keep himself warm and peering in the direction of Harry's car. A few minutes later the ambulance rolled up in front of the block of flats.

That night Harry went home, sat down in his wing chair, lit a cigarette and listened to the Raga Rockers and Duke Ellington. Then he went to work, although he had not been out of his clothes for 48 hours.

Rakel and Harry had their first row one evening in April. He had cancelled a weekend trip at the last moment, and she pointed out that this was the third time he had broken a promise within a very short space of time. A promise to Oleg, she said. He accused her of using Oleg as an excuse and that what she really wanted was for him to prioritise her needs over finding the person who had taken Ellen's life. She said Ellen was a ghost, that he had shut himself up with a corpse, that it wasn't normal, that he was feeding on the tragedy, that it was necrophilia, that it wasn't Ellen who was driving him but his own lust for vengeance.

'You've been hurt,' she said. 'And you've let everything else go so that you can get your revenge.'

As Harry fumed out of the house he caught a glimpse of Oleg's pyjamas and red eyes behind the stair rails.

After that he stopped doing anything that did not have a direct connection with his pursuit of those guilty of Ellen's murder. He read e-mails under the low light of table lamps, stared at the dark windows of detached houses and blocks of flats waiting for people who never came out, and snatched a few hours' sleep in his flat in Sofies gate.

The days grew longer and lighter, but he had made absolutely no progress. One night, out of the blue, a nightmare from his childhood returned: Sis, her long hair trapped, the expression of horror on her face. He was rigid with fear. It returned the following night. And the night after.

Øystein Eikeland, a childhood friend who drank at Malik's when he wasn't driving his taxi, told Harry that he looked shattered and offered him some cheap speed. Harry refused. Exhausted and angry, he continued with the relentless search.

It was just a question of time before it all unravelled. Something as prosaic as an unpaid bill was all it took to trigger it. It was the end of May and he hadn't spoken to Rakel for several days. He was woken in his office chair by the phone ringing. Rakel said that the travel company had reminded her that they hadn't paid for the farm in Normandy. They had a week's grace, after that the travel company would rent the farm out to someone else.

'Friday is the deadline,' were Rakel's last words before ringing off.

Harry went to the lavatory, splashed some cold water over his face and confronted his reflection in the mirror. Beneath his wet, closely cropped fair hair he saw a pair of bloodshot eyes with dark bags under them and drawn, hollow cheeks. He tried a smile. Yellowing teeth grinned back at him. He didn't recognise himself. And he knew that Rakel was right, it was a deadline. For him and Ellen. For him and Tom Waaler.

The same day he went to his closest superior officer, Bjarne Møller, who was the only person at Police HQ he trusted 100 per cent. Møller had alternately nodded and shaken his head as Harry told him what he wanted. Fortunately, he had said, that was not his pigeon and Harry would have to take it up directly with the Chief Superintendent. Nevertheless, he thought that Harry should think twice before he went to see him. Harry went straight from Møller's square office to the oval office of the head of *Kripos*. He knocked, went in and presented what he had to say, about the witness who had seen Tom Waaler together with Sverre Olsen, and the fact that it was none other than Tom Waaler who had shot Olsen while arresting him. That was it. That was all he had after five months' slog, five months' shadowing, five months on the verge of madness.

The head of *Kripos* asked Harry what he thought Tom Waaler's motive might be in killing Ellen Gjelten.

Harry answered that Ellen was in possession of dangerous information. The same evening she was killed she left a message on Harry's answerphone that she knew who Prince was. She knew the name of the ringleader behind the illegal importing of weapons and the person responsible for arming Oslo's criminal community to the teeth with service handguns.

'Unfortunately it was too late when I rang back,' Harry said, trying to read the Chief Superintendent's expression.

'And Sverre Olsen?' the Superintendent asked.

'When we picked up Sverre Olsen's trail, Prince killed him so that he wouldn't be able to reveal the name of Ellen's killer.'

'And this Prince, you said, is . . . ?'

Harry repeated Tom Waaler's name and the head of *Kripos* nodded in silence and said: 'One of our own then. One of our most respected detective inspectors.'

For the next ten seconds Harry felt as if he was sitting in a vacuum, with no air and no sound. He knew that his police career could finish right there on the spot.

'Alright, Hole. I'll meet this witness of yours before I make up my mind what our next step should be.'

The Superintendent stood up.

'I assume that you understand, until further notice, this is a matter which must remain between you and me.'

'How long are we supposed to stay here?'

Harry gave a start at the sound of the taxi driver's voice. He had been asleep.

'Go back,' he said, taking a last look at the timber house.

As they went back down Kirkeveien his mobile phone rang. It was Beate.

'We think we've found the weapon,' she said. 'And you were right. It is a handgun.'

'In that case, congratulations to us both.'

'Well, it wasn't so difficult to find. It was in the rubbish bin under the sink.'

'Make and number?'

'A Glock 23. The number has been filed off.'

'File marks?'

'If you're wondering whether they're the same as the ones we find on most confiscated small arms in Oslo at the moment, the answer is yes.'

'I see.' Harry switched his mobile to his left hand. 'What I don't see is why you're ringing to tell me all this. It's not my case.'

'I wouldn't be so sure about that, Harry. Møller said . . .'

'Møller and the whole fucking Oslo Police Force can go to hell!'

Harry was taken aback by his own screeching voice. He saw the taxi driver's V-shaped eyebrows loom up in the rear-view mirror.

'Sorry, Beate. I . . . Are you still there?'

'Uh-huh.'

'I'm just not quite myself at the moment.'

'It can wait.'

'What can?'

'There's no hurry.'

'Come on.'

She sighed.

'Did you notice the swelling Camilla Loen had on her eyelid?'

'Indeed I did.'

'I thought the murderer may have hit her, or that she got it when she fell, but it turned out it wasn't a swelling.'

'Oh?'

'The pathologist pressed the lump. It was rock hard. So he pulled up her eyelid and do you know what he found on the top of her eyeball?'

'Well, no,' Harry said.

'A small, reddish precious stone cut in the shape of a star. We think it's a diamond. What do you think about that?'

Harry breathed in and checked the time. There were still three hours to go before they stopped serving at Sofie.

'That it's not my case,' he said, switching off his phone.

6

Friday. Water.

THERE IS A DROUGHT, BUT I SAW THE POLICEMAN COMING AWAY FROM the watering hole. Water for the thirsty. Rain water, river water, amniotic waters.

He didn't see me. He staggered over to Ullevålsveien and tried to hail a taxi. No-one wanted to take him. He was like one of the restless souls wandering along the river bank without a ferryman to take him across. I have some experience of what that feels like. Being hounded by those you nourished. Being rejected when for once in your life it is you who needs help. Discovering that you're being spat on and that you have no-one to spit on in return. Quietly considering what you must do. The paradox is, of course, that the taxi driver who takes pity on you, it is his throat you cut.

7

Tuesday. Dismissal.

HARRY WENT TO THE BACK OF THE SHOP, OPENED THE GLASS DOOR of the milk refrigerator and leaned in. He pulled up his sweaty T-shirt, closed his eyes and felt the cool air against his skin.

The forecast was for a tropical night and the few customers there were in the shop wanted grilled food, beer or mineral water.

Harry recognised her by the colour of her hair. She was standing with her back to him at the meat counter. Her broad backside filled her jeans to perfection. When she turned round he saw that she was wearing a zebra-striped top which was just as tight as her leopard-pattern top. Then Vibeke Knutsen changed her mind, put back the ready-cooked pieces of beef, pushed her shopping trolley to the freezer counter and picked out two packets of cod fillets.

Harry pulled down his T-shirt and closed the glass door. He didn't want any milk. Nor did he want any meat or cod. Basically, he wanted as little as possible, just something he could eat, not because he was hungry, but for his stomach's sake. His stomach had started to give him some trouble the night before. And he knew from experience that if he didn't get some solid food down him now, he would not be able to keep down a drop of alcohol. In his trolley there was a loaf of whole-meal bread and a brown paper bag containing a bottle from the Vinmonopol over the road. He added half a chicken, a six-pack of Hansa and fidgeted around at the fruit counter before joining the checkout queue right behind Vibeke Knutsen. It wasn't intentional, but then again perhaps it wasn't quite by chance either.

She half turned without seeing him and wrinkled her nose as if there was a potent smell coming from somewhere, which was a possibility that Harry could not completely exclude. She asked the checkout girl for a pack of 20 Prince Mild cigarettes.

'Thought you were trying to give them up.'

Vibeke turned round in surprise, scrutinised him and gave him three different smiles. The first one, fleeting, automatic. Then one of recognition. Then, after she had paid, one of curiosity.

'And you're going to have a party, I see.'

She put her purchases into a plastic bag.

'Something like that,' Harry mumbled, reciprocating her smile.

She tilted her head to the side. The zebra stripes moved.

'Many guests?'

'A few. All uninvited.'

The checkout girl handed him his change, but he nodded towards the collection box for the Salvation Army.

'You could show them the door, couldn't you?' Her smile had reached her eyes now.

'Course. But these particular guests are not so easy to get rid of.'

The bottle of Jim Beam clinked joyfully against the six-pack as he lifted his bags.

'Oh? Old drinking pals?'

Harry threw a lingering look in her direction. She seemed to know what she was talking about. This struck him as even stranger because she was living with the type of person who gave the impression of being fairly austere. Or to be more precise: it was strange that such an austere person would be living with her.

'I haven't got any pals,' he said.

'Must be the ladies then. The type that doesn't let go easily.'

He intended to hold the door open for her, but it turned out it was automatic. He had only been shopping there a few hundred times. They stood opposite each other on the pavement outside.

Harry didn't know what to say. Perhaps this was why he came out with:

'Three ladies. Perhaps they'll go away if I drink enough.'

'Eh?'

She shaded her eyes from the sun.

'Nothing. Sorry. I'm just thinking aloud. That is, I'm not thinking . . . but I'm doing it aloud anyway. Prattling away, I suppose. I . . .'

He couldn't understand why she was still there.

'They've been running up and down our stairs all weekend,' she said.

'Who?'

'The police, I suppose.'

Harry slowly absorbed the information that a weekend had passed since he had stood in Camilla Loen's flat. He tried to catch a glimpse of himself in the shop window. A whole weekend? What did he look like now?

'They won't tell us anything,' she said. 'And the papers only say they haven't got any leads. Is that true?'

'It's not my case,' he said.

'Right.' Vibeke Knutsen nodded her head. Then she began to smile. 'And do you know what?'

'What?'

'Actually, it's probably a good thing too.'

It took a couple of seconds before Harry realised what she meant. He laughed. The laugh developed into a hacking cough.

'Funny that I've never seen you in this shop before,' he said when he had regained his composure.

Vibeke shrugged her shoulders. 'Who knows? Perhaps we'll see each other here again soon?'

She beamed at him and began to walk away. The plastic bags and her backside swung from side to side.

Yes, you and me and a flying pig.

Harry was thinking furiously and for a moment he was afraid that he had thought out loud.

A man with his jacket slung over one shoulder and a hand pressed against his stomach was sitting on the steps outside the entrance to the apartment block in Sofies gate. His shirt had dark, sweaty patches on the front and under the armpits. On seeing Harry, he stood up.

Harry breathed in and steeled himself. It was Bjarne Møller.

'My God, Harry.'

'My God to you too, boss.'

'Have you seen what you look like?'

Harry took out his keys. 'Not quite peak of fitness?'

'You were told to assist with the murder case at the weekend and no-one has seen hide nor hair of you. Today you didn't even turn up for work.'

'Overslept, boss. And that's not as bloody far from the truth as you might think.'

'Perhaps you overslept during those weeks when you only came in on Fridays as well?'

'Probably. I picked up a bit after the first week. So I rang into work and was told that someone had put my name up on the staff leave list. I reckoned it was you.'

Harry trudged into the hallway with Møller hard on his heels.

'I had absolutely no choice,' Møller said, groaning and holding his hand against his stomach. 'Four weeks, Harry!'

'Well, just a nanosecond in the universe . . .'

'And not one single word about where you were!'

Harry guided the key into the lock with some difficulty. 'It's coming now, boss.'

'What is?'

'A single word about where I was. Here.'

Harry shoved open the door to his flat and an acrid stench of beer, cigarette ends and stale refuse rose up to meet them.

'Would you have felt better if you'd known?'

Harry went in, and hesitantly Møller stepped in after him.

'You don't need to take your shoes off, boss,' Harry shouted from the kitchen.

Møller rolled his eyes and tried not to tread on any of the empty bottles, ashtrays full of cigarette butts and old vinyl records on his way across the sitting-room floor.

'Have you been sitting here drinking for four weeks, Harry?'

'With some breaks, boss. Long breaks. After all, I am on holiday, aren't I? Last week I hardly touched a drop.'

'I've got some bad news for you, Harry,' Møller shouted, releasing the catches on the window and pushing feverishly at the glass. At the third shove the window sprang open. He groaned, loosened his belt and undid the top trouser button. As he turned round he saw Harry standing by the sitting-room door with an open bottle of whisky.

'That bad, is it,' Harry said, noticing the Chief Inspector's slackened belt. 'Am I going to be whipped or ravished?'

'Slow digestion,' Møller explained.

'Mm.' Harry put the top back on the whisky bottle. 'Funny expression that, slow digestion. I've been suffering with my stomach a bit myself, so I read up about it. It takes somewhere between twelve and twenty-four hours to digest food. For everyone. Whoever and whatever. It might keep hurting, but your intestines don't need any longer.'

'Harry . . .'

'A glass, boss? Unless it has to be clean, that is.'

'I've come to tell you it's finished, Harry.'

'Are you resigning?'

'Now that's enough of that!'

Møller banged the table so hard the empty bottles jumped. Then he sank down into a green armchair. He ran his hand across his face.

'I've risked my own job too many times to save yours, Harry. There are people in my life I am closer to than you. People I provide for. This is where it stops, Harry. I can't help you any more.'

'Fine.'

Harry sat down on the sofa and poured whisky into one of the glasses.

'No-one asked you to help me, boss, but thank you anyway. For as long as it lasted. *Skål.*'

Møller took a deep breath and closed his eyes.

'Do you know what, Harry? At times you are the most arrogant, the most selfish and the most unintelligent pile of shit on this planet.'

Harry shrugged his shoulders and emptied his glass in one swallow.

'I've written your dismissal papers,' Møller said.

Harry refilled his glass.

'They're on the Chief's desk. All that's missing is his signature. Do you understand what that means, Harry?'

Harry nodded. 'Sure you won't have a little snifter before you go, boss?'

Møller got up. He paused by the sitting-room door.

'You have no idea how much it hurts me to see you like this, Harry. Rakel and your work were everything you had. First of all you spat on Rakel, and now you're spitting on your job.'

I spat on both exactly four weeks ago, Harry declared roundly in his thoughts.

'I'm really sorry, Harry.'

Møller closed the door gently behind him as he left.

Three-quarters of an hour later Harry was asleep in the chair. He had been visited. Not by his three regular women, but by the head of *Kripos.* Four weeks and three days ago, to be precise.

*

The Chief Superintendent himself had asked to meet at the Boxer, a bar for the exuberantly thirsty a stone's throw from Police HQ and a few teetering steps from the gutter. Just him, Harry and Roy Kvinsvik. He explained to Harry that as long as no official decision had been taken it was best to do everything as unofficially as possible so that he had room for manoeuvre.

He didn't say anything about Harry's room for manoeuvre.

When Harry arrived at the Boxer a quarter of an hour later than they had agreed the Chief Superintendent was sitting at a table at the back of the bar with a beer. Harry could feel his eyes on him as he sat down, his blue eyes shining in their deep sockets on either side of his thin, imperious nose. He had thick, grey hair, an upright posture and he was slim for his age. The Chief was like one of those 60-year-olds you could never really imagine ever having been young. Or ever really being old. In Crime Squad they called him the President because his office was oval and also because he – particularly on public occasions – talked like one. But this was 'as unofficial as possible'. The Chief Superintendent's lipless mouth opened.

'You've come on your own.'

Harry ordered a Farris mineral water from the waitress, picked up the menu lying on the table, studied the front page and remarked casually as if it were redundant information:

'He's changed his mind.'

'Your witness has changed his mind?'

'Yes.'

The head of *Kripos* sipped his beer.

'For five months he said that he would appear as a witness,' Harry said. 'The last time was the day before yesterday. Do you think the knuckle of pork is good?'

'What did he say?'

'We agreed that I would meet him after the Philadelphia meeting today. When I turned up he said that he'd changed his mind and that

51

he'd come to the conclusion that it wasn't Tom Waaler he'd seen in the car with Sverre Olsen anyway.'

The Chief Superintendent fixed Harry with a straight look. Then he pushed up his coat sleeve and checked his watch, a movement which Harry took to mean that the meeting was concluded.

'Then we have no choice but to assume that it was someone else your witness saw and not Tom Waaler. Or what do you think?'

Harry swallowed. And swallowed again. He stared at the menu.

'Knuckle of pork. I think pork.'

'By all means. I have to be running along, but put it on my bill.'

Harry gave a brief laugh. 'Very nice of you, sir, but to be honest I have a horrible feeling that I'm going to be left paying the bill anyway.'

The Chief Superintendent frowned and when he spoke there was a quiver of irritation in his voice.

'May I be absolutely frank, Hole? It is well known that you and Inspector Waaler cannot stand the sight of each other. From the very moment you came to me with these wild accusations I have suspected that you have allowed your personal antipathies to colour your judgment. From where I am sitting, I have just had this suspicion confirmed.'

The Chief Superintendent pushed his unfinished glass of beer away from the edge of the table, stood up and buttoned his coat.

'May I therefore be concise and I hope clear, Hole. Ellen Gjelten's murder has been cleared up and the case is hereby closed. Neither you nor anyone else has successfully presented anything new that is substantial enough to warrant further investigation. If you so much as touch the case again it will be interpreted as countermanding orders and your dismissal papers signed by myself will be sent to the Police Appointments Committee forthwith. I am not saying this because I want to turn a blind eye to corrupt policemen, but because it is my responsibility to maintain the morale of the police force at a reasonable level. So we cannot have policemen crying wolf for no reason. Should I discover that you have made the slightest attempt to proceed with your charges against Inspector Waaler, you will be suspended with immediate effect and the case will be put before SEFO.'

'Which case?' Harry asked in a low voice. 'Waaler versus Gjelten?'

'Hole versus Waaler.'

When the Chief Superintendent had left, Harry sat staring at the half-empty glass of beer. He could do exactly what the head of *Kripos* said, but it would not change a thing. He was finished whatever happened. He had failed and now he had become a risk to the force. A paranoid traitor, a ticking bomb, they would get rid of him at the earliest opportunity. It was simply up to Harry to supply them with that opportunity.

The waitress arrived with the bottle of Farris water and asked him if he wanted anything to eat. Or to drink. Harry moistened his lips as his thoughts collided into one another. It was simply up to Harry to provide them with an opportunity; others would take care of the rest.

He pushed the bottle of Farris to the side and answered the waitress. That was four weeks and three days ago, and that was when it had all started. And finished.

Part Two

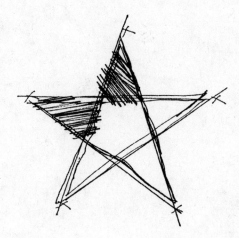

8

Tuesday and Wednesday. Chow Chow.

ON TUESDAY THE TEMPERATURE IN OSLO ROSE TO 29 DEGREES IN THE shade and by three o'clock, office workers were already making for the beaches in Huk and Hvervenbukta. The tourists were flocking to open-air restaurants in Aker Brygge and in Frogner Park where, covered in sweat, they snapped obligatory pictures of the Monolith before drifting down to the Fountain in the hope that a breath of wind would send a cooling mist of fine droplets over them.

Off the tourists' beaten track it was quiet, and what little life there was moved in slow motion. Roadworkers, their torsos bared, leaned over their machines, bricklayers on scaffolding at the building site around the Rikshospital peered down over deserted streets and taxi drivers found places to park in the shade, where they stood in groups discussing the murder in Ullevålsveien. Only in Akersgata were there signs of increased activity. The sensation-seeking rags had released the silly-season news and were greedily milking the latest killing. With many of their colleagues on holiday, the editors were putting everyone to work on the story, from journalism students doing summer jobs to unemployed political commentators. Only the cultural correspondents escaped.

It was still quieter than usual. It may have been because *Aftenposten* had moved from its position in Akersgata, the street the press traditionally occupied, down towards the centre, to the Post House, *Aftenposten* House or Post Giro Building. Whatever you called it, it was an unlovely small-town version of a skyscraper pointing up into a blue, cloudless sky. The golden-brown colossus at the top edge of the building site in Bjørvika had been smartened up, but for the time being crime reporter Roger Gjendem had only a view of Plata, the junkies' market square, and their outdoor shooting gallery behind the sheds where they hoped to meet their brave new world. He occasionally caught himself looking to see if Thomas was down there. But Thomas was in Ullersmo prison serving a sentence for attempting to break into a policeman's flat last winter. How crazy can you get? Or how desperate? At any rate, Roger would not have to worry that he would suddenly be looking down on his little brother shooting an overdose into his arm.

Aftenposten had not formally appointed a new crime editor. The last one had been offered a financial pay-off as part of downsizing and had accepted it with alacrity and left. Crime was then simply placed under the news coverage umbrella and, in practice, that meant that Roger Gjendem had to step in as the crime editor, but was paid the basic journalist's salary. He sat behind his desk with his fingers on the keyboard, his eyes on the smiling face of the woman he had scanned in as his screensaver and his mind on the woman who had packed her bags for the third time and left him and his flat in Seilduksgata. He knew that Devi would not come back this time and that it was time to move on. He went into the control panel on his computer and deleted the screensaver. That was a start. He had been working on a heroin case, but he had put it aside. Good, he hated writing about drugs. Devi insisted that it was because of Thomas. Roger tried to shut out both Devi and his little brother so that he could concentrate on the case he was supposed to be writing about.

He was summarising the details of the murder story in Ullevålsveien, enjoying some respite while they were waiting for developments, new evidence or a suspect or two. This would be an easy job. It was a sexy case in every way, with most of the ingredients that any crime reporter could wish for. A young woman of 23, single, shot in the shower room of her own flat, in broad daylight one Friday. The handgun found in the rubbish bin in the flat turns out to be the murder weapon. None of the neighbours has seen anything, no strangers have been observed roaming the area and just one of the neighbours claims to have heard something that could have been a shot. Since there are no signs of a break-in, the police are working on the theory that Camilla Loen let the killer in herself, but there is no-one in her circle of friends and acquaintances who stands out as suspicious and they all have more or less watertight alibis. The fact that Camilla Loen left her work as a graphic designer at Leo Burnett's at 4.15 to meet two friends in front of Kunstnernes Hus at 6.00 makes it highly unlikely that she would have invited anyone home. It is equally unlikely that anyone would have rung Camilla Loen's doorbell and sneaked into the apartment block using a false identity as she would have seen them on the video camera at the intercom panel at the entrance.

It was bad enough that the news desk could publish headlines like 'Psycho Murder' and 'Neighbour Tasted Blood', but two further details leaked out which gave the front pages two more splashes: 'Camilla Loen's Finger Severed' and 'Red Diamond Star Found Under Eyelid'.

Roger Gjendem began his summary in the present historic in order to give it dramatic emphasis, but he discovered that the material didn't need it and he deleted everything he had written. He sat for a while with his head in his hands. Then he double-clicked the recycle bin icon on the screen, placed the cursor over 'Empty the recycle bin' and hesitated. It was the only picture he had of her. In his flat all vestiges of her had been removed. He had even washed the woollen jumper she used to borrow and which he liked wearing because it smelled of her.

'Bye-bye,' he whispered and clicked.

He reread his introduction and decided to change 'Ullevålsveien' to 'Our Saviour's Cemetery' – it sounded better. Then he began to write, and this time it flowed.

At 7.00 people were reluctantly making a move homewards from the beaches although the sun was still beating down from a cloudless sky. It turned 8.00 and then 9.00. People wearing sunglasses were still drinking beer outside while the waiters in restaurants without terraces were twiddling their thumbs. It was 9.30, the sun was red over Ullernåsen and then it plunged. Unlike the temperature. It was a tropical night and people were returning home from restaurants and bars to lie awake and sweat in their beds.

In Akersgata the deadline was approaching and the editorial staff sat down to discuss the front page for the last time. The police had not made any new announcements. Not that they were holding back information, it was just that four days after the murder it seemed as if they didn't have anything else to say. On the other hand, silence allowed Gjendem and his colleagues even greater scope for speculation. It was time to be creative.

At roughly the same time in Oppsal the telephone rang in a house with yellow timber cladding and an apple orchard. Beate Lønn stretched out an arm from under the sheet and wondered if her mother, who lived on the floor below, had been woken up by the telephone ringing. Probably.

'Were you asleep?' asked a hoarse voice.

'No,' Beate said. 'Is anyone?'

'Right. I've only just woken up.'

Beate sat up in bed.

'How's it going?'

'What can I say? Well, yes, badly, I suppose I can say that.'

Silence. It wasn't the telephone connection that made Harry's voice seem distant to Beate.

'Anything new from Forensics?'

'Just what you've read in the newspapers,' she said.

'What newspapers?'

She sighed. 'Just what you already know. We've taken fingerprints and DNA from the flat, but for the moment there doesn't seem to be a clear link to the murderer.'

'We don't know if there was malice aforethought,' Harry said. 'Killer.'

'Killer,' Beate yawned.

'Have you found out where the diamond came from?'

'We're working on it. The jewellers we've talked to say that red diamonds are not unusual, but there's very little demand for them in Norway. They doubt that the diamond came via Norwegian jewellers. If it came from abroad then that increases the likelihood that the perpetrator is a foreigner.'

'Mm.'

'What is it, Harry?'

Harry coughed loudly. 'Just trying to keep myself up to date.'

'The last thing I heard was that it wasn't your case.'

'It isn't.'

'So what do you want?'

'Well, I woke up because I was having a nightmare.'

'Do you want me to come and tuck you in?'

'No.'

New silence.

'I was dreaming about Camilla Loen. And the diamond you found.'

'Oh yes?'

'Yes. I think there's something in that.'

'What do you mean?'

'I'm not quite sure, but did you know that in the past they used to place a coin on the eyes of a corpse before it was buried?'

'No.'

'It was payment for the ferryman to deliver the soul into the kingdom of the dead. If the soul wasn't delivered, it would never find peace. Think about it.'

'Thank you for the wisdom, but I don't believe in ghosts, Harry.'

Harry didn't answer.

'Anything else?'

'Just one small question. Do you know if the Chief Super starts his holidays this week?'

'Yes, he does.'

'You wouldn't by any chance happen to know . . . when he comes back?'

'Three weeks' time. What about you?'

'What about me?'

Beate heard the click of a lighter. She sighed: 'When are you coming back?'

She heard Harry inhale, hold his breath and slowly let it out again before he answered:

'I thought you said you didn't believe in ghosts.'

As Beate was putting down the phone, Bjarne Møller woke up with abdominal pains. He lay in bed twisting and turning until 6.00 when he gave up and got out of bed. He had a long breakfast without any coffee and immediately felt better. When he arrived at Police HQ just after eight, to his surprise, the pains had completely gone. He took the lift up to his office and celebrated by swinging his feet onto the desk, taking his first mouthful of coffee and grappling with the day's newspapers.

Dagbladet ran a picture of a smiling Camilla Loen on the front page under the headline 'Secret Lover?'. *Verdens Gang* ran the same picture but with a different headline: 'Clairvoyant Sees Jealousy'. Only the article in *Aftenposten* seemed to be interested in reality.

Møller shook his head, cast a glance at his watch and dialled Tom

Waaler's number. Timed to perfection. He would just have finished his morning meeting with the detectives on the case.

'No breakthrough yet,' Waaler said. 'We've been conducting door-to-door inquiries with all the neighbours and we've talked to all the shops nearby. Checked the taxis who were in the area at the relevant time, had a chat with informers and gone through the alibis of old friends with tarnished records. No-one stands out as a suspect, let's put it that way. And, to be frank, in this case I don't think the man is someone we know. No evidence of a sexual assault. No money or valuables touched. No familiar features here and no bells ringing. This finger and the diamond for example . . .'

Møller could feel his guts grumbling. He hoped it was hunger.

'So no good news for me then.'

'Majorstua police station has sent us three men, so now we have ten men working on the strategic side of the investigation. And the technicians at *Kripos* are giving Beate a hand to go through what they found in the flat. We're pretty well staffed, considering it's the holiday period. Does that sound good?'

'Thanks, Waaler, let's hope it stays that way. As regards the staffing, I mean.'

Møller put the phone down and turned his head to look out of the window before going back to the papers. However, he remained in this position, with his head twisted round very uncomfortably and his eyes rooted to the lawn outside Police HQ. He had caught sight of a figure wandering up Grønlandsleiret. The person in question was not walking quickly, but he appeared at any rate to be walking in a moderately straight line and there was no doubt where he was headed: he was coming towards the police station.

Møller got up, went out into the corridor and called for Jenny to come in right away with more coffee and an extra cup. Then he went back, sat down and hastily pulled out some old documents from one of his drawers.

Three minutes later there was a knock at the door.

'Come in!' Møller shouted without looking up from his papers, a twelve-page letter of complaint written by a dog owner accusing the dog clinic in Skippergata of administering the wrong medicine and thus killing his two chow chows. The door opened and Møller casually waved him in as he perused a page about the dogs' breeding, their awards from dog shows and the remarkable intelligence with which both dogs had been blessed.

'My God,' Møller said when he finally looked up. 'I thought we'd given you the boot.'

'Well. Since my dismissal papers are still lying unsigned on the Chief Superintendent's desk, and will be doing so for at least the next three weeks, I thought I might as well turn up for work in the meantime. Eh, boss?'

Harry poured himself a cup of coffee from Jenny's coffee pot and carried the cup with him round Møller's desk and over to the window.

'But that doesn't mean I'll work on the Camilla Loen case.'

Bjarne Møller turned round and contemplated Harry. He had seen it all several times before, how Harry could have a near-death experience one day and the very next be strolling around like some red-eyed Lazarus. For all that, it was still a surprise every time.

'If you think your dismissal is a bluff, Harry, you're wrong. This is not a shot across the bows this time. It's definitive. All the times you've disobeyed instructions it was me who ensured that you were dealt with leniently. For that reason I can't run away from my responsibilities now, either.'

Bjarne Møller searched for hints of an appeal in Harry's eyes. He found none. Fortunately.

'That's how it is, Harry. It's over.'

Harry didn't answer.

'And while I remember, your gun licence is withdrawn with immediate effect. Standard procedure. You'll have to nip down to the armoury and return whatever hardware you have on you today.'

Harry nodded. The department head scrutinised him. Did he detect a faint touch of the bewildered schoolboy who had received an unexpected box around the ears? Møller placed his hand against the lowest buttonhole on his shirt. It wasn't easy to work Harry out.

'If you think you can make yourself useful in your last weeks, and you feel like turning up for work, that's absolutely fine by me. You are not suspended and we have to pay your salary to the end of the month anyway. And we know what your alternative is to sitting here, don't we.'

'Fine,' Harry grunted and stood up. 'I'll just go and see if my office still exists. You'll have to tell me if there's anything you need any help with, boss.'

Bjarne Møller flashed an indulgent smile.

'Yes, I'll take you up on that, Harry.'

'On the chow chow case, for example,' Harry said, closing the door quietly behind him.

Harry stood in the doorway contemplating his shared office. Halvorsen's desk, cleared for his holiday and empty, was set against his. On the wall over the filing cabinet hung a picture of Officer Ellen Gjelten, taken at the time when she used to sit in Halvorsen's seat. The other wall was almost completely covered with a street map of Oslo. The map was decorated with pins, lines and times indicating where Ellen, Sverre Olsen and Roy Kvinsvik were at the time of the murder. Harry went over to the wall and stood in front of the map. Then, in one swift movement, he tore it down and stuffed it into one of the drawers of the filing cabinet. He took a silver hip flask out of his jacket pocket, took a quick swig and rested his forehead against the metal cabinet's cooling surface.

He had worked for more than ten years in this office. Room 605. The smallest office in the red zone on the sixth floor. Even when they hit on the weird idea of promoting him to detective inspector he had insisted on remaining here. Room 605 didn't have any windows, but he observed the world from here. In these ten square metres he had learned his trade, celebrated his victories and suffered his defeats and acquired the little insight he had into the human mind. He tried to remember what else he had done over those ten years. There must have been something. You only work eight to ten hours every day. Not more than twelve, anyway. Plus the weekends.

Harry slumped down into his battered office chair, and the damaged springs screamed joyously. He could happily sit here for another two weeks.

At 5.25 p.m. Bjarne Møller would normally have been at home with his wife and child. However, since they were visiting Grandma he decided to use these days of holiday tranquillity to catch up on neglected paperwork. The shooting in Ullevålsveien had to some extent spoiled these plans, but he determined to make up for lost time.

When he received a call from the control room, Møller answered in an irritated tone that they would have to ring uniformed police as Crime Squad could not start taking responsibility for missing persons.

'Apologies, Møller. Patrol officers were busy dealing with a field fire in Grefsen. The caller is convinced that the missing person has been the victim of a crime.'

'All the staff still here are working on the shooting in Ullevålsveien. That would be . . .' Møller stopped in his tracks. 'Or, just a minute. Wait a sec, let me just check . . .'

9

Wednesday. Missing Person.

THE POLICE OFFICER RELUCTANTLY PUT HIS FOOT ON THE BRAKE AND the police car came to a halt in front of the red traffic lights by Alexander Kiellands plass.

'Or shall we stick the siren on and go for it?' asked the officer, turning towards the passenger seat.

Harry absentmindedly shook his head. He gazed across to the park which used to be a grass area with two benches occupied by boozers trying to drown out the sound of traffic with their songs and streams of abuse. A couple of years ago, though, they had decided to spend a few million on cleaning up the square bearing the writer's name, and the park was cleared, some planting was done, asphalt and paths were laid and an impressive fountain shaped like a salmon ladder was installed. It was without question a much more scenic background for singing songs and hurling abuse.

The police car swung to the right across Sannergata, crossed the bridge over the Akerselva and stopped in front of the address Harry had been given by Møller.

Harry told the officer he'd make his own way back, stepped out onto the pavement and straightened his back. On the other side of the road was a newly erected office building which still stood empty and according to the newspapers would continue to do so for a while. The windows reflected the apartment building whose address he had been given. It was a white building from the '40s or thereabouts, not completely functional, but an indeterminate close relative. The façade was richly appointed with graffiti tags marking territories. At the bus stop there was a dark-skinned girl with her arms folded, chewing gum as she studied a large hoarding for Diesel clothing on the other side of the street. Harry found the name by the top doorbell.

'Police,' Harry said, and prepared himself to tackle the stairs.

A strange figure stood in the doorway at the top, waiting as Harry came panting up the stairs. The man had a large tousled mane of hair, a black beard on a burgundy-red face and a matching tunic-like garment covering him from neck down to sandal-clad feet.

'It's good you could come so quickly,' he said, holding out his paw.

A paw it was in fact, the hand was so large that it completely enclosed Harry's when the man introduced himself as Wilhelm Barli.

Harry gave his name and tried to withdraw his hand. He didn't like physical contact with men, and this handshake belonged more in the category of embrace. However, Wilhelm held on to him as if for his life.

'Lisbeth has gone,' he whispered. His voice was surprisingly clear.

'Yes, we received the message. Shall we go inside?'

'Yes, come in.'

Wilhelm went ahead of Harry. It was only an attic flat, but while Camilla Loen's flat was small and furnished in a strictly minimalist style, this one was large and the decoration was lavish and flashy, like a pastiche of new classicism. However, it was exaggerated to the point that it almost tipped over into being the backdrop for a toga party. Instead of normal sofas and chairs there were reclining arrangements in a sort of Hollywood version of Ancient Rome, and the wooden beams were clad in plaster to form Doric or Corinthian columns. Harry had never grasped the difference, but he did recognise the plaster relief that had been laid directly on the white wall in the hallway. His mother had taken him and Sis to a museum in Copenhagen when they were small and there they had seen Bertel Thorvaldsen's *Jason and the Golden Fleece*. The flat had clearly just been done up. Harry noticed newly painted wood and bits of masking tape and could smell the blissful aroma of solvents.

In the sitting room there was a low table set for two. Harry followed Barli up the staircase and out onto a large, tiled roof terrace looking down onto the central area that was enclosed on four sides by connecting apartment buildings. The outside setting was contemporary Norwegian. There were three charred cutlets smoking on the grill.

'It gets so warm here in the afternoon in these attic flats,' Barli apologised, pointing to a white plastic baroque chair.

'So I've been finding out,' Harry said, walking over to the edge and looking down into the central area.

Generally heights didn't bother him, but after longish spells of drinking relatively modest heights could suddenly make him feel dizzy. Fifteen metres beneath him he saw two ageing bikes, and a white sheet hanging from a rotary clothes dryer and flapping in the wind. He had to look up again smartish.

Facing them across the courtyard, on a balcony with wrought-iron railings, two neighbours raised bottles of beer to him in greeting. Half of the table in front of them was covered in brown bottles. Harry nodded in return. He wondered how it could be that it was windy down in the yard but not up here.

'A glass of red wine?'

Barli had already begun to pour himself a glass from the half-empty bottle. Harry noticed that Barli's hand was shaking. *Domaine La Bastide Sy* he read on the label. The name was even longer but agitated fingers had torn the rest off.

Harry sat down. 'Thanks, but I don't drink when I'm on duty.'

Barli grimaced and quickly put the bottle back down on the table.

'Of course not, I apologise, I'm just beside myself with worry. I shouldn't be drinking either in this situation.'

As he put his glass to his mouth and drank, wine dribbled down the front of his tunic where a red stain began to grow.

Harry looked at his watch so that Barli would appreciate that he would have to be fairly brief.

'She was only supposed to be nipping down to the shop to buy some potato salad to go with the chops,' Barli gasped. 'Only two hours ago she was sitting where you are now.'

Harry adjusted his sunglasses. 'Your wife's been missing for two hours?'

'Yes, well, I'm not very sure any longer, but she was only supposed to be going to Kiwi round the corner and back.'

The sun caught the beer bottles on the opposite balcony. Harry put his hand over his eyes, noticed his moist fingers and wondered where he could wipe off the sweat. He placed the tips of his fingers against the burning hot plastic of the chair arm and felt the moisture being slowly scorched away.

'Have you rung round friends and acquaintances? Have you been down to the supermarket and checked? Perhaps she met someone and they went for a beer. Perhaps –'

'No, no, no!' Barli held up the palms of his hands in front of his chest, his fingers splayed. 'She didn't! She's not like that.'

'Not like what?'

'She's like someone . . . who comes back.'

'Right . . .'

'First of all I rang her on her mobile, but of course she'd left it here. Then I rang people we know whom she might have bumped into. I rang Kiwi, Police Headquarters, three police stations, all the casualty departments, Ullevål hospital and the Rikshospital. Nothing. *Nada. Nichts.*'

'I can see that you're concerned.'

Barli leaned across the table, his moist lips aquiver in his beard.

'I'm not concerned. I'm scared out of my wits. Have you ever heard of anyone going out in just a bikini with a fifty-kroner note while the meat is frying on the grill and then deciding that this is a good opportunity to hop it?'

Harry wavered. Just when he had decided to accept a glass of wine after all, Barli poured the rest of the bottle's contents into his own glass. So why didn't he stand up, say something reassuring about how many people ring in with missing person reports just like his, that almost all of them have a natural, unexceptional explanation, and then, after asking Barli to ring back later if she hadn't turned up by bedtime, take his leave? Perhaps it was the minor detail about the bikini and the 50-kroner note. Or perhaps it was because Harry had been waiting all day for something to happen, and this was at least an opportunity to put off what was waiting for him in his own flat. But most of all it was Barli's obvious and illogical terror. Harry had underrated intuition before, both other people's and his own, and it had been to his cost every time without exception.

'I have to make a couple of calls,' Harry said.

At 6.45 p.m. Beate Lønn arrived at the flat of Wilhelm and Lisbeth Barli in Sannergata, and a quarter of an hour later a police dog handler arrived with a German shepherd. The man introduced both himself and his dog as Ivan.

'It's a coincidence,' the man said. 'It's not my dog.'

Harry saw that Ivan was waiting for some witty comment, but Harry didn't have one.

While Wilhelm Barli went to the bedroom to find some recent photos of Lisbeth and some clothes to give Ivan – the dog – a scent, Harry quickly spoke to the other two in a low voice:

'OK, she could be absolutely anywhere. She could have left him, she could have had a funny turn, she could have said she was going somewhere else and he didn't realise. There are a million possibilities, but she could also be lying in the back seat of a car at this very moment, doped up, being raped by four kids who freaked out at the sight of her bikini. I don't want you to look for anything specific. Just search.'

Beate and Ivan nodded to show they had understood.

'A patrol car will be on its way soon. Beate, you meet them and get them to check the neighbours out, talk to people, especially in the supermarket where she was supposed to be going. Then you talk to the people in this part of the building. I'll just go over to the neighbours sitting on the balcony in the building over the way.'

'Do you think they know anything?' Beate asked.

'They have a perfect view of this flat and, judging by the number of empty bottles, they've been sitting there for a while. According to the husband, Lisbeth has been at home all day. I want to know whether they've seen her on the terrace, and if so, when.'

'Why's that?' the officer asked, jerking Ivan's lead.

'Because if a lady in a bikini in this oven of a flat has not been on the terrace, I'll be damn suspicious.'

'Naturally,' Beate whispered. 'Do you suspect the husband?'

'I suspect the husband on principle,' Harry said.

'Why's that?' Ivan said again.

Beate gave the smile of the initiated.

'It's always the husband,' Harry said.

'Hole's First Law,' Beate said.

Ivan looked from Harry to Beate and back again.

'But . . . wasn't he the one who reported her missing?'

'Yes, he was,' Harry said. 'And still it's always the husband. That's why you and Ivan are not starting the search outside on the street, but in here. You'll have to find an excuse if you have to, but I want the flat and the storage areas in the loft and the cellar checked out first. Afterwards you can continue outside. OK?'

Officer Ivan shrugged his shoulders and looked down at his namesake, who returned his resigned look.

*

The two people on the opposite balcony did not turn out to be two young men, as Harry had assumed when he saw them from Barli's terrace. Harry was aware that because a mature woman had pictures of Kylie Minogue on the wall, lived with a woman of the same age with a fringe and a T-shirt with Trondheim Eagles printed on it, this did not necessarily mean that she was a lesbian, but he drew this provisional conclusion anyway. He sat back in an armchair with the two women facing him, exactly as he had done with Vibeke Knutsen and Anders Nygård five days earlier.

'Apologies for dragging you in from the balcony,' Harry said.

The one who had introduced herself as Ruth put her hand to her mouth to suppress a belch.

'That's alright. We've had enough, haven't we?' she said

She slapped her partner on the knee. In a masculine way, Harry thought, and instantly recalled something Aune, the police psychologist, had said: that stereotypes were self-reinforcing because unconsciously you were looking for things to confirm them. That was why policemen thought – based on so-called experience – that all criminals were stupid, and criminals thought the same about all policemen.

Harry quickly put them in the picture. They stared at him in surprise.

'This will undoubtedly be resolved quickly, but we are obliged to go through standard police procedures. For the moment we are simply trying to establish a timetable.'

They nodded with serious expressions on their faces.

'Excellent,' Harry said, trying out the Hole smile. That, at any rate, was what Ellen used to call the grimace he pulled whenever he tried to appear jolly and good-natured.

Ruth confirmed that they had spent the whole afternoon on their balcony. They had seen Lisbeth and Wilhelm Barli lying on the terrace until about 4.30 when Lisbeth went inside. Immediately afterwards

Wilhelm had got the barbecue going. He had shouted something about potato salad and she had answered from indoors. Then he went in and came out again with the steaks (which Harry corrected to 'chops') about 20 minutes later. After a while – they agreed that it was at 5.15 – they saw Barli making a call on his mobile.

'Sound carries over enclosed spaces like this,' Ruth said. 'We could hear another phone ringing inside the flat. Barli was obviously annoyed. At least, he slammed his phone down on the table.'

'Apparently he was trying to ring his wife,' Harry said.

He noted the immediate exchange of glances and regretted the 'apparently'.

'How long does it take to buy potato salad at the supermarket round the corner?'

'At Kiwi? I can make it there and back in five minutes if there isn't a queue.'

'Lisbeth Barli doesn't sprint,' the partner said in a low voice.

'So you know her?'

Ruth and the Trondheim Eagle exchanged looks as if to harmonise their responses.

'No. But we certainly know who she is.'

'Really?'

'Yes, you must have seen the big spread in *Verdens Gang* about Wilhelm Barli directing a musical at the National Theatre this summer.'

'That was just a five-liner, Ruth.'

'Certainly was not,' snapped Ruth. 'Lisbeth is to play the main role. Big picture and all that. You must have seen it.'

'Mm,' Harry said. 'Haven't got round to . . . much reading of the papers this summer.'

'There was a big row, wasn't there. All the cultural elite thought it was scandalous putting on a summer show at the National Theatre. What's the play called again? My Fat Lady?'

'*Fair* Lady,' the Trondheim Eagle mumbled.

'So you follow the theatre then?' Harry intervened.

'Bit of this and that. Wilhelm Barli is the type to keep himself busy with all sorts of things. Revues, films, musicals . . .'

'He's a producer. And she sings.'

'Really?'

'Yes. I'm sure you can remember Lisbeth from the time before they got married, when she was called Harang.'

Harry regretfully shook his head and Ruth released a deep sigh.

'At that time she sang with her sister in Spinnin' Wheel. Lisbeth was a real babe, a bit like Shania Twain. With a real belter of a voice on her.'

'She wasn't that well known, Ruth.'

'Well, she sang on that programme of Vidar Lønn Arnesen's. And they sold a stack of records.'

'Cassettes, Ruth.'

'I saw Spinnin' Wheel at Momarkedet Country Festival. Pretty good stuff, you know. They should have recorded in Nashville and all that, but then she was discovered by Barli. He was going to make a musical star out of her. Certainly taken its time, though.'

'Eight years,' said the Trondheim Eagle.

'Anyway, Lisbeth Harang stopped singing with Spinnin' Wheel and married Barli. Money and beauty, ever heard that somewhere before?'

'So the wheel stopped spinnin'?'

'Eh?'

'He's asking about the band, Ruth.'

'Oh, yeah. The sister sang solo, but Lisbeth was the real star. Think they're playing holiday hotels and the Denmark ferries now. Sure they are.'

Harry got up.

'Just one last routine question. Do you have any idea what Wilhelm and Lisbeth's marriage was like?'

The Trondheim Eagle and Ruth exchanged further radar communication.

'Sound carries over enclosed spaces like this, as we told you,' Ruth said. 'Their bedroom also looks out over the yard.'

'You could hear them having a row?'

'Not having a row.'

They held Harry's gaze with meaningful expressions. A couple of seconds went by before he twigged what they meant and to his irritation he noticed that he was blushing.

'It's your impression then that the marriage worked especially well?'

'His terrace door is left ajar all summer, so I joked that we should sneak up onto the roof, go round the square and jump down onto his terrace,' Ruth grinned. 'Spy on them a bit, why not? It's not difficult, you just stand on the railing of our balcony and put a foot on the gutter and . . .'

The Trondheim Eagle nudged her partner in the ribs.

'It's not really necessary though,' Ruth said. 'After all, Lisbeth is a professional . . . what do you call it?'

'Communicator,' said the Trondheim Eagle.

'Exactly. All the great imagery is in the vocal cords, you know.'

Harry rubbed the back of his neck.

'Real screamer,' the Trondheim Eagle said with a tentative smile.

When Harry returned, the Ivans were still going through the flat. Officer Ivan was sweating and German Shepherd Ivan's tongue was hanging out of its open mouth like a liver-coloured welcome carpet for VIPs.

Harry sat down carefully on one of the reclining arrangements and asked Wilhelm Barli to tell him everything right from the beginning. His account of the afternoon and the timings confirmed what Ruth and the Trondheim Eagle had said.

Harry recognised genuine despair in the husband's eyes. And he began to suspect that if a crime had taken place, then this might – *might* – be one of the exceptions to the statistics. But most of all it strengthened his belief that Lisbeth would turn up soon enough. If it wasn't the husband, it wasn't anyone. Statistically speaking.

Beate returned and reported that people were at home in only two of the apartments in the building, and they hadn't heard or seen a thing, not in the stairwell and not outside on the street.

There was a knock at the door and Beate opened up. It was one of the uniformed officers from the patrol car. Harry recognised him immediately. It was the same officer who had stood watch at Ullevålsveien. He turned to Beate without showing any awareness of Harry's presence.

'We've been talking to people on the street and at Kiwi. We've checked the entrance and the yard. Nothing. But it is the holiday period and the streets are almost deserted, so the lady could easily have been dragged into a car without anyone noticing a thing.'

Harry felt Wilhelm Barli, who was standing next to him, give a start.

'Perhaps we ought to check with the Pakis who have shops in the area,' the policeman said, sticking his little finger in his ear and revolving it.

'Why them precisely?' Harry asked.

The officer finally turned round and said with exaggerated stress on the last word: 'Haven't you read the crime statistics, Inspector?'

'Indeed I have,' Harry said. 'And as far as I remember, shop owners are way down the list.'

The policeman studied his little finger.

'I know a few things about Muslims that you also know, Inspector. For them, a woman who comes in wearing a bikini is begging to be raped. It's almost a duty, you could say.'

'Oh?'

'That's just the way their religion is.'

'Now I think you're confusing Islam with Christianity.'

'Ivan and I have finished in here now,' the dog handler said, coming down the stairs with his dog.

'We found a couple of chops in the bin, that's all. Have there been any other dogs here recently by the way?'

Harry looked at Wilhelm. He just shook his head. His facial expression suggested that his voice would not have carried.

'In the entrance hall Ivan reacted as if there was another dog there, but it must have been something else. We're ready for the loft and cellar now. Can someone come with us?'

'Yes, of course,' Wilhelm said, getting up onto his feet.

They went out the door, and the police officer from the patrol car asked Beate if he could leave.

'You'll have to ask the boss,' she said.

'He's gone to sleep.'

He nodded scornfully in the direction of Harry who was testing out the Roman reclining chair.

'Constable,' Harry said in a low voice without opening his eyes. 'Please come closer.'

The police officer stood in front of Harry with his legs apart and his thumbs tucked into his belt.

'Yes, *Inspector.*'

Harry opened one eye.

'If you allow Tom Waaler to talk you into handing in another report on me, I'll make sure that you work on patrol cars for the rest of your career. Is that understood, *Constable*?'

The officer's facial muscles twitched. When he opened his mouth Harry was expecting swearing and ill temper. Instead the officer spoke in a controlled, low voice:

'First of all, I don't know any Tom Waaler. Secondly, I see it as my duty to report police officials who put themselves and colleagues at risk by turning up for work intoxicated. And thirdly, I have no desire to work anywhere else except on patrol cars. Can I go now, *Inspector*?'

Harry stared at the officer with his cyclops eye. Then he closed it again, swallowed and said:

'Please do.'

He heard the outer door slam shut and groaned. He needed a drink. And pronto.

'Are you coming?' Beate asked.

'Just go,' Harry said. 'I'll stay here and help Ivan to sniff around the streets as soon as they've finished with the loft and cellar.'

'Sure?'

'Absolutely.'

Harry went up the stairs and out onto the terrace. He watched the swallows and listened to the sounds coming from the open windows in the yard. He lifted up the bottle of red wine from the table. There was just a drop left. He polished it off and waved to Ruth and the Trondheim Eagle, who had not had enough after all, and went inside again.

He felt it immediately he opened the bedroom door. He had often noticed it, but he had never discovered where the stillness of other people's bedrooms came from.

There were still signs of someone's decorating here.

One wardrobe door with a mirror on the inside was ajar and a toolbox lay open beside the neatly made double bed. Over the bed was a photo of Wilhelm and Lisbeth. Harry had not taken a close look at the photograph Wilhelm had given to the patrol car officers, but now he could see that Ruth was right. Lisbeth really was a babe. Blond hair, sparkling blue eyes and a slim, agile body. She had to be at least ten years younger than Wilhelm. They were tanned and happy in the picture – they must recently have returned from a holiday abroad. Behind them he could just make out a magnificent building and a statue of a horseman. Somewhere in France maybe. Normandy.

Harry perched on the edge of the bed and was caught by surprise when the bed moved. A waterbed. He lay back and felt how it moulded to the shape of his body. The cool duvet cover was wonderful against the bare skin of his arm. The water made a slapping sound inside the rubber mattress as he changed position. He closed his eyes.

Rakel. They were on a river. No, a canal. Their canal boat bobbed down and the water slapped against both sides making a kissing sound.

They were below deck and Rakel lay quietly beside him in bed. She gave a low laugh as he whispered to her. Now she was pretending to sleep. He liked that. That she was pretending to sleep. It was a kind of game they played. Harry twisted round to look at her. His gaze fell on the mirror on the wardrobe door which reflected the whole of the bed. He looked at the open toolbox. On the top there was a short chisel with a green wooden handle. He lifted the tool up. Light, small, no sign of rust under the fine layer of builder's plaster.

He was going to put the chisel back when his hand froze. There was a severed part of a body in the toolbox. He had seen the same thing at other crime scenes. Severed sexual parts. It took a second before he realised that the skin-coloured, very realistic-looking penis was merely a dildo.

He lay back on the bed again with the chisel still in his hand. He gulped.

After doing a job for so many years, going through people's private property and personal lives on a daily basis, this was no big deal. That wasn't why he gulped.

Here – in this bed.

Would have to have a drink now.

Sound carries over an enclosed space.

Rakel.

He tried not to think, but it was too late. Her body against his. Rakel.

The erection came. Harry closed his eyes and could feel her hand moving, a sleeping person's unconscious, arbitrary movement, and then resting on his stomach. Her hand just lay there as if it had no intention of going anywhere. Her lips against his ear, her warm breath sounding like the roar of something burning. Her lips began to move as soon as he touched her. Her small, soft breasts with the sensitive nipples that stiffened when he so much as breathed on them; her sex which would open and devour him. There was an explosion in his throat as if he wanted to cry.

Harry gave a start on hearing the door close on the floor below. He sat up, smoothed the duvet, stood up and checked himself over in the mirror. He rubbed his face hard with both hands.

Wilhelm insisted on staying outside to see if the canine Ivan could detect a scent.

As they were coming out of Sannergata, a red bus glided soundlessly away from the bus stop. A little girl stared at Harry through the back window; her round face grew smaller and smaller as the bus disappeared towards Rodeløkka.

They walked to Kiwi and back without any reaction from the dog.

'It doesn't mean your wife hasn't been here,' Ivan said. 'In a busy street with traffic and a lot of people around it's difficult to isolate the scent of one person.'

Harry looked around him. He had the feeling that he was being observed, but the street was deserted, and all he saw in the windows of the row of house fronts was a dark sky and sun. An alkie's paranoia.

'Well,' Harry said. 'Then there's nothing more we can do for the moment.'

Wilhelm stared at them in despair.

'It'll be alright,' Harry said.

'No, it won't be alright,' Wilhelm answered in the same flat voice that radio weather forecasters use.

'Come here, Ivan!' the police officer shouted, jerking the lead. The dog had stuck its nose under the front bumper of a VW Golf parked close to the kerb.

Harry gave Wilhelm a pat on the shoulder and avoided his intense stare.

'All the patrol cars have been informed. If she doesn't turn up before midnight, we'll organise a search party. OK?'

Wilhelm did not answer.

Ivan barked at the Golf and pulled on his lead.

'Wait a moment,' the policeman said.

He went down on all fours, put his head close to the tarmac and stretched out an arm under the car.

'Found anything?' Harry asked.

The officer turned round. He was holding a lady's high-heeled shoe. Harry heard Wilhelm sob behind him and asked: 'Is this her shoe, Wilhelm?'

'It won't be alright,' Wilhelm said. 'It won't be alright.'

10

Thursday and Friday. Nightmares.

ON THURSDAY AFTERNOON A RED MAIL VAN STOPPED OUTSIDE A POST office in Rodeløkka. The contents of the postbox were emptied into a sack, eased gently into the back of the van and driven to the mail centre at Biskop Gunnerus gate 14, better known in Oslo as the Post House. The same evening, at the mail centre, the post was sorted by size and so the brown padded envelope ended up in a tray with other letters of C5 format. The envelope passed through several pairs of hands, though naturally enough no-one paid any special attention to it, nor when it was sorted by geographical area and was put first in the Østland tray and then in the tray for postcode 0032.

When the letter finally lay in a post sack in the back of a red van ready for delivery the following morning, it was night-time and most people in Oslo were sleeping.

'It'll be fine,' the boy said, patting the round-faced girl on the head. He felt her long, thin hair stick to his fingers. It was electric.

He was eleven years old. She was seven and his little sister. They had been visiting their mummy at the hospital.

The lift arrived and they opened the door. A man wearing a white coat pushed the grille to one side, gave them a fleeting smile and left. They entered the lift.

'Why is it such an old lift?' the girl asked.

'Because it's an old house,' the boy said, pulling the grille closed.

'Is it a hospital?'

'Not exactly,' he said, pressing the button for the ground floor.

'It's a house for people who are very tired to rest a little.'

'Is Mummy tired?'

'Yes, but she'll be fine. Don't lean against the door, Sis.'

'What?'

The lift started with a jerk and her long blond hair moved. Electricity, he thought, and stared as the hair on her head slowly rose. Her hands shot up to her head, and she screamed. A thin, piercing scream that fixed him to the spot. Her hair was trapped on the other side of the grille. It must have been caught in the lift door. He tried to move, but it was as if he was stuck, too.

'Daddy!' she screamed and stood on the tips of her toes.

But Daddy had gone ahead to collect the car from the car park.

'Mummy!' she screamed as she was pulled off the lift floor. But Mummy lay in bed with a pallid smile on her face.

She kicked out wildly while clinging to her hair. If only he could move.

'Help!'

Harry sat up in bed with a start. His heart was beating like a bass drum gone wild.

'Christ.'

He heard his own hoarse voice and let his head fall back on the pillow.

The light in the crack between the curtains was grey. He peered over to the red digital figures on his bedside table: 4.12. The summer nights were hell. The nightmares were hell.

He swung his legs out of bed and went to the lavatory. The urine splashed into the water as he stared into the distance. He knew he wouldn't be going back to sleep.

The fridge was empty apart from a bottle of low-alcohol beer that had ended up in his shopping basket because his vision had been blurred. He opened the cupboard over the sink unit. An army of beer and whisky bottles stood to attention and eyed him in silence. All empty. In a sudden fit of rage he knocked them flying and heard them clattering long after he had closed the cupboard doors. He checked the time again. It was Friday morning. The Vinmonopol did not open for another five hours.

Harry sat down by the telephone in the sitting room and rang Øystein Eikeland's mobile phone number.

'Oslo Taxis.'

'What's the traffic like?'

'Harry?'

'Good evening, Øystein.'

'Is it? Haven't had a punter for half an hour.'

'Holiday time.'

'Don't I know it! The owner's gone off to his log cabin on Kragerø and has left me driving Oslo's deadest deadmobile. And in the deadest town in Northern Europe. It's as if someone's dropped a bloody neutron bomb.'

'Thought you didn't like to sweat too much on the job.'

'Hah, I'm sweating like a pig. The tight-fisted bastard buys cars without air conditioning. I have to drink like a bloody camel after shifts just to replace the liquid I've lost. And that costs an arm and a leg. Yesterday it cost me more than I had scraped together all day.'

'I'm genuinely sorry to hear that.'

'Should have stuck to cracking codes.'

'Hacking you mean? That got you booted out of Den Norske Bank and a six-month suspended sentence?'

'Right, but I was good at it. Whereas this . . . By the way, the owner's thinking of cutting down on the hours he drives, but I'm already driving twelve-hour shifts and you can't find new taxi drivers anymore. You don't fancy doing a bit, do you, Harry?'

'Thank you, I'll think about it.'

'What are you after?'

'I need something to make me sleep.'

'Go to the doctor.'

'I did. He gave me Imovane, some sleeping tablets. They didn't work. I asked for something stronger, but he refused.'

'Never a good idea to have the smell of booze on your breath when you go asking your GP for some Rohypnol, Harry.'

'He said I was too young for strong medications. Have you got any?'

'Rohypnol? Are you crazy? It's illegal, isn't it? But I've got Flunipam. Same sort of stuff. Half a tablet and you'll go out like a light.'

'OK. I'm a bit short of cash at the moment, but you'll get the money at the end of the month. Does it get rid of dreams, too?'

'Eh?'

'Will it stop me dreaming?'

The line went quiet for a moment.

'Do you know what, Harry? Now that I think about it, I've run out of Flunipam. On top of that, it's dangerous stuff. And it won't stop you dreaming, more the opposite.'

'You're lying.'

'Maybe, but Flunipam is not what you need, anyway. Try taking it easy, Harry. Have a break.'

'Have a *break*? I don't *have* breaks. You know that.'

Harry could hear someone opening the taxi door and Øystein telling them to go to hell. Then his voice was there again.

'Is it Rakel?'

Harry didn't answer.

'Have you had a row with Rakel?'

Harry could hear a crackling noise and guessed Øystein was listening to the police channel.

'Hello! Harry! Can't you answer when a childhood friend asks you if the foundations of your existence are still in place?'

'They aren't,' Harry mumbled.

'Why not?'

Harry took a deep breath.

'Because I practically forced her to dig them up. Something I was working on for a long time fell apart and I couldn't come to terms with it. I went on a bender and festered in my own shit for three days without answering the phone. On the fourth day she came round and rang the bell. At first she was furious. She said that I couldn't just run away, that Møller had been asking after me, and then she stroked my face. She asked me if I needed help.'

'And knowing you as I do, you showed her the door or something like that, right.'

'I said I was fine. Then she went all miserable.'

'Obviously. The girl's fond of you.'

'That's what she said, but she also said that she couldn't go through it again.'

'Go through what again?'

'Oleg's father's an alkie. It was destroying all three of them.'

'And you answered?'

'I said she was right, and that she should keep away from people like me. She pulled a face. Then she left.'

'And now you have nightmares?'

'Yes.'

Øystein breathed a heartfelt sigh.

'Do you know what, Harry? There's nothing that can help you through this. Well, there is one thing.'

'I know,' Harry said. 'A bullet.'

'You yourself, is what I was going to say.'

'I know that, too. Forget I rang, Øystein.'

'Already forgotten.'

Harry went to get the bottle of low-alcohol beer. He sat down in the armchair and glared at the label. The cap came off with a gasp of relief. He put the chisel down on the coffee table. The wooden handle was green and the blade was covered with a fine layer of yellow builder's plaster.

At 6 a.m. on Friday the sun was already shining down on Ekeberg Ridge, making the Police HQ sparkle like a crystal. The security guard in reception yawned aloud and raised his eyes from *Aftenposten* as the first early riser slid his ID card through the security machine.

'Says it's going to get even hotter,' announced the guard, who was glad he finally had someone he could exchange a few words with.

The tall, fair-haired man with bloodshot eyes glanced at him, but he didn't answer.

The guard noticed that he took the stairs even though neither of the two lifts on the ground floor was being used.

Then he went back to concentrating on the *Aftenposten* article about the woman who had disappeared one bright, sunny morning before the weekend and still had not turned up. The journalist, Roger Gjendem, quoted Chief Inspector Bjarne Møller who had confirmed that the police had discovered one of the woman's shoes under a car directly outside where she lived and that this strengthened suspicions that a crime had taken place. However, as yet they had nothing concrete to this effect.

Harry flicked through the paper on the way to his pigeonhole where he picked up the reports on the last two days' search for Lisbeth Barli. There were five messages on his answerphone, all except one from Wilhelm Barli. Harry ran through the messages, which were almost identical: that they had to deploy more men, that he knew of a clair-voyant and that he wanted to go to the press and offer a reward to anyone who could help the police find Lisbeth.

The last message was someone breathing. That was all.

Harry rewound the tape and played it again.

And then again.

It was impossible to be sure whether it was a man or a woman. Even more impossible to hear if it was Rakel. The display showed that they had received the call at 11.10 p.m. from an 'unknown number', just as when Rakel called from her phone in Holmenkollveien. If it was her, why didn't she try his home number or his mobile?

Harry went through the reports. Nothing. He read them one more time. Still nothing. He cleared his brain and started from the beginning again.

When he was finished he looked at his watch and went out to the pigeonholes to see if anything else had arrived. He took a detective's report with him, put an envelope addressed to Bjarne Møller in the correct pigeonhole and went back into his office.

The detective's report was concise and to the point: nothing.

Harry rewound the answerphone tape, pressed play and turned up the volume. He closed his eyes and leaned back in his chair. He tried to remember her breathing. Feel her breath.

'Irritating when they don't say who they are, isn't it.'

It wasn't the words but the voice that made the hairs on his neck stand on end. He turned round slowly in his chair, which screamed in anguish.

Tom Waaler was standing, leaning against the door frame with a smile on his face. He was eating an apple and proffered the bag.

'Dunno what they are. Australian? Taste wonderful.'

Harry shook his head without taking his eyes off him.

'May I come in?' Waaler asked.

When Harry didn't answer, he stepped in and closed the door behind him. He walked round the desk and sat himself down in the other office chair. He leaned backwards and chomped noisily away at the inviting red apple.

'Have you noticed that you and I are almost always the first two to arrive at work, Harry? Strange, isn't it? Since we're also the last two to go home.'

'You're sitting in Ellen's chair,' Harry said.

Waaler patted the arm of the chair.

'It's about time you and I had a chat, Harry.'

'Chat away,' Harry said.

Waaler held the apple up to the light in the ceiling and screwed up one eye. 'Isn't it depressing not having a window in your office?'

Harry didn't answer.

'There is a rumour going round that you're leaving,' Waaler said.

'Rumour?'

'Well, rumour is perhaps an exaggeration. I have my sources, let's put it that way. You've probably been looking around for other work – security companies, insurance companies, debt collection maybe? Must be lots of places where they need an investigator with a bit of a background in law.'

Strong, white teeth sank into the flesh of the apple.

'Perhaps not so many places where they require a work record with notes on drunkenness, unauthorised absences, abuse of authority, insubordination to superiors and disloyalty to the force.'

His jaw muscles were grinding and chewing.

'But – but,' Waaler said. 'Perhaps it's not such a bad thing if they don't employ you. None of them offers particularly interesting challenges, so to speak. Not for someone who, despite everything, has been an inspector and was reckoned to be one of the very best in his field. And they don't pay particularly well, either. And that's what it's about in the final analysis, isn't it? Being paid for your services. Getting enough money to pay for food and rent. Enough for a beer and a bottle of cognac. Or is it whisky?'

Harry noticed that he was clenching his teeth so hard that his fillings were beginning to ache.

'The best thing,' Waaler continued, 'would undoubtedly be to treat yourself to a few extras over and above purely basic needs, providing you had earned sufficient money, that is. Such as the occasional holiday trip with your family to Normandy, for example.'

Harry felt his head fizzing, as if a fuse had blown.

'You and I are different in many ways, Harry, but that doesn't mean that I don't respect you as a professional. You are goal-orientated, smart, creative and your integrity is unimpeachable. That's what I've always thought. Above all else, though, you are mentally tough. In a society where competition gets harder and harder there is a need for this quality. Unfortunately, the competition doesn't always use the means that we might desire, but if you want to be a winner you have to be willing to employ the same means as your competitors. There is one more thing . . .'

Waaler lowered his voice.

'You have to play on the right team, the team you can win something with.'

'What are you after, Waaler?'

Harry could feel his voice trembling.

'I want to help you.' Waaler stood up. 'It doesn't have to be like this, you know . . .'

'Like what?'

'Like this, that you and I are enemies. Like this, that the Chief Super has to sign those papers. You know.'

Waaler walked over to the door.

'And like this, that you can never afford to do something nice for yourself and those you love . . .'

He rested his hand on the door handle.

'Think about it, Harry. There's only one thing that can help you in the jungle out there.'

A bullet, Harry thought.

'You yourself,' Waaler said, and was gone.

11

Sunday. Departure.

SHE LAY IN BED SMOKING A CIGARETTE. SHE STUDIED HIM AS HE STOOD in front of the low chest of drawers, watched his shoulder blades moving under the waistcoat and making it glisten in shades of black and blue. She shifted her gaze to the mirror and watched the gentle, self-assured movements of his hands tying his tie. She liked his hands, liked to see them moving.

'When will you be back?' she asked.

Their eyes met in the mirror. His smile. That too was gentle and self-assured. She thrust out a sulky bottom lip.

'As quickly as I can, *Liebling*.'

No-one said 'darling' the way he did. *Liebling*. In his strange accent and with that singing intonation that had almost made her like the German language again.

'On the evening flight tomorrow, I hope,' he said. 'Will you be there to meet me?'

She couldn't stop herself smiling. He laughed. She laughed. Damn him, he always managed it.

'I'm sure you've got a throng of women waiting for you in Oslo,' she said.

'I hope so.'

He buttoned up his waistcoat and took his jacket off the hanger in the wardrobe.

'Did you iron the handkerchiefs, *Liebling*?'

'I put them in your suitcase with the socks,' she said.

'Excellent.'

'Have you got a rendezvous with any of them?'

He laughed, went across to the bed and bent down over her.

'What do you think?'

'I don't know.' She put her arms around his neck. 'I think there's a woman's scent on you every time you come home.'

'That's because I'm never away long enough for your scent to fade, *Liebling*. How long ago is it now since I first discovered you? Twenty-six months. I've had your scent on me for twenty-six months now.'

'And no other?'

She wriggled further down the bed and dragged him after her. He kissed her lightly on the mouth.

'And no other. My plane, *Liebling* . . .'

He extricated himself.

She watched him as he walked over to the chest of drawers, opened one, took out his passport and plane tickets, put them in his inside pocket and buttoned up his jacket. It all happened in one sleek movement; this effortless efficiency and self-assurance that she found both sensual and frightening. Had it not been for the fact that he did almost everything with the same minimal effort, she would have said that he must have been in training for this all his life: departing; leaving.

Bearing in mind that they had spent so much time together over the last two years, she knew surprisingly little about him, but he never made a secret of the fact that he had been with a great many women in his previous life. He used to say it was because he had been searching so desperately for her. He had turned them away as soon as he realised they weren't her and he had continued his restless search until one fine autumn day two years ago they had met in the bar of the Grand Hotel Europa in Wenceslas Square.

That was the most wonderful description of promiscuity she had ever heard. More wonderful than hers at any rate, which had been for money.

'What do you do in Oslo?'

'Business,' he said.

'Why will you never tell me exactly what it is that you do?'

'Because we love each other.'

He closed the door quietly behind him, and she heard his footsteps going down the stairs.

Alone again. She closed her eyes and hoped that the smell of him would remain in the bedclothes until he returned. She placed her hand over her necklace. She had not taken it off since he gave it to her, not even when she took a bath. She stroked the pendant with her fingers and thought about his suitcase. About the stiff white clergyman's collar she had seen next to his socks. Why hadn't she asked him about it? Perhaps because she felt that she was asking too many questions already. She mustn't irritate him.

She sighed, looked at her watch and closed her eyes again. The day had no shape. An appointment with the doctor at 2.00, that was all. She began to count the seconds as her fingers continued to stroke the pendant, a red diamond, shaped like a star with five points.

The front-page spread in *Verdens Gang* was about an unnamed celebrity in the Norwegian media having had a 'brief, but intense' relationship with Camilla Loen. They had got hold of a grainy holiday snap of Camilla wearing a minuscule bikini, obviously to underline the intimations made in the article as to what the main ingredient of the relationship had been.

The same day *Dagbladet* ran an interview with Lisbeth Barli's sister, Toya Harang, who in a paragraph entitled 'Always Running Off' gave her little sister's childhood behaviour as a possible explanation for her unexplained disappearance. She was quoted as saying: 'She ran off from Spinnin' Wheel too, so why not now?'

There was a picture of her wearing a Stetson and posing in front of the band's bus. She was smiling. Harry assumed that she hadn't really thought about what she was doing before they took her photo.

'A beer.'

He sank down on the bar stool in Underwater and pulled over *Verdens Gang*. The Springsteen concert in Valle Hovin was sold out. Fine with him. For one thing, Harry hated stadium concerts, and for another, he and Øystein had hitched to Drammenshallen when they were 15 with fake Springsteen tickets that Øystein had made. That was when they had all been right at their peak: Springsteen, Øystein and Harry.

Harry pushed the paper away and opened his own *Dagbladet* with the photograph of Lisbeth's sister. The likeness between the two was striking. He had talked to her in Trondheim on the phone, but she didn't have anything to tell him, or more to the point, she didn't have anything interesting to tell him. The fact that their conversation had lasted 20 minutes had had little to do with him. She had explained to him her name should be pronounced with the stress on the *a*. ToyA. And that she had not been named after Michael Jackson's sister, who is called LaToya with the stress on *oy*.

Four days had gone by now since Lisbeth's disappearance, and the case had, in a nutshell, run aground.

The same was true of the Camilla Loen case. Even Beate was frustrated. She had been working all weekend to help the few detectives who were not on holiday. Nice girl, Beate. Shame that being nice didn't pay off.

Since Camilla had clearly been a sociable young lady, they had managed to put together most of her movements the week before the shooting, but the leads they had didn't take them anywhere.

Actually, Harry had meant to mention to Beate that Waaler had been to his office and had more or less openly suggested that he sell his soul to him, but for some reason he held back. Besides, he had enough to think about. If he told Møller it would only lead to a row and so he immediately rejected the idea.

Harry was well into his second beer when he saw her. She was sitting on her own at one of the tables in the semi-darkness by the wall. She was looking right at him and gave him a little smile. On the table in front of her was a beer and between her index and middle finger a cigarette.

Harry picked up his glass and made his way over to her table.

'Can I sit down?'

Vibeke Knutsen nodded towards the vacant seat.

'What are you doing here?'

'I live just round the corner,' Harry said.

'I thought so, but I haven't seen you here before.'

'No. My local and I have differing interpretations of an incident that took place there last week.'

'They barred you?' she asked with a hoarse laugh.

Harry liked her laugh. And he thought she was attractive, perhaps because of her make-up and because she was sitting in the dark. So what. He liked her eyes; they were playful and full of life, childlike and clever, just like Rakel's but that was where the similarity ended. Rakel had a narrow, sensitive mouth; Vibeke's was large and seemed even larger painted with fire-engine-red lipstick. Rakel was discreetly elegant and agile, almost as slim as a ballerina, no generous curves. Vibeke was wearing tiger stripes today, but they were as eye-catching as the leopard and the zebra stripes. Most things about Rakel were dark: her eyes, her hair and her skin. He had never seen skin glow like hers. Vibeke had red hair and was pale. Her crossed bare legs shone white in the dark.

'What are you doing here on your own?' he asked.

She shrugged her shoulders and took a sip from her glass.

'Anders is away, travelling, and won't be back until this evening. So I am indulging myself a little.'

'Has he gone far?'

'Somewhere in Europe. You know how it is. They never tell you anything.'

'What does he do?'

'He sells fittings for churches and chapels. Altarpieces, pulpits, crosses and suchlike. Used and new.'

'Mm. And he does that in Europe?'

'When a church in Switzerland needs a new pulpit, it could well come from Ålesund. And the old one may well end up being restored in Stockholm or Narvik. He travels all the time. He's away more than he's at home. Especially in the last few months. This last year really.' She took a drag of her cigarette and added while inhaling: 'He's not Christian though.'

'No?'

She shook her head as the smoke rose in a thick coil from the red lips with the small, close-set wrinkles above them.

'His parents were in the Pentecostal sect, and he grew up with that stuff. I've only been to one meeting, but do you know what? I think it's creepy, I do. When they start talking in tongues and all that. Have you been to any meetings like that?'

'Twice,' Harry said. 'With the Philadelphians.'

'Were you saved?'

'Unfortunately not. I just went there to find someone who said he would stand in court as a witness for me.'

'Well, if you didn't find Jesus, at least you found your witness.'

Harry shook his head.

'They said he'd stopped going, and he doesn't live at any of the addresses I've been given. So no, I definitely wasn't saved.'

Harry drained his beer and signalled to the bar. He lit another cigarette.

'I tried to get hold of you during the day,' she said. 'At your work.'

'Oh yes?'

Harry thought of the wordless message on his answerphone.

'Yes, but I was told it wasn't your case.'

'If you're thinking about the Camilla Loen case, then that's correct.'

'So I spoke to the other one who was at our place. The fit-looking one.'

'Tom Waaler?'

'Yes. I told him a few things about Camilla. The sort of thing I couldn't say when you were there.'

'Why not?'

'Because Anders was sitting there.'

She took a long drag on her cigarette.

'He can't stand it when I say anything derogatory about Camilla. He gets absolutely furious. Even though we hardly knew her.'

She shrugged her shoulders.

'I don't think it's derogatory. It's Anders who thinks that. I suppose it's our upbringing. I believe that he actually thinks that all women should go through their lives without having sex with more than one man.' She stubbed out her cigarette and added in a low voice: 'And barely that.'

'Mm. And Camilla had sex with more than one man?'

'The upper-class name says it all.'

'How do you know that? Can you hear noises?'

'Not between floors. So in the winter we didn't hear much. But in the summer, with the windows open. You know, sound . . .'

'. . . carries over enclosed spaces.'

'Exactly. Anders used to get up and slam the bedroom window shut. And if I happened to make a comment, like "now she's got a good head of steam up", well, he would get so angry that he would go and bed down in the sitting room.'

'So you tried to get hold of me to tell me this?'

'Yes. And there was one other thing. I received a phone call. At first I thought it was Anders, but I can usually hear background noise when he calls. As a rule he rings from some street in some European town. The weird thing is that the sound is exactly the same, just as if he were ringing from the same place every time. Anyway, this sounded different. Normally I would have just slammed down the receiver and not given it a second thought, but what with the Camilla business and with Anders away . . .'

'Yes?'

'Well, it was no big deal.'

She gave a tired smile. Harry thought it was a wonderful smile.

'It was just someone breathing on the phone. I thought it was creepy though, so I wanted to tell you. Waaler said he would look into it, but I don't think they could find what number he was calling from. It does happen that these murderers return to the scene of the crime, doesn't it?'

'Think that's mostly in detective novels,' Harry said. 'I wouldn't give it another thought.'

He twirled his glass round. The medicine was beginning to work.

'Do you and your partner know Lisbeth Barli by any chance?'

Vibeke held his gaze, her pencilled eyebrows raised aloft.

'The woman who's disappeared? Why on earth should we?'

'You're right, why on earth should you?' Harry mumbled and wondered what made him ask.

It was close to 9.00 when they stepped out onto the pavement outside Underwater.

Harry had to find his sea-legs.

'I live just down the road,' Harry said. 'What about . . . ?'

Vibeke tilted her head and smiled.

'Don't say anything you'll come to regret now, Harry.'

'Regret?'

'For the last half an hour you've been talking non-stop about this Rakel. You haven't forgotten, have you?'

'She doesn't want me, I said.'

'Yes, and you don't want me, either. You want Rakel. Or a Rakel substitute.'

She put her hand on his arm.

'If things were different, maybe I could have imagined being that person for a while, but they aren't. And Anders will be home soon.'

Harry shrugged his shoulders and steadied himself with a step to the side.

'Well, let me accompany you to your door,' he snuffled.

'It's two hundred metres, Harry.'

'I can manage it.'

Vibeke laughed out loud and linked her arm under his.

They glided slowly down Ullevålsveien as cars and unoccupied taxis cruised past and the evening air caressed their skin as it does in Oslo in July, but only then. Harry listened to the regular hum of her voice and wondered what Rakel was doing right now.

They stopped outside the black wrought-iron entrance.

'Goodnight, Harry.'

'Mm. Are you going to take the lift?'

'How's that?'

'Nothing.' Harry shoved his hands in his trouser pockets in an attempt to keep his balance. 'Take care. Goodnight.'

Vibeke smiled, went over to him, and Harry breathed in her fragrance as she kissed him on the cheek.

'In another life, who knows?' she whispered.

The gate closed after her with a smooth, well-oiled click. Harry stood there trying to orientate himself when something in the show-room window in front of him caught his attention. It wasn't the range of headstones, but something in the reflection. A red car parked by the kerb on the other side of the road. If Harry had been in the slightest bit interested in cars, he would perhaps have known that this exclusive toy was a Tommykaira ZZ-R.

'Fuck you,' Harry muttered under his breath and stepped out to cross the road. A taxi shot past him with a blaring horn. He crossed over to the sports car and stood by the driver's door. A blackened window was lowered without a sound.

'What the fuck are you doing here?' Harry wheezed. 'Are you spying on me?'

'Good evening, Harry,' Tom Waaler yawned. 'I'm keeping Camilla Loen's flat under surveillance, watching who comes and goes. You know, it's not just a hollow phrase that criminals go back to the scene of the crime.'

'Yes, it is. That's exactly what it is,' Harry said.

'But, as you have perhaps realised, it's all we have. The murderer hasn't left us a lot to go on.'

'We don't know that the man . . .' Harry said.

'Or woman,' Waaler interrupted.

Harry shrugged his shoulders and steadied himself. The door on the passenger side flew open.

'Hop in, Harry. I'd like a chat with you.'

Harry squinted at the open door. He wavered. He took another stabilising sidestep. Then he walked round the car and got in.

'Have you had a think?' Waaler asked, turning down the music.

'Yes, I've had a think,' Harry said, squirming in the narrow bucket seat.

'And did you come to the correct conclusion?'

'You obviously like red, Japanese sports cars.' Harry raised his hand and slapped the dashboard with some force. 'Solid stuff. Tell me . . .' Harry concentrated on his diction. 'Was this how you and Sverre Olsen sat in the car and chatted in Grünerløkka the night Ellen was killed?'

Waaler eyed Harry for a long time before he opened his mouth and answered: 'Harry, I have no idea what you're talking about.'

'No? You knew that Ellen had named you as the ringleader behind the arms smuggling, didn't you? It was you who made sure that Sverre Olsen killed her before she could tell anyone else. And when you were told that I was on Sverre Olsen's trail you hurriedly arranged it so that it looked as if he had drawn a gun while you were trying to arrest him. Just like with the other guy in Havnelageret. It's a sort of speciality of yours, executing troublesome prisoners.'

'You're drunk, Harry.'

'I've spent two years trying to get something on you, Waaler. Did you know that?'

Waaler didn't answer.

Harry laughed and struck out again. The dashboard gave an ominous cracking sound.

'Of course you knew! The Prince and heir apparent knows everything. How do you do it? Tell me.'

Through the side window Waaler caught sight of a man coming out of Kebabgården; he stopped and looked in both directions before walking down towards Trinity Church. Neither of them said a word until the man had turned into the road between the cemetery and Our Lady's Hospital.

'Fine,' Waaler growled. 'I can easily make a confession if that's what you want. But just remember that when you hear a confession you can quickly get caught up in unpleasant dilemmas.'

'Unpleasantness is fine by me.'

'I gave Sverre Olsen the punishment he deserved.'

Harry turned his head slowly towards Waaler who was reclining against the headrest with his eyes half closed.

'But not because I was afraid he would reveal that he and I were in league with each other. That part of your theory is incorrect.'

'Yeah?'

Waaler sighed.

'Do you wonder what it is that makes people like us do what we do?'

'I never do anything else.'

'What's your earliest memory, Harry?'

'When?'

'My earliest memory is of night and of my father bending over me in bed.'

Waaler stroked the steering wheel.

'I must have been four or five. He smelled of tobacco and security. You know, how fathers should smell. He used to come home after I'd gone to bed. And I knew that he would have gone to work long before I woke up in the morning. I knew that if I opened my eyes, he would smile, pat me on the head and go again. So I pretended that I was sleeping so he would stay there a little longer. Just sometimes, when I was having nightmares about the woman with the pig's head going round the streets in search of children's blood, I would open my eyes when he got up to go and ask him to sit with me for a little longer. And he sat down while I lay there wide-eyed, staring at him. Was it the same with your father, Harry?'

Harry shrugged his shoulders.

'My father was a teacher. He was always at home.'

'Middle-class home then.'

'Something like that.'

Waaler nodded.

'My father was a workman. Just like the fathers of my two best pals, Geir and Solo. They lived right above us in the block of flats in Oslo Old Town where I grew up. East End of Oslo, grey, but it was a good, well-kept block of flats owned by the union. We didn't see ourselves as working class, we were all entrepreneurs. Solo's father even owned a shop and everyone in the family played their part. All the men in our neighbourhood worked hard, but no-one worked as hard as my father did – dawn to dusk, day and night. He was like a machine that was only switched off on Sundays. Neither of my parents was particularly Christian. My father studied theology for half a year at evening school because Grandfather wanted him to become a priest, but when Grandfather died he gave it up. All the same we went to Vålerenga church every Sunday and afterwards Father went with us to Ekeberg or Østmarka. At five o'clock we changed clothes and had our Sunday meal in the sitting room. This might sound boring, but I'll tell you what, I looked forward all week to Sundays.

'Then it was Monday and he was off again. There was always some building job that needed him to do overtime. "Some money was whiter than white, some grey and some black," he used to say. It was the only way you could save up anything in his line of work. When I was thirteen we moved west to a house with an apple orchard. Father said it was better there. I was the only person in the class whose parents were not lawyers, economists, doctors or other professionals. The neighbour was a judge and he had a son of my age. Father hoped that I would turn out like him. He said that if I ever wanted to take up one of those professions it was important to have friends in the trade, to learn the codes, the language and the unwritten rules. However, I never saw anything of the son, just their dog, a German shepherd that stood barking on the veranda all night. After school I took the train to Oslo Old Town and met Geir and Solo there instead. Mother and Father invited all the neighbours to a barbecue party, but they all made excuses and politely turned down our invitation, except for one person. I can remember the smell of the smoke from the barbecue and the raucous laughter from the other gardens that summer. There was never a return invitation.'

Harry concentrated on his diction. 'Does this story have a point to it?'

'You'll have to decide that. Shall I stop?'

'No, do go on, there's nothing particular I want to watch on TV tonight.'

'One Sunday we were going to church as usual. I was waiting out in the street for Father and Mother and watching the German shepherd going wild in the garden snarling and barking at me from the other side of the fence. I don't know why I did it, but I went and opened the gate. I may have thought it was angry because it was all alone. The dog jumped on me, knocked me to the ground and bit right through my cheek. I still have the scar.'

Waaler pointed, but Harry couldn't see anything.

'The judge called the dog from the veranda. It let go, then he told me to get the hell out of his garden. Mother cried and Father hardly said a word as we drove to casualty. On our return I had a thick black line of stitches running from my chin to right up to underneath my ear. My father went over to see the judge. When he came back his eyes were dark with fury and he said even less than before. We ate our Sunday joint in total silence. That night I woke up and lay awake wondering what had woken me. It was quiet everywhere. Then I realised. The German shepherd. It had stopped barking. I heard the front door close, and I knew instinctively that we would never hear that dog barking again. When the bedroom door was gently opened I closed my eyes tight, but still caught a glimpse of the hammer. He smelled of tobacco and security. And I pretended I was asleep.'

Waaler wiped an invisible speck of dust off the steering column.

'I did what I did because we knew that Sverre Olsen had taken the life of one of our colleagues. I did it for Ellen, Harry. For us. Now you know I have killed a man. Are you going to report me or not?'

Harry simply stared. Waaler closed his eyes.

'We only had circumstantial evidence against Olsen, Harry. He had got away with it. We couldn't allow that to happen. Would you have allowed it to happen, Harry?'

Waaler turned his head and met Harry's unrelenting stare.

'Would you?'

Harry swallowed.

'There was someone who saw you and Sverre Olsen together in a car, someone who was willing to testify to that effect, but you probably knew that, didn't you.'

Waaler shrugged his shoulders.

'I spoke to Olsen on several occasions. He was a neo-Nazi and a criminal. It's our job to keep tabs on that sort, Harry.'

'The person who saw you suddenly does not want to talk any more. You've had a chat with him, haven't you. You've intimidated him into silence.'

Waaler shook his head.

'I can't answer that kind of thing, Harry. Even if you decide to join our team it's a hard and fast rule that you only get to know what is absolutely necessary in order for you to perform your role. It may sound rigid, but it works. It works for us.'

'Did you talk to Kvinsvik?' Harry slurred.

'Kvinsvik is just one of your windmills, Harry. Forget him. You'd be better off thinking about yourself.'

He leaned closer to Harry and lowered his voice.

'What have you got to lose? Have a good look in the mirror . . .'

Harry blinked.

'Right,' Waaler said. 'You're a man of almost forty with an alcohol problem and no job, no family and no money.'

'For the last time!' Harry tried to shout but was too drunk. 'Did you talk to . . . to Kvinsvik?'

Waaler sat up in his seat again.

'Go home, Harry. And think about who you really owe something to here. Is it the force? Who feed on you, don't like the taste and then spit you out? Your bosses who scurry off like frightened mice as soon as they smell trouble? Or do you perhaps owe yourself something? You've slogged away year in, year out to keep the streets of Oslo moderately safe in a country which protects its criminals better than it does its own civil servants. You are in fact one of the best at what you do, Harry. Unlike the others, you've got talent. And yet you earn a pittance. I can offer you five times what you're earning today, but that's not the most important bit. I can offer you a touch of dignity, Harry. Dignity. Think about it.'

Harry struggled to focus his eyes on Waaler, but his face kept drifting off. He fumbled around looking for the door handle, but couldn't find it. Bloody Jap cars. Waaler leaned across him and pushed the door open.

'I know you've been trying to find Kvinsvik,' Waaler said. 'Let me save you the bother. Yes, I talked to Olsen in Grünerløkka that evening, but that does not mean that I had anything to do with Ellen's murder. I kept my mouth shut so that I didn't complicate matters. You can do what you like, but believe me: Roy Kvinsvik has nothing to say that's worth hearing.'

'Where is he?'

'Would it make any difference if I told you? Would you believe me then?'

'Maybe,' Harry said. 'Who knows?'

Waaler sighed.

'Sognsvannveien 32. He is staying in his ex-stepfather's basement sitting room.'

Harry turned round and hailed a taxi coming towards him with its sign lit up.

'But this evening he's at choir practice with the Menna choir,' Waaler said. 'Walking distance. They practise in Gamle Aker church hall.'

'Gamle Aker?'

'He converted from Philadelphia to Bethlehem.'

The unoccupied taxi braked, hesitated, then accelerated again and drove off in the direction of the city centre. Waaler gave a wry smile.

'You don't have to lose your convictions to convert, Harry.'

12

Sunday. Bethlehem.

IT WAS 8 P.M. ON SUNDAY. BJARNE MØLLER YAWNED, LOCKED THE DESK drawer and put his arm out to turn off his work lamp. He was tired but pleased with himself. The worst onslaught from the media after the shooting and the disappearance had let up and he had been able to work all weekend unbothered. The pile of papers that had towered on his desk when the holiday period began was soon halved. Now he could go home and enjoy a smooth Jameson whisky and the repeat on television of *Beat for Beat*. His finger was on the switch; he cast a final look at the now tidy desk top. That was when he noticed the brown padded envelope. He vaguely remembered taking it from his pigeonhole on Friday. Obviously it had been hidden behind the pile of papers.

He hesitated. It could wait until tomorrow. He squeezed the envelope. He could feel an object inside, something he couldn't immediately identify. He opened it with the letter knife. There was no letter. He turned the envelope upside down, but nothing fell out. He shook it hard and heard something detach itself from the bubble-wrap lining.

It hit the desk, bounced across to the telephone and landed on the blotting pad, on top of the duty roster.

His stomach pains came on suddenly. Bjarne Møller doubled up and stood gasping for breath. It wasn't until a few minutes had passed that he was able to stand up straight and dial a number. If he had not been in such pain he might perhaps have noticed that the telephone number he had just dialled belonged to the name that the object from the envelope was now pointing to on the duty roster.

Marit was in love.

Again.

She cast a glance over to the church hall steps. The light shone through the circular window in the door with the inset Bethlehem Star, lighting up the face of the new boy, Roy. He was talking to one of the other girls in the choir. She had been thinking for several days now about how she could get him to notice her, but inspiration had deserted her. Going over to talk to him would not be a bad start. She would have to wait until an opportunity offered itself. At last week's choir practice he had spoken up in a loud, clear voice about his past, about how he had been a Philadelphian, and about how he had been a neo-Nazi before he was saved! One of the other girls had heard a rumour that he had a big Nazi tattoo somewhere on his body. They were agreed that it was terrible, but Marit could feel how the very thought made her body tremble with excitement. She knew deep down that this was the reason she was in love. The newness, the unfamiliarity, this wonderful but transient excitement. She knew that ultimately she would be with someone else. Someone like Kristian. Kristian was the choirleader. Both his parents were in the congregation and he had just begun to preach at the youth meetings. People like Roy so often finished up among the defectors.

They had practised for a long time this evening. They had been rehearsing a new song and had gone through practically their whole repertoire as well. Kristian tended to do that when new members joined, to show how good they were. Usually they practised in their own rooms in Geitmyrsveien, but they were closed because of the national holidays, so they had borrowed Gamle Aker church hall in Akersbakken. Even though it was past midnight they stood outside after choir practice. Their voices were buzzing like a swarm of insects and it was as if there was an extra excitement in the air this evening. Perhaps it was the heat. Or maybe it was because the married and betrothed members of the choir were on holiday and thus they were spared the smiling, tolerant but nevertheless admonishing looks the younger members received when it was considered that the flirting had gone too far. Marit blurted out whatever came into her head when her girlfriends asked as she also stole a glance at Roy. She wondered where you would put a large Nazi tattoo.

One of her girlfriends nudged her and nodded towards a man coming up Akersbakken.

'Look. He's drunk,' one girl whispered.

'Poor man,' one of the others said.

'Those are the lost souls Jesus wants to redeem.'

It was Sofie who said that. She always said things like that. The others nodded. Marit did too. And then she realised. This was it, the opportunity. And without a moment's hesitation she left her throng of girlfriends and stood in the man's path.

He stopped and peered down at her. He was taller than she had anticipated.

'Do you know Jesus?' Marit asked in a loud, clear voice and with a smile.

The man's face was bright red and his vision was blurred. The conversation behind her had suddenly died, and out of the corner of her eye she could see that Roy and the girls on the steps had turned towards them.

'Unfortunately, I don't,' the man snuffled. 'And neither do you, my girl, but perhaps you know Roy Kvinsvik?'

Marit could feel her blushes suffusing her face, and her follow-up –
Do you know he's just waiting to meet you? – became ensnared in her
throat.

'Well?' the man asked. 'Is he here?'

She took in the man's cropped skull and his boots. She suddenly
went very red. Was this man a neo-Nazi, someone from Roy's past?
Someone come to avenge his betrayal? Or to persuade him to return?

'I . . .'

But the man had already sidestepped her.

She turned round, just in time to see Roy beat a hasty retreat into
the church hall and slam the door behind him.

The drunk strode across the crunching gravel, his upper body tipped
like a mast caught in a sudden gust of wind. In front of the steps he
slipped and fell to his knees.

'Oh my God . . .' one of the girls gasped.

The man got up again.

Marit saw Kristian hurriedly draw back as the man ran up the steps.
He stood on the top step, swaying to and fro. For a moment he teetered
on the point of falling backwards. Then he regained control over the
forces of gravity and snatched at the door handle.

Marit held her hand in front of her mouth.

He pushed. Fortunately Roy had locked the door.

'Fuck!' The man shouted in a voice thick with alcohol. He leaned
back and then brought his head forward in a bow.

There was the crisp crack of broken glass as his forehead smashed
the circular window in the door and the splintered glass fell to the
steps.

'Stop it!' Kristian shouted. 'You can't . . .'

The man turned round and gaped at him. A triangular fragment of
glass was protruding from his forehead. Blood ran down from it in a
tiny stream and forked at the ridge of his nose.

Kristian didn't say another word.

The man opened his mouth and began to howl. The sound was as chilling as a steel blade. He began to attack the door again with a fury that Marit had never witnessed before, beating the solid, white door with clenched fists. Howling like a wolf, he struck again and again, flesh against wood. It sounded like axe-blows in the stillness of the morning forest. Then he began to beat the wrought-iron Star of Bethlehem in the circular window. She thought she heard the sound of ripping skin as the splatter of blood began to discolour the white door.

'Someone do something,' a voice screamed. She saw Kristian take out his mobile phone.

The iron star was loose. All of a sudden the man sank to his knees.

Marit went closer. The others had moved back, but she had to go nearer. Her heart was thumping in her chest. In front of the steps she felt Kristian's hand on her shoulder and she stopped. She could hear the man gasping for breath on the steps, like a fish drowning on dry land. It sounded as if he was weeping.

When the police car came to collect him a quarter of an hour later, he was lying in a heap on the steps. They got him to his feet, and he allowed himself to be led to the car without putting up any resistance. One of the policewomen asked if anyone had any damage to report. They just shook their heads, too shocked to give the smashed window another thought.

Then the car was gone and all that was left was the warm summer night. It went through Marit's mind that it was as if nothing had happened. She hardly noticed Roy emerge, pale and worn, and then disappear, or Kristian put his arm around her. She stared at the damaged star in the window. It was bent over and twisted; two of the five points of the star pointed upwards and one down. Despite the heat of the night, she pulled her jacket tighter round her shoulders.

It was well past midnight, and the moon was reflected in the windows of Police HQ. Bjarne Møller walked across the empty car park and into the custody block. As he entered, he took a quick look around. The three reception desks were unmanned; two officers were staring at the TV in the guard room. As an old Charles Bronson fan, Møller recognised the film. *Death Wish.* And he recognised the older of the two officers. It was Groth, also known as the 'Griever' on account of the liver-coloured scar that ran down from his left eye to the top of his cheek. Groth had worked in the custody block for as long as Møller could remember and everyone knew that to all intents and purposes he ran the place.

'Hello?' Møller shouted.

Without taking his eyes off the television screen, Groth raised a finger and pointed to the younger officer who reluctantly twisted in his chair to face him.

Møller flashed his ID card, but apparently that was superfluous. They knew him.

'Where's Hole?' he shouted.

'The idiot?' Groth snorted as Charles Bronson raised his gun to exact revenge.

'Cell five, I think,' the younger officer said. 'Check with one of the warders in there, if you can find one.'

'Thank you,' Møller said, and went through the door leading to the cells.

There were approximately a hundred detention cells and the number of inmates varied according to the season. Now it was definitely low season. Møller didn't bother going to the warders' guard room and began to walk down the corridors between the metal cubicles. His footsteps reverberated. He had always loathed the custody block. Firstly, it was absurd that living people should be incarcerated here. Secondly, there was the atmosphere of the gutter and ruined lives. Thirdly, he knew the kind of thing that went on here. Such as the time a prisoner had reported Groth for using a fire hose on him. SEFO rejected the claim when they took out the fire hose and discovered that it only reached halfway to the cell where the hosing down was

113

alleged to have taken place. It seemed that SEFO were the only people at Police HQ who didn't know that when Groth knew there would be a spot of bother, he would just cut a chunk off the fire hose.

Like all the other cells, number five had no lock and key, just a basic device for opening the door from the outside.

Harry was sitting on the floor with his head in his hands. The first thing that Møller noticed was that the bandage on Harry's right hand was soaked in blood. Harry raised his head slowly and looked at him. He had a plaster on his forehead and his eyes were swollen as if he had been crying. There was the smell of vomit.

'Why don't you lie on the bunk?' Møller asked.

'Don't want to sleep,' Harry whispered in an unrecognisable voice. 'Don't want to dream.'

Møller pulled a face to hide the fact that he was shaken. He had seen Harry down before, but not like this, not so low. Never crushed.

He cleared his throat.

'Let's go.'

'Griever' Groth and the young officer did not even cast a glance their way as they passed the guard room, but Møller caught Groth's telling shake of the head.

Harry threw up in the car park. He stood bent over, spitting and cursing as Møller lit a cigarette and passed it over to him.

'This is out of hours,' Møller said. 'It's staying unofficial.'

Harry choked on his laughter. 'Thanks, boss. It's good to know I'll get the boot with a slightly better record than it might have been.'

'That's not why I said that. It's because otherwise I would have had to suspend you with immediate effect.'

'And so?'

'I need a detective like you for the next few days. That is, the detective you are when you're sober. So the question is whether you can stay sober.'

Harry straightened up and exhaled the cigarette smoke.

'You know I can, boss. But do I want to?'

'I don't know. Do you want to, Harry?'

'You have to have a reason, boss.'

'Yes. I suppose you do.'

Møller surveyed his inspector thoughtfully. He considered the situation. Here they were, standing in the middle of a deserted car park one summer's night in Oslo, under the light of the moon and a lamp full of dead insects. He thought of all the things they had been through together, all the things they had achieved and hadn't achieved. In spite of everything, after all these years, was it going to be here, like this, as banal as it sounded, that they would finally go their separate ways?

'For as long as I've known you, there's only been one thing that's kept you going,' Møller said, 'and that's work.'

Harry didn't answer.

'I've got a job for you. If you want it.'

'And that would be . . . ?'

'I received this in a brown padded envelope today. I've been trying to get hold of you ever since.'

Møller opened his hand and studied Harry's reaction. The moon and the lamp shone on the palm of Møller's hand and one of the Forensics department's plastic bags.

'Mm,' Harry said. 'And the rest of her body?'

In the plastic bag was a long, slim finger with a red-lacquered nail. The finger was wearing a ring. The jewel set in the ring was in the shape of a star with five points.

'That's all we've got,' Møller said. 'The middle finger of the left hand.'

'Did forensics manage to identify the finger?'

Bjarne Møller nodded.

'So quickly?'

Møller pressed his hand against his stomach and nodded again.

'Right,' Harry said. 'So it is Lisbeth Barli then.'

Part Three

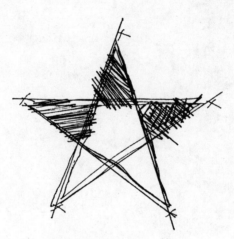

13

Monday. Touch.

YOU ARE ON TELEVISION, DARLING. THERE IS A WHOLE WALL OF YOU. There are twelve clones of you, all moving in step, copies in almost imperceptible variations of colour and shade. You are walking down a catwalk in Paris. You stop, raise a hip and look down at me with that cold, hate-filled look that you learned, and turn your back on me. It works. Rejection works every time, you know that, darling, don't you.

Then the news item is over, and you give me twelve severe looks while you read twelve similar news broadcasts and I read from 24 red lips, but you are silent and I love you for your silence.

Then there are pictures of a flood somewhere in Europe. Look, my love, we are wading through the streets. I drag my finger across a television screen and draw your star sign. Even though the television is dead, I can feel the tension between the dusty screen and my finger. The electricity. The encapsulated life. And it is my touch that brings it to life.

The tip of one of the points of the star meets the pavement outside the red-brick building on the other side of the crossroads, darling. I can stand here in the television shop and study it through the gaps between the sets.

This is one of Oslo's busiest crossroads and usually there are long queues
of cars out there, but today there are only cars on two of the roads which
radiate out from the tarmac heart. Five roads, darling. You have been
in bed all day waiting for me. I just have to do this and then I'm coming.
If you like I can take the letter out from behind the wall and whisper the
words to you. 'My darling! You are in my thoughts all the time. I can
still feel your lips against mine, your skin against mine.'

I open the shop door to go out. The sun floods in. Sun. Flood. I'll soon
be with you.

The day had started badly for Møller.

The previous night he had collected Harry from custody, and then
in the morning he had been awoken by pains in his stomach, which
was shaped like an over-inflated beach ball.

It was to get even worse though.

But at 9.00 things did not seem so bad when an apparently sober
Harry came walking in through the door of the Crime Squad meeting
room on the sixth floor. Already sitting round the table were Tom
Waaler, Beate Lønn and four of the division's detectives responsible
for case strategy along with two specialist colleagues summoned from
their holidays the night before.

'Good morning, everyone,' Møller began. 'I assume you are already
aware of what we have on our hands here: two cases, perhaps two
killings, with some indication that the perpetrator is one and the same
person. In brief, it looks suspiciously like the nightmare that we all
have at some point.'

Møller put the first overhead transparency on the projector.

'What we can see on the left is Camilla Loen's left hand with the
severed index finger. On the right, we can see the middle finger of
Lisbeth Barli's left hand, which was sent to me by post. Although we
don't have a body to match as yet, Beate identified the finger by
comparing the fingerprint with those she had taken in Barli's flat. Good
initiative and good work, Beate.'

Beate blushed while drumming her pencil on her notepad and trying to look unaffected.

Møller changed the overhead transparency.

'We found this precious stone under Camilla's eyelid, a red diamond in the shape of a five-pointed star. This ring on the right was on Lisbeth's finger. As you can see, the diamond on the ring is paler, but the shape is identical.'

'We have tried to find out where the first diamond comes from,' Waaler said. 'Without success. We sent photos to two of the biggest diamond-cutting establishments in Antwerp, but they say that this type of workmanship probably originates from somewhere else in Europe. They suggested Russia or southern Germany.'

'We contacted a diamond expert working for De Beers, by far the biggest buyer of uncut diamonds in the world,' Beate said. 'According to her, it is possible to use spectrometry and microtomography to identify precisely where a diamond comes from. She is flying from London this evening to help us.'

Magnus Skarre, one of the younger detectives and relatively new to Crime Squad, put up his hand.

'Going back to what you said at the beginning, sir, I don't understand why this is such a nightmare if this is a double murder. After all, we are only looking for one killer instead of two, so all of us here can work with the same focus. In my opinion, it should be the opposite . . .'

Magnus Skarre heard a deep clearing of a throat and the meeting's attention turned to where Harry Hole had remained sunken in his chair until now.

'What's your name again?' Harry asked.

'Magnus.'

'Surname.'

'Skarre.' The voice betrayed irritation. 'You'll have to remember –'

'No, Skarre, I won't remember. But you try to remember what I'm saying to you now. When detectives are confronted with a premeditated,

and in this case carefully planned, murder, they know that the perpetrator has a number of clear advantages. He may have removed all the
forensic evidence, established an apparently solid alibi for the time of
the death, disposed of the weapon and so on. But there is one thing
the killer can, so to speak, never hide from an investigation. And what
is that?'

Magnus Skarre blinked a couple of times.

'The motive,' Harry said. 'Basic stuff, isn't it? The motive, that's
where we start our investigation. It's so fundamental that sometimes
we forget it. Until one day, out of the blue, up he pops: the killer out
of every detective's worst nightmare. Or wet dream, all depending on
how your head's wired. And the nightmare is the killer who has no
motive. Or to be more precise: who has no motive that is humanly
possible to comprehend.'

'Now you're just painting a devil on the wall, Inspector Hole, aren't
you.' Skarre looked round at the others. 'We don't know yet whether
there is a motive behind these killings or not.'

Tom Waaler cleared his throat.

Møller saw the muscles in Harry's jaw tighten.

'He's right,' Waaler said.

'Of course I'm right,' Skarre said. 'It's obvious that –'

'Shut up, Skarre, Inspector Hole's right. We've worked on these two
cases for ten and fifteen days respectively without finding one single
thing that might be a connection between these murder victims. And
when the only connection between the victims is the way they were
dispatched, the rituals and things that look like coded messages, then
we begin to think about a word that I suggest we don't say out loud
yet, but all of us have at the back of our minds. I also suggest that
Skarre and the other new boys from college keep their mouths shut
from now on and open their ears when Inspector Hole speaks.'

The room went quiet.

Møller saw Harry staring at Waaler.

'To sum up,' Møller said, 'we're trying to keep two thoughts in our minds at the same time. On the one hand, we are working systematic- ally as if these were two run-of-the-mill killings. On the other hand, we are painting a big, fat, nasty devil on the wall. No-one else speaks to the press except me. The next meeting is at five. Now get cracking.'

The man in the spotlight was elegantly dressed in tweeds, holding a Sherlock Holmes pipe and rocking on his heels as he looked upon the woman in rags in front of him with a sympathetic expression.

'How much do you propose to pay me for the lessons?'

The woman in rags threw back her head and put her hands on her hips.

'Oh, I know what's right. A lady friend of mine gets French lessons for eighteen pence an hour from a real French gentleman. Well, you wouldn't have the face to ask me the same for teaching me my own language as you would for French; so I won't give more than a shilling. Take it or leave it.'

Wilhelm Barli sat in the twelfth row and let his tears flow freely. He could feel them running down his neck and in under his silk Thai shirt, over his chest; he felt the salt make his nipples smart before the tears continued down over his stomach.

They would not stop.

He held a hand in front of his mouth so that his sobs would not distract the actors or the stage director in the fifth row.

He gave a start when he felt a hand on his shoulder. He turned round and saw a tall man towering over him. A premonition rooted him to his chair.

'Yes?' he whispered in a strangulated voice.

'It's me,' the man whispered. 'Harry Hole. Police.'

Wilhelm Barli took his hand away from his mouth and studied Harry's face in detail.

'Of course it is,' he said with relief in his voice. 'Sorry, Inspector. It's so dark. I thought . . .'

The policeman sat down in the seat beside Wilhelm.

'You thought what?'

'You're dressed in black.'

Wilhelm blew his nose in a handkerchief.

'I thought you were a priest. A priest coming . . . with bad news. Stupid, isn't it?'

The policeman didn't answer.

'You caught me at a rather emotional moment, Inspector. We have the first dress rehearsal today. Look at her.'

'Who?'

'Eliza Doolittle. Up there. When I saw her on the stage, I thought for a moment it was Lisbeth and that I had only been dreaming she was gone.'

Wilhelm was taking deep breaths and trembling.

'But then she began to speak, and my Lisbeth disappeared.'

Wilhelm discovered that the policeman was staring at the stage in amazement.

'A striking resemblance, isn't it? That's why I brought her in. It was supposed to be Lisbeth's musical.'

'Is it . . . ?' Harry started to say.

'Yes, that's her sister.'

'Toya? I mean Toy-A.'

'We've managed to keep it secret so far. The press conference is later today.'

'Right. That ought to create a bit of publicity.'

Toya swung herself round and cursed loudly when she stumbled. Her partner raised his arms in desperation and his eyes sought the director.

Wilhelm sighed.

'Publicity isn't everything. As you can see, there is quite a lot of work to do. She has a sort of raw talent, but appearing on the stage of the National Theatre is rather different to singing cowboy songs at the community centre in a small town in central Norway. It took me two years to teach Lisbeth how to behave on stage, but with her up there we'll have to do it in two weeks.'

'If I'm disturbing you, I can run through this very quickly, Herr Barli.'

'Run through it quickly?'

Wilhelm tried to read the expression on Harry's face in the dark. Fear had him in its grip again, and when Harry opened his mouth, instinct took over and Wilhelm interrupted.

'You're not disturbing at all, Inspector. I'm just the producer. You know, someone who gets things moving. The others take over now.'

He waved his hand towards the stage where the man dressed in tweeds was loudly proclaiming at that moment:

'I shall make a duchess of this draggletailed guttersnipe!'

'Director, stage designer, actors,' Barli said. 'As from tomorrow I'll be a mere onlooker watching this . . .' He continued to wave his hand in the air until he found the word. '. . . comedy.'

'Well, we all have to discover our own talents.'

Wilhelm gave a hollow laugh, but stopped when he saw the silhouette of the director's head turn suddenly towards them. He leaned over to the policeman and whispered: 'You're right. I was a dancer for 20 years. A very bad dancer if you have to know, but there's always a desperate shortage of male dancers in opera so they take almost anyone who can half dance. Anyway, we're pensioned off when we reach 40 and then I had to find something new. It was then that I realised that my real talent lay in getting others to dance. Stage management, Inspector. That's the only thing I can do. But do you know what? We become pathetic at the merest hint of success. Because things happen to go our way on a couple of productions we believe we are gods who can control all the variables and that we are the architects of our fortunes in all areas. And then something like this happens, and we discover how helpless we are. I . . .'

Wilhelm suddenly broke off.

'I'm boring you, aren't I?'

The other man shook his head and cleared his throat.

'It's about your wife.'

Wilhelm screwed up his eyes as if waiting to hear an unpleasant, loud noise.

'We received a package. Containing a severed finger. I'm afraid it belonged to her.'

Wilhelm swallowed hard. He had always seen himself as a man of love, but now he could feel it growing again. The lump under his heart that had been there ever since that day. The tumour that was driving him to the edge of insanity. He sensed that it had a colour, he sensed that hatred was yellow.

'Do you know what, Inspector? It's almost a relief. I've known it all the time. That he would harm her.'

'Harm?'

Wilhelm detected a note of anxious surprise in the other man's voice.

'Can you promise me something, Harry? Is it OK if I call you Harry?'

The policeman nodded.

'Find him. Find him, Harry. And punish him. Punish him severely. Will you promise me?'

Wilhelm thought he saw the other man nod, but he wasn't sure. His tears distorted everything.

Then the man was gone. Wilhelm took a deep breath and tried to concentrate on the stage again.

'No! I'll call the police, I will,' Toya shouted.

Harry sat in his office staring at the desk top. He was so tired he didn't know if he was capable of doing any more.

The escapades of the previous day – his time in the cell and another night of nightmares – they had taken their toll. It was the meeting with Wilhelm Barli, however, that had really drained him. Sitting there and promising that they would catch the perpetrator, holding back when Barli said that his wife was 'harmed'. For if there was one thing Harry was certain about, it was that Lisbeth Barli was dead.

Harry had felt the gnawing ache for alcohol from the moment he woke up that morning. First as an instinctive physical craving, then as a panic-stricken fear because he had put a distance between himself and his medicine by not taking his hip flask or any money with him to work. Now the ache was entering a new phase in which it was both a wholly physical pain and a feeling of blank terror that he would be torn to pieces. The enemy below was pulling and tugging at the chains, the dogs were snarling up at him from the pit, somewhere in his stomach beneath his heart. God, how he hated them. He hated them as much as they hated him.

Harry got to his feet. He had stashed away half a bottle of Bell's in the filing cabinet on Monday. Had that just occurred to him now or had he been aware of it the whole time? Harry was used to Harry playing tricks on Harry in hundreds of ways. He was just about to pull out the drawer when suddenly he looked up. He had spotted a movement. Ellen was smiling at him from her photo. Was he going mad or had her mouth just moved?

'What are you looking at, you bitch?' he mumbled, and the very next moment the picture fell from the wall, hitting the floor and smashing the glass to smithereens. Harry stared at Ellen who was smiling imperturbably up at him from the broken frame. He held his right hand where the pain was throbbing under the bandages.

It was only when he turned to open the drawer that he noticed the two of them standing in the doorway. He realised that they must have been standing there for quite a while and that it must have been their reflection in the glass of the picture frame that he had seen moving.

'Hi,' Oleg said, looking at Harry with a mixture of wonder and fear.

Harry swallowed. His hand let go of the drawer.

'Hi, Oleg.'

Oleg was wearing trainers, a pair of blue trousers and the yellow national strip of Brazil. Harry knew that on the back of his shirt there was a number nine with the name of Ronaldo above it. He had bought it at a petrol station one Sunday when Rakel, Oleg and he had been on their way to Norefjell to go skiing.

'I found him downstairs,' Tom Waaler said.

He had his hand on Oleg's head.

'He was asking for you in reception, so I brought him up here. So you play football then, Oleg?'

Oleg didn't answer, he just looked at Harry. With those dark eyes of his mother's that could at times be so unendingly gentle and at others so hard and pitiless. At this moment Harry couldn't read which they were, but then, it was dark.

'A striker, eh?' Waaler asked, smiling and ruffling the young boy's hair.

Harry stared at his colleague's strong, sinewy fingers, Oleg's dark strands of hair against the back of Waaler's tanned hand, hair that stood up on its own. He could feel his legs giving way under him.

'No,' Oleg said, with his eyes still firmly fixed on Harry. 'I play in defence.'

'Hey, Oleg,' Waaler said, looking over at Harry enquiringly. 'Harry has still got a bit of shadow-boxing to do in here – I do the same when something gets on my nerves – but perhaps you and I could go up top and see the view from the roof terrace while Harry tidies up.'

'I'm staying here,' Oleg stated unequivocally.

Harry nodded.

'OK. Nice to meet you, Oleg.'

Waaler patted the boy on his shoulder and left. Oleg stood in the doorway.

'How did you get here?' Harry asked.

'Metro.'

'On your own?'

Oleg nodded.

'Does Rakel know you're here?'

Oleg shook his head.

'Don't you want to come in?' Harry's throat was dry.

'I want you to come home,' Oleg said.

Four seconds after Harry pressed the bell, Rakel tore open the door. Her eyes were black with fury.

'Where've you been?'

For an instant Harry thought that the question was directed to them both before her eyes swept past Harry and beamed in on Oleg.

'I didn't have anyone to play with,' Oleg said with his head bowed. 'I took the metro to town.'

'The metro. On your own? But how . . . ?'

Her voice failed her.

'I slipped out,' Oleg said. 'I thought you would be happy, Mummy. After all you said you also wanted . . .'

She suddenly took Oleg into her arms.

'Do you realise how worried I've been about you, my lad?'

She viewed Harry askance while she hugged Oleg.

Rakel and Harry stood by the fence at the back of the garden and gazed down over Oslo and Oslo fjord. They were silent. The sailing boats stood out against the blue sea like tiny white triangles. Harry turned to face the house. Summer birds took off from the lawn and flitted between the apple trees in front of the open windows. It was a large house, with black timber cladding – a house constructed for winter, not for summer.

Harry looked at her. Her legs were bare and she was wearing a thin, red cotton button-up jacket over a light blue dress. The sun glistened on the droplets of sweat on her bare skin under the necklace with the cross that she had inherited from her mother. Harry mused that he knew everything about her: the smell of the cotton jacket, the gentle curve of her back under the dress, the smell of her skin when it was sweaty and salty, what she wanted from her life, why she didn't say anything.

All this knowledge to no end.

'How's it going?' he asked.

'Fine,' she said. 'I've rented a log cabin. We can't have it until August. I was late getting in.'

The tone was neutral, the accusation scarcely perceptible.

'Have you injured your hand?'

'Just a cut,' Harry said.

A strand of hair blew across her face. He resisted the temptation to brush it away.

'I had someone round to value the house yesterday,' she said.

'To value it? You're not thinking of selling it, are you?'

'The house is too big for only two people, Harry.'

'Yes, but you love this house. You grew up here. And so did Oleg.'

'You don't need to remind me. The thing is that the work over the winter cost twice as much as I had imagined. And now the roof has to be redone. It's an old house.'

'Mm.'

Harry watched Oleg kicking a ball against the garage door. He smashed the ball again and as soon as it left his foot he closed his eyes and raised his arms to an imaginary crowd of fans.

'Rakel.'

She sighed.

'What is it, Harry?'

'Can't you at least look at me when I'm talking?'

'No.' Her voice was neither angry nor upset; she was just establishing a fact.

'Would it make any difference if I gave it up?'

'You can't give it up, Harry.'

'I mean the police.'

'I guessed that.'

He kicked at the grass.

'I may not have a choice,' he said.

'Haven't you?'

'No.'

'Why the hypothetical question then?'

She blew away the strand of hair.

'I could find a quieter job, be at home more, take care of Oleg. We could –'

'Stop it, Harry!'

Her voice was like a whiplash. She bowed her head and crossed her arms as if she were frozen in the burning sun.

'The answer's no,' she whispered. 'It won't make any difference. It's not your job that's the problem. It's . . .'

She breathed in, turned round and looked him in the eyes.

'It's you, Harry. You're the problem.'

Harry saw the tears welling up in her eyes.

'Go now,' she whispered.

He wanted to say something, but changed his mind. Instead he nodded towards the sailing boats on the fjord.

'You're right,' he said. 'I am the problem. I'll have a chat with Oleg and then I'll be off.'

He took a few steps, then stopped and turned round.

'Don't sell the house, Rakel. Don't do it, do you hear? I'll come up with something.'

She smiled through her tears.

'You're a strange man,' she whispered and reached out a hand as if she was going to stroke his cheek, but he was too far away and she let it drop again.

'Take care of yourself, Harry.'

As Harry left, a shiver ran down his spine. It was 5.15. He would have to hurry to get to the meeting.

I'm in the building. It smells of cellar. I'm standing quite still and studying the names on the noticeboard in front of me. I can hear voices and footsteps on the stairs, but I'm not afraid. They cannot see that, but I am invisible. Did you hear? They cannot see that, but . . . It isn't a paradox, darling. *I just expressed it in that way to sound like one. Everything can be formulated as a paradox. It isn't difficult. It's just that true paradoxes don't exist. True paradoxes, ha, ha. Do you see how easy it is? It's just words, the lack of precision in language. I have finished with words. With language. I'm looking at my watch. This is my language. It's clear and there are no paradoxes. I'm ready.*

14

Monday. Barbara.

BARBARA SVENDSEN HAD BEGUN TO THINK A LOT ABOUT TIME OF LATE, not that she was particularly philosophical by nature; most people she knew would have said exactly the opposite. It was just that she had never given it a thought before. She had never considered that there was a time for everything and that this time was being eaten away. She had realised several years ago that she was never going to make it as a model and would have to be satisfied with the title of ex-mannequin. It sounded good even if the word originating from Dutch did mean 'little man'. Petter had told her that. As he had told her most things he thought she ought to know. He had got her the job in the bar at Head On. And because of the pills she hadn't felt like going straight from work to Blindern University, where she was studying to become a sociologist.

However, the time for Petter, pills and dreams of becoming a sociologist was over and one day she found herself alone with debts for unfinished studies and pills to pay off, and a job at the most boring bar in Oslo. So Barbara dropped everything, borrowed money from her parents and went off to Lisbon to get her life back on an even keel and perhaps learn a little Portuguese. Lisbon was a wonderful time. The days passed in a whirl, but this didn't bother her. Time was simply something that came and went, until the money stopped coming, until Marco was no longer 'true until eternity' and the fun was over. She returned home a few experiences older; she had learned, for example, that Ecstasy was cheaper in Portugal than in Norway, but it made a mess of your life in just the same way, that Portuguese was an extremely difficult language and that time was a limited, non-renewable resource.

Then she went with, and allowed herself to be kept by, Rolf, Ron and Roland in chronological order. It sounded like more fun than it was, except in Roland's case. Roland was wonderful, but time passed and Roland with it.

It was only when she moved back into her old room at her parents' house that the world stopped spinning and time slowed down. She stopped going out, managed to give up the pills and she began to play with the idea that she might resume her studies. In the meantime, she did temp work for Manpower. After four weeks' contract work with a firm of solicitors called Halle, Thune & Wetterlid who were geographically situated in Carl Berners plass and hierarchically in the lower reaches of solicitors specialising in debt collection, she was offered a permanent job.

That was four years ago.

The reason she accepted was primarily because she had discovered that at the offices of Halle, Thune & Wetterlid time went slower than anywhere else she had ever been. The tardy advance of time started the moment you entered the red-brick building and pressed number 5 in the lift. Half of eternity passed before the doors glided back into place and the lift rose slowly towards a heaven where time was even slower to pass. Well ensconced behind the counter, Barbara was able to record the movement of the second hand on the clock over the entrance and the snail-like, reluctant ticking of seconds, minutes and hours. Some days she could almost make time stop completely, it was just a question of concentration. The strange thing was that time seemed to go much faster for the other people around her, as if they existed in parallel, but different, time dimensions. The telephone in front of her rang continuously and people flew in and out like in silent movies, but it was all as if it were happening separate from her, as if she were a robot with mechanical parts moving as fast as everyone else while her inner life proceeded in slow motion.

Only last week was a case in point. A fairly large debt collection office had suddenly gone bankrupt and at this everyone had started running around and making telephone calls as if demented. Wetterlid told her that it was open season for vultures to gobble up new shares on the market, and a golden opportunity to move up among the elite market leaders. This morning he asked Barbara if she could stay on a bit longer today. He said there were meetings with customers of the bankrupt company until 6.00, and they did want to give the impression that everything was in order at Halle, Thune & Wetterlid, didn't they. As usual Wetterlid stared at her boobs while talking to her, and as usual she smiled, automatically pulling her shoulders back as Petter had told her when she was working at Head On. It had become a reflex action. Everyone flaunted what they had. At least, that was what Barbara Svendsen had learned. The courier who had just that moment walked in was an example. She would have bet anything that he was nothing to look at under the helmet, racing goggles and the handkerchief tied round his mouth. That was probably why he kept them on. Instead he said that he knew which office the parcel was for and walked slowly down the corridor in his tight cycling shorts so that she could have a really good look at his muscular buttocks. The cleaning lady who was due soon was another example. She was a Buddhist or a Hinduist, or whatever you call them, and Allah said that she had to conceal her body beneath a pile of bed linen, but she had excellent teeth, so what did she do? Yes, she went round smiling like a crocodile on E. Flaunt, flaunt, flaunt.

Barbara was watching the second hand on the clock when the door opened.

The man who walked in was fairly short and plump. He was breathing heavily and his glasses were steamed up, so Barbara assumed that he had walked up the stairs. When she had begun four years ago, she couldn't tell the difference between a two-thousand kroner dress from Dressman and a Prada, but bit by bit she had put in the training and now she could not only judge dresses, but ties too and – the surest determiner of what level of service she should offer – shoes.

The new arrival didn't seem particularly impressive as he stood there cleaning his glasses. In fact, he reminded her of the fatso in *Seinfeld* whose name she didn't know because she didn't actually watch *Seinfeld.* However, if clothes were anything to go by – and they were – the light pinstriped suit, the silk tie and the hand-sewn shoes gave cause for optimism that Halle, Thune & Wetterlid would soon have an interesting customer.

'Good evening. May I help you?' she said, smiling her next best smile. Her best smile she kept in reserve for the day when the man walked in whom she would have as her own.

'I hope so,' the man smiled back, taking a handkerchief out of his breast pocket and pressing it against his forehead. 'I have a meeting, but perhaps you would be so kind as to fetch me a glass of water first?'

Barbara thought she could detect a foreign accent, but she couldn't quite place it. Nevertheless, the courteous yet commanding way he asked strengthened her conviction that this customer was a big cheese.

'Of course,' she said. 'One moment.'

As she walked down the corridor she remembered that Wetterlid had mentioned something about a possible bonus for all employees if their annual figures came up to scratch this year. Perhaps then the firm could also afford to think about getting a water cooler like those she had seen in other places. Then, completely out of the blue, something odd happened. Time accelerated. It jerked forward. It only lasted a few seconds and then time went back to being slow again, but it felt as if, quite unaccountably, the seconds had been taken from her.

She went into the ladies' lavatory and turned on the tap above one of the three basins. She pulled a plastic beaker out of the container and waited as she held her finger under the water. Lukewarm. The man outside would just have to be patient. They said on the radio today that sea temperatures in Nordmarka would be around 22 degrees. Yet, if you let the water run for long enough, the drinking water that came from Lake Maridal was wonderfully cold. While staring at her finger, she wondered how that could be. When the water was really cold, her finger would go white and almost completely lose feeling. The ring finger on her left hand. When would she wear a wedding ring? She hoped before her heart went white and lost feeling. She felt a current of air and then it was gone, so she didn't bother to turn round. The water was still lukewarm. And time was passing. Running out, just as the water was. Nonsense. She wouldn't be 30 for another 20 months. She had plenty of time.

A sound made her look up. In the mirror she saw two white cubicle doors. Had someone come in without her noticing?

She almost gave a start when the water suddenly went ice cold. Deep cavities under the earth. That's what it was, that's why it was so cold. She put the beaker under the tap and it was soon full to the brim. She felt an urge to hurry, to get out. She turned and dropped the beaker on the floor.

'Did I frighten you?'

The voice appeared to be genuinely concerned.

'Sorry,' she said, forgetting to pull her shoulders back. 'I'm a bit jittery today.' She bent down to pick up the beaker and added: 'Actually, you're in the ladies' lavatory.'

The beaker had whirled around and stopped in an upright position.

There was still some water left in it, and as she reached out towards it, she could see her own face reflected in the circular white surface. Beside her face, on the outer edge of the narrow reflection, she saw something move. Again time seemed to pass slowly. Unendingly slowly. Once more she caught herself thinking that time was ticking away.

15

Monday. *Vena Amoris.*

HARRY'S RUSTY RED-AND-WHITE FORD ESCORT PULLED UP IN FRONT of the television shop. Two police cars and Waaler's red sports supercar looked as if they had been strewn randomly across the pavements around the crossroads with the flattering name of Carl Berners plass.

Harry parked, took the green chisel out of his jacket pocket and put it on the passenger seat. As he hadn't been able to find his car keys in his flat he had taken some wire and the chisel with him while he trawled the neighbourhood. He found his beloved car again in Stensberggata. And, sure enough, with the car keys in the ignition. The green chisel was perfect for bending the car door so that he could flip up the locking device with the wire.

Harry crossed the pedestrian crossing on red. He walked slowly; his body wouldn't allow high speeds. His stomach and head ached, and his sweaty shirt was stuck to his back. It was 5.55 and he had managed without his medicine so far, but he wasn't making any promises to himself.

The board in the hallway said the solicitors' firm of Halle, Thune &

Wetterlid was on the fifth floor. Harry groaned. He cast a glance at the lift. Sliding doors. No grille.

The lift was manufactured by KONE and when the shiny metal doors closed, he had the feeling he was inside a welded tin can. Harry tried not to listen to the lift machinery as they rose. He closed his eyes, but opened them again in a hurry when images of Sis appeared on the inside of his eyelids.

One of the uniformed regulars opened the door to the office area.

'She's in there,' he said, pointing down the corridor to the left of the reception desk.

'Any uniformed officers here?'

'On their way.'

'They'd certainly appreciate it if you closed off the lift and the door downstairs.'

'Fine.'

'Anyone here from Forensics?'

'Li and Hansen. They've gathered together all the people who were still here when she was found. They're questioning them now in one of the conference rooms.'

Harry walked down the corridor. The carpets were worn and the reproductions of national romantic treasures faded. It was a firm that had seen better days. Or perhaps it hadn't.

The door to the ladies' lavatory was ajar and the carpets muffled the sound of Harry's steps as he approached. He could hear the sound of Tom Waaler's voice. Harry stopped outside. It sounded as if Waaler was talking on his mobile.

'If it's one of his, he's obviously not going through us anymore. OK, leave it with me.'

Harry pushed open the door and saw Waaler in a squat position. He looked up.

'Hi, Harry. Be with you in a minute.'

Harry stood on the threshold, absorbing the scene and the sound of a distant crackling voice on Waaler's phone in the background.

The room was surprisingly big, roughly four metres by five, with two white lavatory cubicles and three white basins placed below a long mirror. The neon lights in the ceiling cast a harsh glare on the white walls and white floor tiles. The absence of colour was almost conspicuous. Perhaps it was this background that made the body look like a small work of art, a carefully arranged exhibition. The woman was young and slim. She was kneeling with her forehead on the ground, like a Muslim at prayer, except that her arms were beneath her body. Her suit skirt had ridden up over her underwear, revealing a cream-yellow G-string. A narrow, dark red stream of blood ran in the grouting between the woman's head and the drain. It looked almost painted on to achieve maximum effect.

The body was in balance, supported at five points: the two feet, the knees and the forehead. The suit, the bizarre position and the bared posterior made Harry think of a secretary preparing herself to be penetrated by the boss. Stereotypes again. For all he knew, she could be the boss.

'OK, but we can't deal with that now,' Waaler said. 'Call me this evening.'

The detective inspector put the phone back in his inside pocket, but remained in a squat position. Harry noticed that his other hand was on the woman's white skin, just below the edge of her underwear. To support himself, he supposed.

'They'll be good photos, won't they,' Waaler said as if he had been reading Harry's thoughts.

'Who is she?'

'Barbara Svendsen, twenty-eight years old from Bestum. She was the receptionist here.'

Harry squatted down beside Waaler.

'She was shot through the back of her head, as you can see,' Waaler said. 'Must have been with the gun under the basin over there. It still smells of cordite.'

Harry looked at the black gun on the floor in the corner of the room. There was a large, black lump of metal attached to the end of the barrel.

'A Ceská Zbrojovka,' Waaler said. 'Czech, with a specially made silencer.'

Harry nodded. He was tempted to ask if the gun was one of the items that Waaler imported. Or if that was what he had been talking about on the phone.

'Unusual position,' Harry said.

'Yes, it's my guess that she was bending down or kneeling and fell forwards.'

'Who found her?'

'One of the solicitors, a woman. Control room got the call at eleven minutes past five.'

'Witnesses?'

'No-one we've talked to so far saw anything. Nothing untoward, no suspicious persons coming or going in the last hour. A visitor due to meet one of the solicitors says that Barbara left the reception desk to get a glass of water for him at five to five and never came back.'

'And she came here?'

'I suppose so. The kitchen's quite a walk from reception.'

'But no-one else saw her on her way over here from reception?'

'The two people with offices between reception and the toilets had both gone home for the day. And those who were still here were either in their offices or in one of the conference rooms.'

'What did this visitor do when she didn't return?'

'He had a meeting at five and when the receptionist didn't return he became impatient and walked on through until he found the office of the solicitor he was due to meet.'

'So he knew his way around?'

'No, he said it was the first time he'd ever been here.'

'Mm. And he's the last person we know of to see her alive?'

'Yup.'

Harry noticed that Waaler had not moved his hand.

'So it must have happened somewhere between five to five and eleven minutes past.'

'It seems so, yes.'

Harry looked down at his notepad.

'Do you have to do that?' he said in a low voice.

'What?'

'Touch her.'

'Don't you like it?'

Harry didn't answer. Waaler leaned closer.

'Are you implying that you've never touched them, Harry?'

Harry tried to write, but his pen didn't work.

Waaler chuckled.

'You don't have to answer. I can see it in your face. There's nothing wrong with being curious, Harry. That's one of the reasons we joined the police force, isn't it? Curiosity and excitement. Like finding out what skin feels like when they've just died, when they're neither very warm nor very cold.'

'I . . .'

Harry dropped his pen when Waaler grabbed his hand.

'Feel.'

Waaler pressed Harry's hand against the dead woman's thigh. Harry was breathing hard through his nose. His first reaction had been to withdraw his hand, but he didn't. Waaler's hand on his was warm and dry, but his skin didn't feel like human skin. It was like holding rubber. Lightly warm rubber.

'Can you feel it? It's the excitement, Harry. It's got you too, hasn't it. But how will you find it when this job's over? Will you do the same as the other poor guys? Look for it in video shops or at the bottom of one of your bottles? Or do you want it in real life? Feel, Harry. This is what we're offering you. A real life. Yes or no?'

Harry cleared his throat.

'I'm just saying that forensics will want to examine the evidence before we touch anything.'

Waaler kept his eyes on Harry for a long time. Then he blinked cheerily and let go of Harry's hand.

'You're right. My mistake.'

Waaler stood up and walked out.

Harry's stomach pains continued to overpower him, but he tried to take deep breaths and stay calm. Beate would never forgive him if he threw up over her crime scene.

He rested his cheek against the cool floor tiles and lifted up Barbara's jacket so that he could see what was underneath her. Between her knees and beneath the smooth curve of her upper body he saw a white beaker. What really caught his attention though was her hand.

'Fuck,' Harry whispered. 'Fuck.'

At 6.20 Beate came rushing into the offices of Halle, Thune & Wetterlid. Harry was sitting on the floor and leaning up against the wall outside the ladies' lavatory, drinking from a white plastic cup.

Beate pulled up in front of him, put down her metal cases and drew the back of her hand across her moist, bright red forehead.

'Sorry. I was lying on the beach in Ingierstrand. Had to go home first and change and then drive to Kjølberggata to pick up the equipment. Some idiot gave orders to close off the lift, so I had to take the stairs up here.'

'Hmm. The person in question probably did that to protect the evidence. Has the press stuck its snout in yet?'

'There are a few reporters making themselves comfortable in the sun outside. Not many. Holidays.'

'I'm afraid the holidays are over.'

Beate grimaced.

'Do you mean . . . ?'

'Come here.'

Harry went into the lavatory ahead of her and crouched down.

'Look underneath her, her left hand. Her ring finger has been cut off.'

Beate groaned.

'Not much blood,' Harry said. 'So it happened after she was dead. And then we've got this.'

He lifted the hair up over Barbara's left ear.

Beate screwed up her nose: 'An earring?'

'In the shape of a heart. Quite unlike the silver earring she has in her other ear. I found the other earring on the floor in one of the cubicles. So the killer put this earring in her ear. The funny thing is that you can open it. Like this. Unusual contents or what?'

Beate nodded.

'A red diamond in the shape of a five-pointed star,' she said.

'And so what have we got?'

Beate looked at him.

'Can we say the words aloud now?' she asked.

'Serial killer?'

Bjarne Møller was speaking in such a low whisper that Harry instinctively pressed his mobile phone harder against his ear.

'We're at the scene of the crime and it is the same pattern,' Harry said. 'You'll have to get things moving and cancel holidays, boss. We're going to need everyone you can muster.'

'Is it a copycat killing?'

'Out of the question. We're the only ones who know about the mutilation and the diamonds.'

'This is very inconvenient, Harry.'

'Convenient serial murders are rare, boss.'

Møller went quiet for a few moments.

'Harry?'

'I'm still here, boss.'

'I'm going to ask you to spend your final weeks assisting Tom Waaler on this case. You're the only person in Crime Squad who has any experience of serial killings. I know you'll say no, but I'm going to ask you anyway. Just to get us moving, Harry.'

'OK, boss.'

'This is more important than the disagreements between you and Tom . . . What did you say?'

'I said it was fine.'

'Do you mean that?'

'Yes. I'll have to be going now though. We'll be here most of the evening, so it would be good if you could organise the first meeting of those involved in the case for tomorrow. Tom suggests eight o'clock.'

'Tom?' Møller asked in astonishment.

'Tom Waaler.'

'I know who it is. I've just never heard you use his Christian name before.'

'The others are waiting for me, boss.'

'OK.'

Harry slipped the phone back into his pocket, tossed the plastic beaker into the litter bin, locked himself in one of the cubicles in the Gents and clung onto the toilet bowl as he threw up.

Afterwards he stood in front of the basin with the tap running, looking at himself in the mirror. He listened to the buzz of voices from the corridor. Beate's assistant was urging people to keep behind the barriers; Waaler was telling policemen to find out who had been in the vicinity of the building; Magnus Skarre was shouting to a colleague that he wanted a cheeseburger without chips.

When the water finally ran cold, Harry stuck his face under the tap. He let the water run down his cheek, into his ear, down over his neck, inside his shirt, along his shoulder and down his arm. He drank greedily. He refused to listen to the enemy deep inside him. Then he ran into the cubicle and threw up again.

Outside, the evening had drawn in quickly and Carl Berners plass lay deserted as Harry walked out of the building, lit a cigarette and raised a hand in defence to one of the newspaper vultures approaching him. The man stopped. Harry recognised him. Gjendem, wasn't that his name? He had chatted to him after the case in Sydney. Gjendem was no worse than the others, maybe even a little better.

The television shop was still open. Harry went in. There was no-one about except for a fat man in a filthy flannel shirt sitting behind the counter reading a newspaper. On the counter an electric fan was blowing around his carefully placed strands of hair intended to conceal his baldness, and radiating his sweaty odour all over the shop. He sniffed when Harry showed him his ID and asked whether he had seen anyone suspicious inside or outside the shop.

'They're all suspicious here,' he said. 'This area is going to the dogs.'

'Anyone who looked like they might kill someone?' Harry asked drily.

The man squeezed one eye shut. 'Is that why there are so many police cars round here?'

Harry nodded.

The man shrugged his shoulders and began to read the paper again.

'Who hasn't thought about killing someone at one time or another, Constable?'

On his way out Harry stopped when he saw his own car on one of the television screens. The camera swept across Carl Berners plass and stopped when it met the red-brick building. Then the picture went back to TV2 news and the next moment it was a fashion show. Harry sucked hard at his cigarette and closed his eyes. Rakel was coming towards him on a catwalk, no, twelve catwalks. She walked through the wall with the television sets on and stood in front of him with her hands on her hips. She fixed him with a look, tossed her head back, turned round and left him. Harry opened his eyes again.

It was 8.00. He tried not to remember that there was a bar close by, in Trondheimsveien. They had a licence to serve spirits.

The hardest part of the evening lay before him.

Then there was the night.

It was 10.00, and even though the mercury had mercifully dropped by two degrees, the air was still hot and static, waiting for an offshore breeze or an onshore breeze, or any kind of breeze. Forensics was deserted except for Beate's office where a light still burned. The murder in Carl Berners plass had turned the whole day upside down and Beate was still at the crime scene when her colleague Bjørn Holm had rung to say there was a woman in reception from De Beers who had come to examine some diamonds.

Beate had returned in a hurry and now she was concentrating on the short, energetic woman in front of her who spoke the perfect kind of English you would expect from a Dutch person settled in London.

'Diamonds have geological fingerprints which, theoretically, makes it possible for us to trace them right back to the owner as certificates, which go everywhere with the diamond, are issued showing their origin. Not in this case though, I'm afraid.'

'Why not?' Beate asked.

'Because the two diamonds I have seen are what we call blood diamonds.'

'Because of the red colour?'

'No, because they most probably come from the Kiuvu mines in Sierra Leone. All the diamond dealers in the world boycott diamonds from Sierra Leone because the diamond mines are controlled by rebel forces who export diamonds to finance a war that is not about politics, but about money. Hence the name, blood diamonds. I believe these diamonds are new, and I suppose they have been smuggled out of Sierra Leone to another country where false certificates have been issued claiming they come from well-known mines in, say, South Africa.'

'Any idea which country they were smuggled into?'

'Most of them end up in ex-communist countries. When the Iron Curtain came down, the expertise acquired making false ID papers had to find a new outlet. And authentic-looking diamond certificates cost a pretty penny. That's not the only reason, however, that I would go for Eastern Europe.'

'Oh?'

'I have seen these star-shaped diamonds before. They were smuggled in from the former GDR and Czechoslovakia. Like these ones, they were ground into diamonds of mediocre quality.'

'Mediocre quality?'

'Red diamonds may look attractive, but they're cheaper than the white ones, the clear diamonds. The stones you've found also have substantial remains of uncrystallised carbon in them which makes them less clear than one would like. If you have to grind away so much of the diamond to produce the star shape, then you prefer not to use diamonds that are perfect from the very start.'

'So, East Germany and Czechoslovakia.' Beate closed her eyes.

'Just an educated guess. If there's nothing else, I can still make the evening flight back to London . . .'

Beate opened her eyes and got up.

'Please forgive me. It's been a long, hectic day. You've been a great help. Thank you very much for coming.'

'Not at all. I only hope that it can help you catch the person who did this.'

'So do we. I'll call you a taxi.'

While Beate waited for Oslo Taxis to answer she noticed that the diamond expert was looking at her right hand holding the telephone. Beate smiled.

'That's a very attractive diamond you've got there. Looks like an engagement ring.'

Beate blushed without quite knowing why.

'I'm not engaged. It's the engagement ring my father gave my mother. I inherited it when she died.'

'Right. That explains why you are wearing it on your right hand.'

'Eh?'

'Yes, you would usually wear it on your left hand. Or on the middle finger of your left hand, to be precise.'

'The middle finger? I thought your ring finger was next to your little finger.'

'Not if you have the same beliefs as the Egyptians.'

'And what did they believe?'

'They thought that the vein of love, *vena amoris*, went directly from the heart to the middle finger on the left hand.'

After the taxi had arrived and the woman had left, Beate stood for a moment looking at her hand, at the middle finger on her left hand. Then she rang Harry.

'The gun was Czech, too,' Harry said when she finished.

'Perhaps there's something in it,' Beate said.

'Perhaps,' Harry said. 'What was the vein called again?'

'*Vena amoris*?'

'*Vena amoris*,' Harry mumbled. Then he put down the receiver.

16

Monday. Dialogue.

YOU'RE SLEEPING. I PLACE MY HAND AGAINST YOUR FACE. HAVE YOU missed me? I kiss your stomach. I go down lower and you begin to stir. Waves. A dance of elfins. You're silent. You pretend to sleep. You can wake up now, darling. You have been found.

Harry sat bolt upright in bed. It took a few seconds before he realised that it was his own scream that had woken him. He stared out into the semi-darkness and studied the shadows by the curtains and the wardrobe.

He laid his head back on the pillow. What had he been dreaming about? He'd been in a dark room. Two people were moving towards each other in a bed. Their faces were hidden. He switched on his torch and was shining it at them when he was woken by his own scream.

Harry looked at the digits on the clock on his bedside table. It was still two and a half hours away from 7.00. You can dream your way to hell and back in that time. He had to sleep though. Had to. He took a deep breath as if he were going to dive under water, and closed his eyes.

17

Tuesday. Profiles.

HARRY WATCHED THE SECOND HAND ON THE WALL CLOCK OVER TOM Waaler's head.

They'd had to bring in extra chairs to accommodate everyone in the large conference room in the green zone on the sixth floor. There was almost an atmosphere of solemnity in the room: no chatting, no drinking of coffee, no reading of newspapers, just people scribbling on notepads, the silent waiting for the clock to advance to 8.00. Harry counted 17 heads, and that meant that only one person was missing. Tom Waaler stood at the front with his arms crossed, staring at his Rolex wristwatch.

The second hand on the wall clock moved, stopped and, quivering, stood to attention.

'Let's start,' Tom Waaler said.

There was a rustle of movement as everyone, with one accord, sat up in their chairs.

'I'll be leading this investigation, assisted by Harry Hole.'

Heads round the table turned in surprise towards Harry, who sat at the back of the room.

'First of all, I'd like to thank those of you who uncomplainingly cut short your holidays,' Waaler continued. 'I'm afraid you'll be asked to sacrifice more than your holidays in the days to come, and I'm not sure I'll be able to get round to you all to thank you personally, so let's just say that this "thank you" is for the whole month. OK?'

There were smiles and nods round the table. As one smiles and nods to a future divisional commander, Harry thought.

'This is a special day in many ways.'

Waaler switched on the overhead projector. The front page of *Dagbladet* appeared on the screen behind him. SERIAL KILLER ON THE LOOSE? No pictures, just this screaming headline in block capitals. It's rare now for a news desk with any respect for the profession to use question marks on a front page, and what very few people knew – and no-one in Room K615 – was that the decision to add the question mark had been taken only minutes before the paper went to press after the acting editor rang his superior – on holiday in Tvedestrand – for advice.

'We haven't had a serial killer in Norway – as far as we know at least – since Arnfinn Nesset went berserk in the '80s,' Waaler said. 'Serial killers are rare, so rare that this is going to attract attention beyond the borders of Norway. We're already the subject of a lot of interest, folks.'

Tom Waaler's subsequent pause for effect was unnecessary. All those present had already been made aware of the significance of the case when they were briefed on the phone by Møller the previous evening.

'OK,' Waaler said. 'If we're really up against a serial killer now, we have a number of advantages on our side. Firstly, in our midst we have someone who has investigated and caught a serial killer. I assume you all know about Inspector Harry Hole's star turn in Sydney. Harry?'

Harry saw the faces turn towards him and cleared his throat. He could feel his voice threatening to desert him and he cleared his throat again.

'I'm not so sure that the job I did in Sydney was a model investigation.' He attempted a wry smile. 'As you perhaps remember, I ended up shooting the man.'

No laughter, not even so much as the suspicion of a smile. Harry was no future divisional commander.

'We can imagine worse outcomes than that, Harry,' Waaler said, looking at his Rolex again. 'Many of you know the psychologist Ståle Aune, to whom we have turned for expert advice on several cases. He's agreed to come and give us a short presentation on the phenomenon of serial killing. For some of you this is nothing new, but going over some old ground won't do any harm. He should be here at –'

All heads went up as the door swung open. The man who entered was panting loudly. Above the rotund stomach bursting out of a tweed jacket was a floppy orange necktie and glasses so small that you wondered whether it was possible to see through them at all. Beneath a shiny pate was a forehead glistening with sweat and beneath that a pair of dark, possibly dyed, but at any rate neatly tended eyebrows.

'Talk of the devil . . .' Waaler said.

'And here he is!' Ståle Aune completed, pulling out a handkerchief from his breast pocket and drying his forehead. 'And devilishly hot it is too!'

He went up to the end of the table and dropped his worn, brown leather bag onto the floor with a bang.

'Good morning, lady and gentlemen. Nice to see so many young people awake at this time of day. Some of you I have met before, others of you have been spared.'

Harry smiled. He was one of those who had definitely not been spared. Harry first went to see Aune about his drinking problems many years ago. Aune was no expert on drug abuse, but Harry had to admit a relationship had developed between them that bordered on a friendship.

'Notepads out, sluggards!'

Aune hung his jacket over a chair.

'You look as if you're at a funeral, and that's probably true in some respects, but I want to see a few smiles before I leave here. That's an order. And hang onto my coat-tails. I'm going to whistle through this.'

Aune grabbed a marker from the ledge under the flip chart and began to write at breakneck speed while speaking:

'There is every reason to believe that serial killers have existed for as long as there have been men on earth to kill. However, many consider the so-called "Autumn of Terror" in 1888 the first serial killer case of modern times. It's the first documented case of a serial killer with a purely sexual motive. The murderer killed five women before vanishing into thin air. He was given the epithet "Jack the Ripper", but he took his real identity with him to the grave. Our most famous national contribution to the list is not Arnfinn Nesset, who, as you will all remember, poisoned twenty patients or so in the '80s, but Belle Gunness who was that rare thing: a female serial killer. She left for America and married a weed of a man in 1902 and settled down on a farm outside La Porte in the state of Indiana. I say a weed of a man because he weighed seventy kilos and she weighed 120.'

Aune pulled lightly at the braces on his trousers.

'If you ask me, her weight was just right.'

Ripples of laughter.

'This pleasantly plump lady killed her husband, some children and an unknown number of suitors whom she lured to the farm through lonely heart advertisements in the Chicago press. Their bodies were discovered one day in 1908 when the farm burned down under mysterious circumstances. Among them was the burned and unusually voluminous torso of a woman with her head chopped off. The woman was presumably placed there by Belle to dupe investigators into believing it was her. The police received several reports from witnesses who said they had seen Belle in various places throughout America, but she was never found. And that is my point, dear friends. Unfortunately the cases of Jack and Belle are quite typical of serial killers.'

Aune finished writing with a round smack of his marker against the flip chart.

'They do not get caught.'

The assembly looked at him in silence.

'So,' Aune said, 'the concept of the serial murderer is just as controversial as everything else I'm going to tell you now. This is because psychology is a science that is still in its infancy and because psychologists are quarrelsome by nature. I'll tell you what we know about serial killers – it's much the same as what we don't know. By the way, "serial killer" is a term which many competent psychologists consider meaningless since it is used to describe a set of mental illnesses that other psychologists claim do not exist. Is that clear? Well, some of you are smiling anyway, and that's good.'

Aune tapped his index finger against the first point he had written up on the flip chart.

'The typical serial killer is a white man between 24 and 40 years of age. As a rule he acts alone, but he can work with others, in a pair, for example. Brutality against the victim is an indication that he is acting alone. The victims can be anyone, though generally they fall into the same ethnic group as the killer, and in exceptional cases they may be known to him.

'Usually he finds the first victim in an area he knows well. In the public imagination there are always special rituals connected with the murders. This is not true, but when rituals do occur, it is often in connection with a serial killing.'

Aune pointed to the next point where he had written PSYCHOPATH/SOCIOPATH.

'However, the most characteristic trait of the serial killer is that he's American. Only God – and perhaps a couple of psychology professors at Blindern – knows why. That's why it is interesting that the people who know most about serial killings – the FBI and the American legal profession – distinguish between two types of serial murderer: the psychopath and the sociopath. The professors I mentioned believe that both the distinction and the concepts stink, but in the homeland of the serial killer most law courts follow the McNaughten Rules which decree that it is only the psychopath who does not know what he's doing while committing the crime. The psychopath, therefore, unlike the sociopath, escapes a prison sentence or – as is probably the case in God's own country – execution. Apropos serial killers, it is my opinion that, hm . . .'

He sniffed at the marker pen and raised a surprised eyebrow.

Waaler put up his hand. Aune nodded.

'What sentence is apportioned is very interesting,' Waaler began, 'but first we have to catch him. Have you any practical advice we can use?'

'Are you crazy? I'm a psychologist, aren't I?'

Laughter. Aune, gratified, bows.

'Yes, I'll be coming to that, Inspector Waaler. Let me first say that if any of you are already becoming impatient, you have a tough time ahead of you. From experience, nothing takes as long as catching a serial killer. If they are the wrong type, at any rate.'

'What's the wrong type?' It was Magnus Skarre's question.

'First of all, let's have a look at how the people who draw up psychological profiles for the FBI distinguish between psychopaths and sociopaths. The psychopath is often a maladjusted individual without a job, without any education, with a criminal record and a variety of social problems. Unlike the sociopath, who is intelligent, apparently successful and living a normal life. The psychopath stands out and easily falls under suspicion, whereas the sociopath can disappear in the crowd. It always comes as quite a shock to neighbours and friends when a sociopath is uncovered. I was talking to a psychologist who works as a profiler for the FBI and she told me that the first thing she considered was the timing of the killings. Killing takes time of course. A useful lead for her was whether the killings had taken place on weekdays, at weekends or on national holidays. The latter would suggest that the killer had a job and would increase the likelihood that you were dealing with a sociopath.'

'So if our man kills during the national holidays it suggests that he has a job and is a sociopath?' Beate Lønn asked.

'It is somewhat premature to draw such conclusions of course, but taking that into account with what we already know, perhaps. Is that practical enough for you?'

'Practical, yes,' Waaler said, 'but it's also bad news if I read you right?'

'Correct. Our man looks a lot like the wrong type of serial killer. The sociopath.'

Aune gave the gathering a couple of seconds to let that sink in before going on.

'According to the American psychologist, Joel Norris, the serial killer goes through a mental process involving six phases with each killing. The first is called the aura phase where the person gradually loses their grip on reality. The totem phase, the fifth phase, is the killing itself, the serial killer's climax, or, to be more precise, the anti-climax, because the killing is never able to fulfil the hopes and expectations of catharsis and purification that the killer associates with the taking of a life. That's why the killer goes straight into the sixth phase, the depressed phase. This in turn leads into a new aura phase in which he builds himself up, ready for the next killing.'

'Round and round in circles then,' said Bjarne Møller, who had crept in unnoticed and was standing by the door. 'Like a perpetuum mobile.'

'Except that a perpetual motion machine repeats the operations without any changes,' Aune said. 'However, the serial killer goes through a process that changes his behaviour over the long term. Characterised, fortunately, by a decreasing level of control, but, unfortunately, also by an increasing level of brutality. The first murder is always the one that is most difficult to recover from and thus the so-called cooling-down period afterwards is also the longest. It produces a long aura phase in which he builds himself up for the next killing and he gives himself a good long time to plan it. If the killer has taken a great deal of care with details at the scene of a crime, if the rituals have been carried out with precision and the risk of discovery is small, it suggests that he is still at the beginning of the process. In this phase he is perfecting his technique to become even more efficient. This is the worst phase for the people trying to catch him. However, after he has killed a few times, the cooling-down periods typically become shorter and shorter. He has less time to plan, the murder scenes are messier, the rituals less neatly performed and he takes greater risks. All of this indicates that his frustration is growing. Or let me put it another way, that his thirst for blood is escalating. He loses self-control and is easier to catch. But if at this time attempts to capture him fail, he can be frightened off and he will stop killing for a while. In this way he has time to calm down and he will begin at the beginning again. I hope these examples are not too depressing?'

'We're surviving,' Waaler said. 'Could you say a little about this particular case?'

'Fine,' Aune replied. 'Here we have three premeditated murders –'

'Two!' It was Skarre again. 'For the time being, Lisbeth Barli is only reported missing.'

'Three murders,' Aune said. 'Believe me, young man.'

Some of the policemen exchanged glances. Skarre seemed to want to say something, but then changed his mind. Aune continued.

'The three murders have been committed with the same number of days between each one. And the ritual of mutilation and decorating the body has been carried out in all three cases. He cuts off one finger and compensates by giving the victim a diamond. Compensation is, by the way, a familiar feature with this kind of brutality, typical of killers who have been brought up according to strict moral principles. Perhaps this is a lead you can follow up since there is not much morality left in homes around Norway.'

No laughter.

Aune sighed.

'It's called gallows humour. I'm not trying to be cynical and my points could probably be better made, but I am trying not to let this case bury me before we have even started. I recommend you do the same. Anyway, in this particular case, the intervals between the killings and the fact that rituals are being performed indicate self-control and an early phase.'

Someone cleared their throat gently.

'Yes, Harry?' Aune said.

'Choice of victim and place,' Harry said.

Aune rubbed his index finger against his chin, considered for a moment and nodded.

'You're right, Harry.'

Others round the table exchanged enquiring looks.

'Right about what?' Skarre called out.

'The choice of victim and place suggests the opposite,' Aune said. 'That the murderer is moving quickly into the phase where he loses control and begins to kill indiscriminately.'

'How so?' Møller asked.

Harry talked without looking up from the table.

'The first shooting, of Camilla Loen, took place in a flat where she lived alone. The killer could go in and out without any risk of being caught or identified. He could carry out the killing and the rituals without being disturbed, but he's already taking chances when he goes for the second victim. He kidnaps Lisbeth Barli in the middle of a residential area, in broad daylight, probably using a car, and obviously a car has a number plate. The third killing is of course a pure lottery – in the ladies' lavatory in an office area. True, it's after normal office hours, but there are so many people around that luck has to be with him if he's not to be caught or at least identified.'

Møller turned towards Aune.

'So what's the conclusion?'

'That we can't conclude anything,' Aune said. 'The most we can assume is that he is a well-integrated sociopath. And we don't know whether he's about to go bananas or whether he is still in control of himself.'

'What can we hope for?'

'One scenario is that we are about to witness a bloodbath, but there is a chance that we might nab him as he'll be taking risks. The other scenario is that there will be longer intervals between each murder, but all our experience tells us that we will not manage to capture him in the foreseeable future. Make your own choice.'

'But where shall we begin to look?' Møller asked.

'If I believed my statistics-minded colleagues I would say among bedwetters, animal tormentors, rapists and pyromaniacs, particularly pyromaniacs. But I don't believe them. Unfortunately I have no alternative idols, so I suppose the answer is: I have no idea.'

Aune put the top on his marker pen. The silence was oppressive.

Tom Waaler jumped up.

'OK, folks. We've got a bit to do. To begin with, I want everyone we have talked to so far to be interviewed again. I want all convicted murderers checked out and I want a review of all the criminals who have been convicted of rape or arson.'

Harry observed Waaler as he delegated assignments, noted his efficiency and self-assurance, the speed and flexibility with which he dealt with relevant, practical objections, his strength of mind and decisiveness when the objections were not relevant.

The clock above the door showed 9.15. The day had hardly begun and Harry already felt drained of energy, like an old, dying lion who hung back from the pack when once he could have challenged the leader. Not that he had ever nurtured ambitions of leading the pack, but things had taken a nosedive anyway. All he could do was lie low and hope that someone would throw him a bone.

And someone had thrown him a bone. A big one.

The muffled acoustics in the small interview rooms gave Harry the feeling he was talking into a duvet.

'I import hearing aids,' the short, stout man said, running his hand down his silk tie. A discreet gold tiepin held his tie in place against the white shirt.

'Hearing aids?' Harry repeated, looking down at the interview sheet which Tom Waaler had given him. In the box for his name the man had written *André Clausen* and under profession, *Private Businessman.*

'Have you got hearing problems?' Clausen asked. Harry couldn't decide whether this sarcasm was being directed towards himself or whether Clausen was being ironic.

'Mm. So you were at Halle, Thune and Wetterlid's to talk about hearing aids?'

'I just wanted an evaluation of an agency contract. One of your kind colleagues took a copy of it yesterday afternoon.'

'This?' Harry pointed to a folder.

'Exactly.'

'I was looking at it just now. It was signed and dated two years ago. Is it going to be renewed?'

'No. I just wanted to be sure I wasn't being conned.'

'Only now?'

'Better late than never.'

'Haven't you got your own solicitor?'

'Yes, but he's getting on, I'm afraid.' There was the flash of a gold filling when Clausen smiled and continued speaking. 'I asked for an introductory meeting to hear what this firm of solicitors could offer.'

'And you agreed to this meeting before the weekend? With a firm which specialises in debt collection?'

'I only realised that in the course of the meeting. That is, the short while we had before all the uproar.'

'But if you're looking for a new solicitor, you must have arranged meetings with several,' Harry said. 'Can you tell us which ones?'

Harry didn't look at André Clausen's face. That wasn't where a lie would reveal itself. Harry had known immediately they met that Clausen was one of those people who didn't like his facial expression to reveal what he was thinking. Possibly because of shyness, possibly because his profession required a poker face or possibly because, in his past, self-control had been seen as an essential virtue. Accordingly, Harry kept an eye open for other signs, such as if his hand came up from his lap to stroke his tie again. It didn't. Clausen just sat looking at Harry. He wasn't staring, but his eyelids were heavy as if he found the situation irritating, just a little tedious.

'Most solicitors I rang didn't want to arrange a meeting until after the holidays,' Clausen said. 'Halle, Thune and Wetterlid were a great deal more obliging. Tell me: Am I under suspicion for anything?'

'Everyone is under suspicion,' Harry said.

'Fair enough.'

Clausen said this in English with a precise BBC accent.

'I've noticed that you have a slight accent.'

'Oh? I've travelled a lot in recent years. Perhaps that's why.'

'Where do you travel to?'

'In point of fact, mostly inside Norway. I visit hospitals and institutions. Otherwise I'm often in Switzerland, at the factory where they manufacture the hearing aids. The way products are advancing you have to keep up to date professionally.'

Again this indefinable sarcasm in the tone of his voice.

'Are you married? Have you got a family?'

'If you look at the form your colleague filled in, you'll see I haven't.'

Harry looked at the form.

'Yes, I see. So you live on your own . . . let's see . . . in Gimle terrasse?'

'No,' Clausen said. 'I live with Truls.'

'Exactly. I know.'

'Do you?' Clausen smiled, his eyelids sinking a little lower. 'Truls is a golden retriever.'

Harry could feel a headache coming on behind his eyes. A look at his list showed that he had four interviews before lunch, and five after. He didn't have the energy to trade blows with them all.

He asked Clausen to tell him again what had happened, from the time he entered the building in Carl Berners plass until the police arrived.

'More than gladly,' he said, yawning.

Harry sat back in the chair as Clausen, fluently and with self-confidence, told him how he had arrived by taxi, taken the lift up and, after a brief exchange with the receptionist, had waited for five or six minutes for her to return with the water. When she didn't come back, he wandered through to the offices and found Mr Halle's nameplate on his door.

Harry saw from Waaler's notes that Halle had confirmed the time Clausen knocked on the door as 5.05.

'Did you see anyone go into or come out of the Ladies?'

'I couldn't see the door from where I was waiting in reception. And I didn't see anyone on the way in or out when I went to the office. In fact, I have repeated this several times now.'

'And there will be even more times,' Harry said, yawning aloud and running his hand across his face. At that moment Magnus Skarre knocked on the window of the interview room and held up his wristwatch. Harry recognised Wetterlid standing behind him. Harry nodded in assent and cast a last look at his interview sheet.

'It says here that you didn't see any suspicious persons coming into or leaving reception while you were sitting there.'

'That's correct.'

'Well, thank you very much for your cooperation thus far,' Harry said, putting the sheet in the folder and pressing the stop button on the tape recorder. 'We'll certainly contact you again.'

'No *suspicious* persons,' Clausen said, getting up.

'What?'

'I said that I didn't see anyone *suspicious* in reception, but there was the cleaning lady who came in and went into the offices.'

'Yes, we've talked to her. She says she went straight into the kitchen and didn't see anyone.'

Harry got up and ran his eye down the list. The next interview was at 10.15 in room four.

'And the courier of course,' Clausen said.

'Courier?'

'Yes. He went out through the front door just before I went to look for the solicitor. Must have delivered something or picked something up. Why are you looking at me like that, Inspector? A standard courier in solicitors' offices is, quite frankly, not particularly suspicious.'

Half an hour later, after checking with the firm of solicitors and several courier companies in Oslo, Harry was clear about one thing: no-one had registered the delivery or collection of anything at all at the offices of Halle, Thune & Wetterlid on Monday.

Two hours after Clausen had left Police HQ, just before the sun reached its peak, he was picked up at his office and brought back to describe the courier again.

He couldn't tell them very much: height around one metre 80; average build. Clausen had not exactly studied the man's physical details. He considered that sort of thing both uninteresting and inappropriate for men, he said, and repeated that the courier was wearing what bike couriers usually wear: a yellow and black cycle shirt in some tight-fitting material, shorts and cycling shoes which clicked even when he walked on the carpet. His face was masked by the helmet and sunglasses.

'His mouth?' Harry asked.

'White cloth covering his mouth,' Clausen said. 'Like Michael Jackson uses. I thought bike couriers wore them to protect themselves from inhaling exhaust fumes.'

'In New York and Tokyo, yes. This is Oslo.'

Clausen shrugged his shoulders. 'Well, it didn't strike me as unusual.'

Clausen was given leave to go and Harry went to Tom Waaler's office. Waaler was sitting with the phone to his ear, mumbling *uh-huh* and *m-hm* when Harry walked in.

'I think I've got an idea how the killer got into Camilla Loen's flat,' Harry said.

Tom Waaler put down the phone without finishing the conversation.

'There's a video camera connected to the intercom at the main entrance to the block where she lived, isn't there?'

'Yes . . . ?' Waaler leaned forwards.

'Who can ring any bell, stick a masked face up into the camera and still be fairly sure that they'll be let in?'

'Father Christmas?'

'Hardly, but you would let in a person carrying an express package or a bunch of flowers, a courier, wouldn't you.'

Waaler pressed the engaged button on his phone.

'Just a little over four minutes passed from the moment Clausen arrived until he saw the courier leave through reception. A courier runs in, delivers and runs out again, he doesn't spend four minutes hanging about.'

Waaler nodded slowly.

'A courier on a bike,' he said. 'It's ingeniously simple. Someone with a plausible reason for calling in on all manner of people, with a cloth round his mouth. Someone everyone can see, but nobody notices.'

'A Trojan horse,' Harry said. 'What a dream set-up for a serial killer.'

'No-one gives a courier leaving somewhere with great haste a second thought. And he's using an unregistered form of transport, probably the most effective way to make a getaway in a city.' Waaler placed his hand on the telephone.

'I'll get some of the boys to make enquiries about a bike courier at the murder scenes at the relevant times.'

'There's one other thing we'll have to think about,' Harry said.

'Yes,' Waaler said. 'Whether we need to warn people about unfamiliar couriers.'

'Right. Will you take that up with Møller?'

'Yes. And Harry . . .'

Harry stopped in the doorway.

'Bloody good work,' Waaler said.

Harry gave a brief nod and left.

Three minutes later the rumours were swirling around Crime Squad that Harry had a lead.

18

Tuesday. The Pentagram.

NIKOLAI LOEB PRESSED DOWN GENTLY ON THE KEYS. THE NOTES FROM the piano sounded delicate and frail in the bare room. Pyotr Ilyich Tchaikovsky, Piano Concerto No. 1 in B-Flat Minor. Many pianists thought it was weird and lacked elegance, but to Nikolai's ears no-one had ever written more beautiful music. It made him feel homesick just to play the few bars he knew by heart, and it was always these notes that his fingers automatically searched for when he sat down at the untuned piano in the assembly room in Gamle Aker church hall.

He looked out of the open window. The birds were singing in the cemetery. It reminded him of summers in Leningrad and his father, who had taken him to the old battlefields outside the towns where his grandfather and all of Nikolai's uncles lay in long-forgotten mass graves.

'Listen,' his father had said. 'How beautiful and how futile their singing.'

Nikolai became aware of someone clearing his throat and twisted round.

A tall man in a T-shirt and jeans was standing in the doorway. He had a bandage round one hand. The first thing Nikolai thought was that it was one of those drug addicts who turned up from time to time.

'Can I help you?' Nikolai called out. The severe acoustics in the room made his voice sound less friendly than he had intended.

The man stepped in over the threshold.

'I hope so,' he said. 'I've come to make amends.'

'I'm so pleased,' Nikolai said. 'But I'm afraid I can't receive confessions here. There's a list in the hall with a timetable. And you'll have to go to our chapel in Inkognitogata.'

The man came over to him. Nikolai concluded from the dark circles under his bloodshot eyes that the man had not slept for a while.

'I want to make amends for destroying the star on the door.'

It took Nikolai a few seconds to take in what the man was referring to.

'Oh, now I'm with you. That's not really anything to do with me. Except that I can see that the star is loose and is hanging upside down.' He smiled. 'A little inappropriate in a religious house, to put it mildly.'

'So you don't work here?'

Nikolai shook his head.

'We have to borrow these rooms on occasion. I'm from the church of the Holy Apostolic Princess Olga.'

Harry raised his eyebrows.

'The Russian Orthodox Church,' Nikolai added. 'I am a pastor and chief administrator. You need to go to the church office and see if you can find someone to help you there.'

'Mm. Thank you.'

The man didn't make a move to leave.

'Tchaikovsky, wasn't it? First Piano Concerto?'

'Correct,' Nikolai said with surprise in his voice. Norwegians were not exactly what you might call a cultured people. On top of that, this one was wearing a T-shirt and looked like a down-and-out.

'My mother used to play it to me,' the man said. 'She said it was difficult.'

'You have a good mother. Who played pieces she thought were too difficult for you.'

'Yes, she was good. Saintly.'

There was something about the man's lopsided smile that confused Nikolai. It was a self-contradictory smile. Open and closed, friendly and cynical, laughing and pained. But he was probably reading too much into things, as usual.

'Thank you for your help,' the man said, moving towards the door.

'Not at all.'

Nikolai turned his attention to the piano and focused his concentration. He pressed down a key gently enough for it to touch, but make no sound – he could feel the felt lying against the piano string – and it was then he became aware that he had not heard the door shut. He turned round and saw the man standing there, his hand on the door handle, staring at the star in the smashed window.

'Something wrong?'

The man looked up.

'No. I was just wondering what you meant when you said it was inappropriate that the star was hanging upside down.'

Nikolai released a laugh which rebounded off the walls.

'It's the upside-down pentagram, isn't it.'

From the expression on the man's face it was clear to Nikolai that he didn't understand.

'The pentagram is an old religious symbol, not just for Christianity. As you can see, it is a five-pointed star made up of a continuous line that intersects itself a number of times: it has been found carved into headstones dating back several thousand years. However, when it hangs upside down with one point downwards and two points upwards, it's something completely different. It's one of the most important symbols in demonology.'

'Demonology?'

The man asked questions in a calm yet firm voice, like someone who was used to getting answers, Nikolai thought.

'The study of evil. The term originates from the time when people thought that evil emanated from the existence of demons.'

'Hm. And now the demons have been abolished?'

Nikolai swivelled round on his piano stool. Had he misjudged the man? He seemed to be a bit too sharp for a drug addict or a down-and-out.

'I'm a policeman,' the man said, as if answering his thoughts. 'We tend to ask questions.'

'Alright, but why are you asking about this in particular?'

The man shrugged his shoulders.

'I don't know. I've seen this symbol just recently, but I can't put my finger on where. I'm not sure if it's significant or not. Which demon uses this symbol?'

'Tchort,' Nikolai said, gently pressing down three keys. Dissonance. 'Also called Satan.'

In the afternoon Olaug Sivertsen opened the French doors to the balcony facing Bjørvika, sat down on a chair and watched the red train glide past her house. It was quite an ordinary house, a detached red-brick building dating back to 1891; what was so extraordinary was its location. Villa Valle – named after the man who designed it – stood on its own beside the railway track just outside Oslo Central Station, inside railway domain. The nearest neighbours were some low sheds and workshops belonging to Norwegian Railways. Villa Valle was built to accommodate the station master, his family and servants and was designed with extra thick walls so that the station master and his wife would not be awakened every time a train passed. In addition, the station master had asked the builder – who had got the job because it was well known that he used a special mortar to make the walls extra solid – to strengthen it even further. In the event that a train came off the rails and hit the house, the station master wanted the train driver to take the brunt of the collision and not him and his family. So far no train had crashed into the elegant station master's house that stood in such strange isolation, like a castle in the air above a wilderness of black gravel in which the rails gleamed and wriggled like snakes in the sun.

Olaug closed her eyes and basked in the warmth of the sun.

As a young woman she hadn't liked the heat. Her skin went red and itched and she had longed for the cool, damp summers of north-west Norway. Now she was old – almost 80 – she preferred the hot to cold, light to darkness, company to solitude, sound to silence.

It hadn't been like that when, in 1941 and at 16 years of age, she had left Averøya and gone to Oslo on those same rails and begun work as a maidservant for Gruppenführer Ernst Schwabe and his wife Randi in Villa Valle. He was a tall, good-looking man, and she came from an aristocratic family. Olaug was terrified in the first few days. However, they treated her well and showed her respect, and soon Olaug realised that she had nothing to fear so long as she did her job with the thoroughness and punctuality that Germans are, not unjustifiably, famous for.

Ernst Schwabe was responsible for the WLTA, the Wehrmacht's *Landtransportabteilung*, their transport division, and he himself chose the house by the railway station. His wife, Randi, probably also worked in the WLTA, but Olaug never saw her in uniform. Olaug's room faced south, overlooking the garden and the tracks. During the first weeks the clattering of the long trains, the shrill whistles and all the other noises of a town kept her awake at night, but gradually she became used to it. When she went home on her first holiday the year after, she lay in bed in the house she had grown up in, listening to the silence and the nothingness and longed for the sounds of life and living people.

Living people, there had been many of them in Villa Valle during the war. The Schwabes were very active socially, and both Germans and Norwegians were present at social engagements. If only people knew which heads of Norwegian society had been here, eating, drinking and smoking with the Wehrmacht as their hosts. One of the first things she was told to do after the war was to burn the seating cards she had been hoarding. She did what she was told and never said a word to anyone. Of course, she had felt an occasional urge to disobey when photographs of the self-same persons appeared in the press, which went on about living under the yoke of the German occupation. However, she kept her mouth shut for one reason only: when peace came, they threatened to take away her young son and he was all she had ever had or valued in the world. The fear was still well entrenched within her.

Olaug screwed up her eyes in the weak sun. It was flagging now, not so unremarkable since it had been shining all day and had done its best to kill her flowers in the window boxes. Olaug smiled. My goodness, she had been so young, no-one had ever been so young. Did she yearn to be young again? Maybe not, but she yearned for company, life, people milling around. She had never understood what they meant when they said that old people were lonely, but now . . .

It was not so much being alone as not being there for someone. She had become so deeply sad from waking up in the morning knowing that she could stay in bed all day and it would not make any difference to anybody.

That was why she had taken in a lodger, a cheerful young girl from Trøndelag.

It was odd to think that Ina, who was only a few years older than she had been when she moved to Oslo, was now staying in the same room as she had. She probably lay awake at night thinking about how she longed to be far from the din of town life, back in the silence of somewhere small in North Trøndelag.

Olaug may have been wrong, though. Ina had a gentleman friend. She hadn't seen him, let alone met him, but from her bedroom she had heard his footsteps up the back staircase, the entrance to Ina's room. It was not possible to forbid Ina from receiving men in her room, unlike when Olaug had been a maid, not that she wanted to, anyway. Her only hope was that no-one would come and take Ina away. She had become a close friend, even like a daughter, the daughter she had never had.

However, Olaug was aware that in a relationship between an old lady and a young girl such as Ina it would always be the young girl who offered friendship and the old lady who received it. Consequently, she took care not to be obtrusive. Ina was always friendly, but Olaug thought that may have had something to do with the low rent.

It had become a sort of fixed ritual: Olaug made some tea and knocked on Ina's door carrying a tray of biscuits at around 7.00 in the evening. Olaug preferred them to be there. It was strange, but this room was still the room where she felt most at home. They chatted about everything under the sun. Ina was especially interested in the war and what had gone on in Villa Valle. And Olaug told her. About how much Ernst and Randi had loved each other, about how they would sit for hours in the living room just talking and tenderly touching, brushing away a lock of hair, resting a head on a shoulder. Olaug told her how sometimes she secretly observed them from behind the kitchen door. She described Ernst Schwabe's erect figure, his thick black hair and his high, open forehead, how the expression of his eyes could alternate between joking and seriousness, anger and laughter, self-assurance in the larger things of life and boyish confusion in smaller, trivial things. Mostly, though, she watched Randi Schwabe with her shiny red hair, her slim white neck and bright eyes with a pale blue iris surrounded by a circle of dark blue. They were the most beautiful eyes Olaug had ever seen.

Seeing them like this, Olaug thought the two were made for each other, that they were soulmates and nothing would ever be able to tear them apart. Yet, she told Ina, the happy atmosphere at parties in Villa Ville could disintegrate into furious rows as soon as the guests had gone home.

It was following one such row, after Olaug had gone to bed, that Ernst Schwabe knocked on her door and entered her bedroom. Without switching on the light, he sat down on the edge of her bed and told her that his wife had left the house in a rage and had gone to a hotel for the night. Olaug could smell from his breath that he had been drinking, but she was young and didn't know what you do when a man 20 years her senior, a man she respected, admired and was even a little in love with, asked her to take off her nightdress so that he could see her naked.

He didn't touch her the first night, he just looked at her, caressed her cheek, told her she was beautiful, more beautiful than she would ever be able to understand, and then he got up. As he was leaving he appeared to be on the verge of tears.

Olaug stood up and closed the balcony doors. It was almost 7.00. She took a peek at the door at the top of the back steps and saw a pair of smart men's shoes on the doormat outside Ina's door. So she had a visitor. Olaug sat down on the bed and listened.

At 8.00 the door opened. She could hear someone putting on their shoes and going down the steps, but there was another sound, a scuffling, scratching sound, like a dog's paws. She went into the kitchen and put on some hot water for tea.

When she knocked on Ina's door a few minutes later, she was surprised to find that Ina didn't answer, especially since she could hear the sound of soft music coming from her room.

She knocked again, but still there was no answer.

'Ina?'

Olaug pushed the door and it swung open. The first thing she noticed was how stuffy the air was. The window was closed and the curtains were drawn so it was almost completely black inside.

'Ina?'

No-one answered. Perhaps she was asleep. Olaug went in and had a look behind the door where the bed was. Empty. Strange. Her old eyes were used to the darkness now, and she spotted Ina. She was sitting in the rocking chair by the window and it did look as if she was sleeping. Her eyes were closed and her head hung to the side. Olaug still couldn't make out where the low hum of music was coming from.

She went over to the chair.

'Ina?'

Her lodger didn't react now, either. Olaug held the tray with one hand and gently placed her other hand against the young girl's cheek.

There was a soft thud as the teapot met the carpet. Followed immediately by two teacups, a silver sugar bowl with the German imperial eagle on, a plate and six Maryland cookies.

At the same moment that Olaug's – or, to be more precise, the Schwabe family's – teacups hit the floor, Ståle Aune raised his cup – or, to be more precise, Oslo Police Department's.

Bjarne Møller studied the plump psychologist's distended little finger and wondered to himself how much was play-acting and how much was just a distended little finger.

Møller had called a meeting in his office and in addition to Aune he had asked those leading the investigation – Tom Waaler, Harry Hole and Beate Lønn – to attend.

They all looked jaded, largely perhaps because the hope that had sprung into life with the discovery of the bogus courier was beginning to fade.

Tom Waaler had just gone through the results of the appeal for information they had put out over TV and radio. Twenty-four calls they had received, 13 of which were from their regulars who always rang in whether they had seen something or not. Of the other eleven calls, seven turned out to be genuine couriers on genuine jobs. Four callers told them what they already knew: that there had been a courier near Carl Berners plass on Monday at around 5 p.m. What was new was that he had been seen cycling down Trondheimsveien. The only interesting call came from a taxi driver who had seen a cyclist wearing a helmet, glasses, and a yellow and black shirt outside the Art and Technical School on his way up Ullevålsveien at around the time when Camilla Loen was killed. None of the courier services had taken on jobs anywhere near the Ullevålsveien area at that time of day. Then someone from Førstemann Courier Services had called in to say that he had nipped up Ullevålsveien on his way to the terrace restaurant in St Hanshaugen for a beer.

'In other words, our inquiries have led nowhere.' Møller said.

'Still early days,' Waaler said.

Møller nodded, but his expression indicated that he was not encouraged. Apart from Aune, everyone in the room knew that the first responses were the important ones. People forget quickly.

'What do they say in the understaffed Institute of Forensic Medicine?' Møller asked. 'Have they found anything that can help identify our man?'

''Fraid not,' Waaler said. 'They've put the other autopsies to one side and prioritised ours, but so far nothing. No semen, no blood, no hair, nothing. The only physical clue the murderer has left is bullet holes.'

'Interesting,' Aune said.

Somewhat dejectedly, Møller asked what was so interesting.

'It's interesting because it suggests that he didn't attack the victims sexually,' Aune said. 'And that's very unusual for serial killers.'

'Perhaps this is not about sex,' Møller said.

Aune shook his head. 'It's always sexually motivated. Always.'

'Perhaps he's like Peter Sellers in *Being There*,' Harry said. '"I like to watch."'

The others stared at him in total incomprehension.

'I mean, perhaps he doesn't have to touch them to get sexual satisfaction.'

Harry avoided Waaler's gaze.

'Perhaps the killing and the sight of the body are enough.'

'That could be right,' Aune said. 'What usually happens is that the murderer wants an orgasmic release, but he may have ejaculated without leaving his seed at the scene of the crime. Or he might have had enough self-control to wait until he was in safety.'

It went quiet for a few seconds. Harry knew they were all thinking the same as he was. What had the killer done with the woman who had disappeared, Lisbeth Barli?

'What about the weapons we found at the crime scene?'

'We've checked them,' Beate said. 'The tests show that they are ninety-nine point nine per cent certain to be the murder weapons.'

'That's good enough,' Møller said. 'Any idea where the weapons came from?'

Beate shook her head. 'As before, the serial numbers have been filed off. The marks are the same as those we see on most of the weapons we confiscate.'

'Hm,' Møller said. 'So, the great gun-running fraternity myth again. Surely the security service guys, POT, will get their hands on them soon, won't they?'

'Interpol has been working on the case for more than four years without anything to show for their efforts,' Waaler said.

Harry rocked back on his chair and stole a furtive glance at Waaler. While doing that, to his consternation, he felt something he had never felt for Waaler before: admiration. The same kind of admiration you feel for beasts of prey that have perfected what they do to survive.

Møller sighed. 'I know. We're three-nil down and our opponent still hasn't given us a sight of the ball. Does no-one have any bright ideas?'

'I'm not exactly sure if it's an idea . . .'

'Come on, Harry.'

'It's more like a gut feeling about the crime scenes. They've all got something in common, but I can't put my finger on what it is yet. The first shooting was in an attic flat in Ullevålsveien. The second about a kilometre north-west, in Sannergata. And the third about the same distance again from there, this time towards the east, in an office block by Carl Berners plass. He moves, but I have the feeling that there is a logic behind it.'

'How's that?' Beate asked.

'His territory,' Harry said. 'The psychologist can probably explain.'

Møller turned to Aune, who was just taking a gulp of tea.

'Any comment, Aune?'

Aune grimaced. 'Well, it's not exactly Earl Grey.'

'I didn't mean the tea.'

Aune sighed.

'It was a joke, Møller. I know what you're getting at though, Harry. The killer has strong preferences with respect to the geographical location of the crime. Here, in rough terms, we can distinguish between three types.'

Aune counted on his fingers:

'There is the stationary killer who entices or forces victims into his home and kills them. There is the territorial killer who operates in a restricted area, like Jack the Ripper who only killed in the red-light district, but their territory could easily be a whole town. Finally, there is the nomadic killer who is probably the one with most killings on his conscience. Ottis Toole and Henry Lee Lucas went from state to state in the US and killed more than three hundred people between them.'

'Right,' Møller said. 'Though I can't quite see the logic you were talking about, Harry.'

Harry shrugged his shoulders.

'As I was saying, boss, just a gut feeling.'

'There is one thing they've got in common,' Beate said.

As if operated by remote control, the others turned to face her. Her cheeks immediately flushed and she seemed to regret saying anything. However, she ignored it and went on:

'He intrudes where women feel at their most secure. Into their home. Into a street in broad daylight. Into the Ladies at work.'

'Well done, Beate,' Harry said, and received a quick flash of gratitude.

'Well observed, young lady,' Aune chimed in. 'Since we're talking about patterns of movement, I'd like to add one more thing. Killers of the sociopath variety are often very self-assured, just as it seems to be in this case. A characteristic feature of theirs is that they follow the investigation closely and tend to take every opportunity to be physically close to whatever is going on. They may interpret the investigation as a game between themselves and the police. Many have expressed pleasure at seeing the police in confusion.'

'Which means that somewhere out there someone is sitting and lapping it up right now,' Møller said, clapping his hands together. 'That's all for today.'

'Just one more little thing,' Harry said. 'The diamonds that the murderer has placed on the victims . . .'

'Yes?'

'They've got five points. Almost like a pentagram.'

'Almost? As far as I know, it's exactly like a pentagram.'

'A pentagram is drawn with one unbroken line which intersects itself.'

'Aha!' Aune exclaimed. 'That pentagram. Drawn using the golden section. Very interesting shape. By the way, did you know that there is a theory that in Viking times the Celts were going to convert Norway to Christianity, so they drew a holy pentagram which they placed over southern Norway and used it to determine the location of towns and churches?'

'What's that got to do with diamonds?' Beate asked.

'It's not the diamonds,' Harry said. 'It's the shape, the pentagram. I know I've seen it somewhere, at one of the crime scenes, I just can't remember which and where. This may sound like rubbish, but I think it's important.'

'So,' Møller said, supporting his chin on his hands. 'You can remember something you can't quite remember, but you think it's important?'

Harry rubbed his face hard with both hands.

'When you go to the scene of a crime, you're concentrating so hard that the most peripheral things your brain takes in are much more than you can work through. They simply remain there until something happens, until something new crops up, one piece of the jigsaw fits another, but then you can't remember where you got the first piece from. Your gut feeling tells you that it's important, though. How does that sound?'

'Like a psychosis,' Aune said, yawning.

The other three looked at him.

'Can you not at least smile when I'm being funny?' he said. 'Harry, it sounds like an absolutely normal working brain. Nothing to be frightened of.'

'I think there are four brains here that have done enough for one day,' Møller said and got up.

At that moment the telephone in front of him rang.

'Møller here . . . Just a minute.'

He passed the telephone over to Waaler, who took it and placed it against his ear.

'Yes?'

There was a scraping of chairs, but Waaler motioned with his hand that they should wait.

'Great,' he said, hanging up.

The others turned to him with renewed interest.

'A witness has called in. She saw a cyclist coming out of an apartment block in Ullevålsveien near Our Saviour's Cemetery on the Friday afternoon when Camilla Loen was killed. She remembered it because she thought it was so peculiar that he was wearing a white cloth round his mouth. The courier who nipped off for a beer in St Hanshaugen wasn't wearing one.'

'And?'

'She didn't know which number it was in Ullevålsveien, but Skarre drove her past. She pointed out the building and it was Camilla Loen's.'

Møller slammed his hand down hard on the surface of the table.

'At last!'

Olaug was sitting on the bed with her hand around her throat and feeling her pulse slowly return to normal.

'How you frightened me,' she whispered in a voice which was hoarse and unrecognisable now.

'I'm so sorry,' Ina said, taking the last Maryland cookie. 'I didn't hear you come in.'

'It's me who should apologise,' Olaug said. 'Bursting in like that. I didn't see that you were wearing those . . .'

'Headphones,' Ina laughed. 'I probably had the music on pretty loud. Cole Porter.'

'You know I'm not so up to date with modern music.'

'Cole Porter is an old jazz musician. He's dead, in fact.'

'Dear me, someone as young as you shouldn't be listening to dead people.'

Ina laughed again. When she had felt something touch her cheek she had automatically struck out with her hand and had hit the tray with the teaset on. There was still a fine layer of white sugar on the carpet.

'Someone played me his records.'

'That's such a secretive smile,' Olaug said. 'Was it your gentleman friend?'

She regretted her question the moment she asked it. Ina would think she was spying on her.

'Perhaps,' Ina said, her eyes a-twinkle.

'He's older than you then, is he?' Olaug wanted to intimate indirectly that she hadn't gone out of her way to catch a glimpse of him. 'Since he likes old music, I mean.'

She could hear that was the wrong thing to say, too. Now she was asking questions and probing like an old tittle-tattle. In a flash of panic, she saw Ina mentally looking for somewhere else to live already.

'A bit older, yes.'

Ina's playful smile confused Olaug.

'Much like you and Herr Schwabe perhaps.'

Olaug laughed happily along with Ina, mostly out of relief.

'Just imagine. He was sitting exactly where you're sitting now,' Ina said out of the blue.

Olaug ran her hand across the blanket on the bed.

'Yes, just imagine.'

'When he was crying that evening was it because he couldn't have you?'

Olaug was still stroking the blanket. The rough wool felt good under her hand.

'I don't know,' she said. 'I didn't dare ask. Instead I made up my own answers, the ones I liked best, dreams I could cosset at night. That was probably why I was so much in love as I was.'

'Did you ever go out together?'

'Yes. He took me once in his car to Bygdøy. We went swimming. That is, I went swimming while he sat and watched. He called me his very own nymph.'

'Did his wife find out that her husband was the father when you became pregnant?'

Olaug gave Ina a lingering look. Then she shook her head.

'They left the country in May of 1945. I never saw them again. It was only in July that I discovered I was pregnant.'

Olaug slapped the blanket with her hand.

'But you must be sick and tired of my old stories, my dear. Let's talk about you. Who is your gentleman friend?'

'He's a fine man.'

Ina still had the dreamy expression on her face that she usually wore when Olaug was telling her about her first and last lover, Ernst Schwabe.

'He's given me something,' Ina said, opening a drawer in the desk and holding up a little packet tied with a golden ribbon.

'He said I couldn't open it until we got engaged.'

Olaug smiled and stroked Ina's cheek. She was happy for her.

'Are you fond of him?'

'He's different from all the others. He's not so . . . he's old-fashioned. He wants us to wait. With . . . you know what.'

Olaug nodded. 'It sounds like he's serious.'

'Yes.' A little sigh escaped her.

'You'll have to make sure he's the man for you before you let him go any further,' Olaug said.

'I know,' Ina said. 'That's what's so difficult. He's just been here, and before he left, I told him I needed time to think. He said he understood, I am so much younger than him.'

Olaug was going to ask if he had a dog, but caught herself in time. She had done enough prying and probing. She ran her hand across the blanket for the last time and stood up.

'I'm going to go back and put on some more tea, my dear.'

It was a revelation. Not a miracle, just a revelation.

It was half an hour since the others had left and Harry had just finished reading the interview transcripts of the two women who lived together across from Lisbeth Barli. He turned off the reading lamp on the desk, blinked in the dark and suddenly it came to him. Perhaps because he had turned off the light as you do when you go to bed. Or perhaps because he had stopped thinking for a moment. Whatever the reason, it was as if someone had thrust a clear, sharp photograph in his face.

He went into the office where the keys for the crime scenes were kept and found the one he was looking for. Then he drove to Sofies gate, collected his torch and walked to Ullevålsveien. It was almost midnight. The first floor was locked and the launderette was closed. In the shop selling headstones there was a spotlight in the window lighting up 'Rest in Peace'.

Harry let himself into Camilla Loen's flat.

None of the furniture or anything else had been removed, but still his footsteps echoed. It was as if the demise of the owner had lent the flat a physical void it hadn't had before. At the same time he had the feeling that he wasn't alone. Harry believed in the existence of the soul. Not that he was particularly religious as such, but it was one thing which always struck him when he saw a dead body: the body was bereft of something, something that wasn't to do with the processes of physical change that bodies undergo. Bodies looked like the empty shells of insects in a spider's web – the creature had gone, the light had gone, there was not the illusory afterglow that long-since burned-out stars have. The body was missing its soul and it was this absence of the soul that made Harry believe.

He didn't put on the light; the light of the moon through the skylights was enough. He went straight into the bedroom where he switched on his torch and shone it at the load-bearing beam beside the bed. A sharp intake of breath. It wasn't a heart round a triangle as he had first thought.

Harry sat down on the bed and ran the tips of his fingers over the grooves in the beam. The cuts in the brown, aged wood were so clear that they had to be fresh. And it was clear it had to be one cut. One long cut consisting of straight lines which doubled back and inter-sected each other. A pentagram.

Harry shone the torch on the floor. There were a fine layer of dust and a couple of hefty dustballs on the wood. Camilla Loen obviously had not done the cleaning before she departed. But there, by one of the legs at the top of the bed, he saw what he had been looking for. Wood shavings.

Harry lay back on the bed. The mattress was soft and giving. He stared up at the slanting ceiling while trying to think. If it really was the killer who had carved the star in the beam above the bed, what did it mean?

'Rest in peace,' Harry mumbled, closing his eyes.

He was too tired to think clearly. There was another question churning around in his brain. Why hadn't he actually noticed the pentagram? Why hadn't he put the two things together, the star and the diamonds? Or had he? Perhaps he had been too quick, perhaps his subconscious had connected the pentagram with something else, something he had seen at one of the killings, but he hadn't managed to draw out.

He tried to establish a mental picture of the crime scenes.

Lisbeth in Sannergata. Barbara in Carl Berners plass. And Camilla here in the shower, in the room next door. She was almost naked. Wet skin. He had felt it. The hot water had made it seem as if she had been dead for less time than she really had. He had felt her skin. Beate watched him. He couldn't stop touching her. It was like running your fingers over warm, smooth rubber. He looked up and saw that they were alone, and it was only then that he felt the warm stream of water from the shower. His eyes wandered down again; he saw her staring up at him with an odd gleam in her eyes. He gave a start and withdrew his hands; her stare faded away like on a television screen when the set has been switched off. Odd, he thought, and put a hand against her cheek. He waited while the hot water from the shower soaked through his clothes. The gleam came slowly back. He placed his other hand on her stomach. Her eyes became alive and he could feel her body stir beneath his fingers. He knew that it was touch that brought her back to life, that without touch she would disappear, die. He rested his forehead against her forehead. The water ran down the inside of his clothing, soaked his skin and lay like a warm filter between them. It was then that he noticed that her eyes were not blue, but brown. And her lips were no longer pale, but red and full of life. Rakel. He put his lips against hers. He recoiled when he discovered that they were ice cold.

She stared at him. Her mouth moved.

'What are you doing?'

Harry's heart stopped beating, partly because the echo of the words still hung in the room so that he knew it could not have been a dream, and partly because the voice did not belong to a woman, but mostly because there was someone standing in front of the bed, leaning over him.

His heart began to race again and he flung himself round in an attempt to grope for the torch that was still switched on. It fell on the floor with a soft thud and rolled around in a circle as the beam of light and the shadow of the figure ran across the walls.

Then the ceiling lights came on.

Harry was blinded and his first reflex action was to hold up his arms in front of his face. A second came and went. Nothing happened. No shots, no blows. Harry lowered his arms.

He recognised the man standing in front of him.

'What on earth are you up to?' the man asked.

He was wearing a pink dressing gown, but otherwise did not look as if he had just got up. The side parting in his hair was immaculate.

It was Anders Nygård.

'I was woken up by the noise,' Nygård said, pushing a cup of filter coffee in front of Harry. 'My first thought was that someone had realised that it was vacant upstairs and had broken in. So I went up to check.'

'Understandable,' said Harry. 'Though I thought I had locked the door after me.'

'I've got the caretaker's key. Just in case.'

Harry heard the shuffle of feet and turned round.

Vibeke Knutsen, wearing a dressing gown, appeared in the doorway with a sleepy face and red hair sticking out in all directions. Without make-up and in the harsh light of the kitchen she looked older than the version Harry had seen before. She gave a start when she discovered he was there.

'What's going on?' she mumbled, her eyes darting between Harry and her partner.

'I was checking a few things out in Camilla's flat,' Harry quickly interposed when he saw her forebodings. 'I was sitting on the bed and resting my eyes for a couple of seconds and then I nodded off. Nygård, here, heard noises and woke me up. It's been a long day.'

Without being absolutely sure why, Harry yawned demonstratively.

Vibeke peered at her partner.

'What are you wearing?'

Anders Nygård looked at the pink dressing gown as if he had only just realised he was wearing it.

'Wow, I must look like a regular drag queen.'

He sniggered.

'It's a present I bought you, love. It was still in my suitcase and it was all I could find in my haste. Here you are.'

He loosened the belt, tore the gown off and threw it to Vibeke. She was taken aback but caught it.

'Thank you,' she said, bewildered.

'It's a surprise to see you up, by the way,' he purred. 'Didn't you take your sleeping pill?'

Vibeke cast an embarrassed glance over to Harry.

'Goodnight,' she mumbled and left.

Anders went to the coffee machine and put back the jug of coffee. His back and upper arms were pale, almost white, but his lower arms were brown, exactly the way lorry drivers' arms are in the summer. The same sharp division was apparent on his knees.

'Normally she sleeps like a log all night,' he said.

'But you don't?'

'How's that?'

'Well, since you know that she sleeps like a log.'

'That's what she says.'

'And so someone only has to walk across the floor above you and you're awake?'

Anders looked at Harry. He nodded.

'You're right, Inspector. I don't sleep. It's not so easy after all that has happened. You lie awake thinking and come up with all sorts of possible theories.'

Harry took a sip of his coffee. 'Any you want to share with the rest of us?'

Anders shrugged his shoulders.

'I don't know that much about mass murderers. If that's what it really is.'

'It's not. It's a serial killer. Big difference.'

'Right, but haven't you noticed that the victims have something in common?'

187

'They're young women. Anything else?'

'They're promiscuous, or they were.'

'Oh?'

'You can read about it in the papers. What you read about these women's pasts speaks for itself.'

'Lisbeth Barli was a married woman and, as far as I know, faithful.'

'After she was married, yes, but before that she was in a band travelling all over the country playing at dances. You're not so naive, are you, Inspector?'

'Mm. What do you conclude from this similarity then?'

'This kind of murderer who acts as an arbiter over life and death has elevated himself into the position of God. And, in our Bible, in Hebrews, chapter 13, verse 4, it says that God will judge whosoever commits fornication.'

Harry nodded and raised his wrist to check the time.

'I'll make a note of that.'

Nygård fidgeted with his cup.

'Did you find what you were looking for?'

'You could say that. I found a pentagram. I suppose that since you deal with the interiors of churches you'll know what that is.'

'You mean a five-pointed star?'

'Yes, drawn with one continuous line. Do you have any idea what a sign like that might symbolise?'

Harry's head was bent over the table, but he was furtively studying Nygård's face.

'Quite a lot,' Nygård said. 'Five is the most important figure in black magic. Did it have one or two points sticking upwards?'

'One.'

'So it's not the sign of evil then. The sign you're describing might symbolise both vitality and passion. Where did you find it?'

'On a beam above her bed.'

'Oh, I see,' Nygård said. 'That's a simple one then.'

'Oh?'

'It's what we call a mare cross, or a devil's star.'

'A mare cross?'

'A pagan symbol. They used to carve it over beds or doorways to keep away the mare.'

'The mare?'

'The mare, yes. As in *night-mare*. A female demon who sits on the chest of a sleeping person and rides him so that he has bad dreams. The pagans thought she was a spirit. Not that strange since "mare" is derived from the Indo-Germanic "mer".'

'Have to confess that my Indo-Germanic is not up to much.'

'It means "death".' Nygård stared down into his cup of coffee. 'Or to be more precise, "murder".'

There was a message on Harry's answerphone when he arrived home. It was from Rakel. She wondered if Harry could possibly stay with Oleg in the swimming pool in Frogner the following day as she had an appointment at the dentist's from three till five. Oleg had asked, she said.

Harry sat and played the recording over and over again to see if he could hear any breathing, like the call he had received a few days previously, but without any success.

He undressed and got into bed naked. The night before he had taken the duvet out of the cover and slept with only the cover over him. He kicked it around for a while, slept, got his foot caught in the opening, panicked and woke up to the splitting sound of the cotton material. The darkness outside had already taken on a grey hue. He threw what remained of the duvet cover onto the floor and lay facing the wall.

And then she came. She sat astride him. She pushed the bridle into his mouth and pulled. His head spun round. She leaned down over him and blew her hot breath into his ear. A fire-breathing dragon. A wordless message, a hiss, on the telephone answerphone. She whipped his flanks, his haunches, and the pain was sweet, and soon, she said, she would be the only woman he would be able to love, so he may as well learn that from the outset.

She didn't let go until the sun shone over the highest roof tiles.

19

Wednesday. Under Water.

WHEN HARRY PARKED OUTSIDE THE OPEN-AIR POOL IN FROGNER A little before 3.00 he realised where all the people who were left in Oslo had gone. There was a queue a hundred metres long in front of the ticket window. He read *Verdens Gang* while the queue shuffled forward towards their chlorine redemption.

There was nothing new in the serial killer case, but they had still dug up enough material to cover four whole pages. The headlines were somewhat cryptic and directed at readers who had been following the case for a while. They referred to the murders as the 'courier killings' now. Everything was in the open, the police were no longer one step ahead of the press, and Harry guessed that the morning meetings with the editors would be identical to those he had with other detectives on the case. He read the statements of the witnesses they had themselves interviewed at Police HQ, but who remembered even more for the papers. He read newspaper surveys in which people said that they were afraid, very afraid or terrified, and about courier businesses who thought they should receive compensation because they couldn't do their jobs if people wouldn't let them in, and ultimately it was the authorities' responsibility to catch this man, wasn't it? The connection between the courier killings and Lisbeth Barli's disappearance was no longer referred to as speculative, it was a fact. A big photograph below the headline 'Takes Over From Sister' showed Toya Harang and Wilhelm Barli standing in front of the National Theatre. The caption under the photograph ran: 'The dynamic producer has no intention of cancelling.'

Harry's eyes ran down to the main text where Wilhelm Barli was quoted as saying:

'"The show must go on" is more than a cheap cliché, it is deadly serious in our line of business, and I know that Lisbeth is behind us on this, whatever has happened to her. Naturally, the situation has had an impact, but, nevertheless, we are trying to stay positive. The show will be a tribute to Lisbeth; she is a great artist who has still not realised her potential, but she will. I simply cannot allow myself to think otherwise.'

When Harry finally made his way through the entrance, he stopped and looked around. It must have been 20 years since he last came to the open-air pool in Frogner, but apart from the renovated exteriors of the buildings and a large blue water slide in the shallow end, not a great deal had changed. There was still the smell of chlorine, the fine spray which drifted from the showers into the pools making small rainbows, the sound of the patter of feet on the asphalt, shivering children in wet bathing costumes queuing in the shade in front of the kiosk.

He found Rakel and Oleg on the grass slope beneath the children's pool.

'Hi.'

Rakel smiled with her mouth, but it was difficult to see what her eyes were doing behind the large Gucci sunglasses. She was wearing a yellow bikini. There are not many women who can make a yellow bikini look good, but Rakel was one of them.

'Do you know what?' Oleg burst out, his head cocked to one side as he tried to shake the water out of his ears. 'I jumped off the five-metre board.'

Harry sat down on the grass beside them, even though there was plenty of space on the rug.

'Now you're telling me whoppers.'

'I'm telling you the truth, I am.'

'Five metres? You're a real stunt man.'

'Have you ever jumped from five metres, Harry?'

'Only just.'

'From seven?'

'Well, I did a belly flop.'

Harry sent Rakel a meaningful look, but she was looking at Oleg who suddenly stopped shaking his head and asked in a low voice:

'From ten?'

Harry glanced up at the diving pool, from where all the screams of pleasure and the braying voice of the lifeguard on the loudhailer were coming. Ten metres. The diving tower stood out like a black-and-white T against the blue sky. It wasn't true that the last time he had been here was 20 years ago. He had come here one summer's night a few years after that. He and Kristin had clambered over the fence, gone up the steps on the diving tower and lay side by side on the top board. They had stayed like that and just talked and talked, with the rough, rigid matting sticking into their skin and the starry sky twinkling above them. He had thought she was the only love he would ever have.

'No, I've never jumped from ten metres,' he said.

'Never.'

Harry could hear the disappointment in Oleg's voice.

'Never. Just dived.'

'Dived?' Oleg leapt up. 'But that's even cooler. Did many people see you?'

Harry shook his head. 'I did it at night. All on my own.'

Oleg groaned. 'What's the point of that? What's the point of being brave if no-one sees you . . . ?'

'I wonder about that too now and then.'

Harry tried to catch Rakel's eye, but her sunglasses were too dark. She had packed her bag, put on a T-shirt and a blue denim miniskirt over her bikini.

'But that's what the most difficult thing about it is,' Harry said. 'Being alone with no-one watching.'

'Thanks for doing me this favour, Harry,' Rakel said. 'It's really good of you.'

'The pleasure's all mine,' he said. 'Take all the time you need.'

'The dentist needs,' she said. 'Which is not too long, I hope.'

'How did you land?' Oleg asked.

'The usual way,' Harry said without taking his eyes off Rakel.

'I'll be back at five,' she said. 'Don't move position.'

'We won't move a thing,' Harry said and regretted it the instant he had said it. This was not the time and place to be pathetic. There would be more suitable occasions.

Harry watched her go until she had disappeared. He wondered how difficult it had been to get an appointment in the middle of the national holiday.

'Will you watch me jumping from five?' Oleg asked.

'Of course,' Harry said, taking off his T-shirt.

Oleg stared at him.

'Don't you ever sunbathe, Harry?'

'Never.'

After Oleg had jumped twice, Harry took off his jeans and joined him on the diving board. His droopy boxer shorts with the EU flag on were attracting disapproving stares from a couple of boys in the queue as he was telling Oleg how to do a jack-knife. He held his hand out flat.

'The trick is to stay horizontal in the air. It looks really weird.

People think you're going to land as flat as pancake. But then at the last minute . . .'

Harry pressed his thumb against his index finger.

'. . . you bend in the middle, like a jack-knife, and break the surface of the water with your hands and feet at the same time.'

Harry took a run up and jumped. He just caught the lifeguard's whistle as he jack-knifed and the surface of the water hit his forehead.

'Hey, you, I said five was off-limits,' he heard the megaphone voice bray as he re-emerged from the water.

Oleg made a sign from the diving platform and Harry raised his thumb to show that he had understood.

He got out of the water, stepped gingerly down the stairs and stood by one of the windows looking into the diving pool. He ran two fingers across the cool glass and made a drawing in the condensation while staring through the green and blue underwater landscape. Up at the surface he could see swimming costumes, kicking legs and the contours of a cloud in the blue sky. He thought of Underwater.

Then Oleg arrived. He braked sharply with a cloud of bubbles, but instead of swimming up to the surface he gave a couple of kicks and swam to the window where Harry was standing.

They looked at each other. Oleg was smiling, waving his arms and pointing. His face was pale, greenish. Harry couldn't hear a sound from inside the pool; he could just see Oleg's mouth moving and his black hair floating weightlessly above his head, dancing like sea grass, and him pointing upwards. It reminded Harry of something, something he didn't want to think about at this moment. Standing there, with Oleg on the opposite side of the glass, with the sun burning down from the sky, amid all the joyful sounds of life around him, yet in absolute stillness, Harry had a sudden premonition that something terrible was going to happen.

The very next minute he had forgotten and the premonition was replaced by another feeling when Oleg gave a kick and disappeared from view. Harry stayed with his eyes glued to the vacant TV screen. The vacant TV screen. With the lines he had drawn in the condensation. Now he knew where he had seen it.

'Oleg!' He sprinted up the stairs.

By and large, Karl was not that interested in people. Although he had been running the television shop in Carl Berners plass for more than 20 years, he had never been interested enough, for example, to find out a few details about his namesake, who had given his name to the square. Nor was he interested in finding out anything about the tall man standing in front of him with the police ID card, or the boy with wet hair standing beside him. Or the girl the policeman was talking about, the one they had found in the toilet at the solicitors' place across the street. The only person Karl was interested in right now was the girl on the front of *Vi Menn* and how old she was, and if she really came from Tønsberg and liked sunbathing in the nude on the balcony of her flat so that men passing by could see her.

'I was here the day Barbara Svendsen was murdered,' the policeman said.

'If you say so,' Karl said.

'Can you see the TV by the window? It's not plugged in,' the policeman said, pointing with his finger.

'Philips,' Karl said, shoving *Vi Menn* to one side. 'Nice, isn't it? Fifty Hertz. Flat screen. Surround sound, teletext and radio. It sells for seven nine, but you can have it for five nine.'

'Someone's been drawing in the dust on the screen. Can you see?'

'OK then,' Karl sighed. 'Five six.'

'I don't give a shit about the TV,' the policeman said. 'I want to know who did it.'

'Why?' Karl said. 'I wasn't really thinking of reporting it.'

The policeman leaned over the counter. Karl could see by the colour of his face that he didn't like the answers he was getting.

'Listen to me carefully. We are trying to find a killer and I have reason to believe that he's been in here drawing on that TV screen. Is that good enough?'

Karl nodded mutely.

'Excellent. And now I want you to have a good think.'

The policeman turned as a bell rang behind him. A woman with a metal case appeared in the doorway.

'The Philips TV,' the policeman said, pointing.

She nodded without saying a word, crouched down in front of the wall where the TV was and opened her case.

Karl stared at them with his eyes open wide.

'Well?' said the policeman.

It had begun to dawn on Karl that this was more important than Liz from Tønsberg.

'I can't remember everyone who's been in here, can I,' he stammered, meaning he couldn't remember anyone.

That was just how it was. Faces didn't mean a thing to him. Even Liz's face was already forgotten.

'I don't need to know about all of them,' the policeman said. 'Just this one. Things seem to be a bit quiet here today.'

Resigned, Karl shook his head.

'What about looking at a few pictures?' the policeman asked. 'Would you recognise him?'

'Dunno. I didn't recognise you . . .'

'Harry . . .' the boy said.

'But did you see anyone drawing on the TV?'

'Harry . . .'

Karl had seen someone in the shop that day. It had occurred to him the time the police came in and asked him if he had seen anything suspicious. The problem was that this person had not done anything in particular, apart from stand and stare at TV screens. So what should he have said? That someone whose face he couldn't remember had been in his shop and behaved suspiciously? And got a whole load of hassle and unwanted attention into the bargain?

'No,' Karl said. 'I didn't see anyone drawing on the TV.'

The policeman mumbled something or other.

'Harry . . .' The boy caught hold of the policeman's T-shirt. 'It's five o'clock.'

The policeman straightened up and consulted his wristwatch.

'Beate,' he said. 'Can you see anything?'

'Too early to say,' she said. 'There are marks right enough, but he's dragged his finger along, so it is difficult to find a complete fingerprint.'

'Call me.'

The bell over the door clanged again, and Karl and the woman with the metal case were alone in the shop.

He picked up Liz from Tønsberg again, but changed his mind. He left her face down and went over to the policewoman. With a tiny brush she was delicately brushing away a kind of powder she had sprinkled over the screen. He could see it now, the drawing in the dust. He had been on an economy drive, with cleaning too, so it was no surprise that the drawing was still there after a few days. The drawing was a surprise though.

'What's that supposed to be?' he asked.

'Don't know,' she said. 'I've only just been told what it's called.'

'And that is?'

'A devil's star.'

20

Wednesday. Cathedral Builders.

HARRY AND OLEG MET RAKEL ON HER WAY OUT OF THE FROGNER open-air pool. She ran over to Oleg and flung her arms round him while looking daggers at Harry.

'What do you think you're doing?' she whispered.

Harry stood there with his arms down by his sides, shifting weight from one foot to the other. He knew he could give her an answer. He could have said that what he was 'doing' was trying to save lives in the city, but even that would have been a lie. The truth was he was 'doing' his own thing and letting everyone around him pay the price. It had always been like that, and it always would be, and if it happened to save lives, then that was a bonus.

'I'm sorry,' he said instead. At any rate, that was the truth.

'We went somewhere where the serial killer's been,' Oleg said over-joyed, but stopped in his tracks when he saw his mother's look of disbelief.

'Well –' Harry began.

'Don't,' Rakel interrupted. 'Don't even *try.*'

Harry shrugged, and smiled sadly at Oleg.

'Let me drive you home anyway.'

He knew what the response would be before it came. He stood and watched them go. Rakel strode ahead briskly. Oleg turned and waved. Harry waved back.

The sun was pumping behind his eyelids.

The canteen was on the top floor of Police HQ. Harry stood inside the door and his eyes swept around the room. Apart from a person sitting with his back to one of the tables, the large area was totally empty. Harry had driven from Frogner Park straight to Police HQ. On his way through the corridors on the sixth floor he established that Tom Waaler's office was unoccupied, but the light was on.

Harry went to the counter where the steel shutters were down. On the TV suspended in the corner the draw was being made for the lottery. Harry watched the ball roll down the funnel. The volume was down low, but Harry could hear a woman's voice say 'Five, the number is five'. Someone had been lucky. A chair scraped by the table.

'Hi, Harry. The counter's closed.'

It was Tom.

'I know,' Harry said.

Harry thought about what Rakel had asked, about what he was actually doing.

'Thought I would just have a smoke.'

Harry nodded towards the door to the roof terrace, which in practice functioned as a year-round smoking room.

The view from the roof terrace was wonderful, but the air was just as hot and still as it was down on the street. The afternoon sun angled across the town and came to rest in Bjørvika, an area of Oslo containing a motorway, a deposit for shipping containers and a refuge for junkies, but it was soon to have an opera house, hotels and millionaires' apartments. Wealth was beginning to take the whole city by storm. It made Harry think of the catfish in the rivers in Africa, the large, black fish that didn't have the sense to swim into deeper waters when the drought came and in the end were trapped in one of the muddy pools that slowly dried up. All the building works had started; the cranes stood out like the silhouettes of giraffes against the afternoon sun.

'It's going to be really great.'

He hadn't even heard Tom approach.

'We'll see.'

Harry pulled on his cigarette. He wasn't sure what he had responded to.

'You'll like it,' Waaler said. 'It's just a question of getting used to it.'

Harry could see the catfish lying in front of him in the mud after the last water had gone, their tails beating, their mouths wide open as they tried to get used to breathing air.

'But I need an answer, Harry. I have to know if you're in or out.'

Drowning in air. The death of the catfish was perhaps no worse than the death of anything else. Death by drowning was supposed to be relatively pleasant.

'Beate rang,' Harry said. 'She's checked the fingerprints from the TV shop.'

'Oh?'

'Just partial prints. And the owner doesn't remember a thing.'

'Shame. Aune says that they get good results from hypnosis with forgetful witnesses in Sweden. Perhaps we should try that.'

'Sure.'

'And there was an interesting bit of information from Forensics this afternoon. About Camilla Loen.'

'Mm?'

'Turns out she was pregnant. Second month. But no-one we've talked to in her circle had a clue about who the father could have been. I don't suppose it has much to do with her death, but it would be interesting to know.'

'Mm.'

They stood in silence. Waaler went over to the railing and leaned over the edge.

'I know that you don't like me, Harry. And I'm not asking you to begin liking me over night.'

He paused.

'But if we're going to work together we have to begin somewhere, be a little more open with each other perhaps.'

'Open?'

'Yes. Does that sound dodgy?'

'A bit.'

Tom Waaler smiled. 'Agreed, but you can start. Ask me anything you'd like to know about me.'

'Know?'

'Yes. Anything at all.'

'Was it you who shot . . . ?' Harry stopped. 'OK,' he said. 'I want to know what it is that makes you tick.'

'What do you mean?'

'What it is that makes you get up in the morning and do what you do. What you're after and why.'

'I understand.'

Tom thought it over. For quite a while. Then he pointed at the cranes.

'Do you see those? My great-grandfather emigrated from Scotland with six Sutherland sheep and a letter from the bricklayers' guild in Aberdeen. He helped to build the houses you can see along the Akerselva and to the east along the railway line. Later his sons followed in his footsteps, and their sons too, right down to my father. My grandfather took a Norwegian surname, but when we moved to the west of Oslo, my father changed it back. Waaler. *Wall.* There was a little pride involved, but he also thought that Andersen was too common a name for a future judge.'

Harry watched Waaler. He tried to locate the scar on his chin.

'You were training to become a judge then?'

'That was the plan when I started law. And I would probably have continued if it hadn't been for what happened.'

'What was that?'

Waaler shrugged his shoulders.

'My father died in an accident at work. It's strange, but when your father has gone you suddenly discover that the choices you have made were as much for him as for yourself. I was immediately aware that I had nothing in common with the other law students. I suppose I was a kind of naive idealist. I thought it was all about raising the banner for justice and driving the modern democratic state forward. However, I discovered that for most people it was about getting a title and a job and creaming enough to be able to impress the girl next door in Ullern. Well, you did law yourself . . .'

Harry nodded.

'Perhaps it's in the genes,' Waaler said. 'At any rate, I've always liked building things. Big things. Right from when I was small. I built huge palaces with Lego bricks, much bigger than the things all the other kids built. On the law course I realised I was wired differently from all these tiny-minded people with their tiny-minded thoughts. Two months after my father's funeral I applied to go to Police College.'

'Mm. And left as top cadet, according to the rumours.'

'Second.'

'And here at Police HQ you had to build your palace?'

'I didn't *have* to. There's no *had to*, Harry. When I was small I took Lego bricks off the other children to make my buildings large enough. It's a question of what you want. Do you want a small, poky house for people with small, poky lives or do you want to have opera houses and cathedrals, majestic buildings that point the way towards something greater than you yourself, something you can strive for.'

Waaler ran his hand along the steel railing.

'Building cathedrals is a calling, Harry. In Italy they gave masons who died during the construction of a church the status of a martyr. Even though cathedral builders built for humanity there isn't a single cathedral in human history that was not founded on human bones and human blood. My grandfather used to say that. And that's the way it will always be. The blood of my family has been used as the mortar of many of the buildings you can see from here. I simply want more justice. For everyone. And I'll use the building materials that are necessary.'

Harry studied the glow of his cigarette.

'And I'm a building material?'

Waaler smiled.

'That's one way of putting it. But the answer is yes. If you want it. I have alternatives . . .'

He didn't complete the sentence, but Harry knew how it ended: '. . . but *you* don't.'

Harry took a long drag on his cigarette and asked in a low voice: 'What if I agree to come on board?'

Waaler raised an eyebrow and fixed Harry with an intent look before answering.

'You'll receive your first assignment, which you will carry out on your own and without asking any questions. Everyone before you has done this. As a mark of loyalty.'

'And it is?'

'You'll find that out in good time. But it means burning bridges.'

'Does it mean breaking Norwegian law?'

'Probably.'

'Aha,' Harry said. 'So that you've got something on me, so that I won't be tempted to rat on you.'

'I would perhaps have expressed that in a different way, but you've got the idea.'

'What are we talking about here? Smuggling?'

'I can't tell you that yet.'

'How can you be sure that I'm not a mole from POT or SEFO?'

Waaler leaned further over the railing and pointed down.

'Do you see her, Harry?'

Harry went to the edge and peered down at the park. People were still lying on the green grass catching the last rays of the sun.

'Her in the yellow bikini,' Waaler said. 'Nice colour for a bikini, isn't it.'

Harry's stomach churned, and he stood up straight again.

'We're not stupid,' Waaler said, without taking his eyes off the lawn. 'We follow the ones we want to join us. She wears well. Smart and independent, from what I can see. But of course she wants what all women want in her position. A man who can provide for her. It's pure biology. And you don't have a lot of time. Women like her are not on their own for long.'

Harry's cigarette fell over the edge. It left behind a stream of sparks.

'There was a warning about forest fires for all Østland yesterday,' Waaler said.

Harry didn't answer. He just shuddered when he felt Waaler's hand on his shoulder.

'Strictly speaking, the deadline has already passed, Harry. But to show how kind we are, I'll give you two more days. If I don't hear anything in that time, the offer is rescinded.'

Harry swallowed hard and tried to get out the one word, but his tongue refused to obey and his salivary glands felt like the dry river beds in Africa.

Finally, he managed it.

'Thanks.'

Beate Lønn enjoyed her work. She like the routines, the security, the knowledge that she was competent, and she knew that the others at the Forensics Institute at Kjølberggata 21A knew that too. Since work was the only thing in her life she considered important, it was reason enough to get up in the morning. Everything else was a musical interlude. She lived in her mother's house in Oppsal and had the whole of the top floor to herself. They got on extremely well. She had always been Daddy's girl when he was alive; she assumed that was why she joined the police force, like him. She had no hobbies. Even though she and Halvorsen, the officer Harry shared his office with, had become a sort of couple, she was not convinced about it. She had read in a women's magazine that this kind of doubt was natural and that you should take risks. Beate didn't like taking risks. Or being in doubt. That was why she enjoyed her work.

As she was growing up she blushed at the thought that anyone could be thinking about her and she spent most of her time devising different ways to hide. She still blushed, but she had found good places to hide. She could sit for hours inside the worn red-brick walls of Forensics studying fingerprints, ballistics reports, video recordings, comparisons of voices, the analyses of DNA or textile fibres, footprints, blood and an endless number of technical leads which might resolve important, complicated, controversial cases in total peace and quiet. She had also discovered that working was not nearly as dangerous as it seemed. So long as she spoke loudly and clearly and managed to repress her panic about blushing, losing face, her clothes, standing there exposed and full of shame, for what reason she didn't know. The office in Kjølberggata was her castle; the uniform and her professional duties her mental armour.

The clock showed 12.30 a.m. when the telephone on her office desk rang, interrupting her reading of the laboratory report on Lisbeth Barli's finger. Her heart began to quicken with fear when she saw on the display that the caller was ringing from an 'unknown number'. It could only mean that it was him.

'Beate Lønn.'

It was him. His words came out in a flurry of blows.

'Why didn't you ring me about the fingerprints?'

She held her breath for a second before she replied.

'Harry said he would pass on the message.'

'Thank you. I received it. Next time, you ring me first. Is that understood?'

Beate gulped. She didn't know whether out of fear or anger.

'Fine.'

'Anything else you told him that you didn't tell me?'

'No. Except that I've got the results from the lab on what was under the finger we were sent through the post.'

'Lisbeth Barli's? And it was?'

'Excrement.'

'What?'

'Pooh.'

'Thank you very much. I know what it is. Any idea where it came from?'

'Er, yes.'

'Correction. *Who* it came from.'

'I don't know for certain, but I can guess.'

'Would you be so kind . . .'

'The excrement contains blood, perhaps from a haemorrhoid. In this particular case, blood group B. Only seven per cent of the country has this blood group. Wilhelm Barli is a registered blood donor. He has –'

'Right. And what do you conclude from this?'

'I don't know,' Beate said quickly.

'But you know that the anus is an erogenous zone, Beate? In men and women. Or had you forgotten?'

Beate squeezed her eyes shut. Please don't let him start again. Not again. It was a long time ago, she had begun to forget, to get it out of her system. But his voice was there, smooth and tough, like snakeskin.

'You're good at playing the very ordinary girl, Beate. I like that. I liked it when you pretended you didn't want to.'

You know something, I know something, no-one else knows anything, she thought.

'Does Halvorsen do it to you as well as I did?'

'I'm putting the phone down now,' Beate said.

His laughter crackled in her ears. She knew it then. There was nowhere to hide. They could find you anywhere, just as they had found the three women where they felt safest. There was no castle. And no armour.

Øystein was sitting in his cab at the taxi rank in Thereses gate and listening to a Rolling Stones tape when the telephone rang.

'Oslo Ta –'

'Hi, Øystein. Harry here. Have you got anyone in the car?'

'Just Mick and Keith.'

'What?'

'The world's greatest band.'

'Øystein.'

'Yep?'

'The Stones are not the world's greatest band. Not even the world's second greatest band. What they are is the world's most overrated band. And it wasn't Keith or Mick who wrote "Wild Horses". It was Gram Parsons.'

'That's lies and you know it! I'm ringing off –'

'Hello? Øystein?'

'Say something nice to me. Quickly.'

'"Under My Thumb" is not a bad tune. And "Exile On Main Street" has its moments.'

'Fine. What do you want?'

'I need help.'

'It's three o'clock in the morning. Shouldn't you be asleep now?'

'Can't do it,' Harry said. 'I'm terrified every time I close my eyes.'

'Same nightmare as before?'

'The listeners' request from hell.'

'The stuff with the lift?'

'I know exactly what's coming and I'm just as frightened every time. How quickly can you get here?'

'I don't like this, Harry.'

'How quickly?'

Øystein sighed.

'Give me six minutes.'

Harry was standing in the doorway wearing just his jeans when Øystein came up the stairs.

They sat down in the sitting room without putting on the lights.

'Have you got a beer?' Øystein took off his black cap with the PlayStation logo and brushed back a thin, sweaty lock of hair.

Harry shook his head.

'Take this,' Øystein said and placed a black camera-film tube on the table.

'This is on me. Flunipam. Definite knockout. One pill is more than enough.'

Harry stared at the tube.

'That's not why I asked you to come, Øystein.'

'It isn't?'

'No. I need to know how to crack a code. How you go about it.'

'Do you mean hacking?' Øystein sent Harry a surprised look. 'Have you got to crack a password?'

'In a way. Have you read about the serial killer in the newspaper? I think he's sending us codes.'

Harry switched on a lamp. 'Look at this.'

Øystein perused the sheet of paper Harry had put on the table.

'A star?'

'A pentagram. He left signs at two of the crime scenes. One was carved into a beam over a bed and the other traced in the dust on a TV screen in a shop opposite the murder scene.'

Øystein examined the star and nodded. 'And you think I can tell you what it means?'

'No.' Harry held his head in his hands. 'But I hoped you could tell me something about the principles behind cracking codes.'

'The codes I cracked were mathematical codes, Harry. With inter-personal codes there's a completely different semantics. For example, I still can't decode what women are actually saying.'

'Imagine that this is both. Simple logic and a subtext.'

'OK, let's talk about cryptography. Ciphers. To see that you need both logical and what is called analogical thinking. The latter means that you use the subconscious and intuition, in other words, what you don't realise you already know. And then you combine linear thinking with the recognition of patterns. Have you heard of Alan Turing?'

'No.'

'Englishman. He cracked the German codes during the war. In a nutshell, he lost them the Second World War. He said that in order to crack codes, first of all you have to know what dimension your opponent is operating in.'

'And that means?'

'If I can put it this way, it is the level that lies above letters and numerals. Above language. The answers that don't tell you how, but why. Do you understand?'

'No, but tell me how you do it.'

'No-one knows. It has something in common with religious visions and is more like a gift.'

'Let's assume that I know why. What happens after that?'

'You can take the long road. Going through all the permutations until you die.'

'It's not me who's going to die. I've only got time for the short road.'

'I only know of one method.'

'Yes?'

'A trance.'

'Of course, a trance.'

'I'm not kidding. You keep staring at the data until you stop thinking conscious thoughts. It's like straining a muscle until it gets cramp and starts doing its own thing. Have you ever seen a climber's leg go into convulsions when he is stuck in the mountains? No, well, it's like that. In '88 I got into the accounts of Den Danske Bank in four nights, on a few frozen drops of LSD. If your subconscious cracks the code, you'll get there. If it doesn't . . .'

'Yes?'

Øystein laughed. 'It'll crack you. Psychiatric departments are full of people like me.'

'Mm. Trance?'

'Trance. Intuition. And a tiny bit of pharmaceutical help . . .'

Harry took the black tube and held it up in front of him.

'Do you know what, Øystein?'

'What?'

He threw the tube over the table and Øystein caught it.

'I was lying about "Under My Thumb".'

Øystein put the tube on the edge of the table as he tied the laces of a pair of unusually battered Puma trainers bought long before the fashion for retro.

'I know. Do you see anything of Rakel?'

Harry shook his head.

'That's what bothers you, isn't it?'

'Maybe,' Harry said. 'I've been offered a job. I don't know that I can turn it down.'

'Well, it's obviously not the job my boss offered you that you're talking about.'

Harry smiled.

'Sorry, I'm not the right man to ask about career advice,' Øystein said and got up. 'I'll put the tube here. Do what you like with it.'

21

Thursday. Pygmalion.

THE HEAD WAITER SCRUTINISED HIM FROM TOP TO TOE. THIRTY YEARS
in the job had given him a bit of a nose for trouble and this man stank
from a long way off. Not that all trouble was bad. A good scandal from
time to time was, in fact, what customers at the Viennese Theatre Café
had come to expect. It had to be the right kind of trouble, though,
such as when young, aspiring artists sang from the gallery in the
Theatre Café that they were the next big thing or when a drunken ex-
romantic lead from the National Theatre loudly proclaimed that the
only positive remark he could make about the famous financier at
the neighbouring table was that he was a homosexual, and therefore
unlikely to reproduce himself. The person standing in front of the
head waiter, however, did not seem as if he had anything witty or original to say; his appearance suggested more the tedious kind of trouble:
unpaid bill, pissed and a scuffle. The external indications – black jeans,
red nose and skinhead – had made him think he was one of the drunken
stage hands who belonged in the cellar at Burns. But when the man
asked to speak to Wilhelm Barli he knew he had to be one of the sewer

rats from the journalists' pub Tostrupkjelleren, which was under the aptly named open-air restaurant the Loo Lid. He had no respect for the vultures who had gorged so uninhibitedly on what remained of poor Barli after his charming wife had so tragically disappeared.

'Are you sure that the gentleman in question is here?' the head waiter asked, looking in the reservations book even though he knew perfectly well that Barli had turned up at 10.00 on the dot, as always, and sat down at his usual table on the glass veranda facing Stortingsgata. The unusual thing – which gave the head waiter some cause for concern about Barli's mental state – was that the jovial producer had made a mistake with the day and come on a Thursday instead of on his regular day, Wednesday.

'Forget it. I can see him,' the man in front of him said. And he was gone.

Harry had recognised Wilhelm Barli by his mane of hair, but as he drew closer he began to wonder if he was mistaken.

'Herr Barli?'

'Harry!'

Wilhelm's eyes lit up, but died just as quickly. His cheeks were sunken and the healthy, suntanned skin of just a few days before was now covered with a layer of white, lifeless powder. Wilhelm Barli seemed to have shrunk; even his broad shoulders appeared to be narrower.

'Herring?' Wilhelm pointed to the table in front of him. 'Oslo's best. I eat them every Wednesday. Good for the heart, they say. But that presupposes that you have one, and the people who come to this café . . .' Wilhelm spread out his arm to present the almost deserted room.

'No, thanks,' Harry said, taking a seat.

'Have a piece of bread, anyway.' Wilhelm held out the bread basket. 'This is the only place in Norway where you can get genuine fennel bread with whole fennel seeds. Perfect for herring.'

'Just coffee, thank you.'

Wilhelm signalled to the waiter.

'How did you find me here?'

'I went to the theatre.'

'Oh? They were told to say I was out of town. The journalists . . .'

Wilhelm imitated a stranglehold. Harry was not sure if that was supposed to demonstrate Wilhelm's own situation or what he would like to do to the journalists.

'I showed them police ID and said it was important,' Harry said.

'Good. Good.'

Wilhelm's attention was focused somewhere in front of Harry when the waiter arrived with a second cup and poured coffee from the pot already on the table. The waiter withdrew, and Harry cleared his throat. Wilhelm gave a start, and his attention returned.

'If you've come with bad news I want it straightaway, Harry.'

Harry shook his head while drinking his coffee.

Wilhelm closed his eyes and mumbled something inaudible.

'How's the play going?' Harry asked.

Wilhelm smiled weakly.

'A woman rang from the culture desk at *Dagbladet* yesterday and asked exactly the same question. I explained how the artistic side of things was going, but then it turned out that what she really wanted to know was if all the publicity surrounding Lisbeth's mysterious disappearance and her sister's jumping into the breech was good for ticket sales.'

He rolled his eyes.

'Well,' said Harry, 'is it?'

'Are you crazy, man?'

Wilhelm's voice boomed forebodingly.

'It's summer. People want to have fun, not mourn for some woman they don't even know. We have lost our main attraction: Lisbeth Barli, the undiscovered singing star from C&W land. Losing her just before opening night is *not* good for business!'

A couple of heads deeper into the room turned, but Wilhelm continued in the same loud voice.

'We've sold almost no tickets. Well, apart from for the opening night – for that the tickets went like hot cakes. People are so blood-thirsty, they can smell a scandal. Basically, Harry, we are entirely dependent on rave reviews to pull this one off. But right now . . .'

Wilhelm banged a fist on the white tablecloth and the coffee jumped in the air.

'. . . I can't think of anything less important than bloody *business*!'

Wilhelm stared at Harry. All the signs were that the outburst would continue when, without any prior indication, an invisible hand wiped the fury from his expression. He was dazed for a moment, as if he didn't know where he was. Then his face fell apart and he quickly hid it in his hands. Harry saw the head waiter send them a strange, hope-filled look.

'I apologise,' Wilhelm mumbled from behind his fingers. 'I don't usually . . . I'm not asleep . . . Oh shit, I'm so theatrical!'

He sobbed, a sound that was somewhere between laughing and crying, he hit the table again with his hand and pulled a grimace which he managed to twist into a kind of desperate smirk.

'What can I help you with, Harry? You look sorry for yourself.'

'Sorry for myself?'

'Saddened. Melancholic. Cheerless.'

Wilhelm shrugged and piled a forkful of herring and bread into his open mouth. The skin of the fish glistened. The waiter glided sound-lessly by the table and poured Chatelain Sancerre from a bottle into Wilhelm's glass.

'I have to ask about something that is perhaps unpleasantly intimate,' Harry said.

Wilhelm shook his head as he washed down the food with wine.

'The more intimate, the less unpleasant, Harry. Remember, I'm an artist.'

'Fine.'

Harry took another gulp of coffee to give himself a mental run-up.

'We found traces of excrement and blood under Lisbeth's nail.

Preliminary analyses match your blood group. I would like to know if we need to run a DNA test on it.'

Wilhelm stopped chewing, put the index finger of his right hand against his lips and stared pensively into the air.

'No,' he said. 'You don't need to bother.'

'So her finger has been in contact with your . . . excrement.'

'We made love the night before she disappeared. We make love every night. We would have made love during the day too, if it hadn't been so hot in the flat.'

'And then . . .'

'You're wondering if we practise postillioning?'

'Eh . . . ?'

'If she fingerfucks me up the backside? As often as she can. But carefully. Like sixty per cent of Norwegian men of my age, I have haemorrhoids. That was why Lisbeth never let her nails grow too long. Do you practise postillioning, Harry?'

Harry choked on his coffee.

'On yourself or with others?' Wilhelm asked.

'You should, Harry. As a man especially. Letting yourself be penetrated touches on absolutely fundamental things. If you dare, you will discover that you have a much greater emotional range than you imagine. If you clench up, you close others out and yourself in. But by opening yourself, making yourself vulnerable and showing trust, you quite literally give others the chance to come inside you.'

Wilhelm was waving his fork around.

'Of course, it is not without risk. They can destroy you, cut you up from the inside. But they can also love you. And then you embrace all their love, Harry. It's yours. We say that the man takes possession of the woman during sexual intercourse, but is that true? Who takes possession of whose sex? Think about it, Harry.'

Harry thought about it.

'It's the same for artists. We have to open up, make ourselves vulnerable, let them in. To have the chance of being loved we have to take a chance on being destroyed inside. We're talking about serious high-risk sports, Harry. I'm glad I don't dance any more.'

As Wilhelm smiled, two tears rolled down – one from each eye in turn – in a jerky parallel slalom down his cheeks where they disappeared into his beard.

'I miss her, Harry.'

Harry concentrated on the tablecloth. He considered whether he should leave, but stayed put.

Wilhelm pulled out a handkerchief and blew his nose with a loud trumpeting sound before he poured the rest of the bottle of wine into his glass.

'I don't wish to impose myself, Harry, but when I said you looked sorry for yourself I realised that you always look sorry for yourself. Is it a woman?'

Harry fidgeted with his coffee cup.

'Several?'

Harry was going to give an answer that would fend off further questions, but something made him change his mind. He nodded.

Wilhelm raised his glass.

'It's always women. Have you noticed that? Whom did you lose?'

Harry looked at Wilhelm. There was something in the expression of the bearded producer, a pained sincerity, an unguarded openness he recognised and which said he could trust him.

'My mother fell ill and died when I was young,' Harry said.

'And you miss her?'

'Yes.'

'But there are several, aren't there?'

Harry hunched his shoulders.

'Six months ago a female colleague of mine was killed. Rakel, my girl . . .'

Harry paused.

'Yes?'

'This is hardly of any interest.'

'I guess we've got to the heart of the matter,' Wilhelm sighed. 'You're going your separate ways.'

'We aren't. She is. I'm trying to make her change her mind.'

'Aha. And why does she want to go?'

'Because I am the way I am. It's a long story, but the short version is that I am the problem. And she would like me to be different.'

'Do you know what? I've got an idea. Take her to my production.'

'Why?'

'Because *My Fair Lady* is based on a Greek myth about the sculptor Pygmalion, who falls in love with one of his sculptures, the beautiful Galatea. He begs Venus to bring the statue to life so that he can marry her, and his prayer is heard. The performance will perhaps show Rakel what can happen when you try to change another person.'

'That it goes wrong?'

'On the contrary. Pygmalion, in the form of Professor Higgins, is entirely successful in his intentions in *My Fair Lady*. I only put on shows that have happy endings. That's my motto in life. If there is no happy ending, I make one.'

Harry shook his head and gave a lopsided smile.

'Rakel is not trying to change me. She's a smart woman. She'll go her own way instead.'

'Something tells me that she wants you back. I'll send you two tickets for opening night.'

Wilhelm signalled to the waiter for the bill.

'What on earth makes you think she wants me back?' Harry asked. 'You don't know anything about her.'

'You're right. I'm talking rubbish. White wine with brunch is a good idea, but only in theory. I'm drinking more than I should at the moment. My apologies.'

The waiter came with the bill. Wilhelm signed it without even looking and asked him to put it with the others. The waiter left.

'Taking a woman to a play on opening night with top-class tickets can never go completely awry, though.' Wilhelm smiled. 'Believe me; I have tested this one out thoroughly.'

Wilhelm's smile reminded Harry of his father's sad, resigned smile, the smile of a man looking backwards because that's where the things that made him smile were.

'Thank you very much, but –'

'No buts. If nothing else, it's a pretext for you to ring her if you're not on speaking terms at the moment. Let me send you the two tickets, Harry. I think Lisbeth would have liked it. And Toya's improving. It'll be a good production.'

Harry fidgeted with the tablecloth.

'Let me think about it.'

'Excellent. I'll get things moving before I go for a nap.' Wilhelm got up.

'By the way.' Harry put his hand in his jacket pocket. 'We found this symbol near two of the other crimes. It's called a devil's star. Can you remember if you've seen it anywhere after Lisbeth disappeared?'

Wilhelm studied the photograph.

'Can't say that I have, no.'

Harry put his hand out for the photo.

'Wait a moment.' Wilhelm peered again while scratching his beard.

Harry waited.

'I've seen it,' Wilhelm said. 'But where?'

'In the flat? By the stairs? Down on the street?'

Wilhelm shook his head.

'None of those places. And not recently. Somewhere else, a long time ago. But where? Is this important?'

'It could be. Ring me if anything occurs to you.'

When they separated Harry stood and stared up Drammensveien where the sun was shining on the tramlines and the shimmering hot air gave the impression that the tram was floating away.

22

Thursday and Friday. The Revelation.

JIM BEAM IS MADE WITH RYE, BARLEY AND A WHOLE 75 PER CENT of maize which gives bourbon the sweet, round taste that marks it out from straight whisky. The water in Jim Beam comes from a source near the distillery in Clermont, Kentucky, where they also make the special yeast that some people maintain is taken from the same recipe Jacob Beam used in 1795. The result is stored for at least four years before it is sent all over the world and bought by Harry Hole, who doesn't give a shit about Jacob Beam and knows that the guff about the water source is a marketing gimmick on a par with Farris, the Norwegian mineral water, and the Farris source. And the only percentage he cares about is the one in small letters on the label.

Harry stood in front of the fridge with a sheath knife in his hand staring at the bottle of golden-brown liquid. He was naked. The heat in the bedroom had forced him to strip off his underpants, which were still damp and smelled of chlorine.

He had been abstinent for four days now. The worst was over, he had said to himself. It wasn't true; the worst was far from over. Aune had once asked him why he thought he drank. Harry had answered without hesitation: 'Because I'm thirsty.' Harry, in a variety of ways, bemoaned the fact that he was living in a society at a time when the disadvantages of drinking outweighed the advantages. His reasons for staying sober had never been principled, merely practical. It was extremely wearing to be a hard drinker and the reward was a brief, miserable life of boredom and physical pain. For an alcoholic, life consisted of being drunk and the intervals between being drunk. Which part was real life was a philosophical question he had never had sufficient time to study since the answer would not be able to offer him a life that was any better anyway. Or worse. According to the alcoholic's basic law of life – The Big Thirst – everything that was good, everything, would be lost sooner or later. That was how he had viewed the equation until he met Rakel and Oleg. It had given temperance a new dimension. But it didn't invalidate the alcoholic's law. And now he couldn't bear the nightmares any longer. Couldn't bear the sound of her screams. Couldn't bear to see the shock in her rigid, lifeless eyes as her head rose towards the ceiling in the lift. His hand moved towards the cupboard. He could leave no stone unturned. He put the sheath knife down beside Jim Beam and closed the cupboard door. Then he went back to the bedroom.

He didn't switch on the light; a shaft of moonlight fell between the curtains.

The pillows and the mattress seemed to be trying to rid themselves of the clammy, twisted bed linen.

He crawled into bed. The last time he had slept without having a nightmare was when he fell asleep for a few minutes on Camilla Loen's bed. He had dreamed about death then too, but the difference was that he hadn't been frightened. A man can lock himself in, but he has to sleep. And in sleep no-one can hide.

Harry closed his eyes.

The curtains moved and the shaft of moonlight trembled. It shone onto the wall over the bedhead and the black marks of a knife. It must have been done with a great deal of force because the cut went deep into the wood behind the white wallpaper. The continuous groove formed a large, five-pointed star.

She lay listening to the traffic outside the window in Trojská, and to his deep, regular breathing beside her. Now and then she thought she could hear screams from the zoological garden, but it might just have been the night trains on the other side of the river braking before they entered the main station. He said he liked the sound of trains when they moved out to Troja, which was located at the top of the brown question mark that the River Vltava formed on its way through Prague.

It was raining.

He had been away all day. In Brno, he had said. When she finally heard him unlocking the front door of their flat, she calmed down. She heard the scrape of his suitcase on the hall floor before he came into the bedroom. She pretended to be asleep, but she observed him in secret as he slowly and calmly hung his clothes up and occasionally cast a glance in the mirror beside the cupboard to look at her. Then he crept into bed; his hands were cold and his skin sticky with dried sweat. They made love to the sound of rain on the tiled roof and he tasted of salt and slept like a baby afterwards. Usually she was also sleepy after making love, but now she lay awake as his juices ran out of her and soaked into the sheet.

She pretended that she didn't know what was keeping her awake, even though her mind always returned to the same thing. That she had found a longish blond hair on the sleeve of his suit jacket when she was brushing it the day after he had returned home from Oslo. That he was going back to Oslo on Saturday. That it was the fourth time in four weeks. That he still wouldn't tell her what he did there. Of course, the hair could have come from anything, from a man or maybe even a dog.

He began to snore.

She thought back to the time they met. To his open face and his open-hearted confidences which she had misinterpreted as meaning that he was an open person. He had melted her like the spring snows in Václav Square, but when you fell so easily for a man there would always be a suspicion gnawing at you that you were not the only one to have fallen in the same way.

He treated her with respect, though, almost like an equal, although he could have bought her as he could any of the prostitutes in Perlová. He was a windfall, the only one she had ever had, the only one she could lose. It was the certainty of this that made her cautious, that kept her from asking where he had been, with whom he had been, what he actually did.

However, something had happened which made it necessary for her to know that she could trust him. She had something even more precious to lose. She hadn't said anything to him yet; she hadn't been sure herself before she went to the doctor three days ago.

She slipped out of bed and tiptoed across the floor. Carefully, she pressed down the door handle while watching his face in the mirror over the dressing table. Then she was in the hallway and, carefully, she closed the door behind her.

The suitcase was a leaden grey colour, modern and bore the Samsonite trademark. It was almost new, yet the sides were scratched and covered with torn stickers from security checks and the names of destinations she had never heard of.

In the dim light she could see that the combination dial showed 0-0-0. It always did. And she didn't need to feel; she knew the case wouldn't open. She had never seen the case open, except for when she was lying in bed as he was taking clothes from drawers and putting them in the case. It was pure chance that she had seen it the last time he was packing. Lucky that the number of the combination lock was on the inside. It wasn't particularly difficult to remember three numbers. Not when you have to. Wasn't difficult to forget everything else and remember the three numbers of a room in a hotel when they rang and told her that her services were required, told her what she was to wear and about any other special requests.

She listened. His snoring was like the low sound of sawing from behind the door. There were things he didn't know. Things he didn't need to know, things she had been forced to do, but it was in the past now. She placed the tips of her fingers on the serrated cogs above the numbers and turned. The future was the only thing that mattered from now on.

The lock sprang open with a soft click.

She stared from her crouching position.

Under the lock, on top of a white shirt, lay an ugly, black metal object.

She didn't need to touch it to know that the gun was genuine. She had seen them before, in her earlier life.

She swallowed and could feel the tears coming. Pressed her fingers against her eyes. Twice whispered her mother's name to herself.

It lasted only a few seconds.

Then she took a deep, calming breath. She had to get through this. They had to get through this. At least it explained why he wasn't able to tell her much about his profession, what allowed him to earn as much money as he obviously did. And the thought had occurred to her, hadn't it?

She made up her mind.

There were things she didn't know. Things she didn't need to know.

She locked the case and turned the dials on the lock back to zero. She listened at the door before she carefully opened it and slipped inside. A rectangle of light fell onto the bed. Had she cast a glance at the mirror before she closed the door, she would have seen one of his eyes open. But she was too preoccupied with her own thoughts. Or rather, the one thought that she returned to again and again as she lay listening to the traffic, the screams from the zoological gardens and his deep, regular breathing. The future was the only thing that mattered from now on.

*

A scream, a bottle smashed on the pavement, followed by raucous laughter. Cursing and the clatter of running feet dying away up Sofies gate in the direction of Bislett Stadium.

Harry stared at the ceiling and listened to the sounds of the night outside. He had slept three dreamless hours before he woke up and started thinking. About three women, two crime scenes and one man offering a good price for his soul. He tried to find a system in it. To decipher the code. To see the pattern. To understand the dimension above the pattern that Øystein had referred to, the question that preceded 'how'. Why.

Why did a man dress up as a courier, kill two women and prob-ably also a third? Why did he make it so difficult for himself when he chose the scene of the crime? Why did he leave messages? When all the past models of serial killers suggested they were sexually moti-vated, why were there no indications of sexual abuse in the cases of Camilla Loen and Barbara Svendsen?

Harry felt a headache coming on. He kicked off the duvet cover and lay on his side. The red numbers on the alarm clock glowed: 2.51. Harry's last two questions were for himself. Why hold onto your soul so desperately if it broke your heart? And why bother about a system that hated him?

He dropped his feet onto the floor and went into the kitchen and stared at the cupboard door over the sink. He poured water from the tap into a glass and filled it to the brim. Then he opened the cutlery drawer, picked up the black tube, peeled off the grey lid and poured the contents into his palm. A pill would make him sleep. Two with a glass of Jim Beam would make him hyper. Three or more would have more unforeseen consequences.

Harry opened his mouth wide, threw in three tablets and washed them down with lukewarm water.

Then he went into the sitting room, put on a Duke Ellington record he had bought after seeing Gene Hackman sitting on the overnight bus in *The Conversation* to the sound of some fragile piano notes that were the loneliest Harry had ever heard.

He sat down in the wing chair.

'I only know of one method,' Øystein had said.

Harry started at the beginning. With the day when he staggered past Underwater on his way to the address in Ullevålsveien. Friday. Sannergata. Wednesday. Carl Berner. Monday. Three women. Three severed fingers. Left hand. First the index finger, then the middle finger and then the ring finger. Three places. Places with neighbours, no family accommodation. An old apartment building from the turn of the last century, one from the '30s and an office block from the '40s. Lifts. He could see the floor numbers over the lift doors. Skarre had talked to the specialist couriers in Oslo and the surrounding district. They hadn't been able to help with cycle equipment or yellow jerseys, but via an insurance arrangement with emergency services they had at least managed to procure a summary of all the people who in the last six months had bought expensive bikes of the type that couriers used.

He could feel the numbing sensation coming. The rough wool on the chair stung his naked thighs and buttocks.

The victims: Camilla, copywriter for an advertising bureau, single, 28 years old, dark, slightly chubby; Lisbeth, singer, married, 33 years old, fair, slim; Barbara, receptionist, 28, living with her parents, medium blonde. All three had been good-looking, nothing outstanding. The times of the murders. Provided that Lisbeth had been murdered immediately, all on weekdays. In the afternoon, after working hours.

Duke Ellington was playing fast. As if his head was full of notes he had to squeeze in. And now he had almost completely stopped. He was just adding the essential full stops.

Harry had not gone into the backgrounds of the victims, he hadn't talked to relatives or friends, he had just skimmed through the reports without finding anything to catch his attention. That wasn't where the answers lay. It wasn't who the victims were, but what they were, what they represented. For this killer the victims were no more than an exterior, more or less randomly chosen, like everything around them. It was just a question of catching a glimpse of what it was, seeing the pattern.

Then the chemicals kicked in with a vengeance. The effect was more like that of a hallucinogen than sleeping tablets. Thinking gave way to thoughts, and completely out of control – as if in a barrel – he sailed down a river. Time pulsated, pumped like an expanding universe. When he came to, everything around him was still, there was only the sound of the stylus on the record player scratching against the label.

He went into the bedroom, sat cross-legged at the foot of the bed and fixed his attention on the devil's star. After a while it began to dance in front of his eyes. He closed them. It was just a question of keeping it in sight.

When it became light outside he was beyond everything. He sat, he heard and he saw, but he was dreaming. The thud of the *Aftenposten* on the stairs woke him up. He lifted his head and focused on the devil's star, which was no longer dancing.

Nothing danced. It was over. He had seen the pattern.

The pattern of a benumbed man in a desperate search for genuine feelings. A naive idiot who believed that where there was someone who loved, there was love, that where there were questions, there were answers. Harry Hole's pattern. In a fit of fury he headbutted the cross on the wall. He saw sparks in front of his eyes and he dropped onto his bed. His gaze fell on the alarm clock: 5.55. The duvet cover was wet and warm.

Then – as if someone had switched off the light – he passed out.

She was pouring coffee into his cup. He grunted a *Danke* and turned the pages of the *Observer* which he would buy at the hotel on the corner. Along with fresh croissants that Hlinka, the local baker, had started making. She had never been abroad, only to Slovakia, which wasn't really abroad, but he assured her that now Prague had every-

thing they had in other big cities in Europe. She had wanted to travel.
Before she met him, an American businessman had fallen in love with
her. She had been bought for him as a present by a business connection in Prague, an executive from a pharmaceutical company. He was
a sweet, innocent, rather plump man and would have given her everything so long as she had gone home with him to Los Angeles. Of
course, she had said yes. But when she told Tomas, her pimp and half-
brother, he went to the American's room and threatened him with a
knife. The American left the following day and she had never seen
him since. Four days later she was sitting, downcast, in the Grand
Hotel Europa drinking wine when he turned up. He sat on a chair at
the back of the room and watched her giving importunate men the
brush-off. That was what he fell for, he always said, not the fact that
she was very much in demand by other men, but that she was
absolutely unmoved by their courtship, so effortlessly apathetic, so
completely chaste.

She let him buy her a glass of wine, thanked him and walked home
alone.

The following day he rang at the door of her tiny basement flat in
Strasnice. He never told her how he had found out where she lived.
But life went from grey to rosy red in the blink of an eye. She was
happy. She was happy.

The newspaper rustled as he turned a page.

She should have known. If it hadn't been for the gun in the suitcase she would not have given it a second thought.

She decided she would forget it, forget everything except what was
important. They were happy. She loved him.

She was sitting in the chair, still wearing her apron. She knew that
he liked her in an apron. After all, she knew a bit about what made
men tick, the trick was not to let on. She looked down at her lap. She
began to smile; she couldn't stop.

'I've got something to tell you,' she said.

'Ye-es?' The newspaper flapped like a sail in the wind.

'Promise me you won't get angry,' she said and could feel her smile spreading.

'I can't promise that,' he said without looking up.

Her smile stiffened. 'What . . .'

'I'm guessing that you're going to tell me that you went through my suitcase when you got up in the night.'

She noticed for the first time that his accent was different. The sing-song wasn't there. He put the paper down and looked her in the eye.

Thank God, she didn't have to lie to him and she knew that she could never have done. She had the proof now. She shook her head, but noticed that she couldn't control the expression on her face.

He raised an eyebrow.

She swallowed.

The second hand on the clock, the large kitchen clock she had bought at IKEA with his money, ticked soundlessly.

He smiled.

'And you found piles of letters from my lovers, didn't you?'

She blinked, totally at sea.

He leaned forward. 'I'm kidding, Eva. Is anything wrong?'

She nodded.

'I'm pregnant,' she whispered quickly, as if there were some sudden rush. 'I . . . we . . . are going to have a baby.'

He sat there, stunned, staring in front of him as she talked about her suspicions, the visit to the doctor and then, finally, the certainty. When she had finished, he got up and left the kitchen. He came back and gave her a little black box.

'Visit my mother,' he said.

'What?'

'You were wondering what I was going to do in Oslo. I'm going to visit my mother.'

'Have you got a mother . . .'

That was her first thought. Had he really got a mother? But she added: '. . . in Oslo?'

He smiled and nodded towards the box.

'Aren't you going to open it, *Liebling*. It's for you. For the child.'

She blinked twice before she could collect herself sufficiently to open it.

'It's beautiful,' she said and felt her eyes welling up with tears.

'I love you, Eva Marvanova.'

The sing-song was back in his accent.

She smiled through her tears as he held her in his arms.

'Forgive me,' she whispered. 'Forgive me. That you love me is all I need to know. The rest is unimportant. You don't need to tell me about your mother. Or the gun . . .'

She felt his body harden in her arms. She put her mouth to his ear.

'I saw the gun,' she whispered. 'But I don't need to know anything. Nothing, do you hear?'

He freed himself from her clasp.

'Yes, well,' he said. 'I'm sorry, Eva, but there's no way out. Not now.'

'What do you mean?'

'You'll have to know who I am.'

'But I know who you are, darling.'

'You don't know what I do.'

'I don't know that I want to know.'

'You have to.'

He took the box from her, took out the necklace inside it and held it up.

'This is what I do.'

The star-shaped diamond shone like a lover's eye as it reflected the morning light from the kitchen window.

'And this.'

He pulled his hand out of his jacket pocket. In his hand was the same gun she had seen in the suitcase. But it was longer and had a large black piece of metal attached to the end of the barrel. Eva Marvanova did not know much about weapons, but she knew what this was. A silencer, an appropriate name.

*

Harry was woken up by the telephone ringing. He felt as if someone had stuffed a towel in his mouth. He tried to moisten it with his tongue, but it rasped like a piece of stale bread against his palate. The clock on his bedside table showed 10.17. Half a memory, half an image entered his brain. He went into the sitting room. The telephone rang for the sixth time.

He picked up the receiver:

'Harry. Who is it?'

'I just wanted to apologise.'

It was the voice he always hoped to hear.

'Rakel?'

'It's your job,' she said. 'I have no right to be angry. I'm sorry.'

Harry sat in the chair. Something was trying to struggle out of the undergrowth of his half-forgotten dreams.

'You have every right to be angry,' he said.

'You're a policeman. Someone has to watch over us.'

'I'm not talking about the job,' Harry said.

She didn't answer. He waited.

'I long for you,' she said in a tear-filled voice.

'You long for the person you wish I could be,' he said. 'Whereas I long for –'

'Bye,' she said, like a song cutting out in the middle of the intro.

Harry sat staring at the telephone, elated and dejected at the same time. A fragment of the night's dream made a last attempt to come to the surface, bumping against the underside of ice which grew thicker by the second as the temperature sank. He ransacked the coffee table for cigarettes and found a dog-end in the ashtray. His tongue was still semi-numb. Rakel had probably concluded from his slurred diction that he was out of it again, which was not so far from the truth, except that he was in no mood to have more of the same poison.

He went into the bedroom and glanced at the clock on the bedside table. Time to go to work. Something . . .

He closed his eyes.

An echo of Duke Ellington hung in his auditory canals. It wasn't there; he would have to go in further. He kept listening. He heard the pained scream of the tram, a cat's footsteps on the roof, and an ominous rustling in the bursting green birch foliage in the yard. Even further in. He heard the yard groan, the cracking of the putty in the window frames, the rumble of the empty basement room way down in the abyss. He heard the piercing scraping sound of the sheets against his skin and the clatter of his impatient shoes in the hall. He heard his mother whispering as she used to do before he went to sleep: '*Bak skapet bakenfor skapet bakenfor skapet til hans madam . . .*' And then he was back in the dream.

The dream from the night. He was blind; he must be blind because he could only hear.

He heard a low chanting voice together with a kind of mumbling of prayers in the background. Judging by the acoustics he was in a large, church-like room, but then there was the continuous drip. From under the high vaulted ceiling, if that was what it was, resounded wildly flapping wings. Pigeons? A priest or a preacher may have been leading a gathering, but the service was strange and alien. Almost like Russian, or speaking in tongues. The congregation joined in a psalm. Odd harmony with short, jagged lines. No familiar words like Jesus or Maria. Suddenly the congregation began to sing and an orchestra began to play. He recognised the melody. From television. Wait a minute. He heard something rolling. A ball. It stopped.

'Five,' said a woman's voice. 'The number is five.'

The code.

23

Friday. A Human Number.

Harry's revelations used to be small, ice-cold drips that hit him on the head. Not any more, but, of course, by looking up and following the fall of the drips he could establish the causal connection. This revelation was different. This was a gift, theft, an undeserved favour from an angel, music that could come to people like Duke Ellington, ready-made, straight out of a dream. All you had to do was to sit down and play it.

And Harry was in the process of doing just that. He had summoned the concert audience to his own office at 1.00. That was enough time for him to fit the most essential part, the last part of the code. For that he needed the Pole Star. And a star chart.

On his way to work he slipped into a stationer's to buy a ruler, a protractor, a pair of compasses, a felt tip with the finest point they had and a couple of overhead transparencies. He set to work as soon as he got to his office. He found the large Oslo map he had torn down, mended a rip, smoothed the surface of the noticeboards and pinned the map up again on the long wall in his office. Then he drew a circle on the transparency, divided it up into five sectors of exactly 72 degrees each and then, using the felt pen and the ruler, joined up each of the two points furthest away from each other in one continuous line. When he had finished he lifted the transparency up to the light. The devil's star.

The overhead projector in the conference room had gone missing, so Harry went into the Crime Division's conference room where Chief Inspector Ivarsson held his regular lecture – known as 'How I became so clever' among colleagues – to a group of press-ganged holiday stand-ins.

'High priority,' Harry said, pulling out the plug and rolling out the projector trolley past an astonished Ivarsson.

Back in his office, Harry put the transparency on the projector, pointed the square of light towards the map and switched off the main light.

In the darkened, windowless room he could hear his own breathing as he twisted the transparency round, moved the projector closer and further away and adjusted the focus of the black outline of a star until it matched. It did match. Of course it matched. He stared at the map, circled two street numbers and made a couple of telephone calls.

Then he was ready.

At 1.05 Bjarne Møller, Tom Waaler, Beate Lønn and Ståle Aune were sitting on borrowed chairs, crushed into Harry and Halvorsen's shared office, as quiet as mice.

'It's a code,' Harry said. 'A very simple code. A common denominator we should have seen ages ago. We were given it very clearly. A numerical figure.'

They looked at him.

'Five,' Harry said.

'Five?'

'The number is five.'

Harry watched the four puzzled faces.

Then something happened which he had experienced now and then, more frequently as time went on, after long periods of drinking. Without any prior warning, the ground suddenly gave way. He had a falling sensation and he lost all sense of reality. There weren't four colleagues sitting in front of him in an office, it wasn't a murder case, it wasn't a warm summer's day in Oslo, no-one called Rakel and Oleg ever existed. He knew that this brief panic attack could be followed by others and he hung on by his fingertips.

Harry lifted his mug of coffee and drank slowly while he collected himself.

He determined that when he heard the sound of the mug being put down on the desk he would be back, here, in this reality.

He put the mug down.

It landed with a soft thud.

'First question,' Harry said. 'The killer has left his mark on all the victims with a diamond. How many sides does it have?'

'Five,' Møller said.

'Second question. He also cut off one finger on the left hand of every victim. How many fingers are there on a hand? Third question. The killings and the disappearance took place over three consecutive weeks on Friday, Wednesday and Monday respectively. How many days are there between each of them?'

It was quiet for a moment.

'Five,' said Waaler.

'And the time?'

Aune cleared his throat: 'Around five o'clock.'

'Fifth and last question. The addresses of the victims appear to have been chosen at random, but the crime scenes have got one thing in common. Beate?'

She pulled a face. 'Five?'

All four of them stared vacantly at Harry.

'Oh, bloody . . .' Beate exclaimed, stopping in her tracks and blushing. 'Sorry, I meant . . . on the fifth floor. All the victims died on the fifth floor.'

'Exactly.'

Realisation began to dawn on the others' faces as Harry went to the door.

'Five.'

Møller spat it out as if it were a revolting word he had just eaten.

It was pitch black when Harry switched off the light. They could only hear his voice as he moved around.

'Five is a familiar number in a variety of rituals. In black magic. Witchcraft. And in devil worship. Also in Christianity. Five is the number of wounds Christ had on the cross. And there are the five pillars and the five calls to prayer in Islam. In several writings five is referred to as the human number, as we have five senses and go through five stages of life.'

There was a click and all of a sudden a pale illuminated face with black sunken eye sockets and a star on the forehead materialised in front of them in the darkness. A low buzz of whispers ensued.

'Sorry . . .'

Harry twisted the projector round so that the square of light shifted from his face and onto the white wall.

'This is, as you can see, a pentagram or devil's star, the same as we found carved and drawn near the bodies of Camilla Loen and Barbara Svendsen. Based on the golden section, as it's known. How's that worked out again, Ståle?'

'I really haven't a clue,' the psychologist sniffed. 'I loathe exact sciences.'

'OK,' Harry said. 'I made a simple version with a protractor. It's good enough for our purposes.'

'Our purposes?' Møller asked.

'So far I've shown you some numerical coincidences that could well have been chance. This is the proof that they aren't.'

'The three killings took place on the edge of a circle with its centre in the heart of Oslo,' Harry said. 'In addition, they are separated by an interval of exactly seventy-two degrees. As you can see here, the crime scenes are located . . .'

'. . . on the tips of three points of the star,' Beate whispered.

'My God,' Møller said in amazement. 'Do you mean that he . . . that he has given us . . .'

'He's given us a Pole Star,' Harry said. 'It's his code . . . to tell us about the five murders. Three have already been carried out and there are still two to come. Which, according to the star, should occur here and here.'

Harry pointed to the rings he had drawn on the map around two of the points.

'And we know when,' Tom Waaler said.

Harry nodded.

'My God,' Møller said. 'With five days between each murder, that'll be . . .'

'Saturday,' Beate said,

'Tomorrow,' Aune said.

'My God,' Møller said for the third time. The invocation sounded heartfelt.

Harry continued talking, interrupted by the excited voices of the others, as the sun arced high across the pale, scorched summer sky above the small white sails of boats making drowsy, half-hearted attempts to find their way back to land. In Bjørvika at the raised intersection known popularly as the Traffic Machine, a carrier bag floated on the warm air currents above the roads, which wound in and out of one another like entangled vipers in a nest. On the seaward side of a storage shed on the future building site of the opera house, a man was working hard to find a vein under an already inflamed sore; he was scowling around him like an emaciated leopard over its prey, conscious that he would have to hurry before the hyenas appeared.

'Wait a moment,' Tom Waaler said. 'How could the killer know that Lisbeth Barli lived on the fifth floor if he was waiting down on the street?'

'He wasn't waiting around on the street,' Beate said. 'He was in the stairwell. We checked out what Barli said about the door not closing properly, and it's true. He kept an eye on the lift to see if anyone was coming down from the fifth floor and hid in the passage down to the basement if anyone turned up.'

'Good, Beate,' Harry said. 'And then?'

'He followed her out onto the street and . . . no, that's too risky. He stopped her as she got out of the lift. And used chloroform.'

'No,' Waaler said firmly. 'Too risky. Then he would have had to carry her out to a car parked outside and if anyone had seen them, they would have certainly taken note of the car and perhaps the number.'

'No chloroform,' Møller said. 'And the car was parked some distance away. He threatened her with a gun and made her walk in front of him while he followed with the gun hidden in his pocket.'

'Whatever happened, the victims are chosen at random,' Harry said. 'The key is the place the murder is committed. If Wilhelm Barli had taken the lift down from the fifth floor instead of his wife, he would have been the victim.'

'If it is as you say, it might also explain why the women were not sexually abused,' Aune said. 'If the murderer . . .'

'The killer.'

'. . . the killer did not choose the victims, it means that the fact that they are all women is coincidence. In this case, the victims are not specifically sexual objects. It is the action itself which gives him his satisfaction.'

'What about the Ladies?' Beate said. 'That wasn't random. Wouldn't it have been more natural for a man to go to the Gents if the sex of the victim is of no consequence? Then he wouldn't have risked attracting attention on his way in or out.'

'Maybe,' Harry said. 'But if he'd prepared as thoroughly as it appears he did, he would have known that there are a lot more men than women in a solicitor's office. Do you see?'

Beate blinked hard with both eyes.

'Good thinking, Harry,' Waaler said. 'In the Ladies there was much less chance of him being disturbed during the ritual.'

It was 2.08 and it was Møller who finally brought the proceedings to an end.

'OK, folks, that's enough about the dead. Shall we concentrate on the living?'

The sun had started on the second half of its parabola, and the shadows were edging out into a deserted schoolyard in Tøyen where all that could be heard was the monotonous smack of a football being kicked against a wall. In Harry's hermetically sealed office the air had become a thick broth of evaporated human fluids. The point of the star to the right of Carl Berners plass lay above a property just by Ensjøveien in Kampen. Harry had explained that the building under the tip of the point had been built in 1912 as what was known then as a 'tuberculosis home', but had since been converted into a student building. At first, for home economics students, then for student nurses and finally for students in general.

The final tip of the pentagram pointed to a grid of black parallel lines.

'Railway lines from Oslo Station?' Møller asked. 'Nobody lives there, do they?'

'Careful,' Harry said, pointing to a small square that had been shaded in.

'That must be a storage shed. It's –'

'No. The map's right,' Waaler said. 'There is in fact a house there. Haven't you noticed it when you come in by train? That strange detached brick-built house standing completely on its own. There's a garden and so on . . .'

'You mean Villa Valle,' Aune said. 'The station master's house. It's very well known. I suppose they're offices now.'

Harry shook his head and informed them that the National Registry Office had a record of one person living there, an elderly lady, Olaug Sivertsen.

'There's no fifth floor in the student building or in the station master's house,' Harry said.

'Will that stop him?' Waaler asked, turning to Aune.

Aune shrugged his shoulders.

'I don't believe so. But now we're talking about predicting features of individual behaviour and here your guess is as good as mine.'

'OK,' Waaler said. 'We can take it that he's going to strike in the student building tomorrow, and our best chance is to organise a carefully planned operation. Are we agreed?'

Everyone round the table nodded.

'Good,' Waaler said. 'I'll get in touch with Sivert Falkeid of Special Forces and start working on the details right away.'

Harry could see the spark of flint in Tom Waaler's eyes. He understood him. Action. The arrest. The felling of the prey. The tenderloin of police work.

'I'll go with Beate to Schweigaards gate to see if we can meet up with Sivertsen,' Harry said.

'Be careful,' Møller shouted to drown the sound of scraping chairs. 'There mustn't be any leaks. Remember what Aune said about these Special Forces guys sniffing around close to the investigation.'

The sun was sinking. The temperature was rising.

24

Friday. Otto Tangen.

OTTO TANGEN ROLLED OVER ONTO HIS SIDE. HE WAS SOAKING WITH sweat after another tropical night, but that was not what had woken him. He stretched out for the telephone and the broken bed creaked ominously. It had sunk in the middle one night more than a year ago when Otto had been humping Aud-Rita, from the bakery, across the bed. Now, Aud-Rita was only a slip of a girl, but Otto had passed the 110 kilo mark that spring, and it was pitch black in the room when they discovered that beds were built for movement along their length, not across it. Aud-Rita had been underneath him, and Otto had had to drive her to casualty in Hønefoss with a fractured collarbone. She was furious, and in her ranting and raving threatened to tell Nils, her partner and Otto's best, and for that matter only, pal. At that time Nils weighed 115 kilos and was well known for his fiery temperament. Otto had laughed so much that he could hardly breathe and since then Aud-Rita just scowled angrily at him every time he went into the bakery. This saddened him because that night was, despite everything, a very dear memory to him. It was also the last time he had got laid.

'Harry Sounds,' he puffed into the phone.

He had named the company after the role Gene Hackman played in the film which had in many ways determined Otto's professional and future life: *The Conversation*, a Francis Ford Coppola film from 1974 about a bugging expert. No-one in Otto's limited circle of acquaintants had seen it. As for himself, he had seen it 38 times. When he realised what insights into other people's lives a little technical equipment gave you, at the age of 15 he had bought his first microphone and discovered what his mother and father talked about in the bedroom. The following day, he began saving for his first camera.

Now he was 35 years old and had around 100 microphones, 24 cameras and a son of eleven from a woman he had spent the night with in his detector bus in Geilo one damp autumn night. At least he had managed to persuade her to christen the boy Gene. Nevertheless, he would still have said, without batting an eyelid, that emotionally speaking he was closer to his microphones. But then his collection did include Neuman boom microphones from the '50s and Offscreen directional microphones. The latter were specially designed to be used with military cameras and he had had to go to America to buy them under the counter, but now he bought them off the Net, no trouble at all. Pride of place in his collection, however, went to three Russian espionage microphones the size of pinheads. There was no brand name on them and he had got hold of them at a trade fair in Vienna.

In addition, Harry Sounds was the owner of one of Norway's only two mobile professional surveillance studios. This meant that he was contacted on the odd occasion by the police, POT and, more rarely, by the intelligence service working at the Ministry of Defence. He wished it were more often; he was sick and tired of setting up surveillance cameras in 7-Eleven shops and Videonova and training the staff who had no understanding of the more sophisticated elements involved in monitoring unsuspecting customers. As far as surveillance work was concerned, it was easier to find kindred spirits in the police force and at the Ministry of Defence, but Harry Sounds' high-quality equipment cost money and to Otto's mind he was getting the same old story about budgetary cuts more and more often. They said it was cheaper for them to set up their own equipment in a flat or a house near the surveillance target, and of course they were right. However, occasionally there was not a house in reasonable condition nearby, or the job required quality equipment they didn't have. Then they would ring Harry Sounds. As they were doing now.

Otto listened. It sounded like a terrific assignment. Since there were obviously a lot of flats near the target, he suspected that they were after a big fish. And at this moment in time there was only one fish that big in the water.

'Is this the courier case?' he asked, sitting up carefully in bed so that it didn't sink in the middle. He should have bought another bed. He wasn't sure whether his constant procrastination was due primarily to his economic circumstances or to sentimentality. Whatever the reason, if this conversation fulfilled the promise it held, he would soon be able to afford a decent, solid, bespoke bed. One of those round ones perhaps. And then maybe he would try a fresh assault on Aud-Rita. Nils weighed 135 kilos now, and he looked revolting.

'It's urgent,' Waaler said without answering his question, which was a good enough answer for Otto. 'I want everything set up tonight.'

Otto laughed out loud.

'You want the stairwell, the lift and various corridors running through a building of four floors covered for sound and image set up in one night? Sorry, chum, that's not on.'

'This is a high-priority special case and we have set aside –'

'N-O-T-O-N. *Capisce?*'

The thought made Otto chortle and the bed began to sway.

'If it's so urgent we can start tonight, Waaler. Then I can promise you that it'll be finished by Monday morning.'

'I see,' Waaler said. 'Apologies for my naivety.'

Had Otto been as skilful at interpreting voices as he was at recording them, he would perhaps have detected from Waaler's intonation that his spelling things out had not gone down well with the inspector. However, right now he was more preoccupied with talking down the urgency and talking up the number of hours the job would take.

'Fine, now we're more or less on the same wavelength,' Otto said, looking for his socks under the bed. But all he could see were dust-balls and empty beer cans.

'I'll have to add on an extra fee for working evenings. And the weekend, of course.'

Beer! Perhaps he should buy a crate and invite Aud-Rita to cele-brate getting the job? Or – if she couldn't – Nils.

'And a little advance for the equipment I'll have to hire. I don't have all of this on tap.'

'No,' Waaler said. 'It's probably in Stein Astrup's barn in Asker.'

Otto Tangen almost dropped the receiver.

'Oh dear,' Waaler said softly and sarcastically. 'Did I touch a raw nerve? Something you forgot to declare? Some equipment sent by boat from Rotterdam?'

The bed collapsed on the floor with a crash.

'You can have a few of our guys to help you set up,' Waaler said. 'Tuck your gut into a pair of trousers, get your superbus into gear and meet me at my office for a briefing and a run-through of the draw-ings.'

'I . . . I . . .'

'. . . am overwhelmed with gratitude. It's great that good friends can work together, isn't it, Tangen. Just be smart, keep mum and make this the best job you've ever done and everything will be fine.'

25

Friday. Speaking in Tongues.

'Do you live here?' Harry asked, stunned.

He was stunned because the likeness was so striking that it startled him when she opened the door. He focused on the pale, elderly face. It was her eyes. There was exactly the same calm, the same warmth in them. Above all it was her eyes. But also her voice when she confirmed that she was indeed Olaug Sivertsen.

'Police,' he said, holding up his ID.

'Really? I hope there's nothing wrong?'

An expression of concern crossed the network of fine lines and wrinkles on her face. Harry wondered if her concern was on someone else's behalf. Perhaps he thought that because of the similarity, because her concern had always been for others.

'Not at all,' he said automatically and repeated the lie with a shake of the head. 'May we come in?'

'Naturally.'

She opened the door and made way for them. Harry and Beate stepped inside. Harry closed his eyes. It smelled of soft soap and old clothes. Of course. When he opened them she was looking at him with a questioning smile playing around her lips. Harry smiled in return. She could not possibly guess that he had been expecting a hug, a pat on the head and a few whispered words to tell him that Grandad was waiting for him and Sis with a nice surprise.

She led them into a sitting room, but no-one was there. The sitting room – or rooms, because there were three of them one after the other – had circular mouldings in the ceiling capped with glass crowns and was furnished with elegant antiques. Both the furniture and the carpets were worn, but it was as spotlessly clean and tidy as only a house with a single occupant can be.

Harry wondered why he had asked if she lived there. Was there something about the way she opened the door? Or let them in? At any rate, he had half expected to see a man, the man of the house, but it seemed that the National Registry Office was right. She was the only occupant.

'Do sit down,' she said. 'Coffee?'

It sounded more like an entreaty than an offer. Harry, ill at ease, cleared his throat, unsure whether he should tell her why they were there at the beginning or at the end of their conversation.

'Sounds lovely,' Beate said with a smile.

The old lady returned the smile and shuffled out to the kitchen. Harry passed Beate a look of gratitude.

'She reminds me of . . .' he began to say.

'I know,' Beate said. 'I could see it in your face. My grandmother was a bit like her too.'

'Mm,' Harry said, looking around.

There were not many family photos. Just earnest faces on two faded black-and-white images which must have been taken before the war and four pictures of a boy taken at different ages. In the teenage photograph he had spots, an early '60s mod haircut, the teddy-bear eyes that had met them in the doorway and a smile which was exactly that – a smile. Not the pained face that Harry, with more than a little difficulty, had managed to pull in front of a camera at that age.

The elderly lady returned with a tray, sat down, poured coffee and passed round a plate of Maryland cookies. Harry waited until Beate had finished complimenting her on the coffee.

'Have you read about the young women who have been recently murdered in Oslo, Fru Sivertsen?'

She shook her head.

'I caught the headlines. They were on the front page of *Aftenposten.* You couldn't miss them. But I never read about that sort of thing.'

The wrinkles around her eyes pointed downwards when she smiled.

'And I'm afraid I'm just an old frøken, not a fru.'

'I apologise. I thought . . .' Harry glanced at the photos.

'Yes,' she said. 'That's my boy.'

It went quiet. The wind brought with it the distant barking of dogs and a metallic voice announcing that the train for Halden was about to depart from platform 17. It barely moved the curtains at the balcony doors.

'Right.' Harry raised his coffee cup, but decided he'd rather speak and put it down again. 'We have reason to believe that the person who killed the girls is a serial killer and that one of his next two targets is –'

'Wonderful biscuits, Fru Sivertsen,' Beate suddenly interrupted, with her mouth full. Harry looked at her, bewildered. From the balcony doors came the hissing sound of a train arriving at the station.

The old lady smiled, somewhat confused.

'Oh, they're just bought biscuits,' she said.

'Let me start again, Fru Sivertsen,' Harry said. 'First of all, I would like to say that there is no reason for concern, that we have the situation completely under control. Next . . .'

'Thanks,' Harry said as they walked down Schweigaards gate past the sheds and the low factory buildings. They stood in sharp contrast to the detached house with the garden which was like a green oasis amid the black gravel.

Beate smiled without a blush.

'Thought we should avoid the mental equivalent of a fractured thigh bone. We are allowed to beat around the bush a little, present things in a somewhat gentler way, as it were.'

'Yes, I have heard that said.'

He lit a cigarette.

'I've never been much good at talking to people. I'm better at listening. And perhaps . . .'

He broke off.

'What?' Beate asked.

'Perhaps I've become a little insensitive. Perhaps I don't care so much any more. Perhaps it's time I . . . did something else. Are you OK to drive?'

He threw the keys over the car roof.

She caught them and looked down at them with a concerned frown.

At 8.00 the four detectives heading the investigation, plus Aune, were sitting together in the conference room again.

Harry reported back on the meeting in Ville Valle and said that Olaug Sivertsen had taken the news calmly. She was obviously frightened, but far from panic-stricken at the thought that she might be on a serial killer's death list.

'Beate suggested that she might move in with her son for a while,' Harry said. 'I think that would be a good idea –'

Waaler shook his head.

'No?' Harry said, surprised.

'The killer may be keeping a lookout for future murder scenes. If unusual things begin to happen, we may scare him away.'

'You mean that we should use an innocent old lady as . . . as . . . as . . .' Beate tried to hide her anger, but managed to stutter out, with a red face, 'bait?'

Waaler held Beate's stare. And for once she held his. In the end the silence became so oppressive that Møller opened his mouth to say something, anything, any random selection of words, but Waaler beat him to it.

'I just want to be sure that we catch the guy so that we can all sleep soundly at night. And as I understand it, it isn't the old dear's turn until next week.'

Møller laughed a loud, strained laugh. And it became even louder when he noticed that the tense atmosphere had not been smoothed over.

'Anyway,' Harry said. 'She stays put. The son lives too far away, abroad somewhere.'

'Good,' Waaler said. 'As for the students' building, it's pretty empty now because of the holiday, but all of the occupants we've talked to have been told in no uncertain terms that they have to stay in their rooms tomorrow. Other than that, they've been given minimal information. We told them all this was to do with a burglar we were trying to catch red-handed. We're going to put in the surveillance equipment tonight while the killer's asleep, we hope.'

'And the Special Forces?'

Waaler smiled. 'They're happy.'

Harry gazed out of the window. He tried to remember what it was like to be happy.

Møller concluded the meeting and Harry noticed that the patches of sweat forming on both sides of Aune's shirt were shaped like Somalia.

The three of them sat down again.

Møller produced four Carlsbergs from the kitchen fridge.

Aune nodded, with a happy expression on his face. Harry shook his head.

'But why?' Møller asked as he opened the bottles of beer. 'Why is he voluntarily giving us the key to the code and thus to his next moves?'

'He's trying to tell us how we can catch him,' Harry said, pushing up the window.

In flooded the sounds of city life on a summer's night: the desperate life cycle of the mayfly, music from a cruising cabriolet, exaggerated laughter, high heels clicking frenetically against tarmac. People enjoying themselves.

Møller stared at Harry in disbelief and cast Aune a glance in the hope that he would receive confirmation that Harry had lost his senses.

The psychologist placed his fingertips together in front of his floppy bow tie.

'Harry may be right,' he said. 'It's not unusual for a serial killer to court and assist the police because he wants, deep down, to be stopped. There's a psychologist called Sam Vaknin who maintains that serial killers want to be caught and punished to satisfy their sadistic superego. I incline more to the theory that they need help to stop the monster in them. I put their desire to be caught down to a degree of objective understanding of their illness.'

'Do they know they're insane?'

Aune nodded.

'It must be hell,' Møller said softly, raising his bottle of beer.

Møller went off to return a call to a journalist on *Aftenposten* who wanted to know whether the police supported the Children's Council's appeal for children to be kept indoors.

Harry and Aune stayed where they were, listening to the distant sounds of a party, the indistinct shouting and the Strokes, broken by a call to prayer which for some reason or other suddenly reverberated metallically and probably blasphemously, yet in a strangely beautiful way, from the same open window.

'Just out of curiosity,' Aune said, 'what triggered it off? How did you know it was five?'

'What do you mean?'

'I know a little about creative processes. What happened?'

Harry smiled.

'You tell me. Anyway, the last thing I saw before I went to sleep this morning was the clock on the bedside table showing three fives. Three women. Five.'

'The brain is a wondrous instrument,' Aune said.

'I suppose so,' Harry said. 'According to a code-savvy friend of mine we have to find the answer to the question "why" before the code is fully cracked. And the answer is not five.'

'So, why?'

Harry yawned and stretched.

'"Why" is your field, Ståle. I'll just be happy if we catch him.'

Aune smiled, looked at his watch, then got up.

'You're a very strange person, Harry.'

He put on his tweed jacket.

'I know you've been drinking a bit recently, but you look a little better. Are you over the worst this time?'

Harry shook his head.

'I'm just sober.'

As Harry walked home the sky arced over him in all its splendour.

A woman wearing sunglasses stood on the pavement below the neon sign over Niazi, the little grocery in the block next to where Harry lived. She had one hand on her hip; in her other hand she was holding one of Niazi's anonymous white plastic bags. She smiled and pretended that she had been standing there waiting for him.

It was Vibeke Knutsen.

Harry knew that she was play-acting. It was a joke she wanted him to join in, so he slowed down and sent her the same smile in return. To show that he had been waiting to see her there. The odd thing was that he had been. He just hadn't realised it until that moment.

'Haven't seen you at Underwater recently, precious,' she said, lifting her sunglasses and peering out as if the sun still hung low over the rooftops.

'I've been trying to keep my head above water,' Harry said, taking out a packet of cigarettes.

'Ooh, a play on words,' she said, stretching.

She wasn't wearing anything exotic this evening – a blue summer dress with a plunging neckline. She filled it well and she knew it. He passed her the packet, and she took a cigarette, which she managed to place between her lips in a way that Harry could only characterise as indecent.

'What are you doing here?' he asked. 'I thought you usually shopped at Kiwi?'

'Closed. It's almost midnight, Harry. I had to come down your way to find somewhere still open.'

Her smile spread and her eyes narrowed, like those of a playful cat.

'This is a dodgy area for a little girl on a Friday night,' Harry said, lighting her cigarette. 'You could've sent your man out if you needed a bit of shopping . . .'

'Mixers,' she said holding up her bag. 'To mix drinks so that they aren't too strong. And my betrothed is away. If it's so dodgy here, you ought to rescue the girl and take her somewhere safe.'

She nodded towards his block of flats.

'I can make you a cup of coffee,' he said.

'Oh?'

'Nescafé. That's all I have to offer.'

When Harry came into the sitting room carrying boiling water and a coffee glass, Vibeke Knutsen was sitting on the sofa with her legs drawn up underneath her and her shoes on the floor. Her milky white skin shone in the semi-darkness. She lit another cigarette, her own this time. A foreign brand Harry had not seen before. No filter tip. In the flickering light from the match he could see that the dark red varnish on her toenails was chipped.

'I don't know that I can go on any longer,' she said. 'He's changed. When he comes home he's just restless and either paces up and down in the sitting room or goes out training. It feels as if he can't wait to get away and travel again. I try to talk to him, but he cuts me short or else just looks at me in total incomprehension. We really do come from two different planets.'

'It's the combination of the distance between the planets and the mutual attraction that keeps them in orbit,' Harry said, spooning out the freeze-dried coffee grains.

'More playing with words?' Vibeke plucked a strand of tobacco off the tip of her pink, wet tongue.

Harry chuckled. 'Something I read in a waiting room. I probably hoped it was true. For my own sake.'

'Do you know what the strangest part is? He doesn't like me. And yet I know that he'll never let me go.'

'How do you mean?'

'He needs me. I don't know what for, exactly, but it's like he's lost something and that's why he needs me. His parents . . .'

'Yes?'

'He doesn't have any contact with them. I've never met them. I don't think they even know I exist. Not so long ago the telephone rang and there was a man asking after Anders. I immediately sensed it was his father. You can sort of hear it in the way that parents say the names of their children. In one way it's something they've said so many times it's the most natural thing in the world. But then in another way it's so intimate that the word strips them bare to the skin so they say it quickly, almost with embarrassment. 'Is Anders there?' When I said that I would have to wake him first the voice suddenly started to babble away in a foreign language, or . . . not foreign exactly, but more like you and I would speak if we had to find words in a hurry. The way they speak at religious meetings in chapels when they're well underway, sort of.'

'Speaking in tongues?'

'Yes, that's probably what it's called. Anders grew up with this stuff, though he never talks about it. I listened for a while. First of all, there was a fair sprinkling of words like "satan" and "sodom". Then it got dirtier. "Cunt" and "whore" and things like that. So I put the phone down.'

'What did Anders say to that?'

'I never mentioned it to him.'

'Why not?'

'I . . . it's like a place I've never been allowed to enter. And I don't want to go there, either.'

Harry drank his coffee. Vibeke didn't touch her own.

'Don't you get lonely sometimes, Harry?'

His eyes rose to meet hers.

'Sort of alone. Don't you wish you were with someone?'

'That's two different things. You're together with someone and you're lonely.'

She shivered as if a cold front was passing through the room.

'Do you know what?' she said. 'I feel like a drink.'

'Sorry, I've run out of that sort of thing.'

She opened her handbag. 'Can you fetch two glasses, precious?'

'We'll only need one.'

'Well, OK.'

She unscrewed the lid of her hip flask, tipped back her head and drank.

'I'm not allowed to move at all,' she said laughing. A shiny brown droplet ran down her chin.

'What?'

'Anders doesn't like me to move. And I have to lie still, without moving. I mustn't say a word or moan. I have to pretend that I'm asleep. He says that he loses the urge when I show passion.'

'And?'

She took another swig and screwed the lid back while looking at him.

'It's a nigh on impossible feat.'

Her stare was so direct that Harry automatically breathed a little deeper, and to his irritation he could feel his erection beginning to throb against the inside of his trousers.

She raised an eyebrow as if she could feel it too.

'Come and sit on the sofa,' she whispered.

Her voice had become rough and husky. Harry saw the bulge in the thick blue artery in her white neck. It's just a reflex action, Harry thought. A slavering Pavlovian dog that stands up when it hears the signal for food, a conditioned reaction, that's all.

'I don't think I can,' he said.

'Are you afraid of me?'

'Yes,' Harry said.

A sad sweetness filled his lower abdomen, the silent lament of his sex.

She laughed out loud, but stopped when she saw his eyes. She pouted and said in a pleading child's voice: 'But Harry, go on . . .'

'I can't. You're so wonderful, but . . .'

Her smile was intact but she blinked as if he had slapped her.

'It's not you I want,' Harry said.

Her eyes wavered. The corners of her mouth pulled as if she were going to laugh.

'Hah,' she said.

It was meant ironically, it was supposed to have been an exaggerated theatrical exclamation. Instead it came out as a weary, resigned groan. The play was over, they had both forgotten their lines.

'Sorry,' Harry said.

Her eyes filled with water.

'Oh, Harry,' she whispered.

He wished she hadn't said that, so he could have asked her to leave right away.

'Whatever it is you want from me, I haven't got it,' he said. 'She knows it. Now you know it, too.'

Part Four

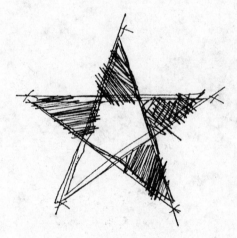

26

Saturday. The Soul. The Day.

As the sun streamed across Ekeberg Ridge on Saturday morning, with the promise of another record-breaking temperature, Otto Tangen was going over the mixing console for the last time.

It was dark and cramped in the bus, and there was the smell of mouldy clothes that neither Otto's Elvis Presley car fresheners nor his roll-up tobacco would ever succeed in dispersing. Sometimes he felt like he was sitting in a bunker in the trenches with the stench of death in his nostrils, but still isolated from what was going on immediately outside.

The student building stood in the middle of a piece of land at the top of Kampen with a view down towards Tøyen. On each side of and almost parallel with the old four-storey red-brick building were two taller blocks of flats from the '50s. The same paint and the same type of windows were used in the student building as in the blocks of flats, presumably in an attempt to give the area a unified look. However, the age difference could not be camouflaged; it still looked as if a waterspout had sucked up the student building and gently planted it down in the middle of a housing cooperative.

Harry and Waaler agreed to locate the bus in the car park with all the other cars, directly in front of the student building, where reception was good and the bus was not too conspicuous. Passers-by who still might cast a cursory glance its way would assume that the rusty, blue Volvo bus with the isoprene-covered windows belonged to the rock band 'Kindergarden Accident', which was painted in black letters on the side with skulls as dots over the two 'i's.

Otto dried his sweat and checked that all the cameras were working, that all the angles were covered and that everything that moved outside the building was picked up by at least one camera, so that they could follow the target from the moment he entered the hallway to the doorway of any one of the 80 student rooms in the eight corridors on the four floors.

They had been assembling, lining up and screwing in cameras to the wall all night. Otto still had the metallic, bitter taste of dry mortar in his mouth and yellow wall plaster dusted the shoulders of his filthy denim jacket, like the scaly scurf of dandruff.

Waaler had listened to reason in the end and realised that if they were to keep to the deadline, they would have to manage without sound. It wouldn't affect the arrest in the slightest; the only thing was that they would lose material proof if the target were to say anything incriminating.

They had not managed to put cameras in the lift, either. Using a cable-free camera, Otto couldn't get a decent picture in the bus because the concrete shaft blocked the signals, and the problem with using cables was that, however they placed them, they were either visible or there was the chance that they would get entangled in the lift machinery. Waaler had given the OK on that since the target would be on his own in the lift anyway. The occupants of the house had been sworn to secrecy and had received strict instructions to lock their doors and stay inside their rooms from 4.00 till 6.00.

Otto Tangen moved the mosaic of small pictures round on the three large data screens and increased the size of them until they formed a logical whole. On the screen to the left: the corridors running north, the fourth floor at the top and the ground floor at the bottom. On the middle screen: the entrance to the block, all the stair landings and the doors to the lift. On the screen to the right: the corridors running south.

Otto clicked 'Save', put his hands behind his head and leaned backwards in his chair with a satisfied grunt. He could monitor the whole building. Of young students. If they had had more time, he might have set up a few cameras in some of the student rooms. Without any of the students knowing, of course. Tiny little fish-eye lenses placed where they would never be discovered. Along with Russian microphones. Randy young trainee nurses from Norway. He could have videoed them and sold the videos through his contacts. Screw that bastard Waaler. How the hell could he have known about Astrup and the barn in Asker! A suspicion of an idea fluttered through Otto's brain and disappeared again. He had long suspected that Astrup was paying someone to spread a protective wing over his operation.

Otto lit up a cigarette. The pictures were like stills; not a single movement in the yellow-painted corridors or on the stairs betrayed that this was a live transmission. Those students who were spending the summer in their rooms were probably still in bed sleeping. But if he waited for a couple of hours he might catch sight of the guy who was let in by the doll in room 303 at 2.00 in the morning. She had looked drunk. Drunk and ready. He had just looked ready. Otto thought about Aud-Rita. The first time he had met her for pre-drinks at Nils's place everyone had had their fat paws out to shake hands, and when she put out her own little white hand to Otto and drawled 'Aud-Rita' it had sounded as though she was asking if he was pissed: *Er'u drita*.

Otto released a deep sigh.

That bastard Waaler had been going over the course with people from Special Forces right up until midnight. Otto had caught the discussion between Waaler and the head of the soldiers outside his bus. Later in the day some soldiers from a special unit were to be deployed in threes in every corridor on each floor, 24 in all, dressed in black with balaclavas and carrying loaded MP5s, tear gas and gas masks. At a signal from the bus they would jump into action immediately the target knocked on a door or tried to enter one of the rooms. The thought made Otto tremble with excitement. He had seen them in action twice before and the guys were bloody unreal. There were bangs and flashes of light, just like at a heavy-rock concert, and on both occasions the targets were so numb with fear that the whole thing was over in seconds. Otto had been told that was the point of it, to frighten the wits out of the target so that he couldn't raise the mental capacity to resist.

Otto stubbed out his cigarette. The trap was set. It was just a question of waiting for the rat.

The police were due to arrive at about 3.00. Waaler had banned any movement into and out of the bus before or after that time. It was going to be a long, hot day.

Otto threw himself down on the mattress on the floor. He wondered what was going on in room 303 right now. He missed his own bed. He missed its movement. He missed Aud-Rita.

At that same moment the entrance gate slammed behind Harry. He stood still to light his first cigarette of the day as he peered up at the sky where the morning mist lay, like a thin veil that the sun was in the process of burning through. He had slept. A deep, continuous, dreamless sleep. It hardly seemed possible.

'That one gonna stink today, Harry! The weather forecast say it's gonna be hottest day since 1907. Maybe.'

It was Ali, who lived in the flat below Harry and owned Niazi. It didn't matter how early Harry got up, Ali and his brother were always busy at work when he was leaving for the office. Ali had raised his broom and pointed to something on the pavement.

Harry squinted to see what it was Ali was pointing at. A dog turd.

He hadn't seen it when Vibeke was standing on exactly the same spot the previous evening. Someone had obviously been a little distracted when they took the dog for a walk this morning. Or last night.

He looked at his watch. This was the day. In a few hours they would have an answer.

Harry inhaled the smoke deep into his lungs and felt how the mixture of fresh air and nicotine perked up the system. For the first time in a very long time he could taste the tobacco. It even tasted good. And for a moment he had forgotten all the things he was going to lose: his job, Rakel and his soul.

For this was the day.

And it had started well.

Once again, it hardly seemed possible.

Harry could feel that she was happy when she heard his voice.

'I've talked to Dad. He's more than happy to look after Oleg. Sis will be there, too.'

'Opening night?' She said it with a cheery laugh in her voice. 'At the National Theatre? Goodness me.'

She was exaggerating – she liked to do that now and then – but Harry noticed that he was getting excited all the same.

'What will you wear?' she asked.

'You haven't said "yes" yet.'

'It depends.'

'A suit.'

'Which one?'

'Let me see . . . the one I bought in Hegdehaugsveien on May 17 the year before last. You know, the grey one with –'

'That's the only suit you've got.'

'Then I'll definitely wear that one.'

She laughed. The soft laugh, as soft as her skin and kisses, but it was still her laugh he liked best. It was as simple as that.

'I'll come and pick you up at six,' he said.

'Fine. But Harry . . .'

'Yes?'

'Don't think . . .'

'I know. It's just a play.'

'Thanks, Harry.'

'Oh, it's my pleasure.'

She laughed again. Once she had started he could get her to laugh at almost anything, as if they were in the same head looking out through the same eyes, and he could just point without saying anything in particular. He had to force himself to put the phone down.

This was the day. And it was still good.

They had agreed that Beate would stay with Olaug Sivertsen during the operation. Møller didn't want to risk the target (two days before, Waaler had started calling the killer 'the target' and now everyone was saying it) discovering the trap and changing the order of the crime scenes.

The telephone rang. It was Øystein. He wondered how things were going. Harry told him that things were going well and asked what he wanted. Øystein said that was what he wanted: to know how things were going. Harry became self-conscious – he wasn't used to that kind of thoughtfulness.

'Are you sleeping?'

'I slept last night,' Harry said.

'Good. And the code? Did you crack it?'

'Partly. I know where and when. I just don't know why.'

'So now you can read the text, but you don't know what it means?'

'Something like that. We'll have to wait for the rest when we've got him.'

'What don't you understand?'

'Loads. Like why hide one of the bodies? Or trivial things like him cutting all the fingers from the victims' left hands, but different fingers. The index finger with the first victim, the middle finger with the second and the ring finger with the third.'

'In sequence then. Must like systems.'

'Yes, but why not start with the thumb? Is there a message there?'

Øystein burst out laughing.

'Take care, Harry. Codes are like women: if you can't crack them, they'll crack you.'

'You're telling me.'

'Am I? Good, because that means I'm a caring person. I can't believe my own eyes, but it looks to me as if I've just got a customer in the car, Harry. Talk to you later.'

'OK.'

Harry watched the smoke dance pirouettes in slow motion. He looked at his watch. There was one thing he hadn't told Øystein: that he had a hunch the rest of the details would soon fall into place. It was a little too pat because, despite the rituals, there was something unemotional about the killings, an almost conspicuous lack of hatred, desire or passion. Or love for that matter. They had been carried out too perfectly, almost mechanically, according to the book. It felt as if he was playing chess against a computer, not against someone whose mind was agitated or unbalanced. Time would tell, though.

He looked at his watch again.

His heart was beating faster.

27

Saturday. Into Action.

OTTO TANGEN'S MOOD WAS IN THE ASCENDANT.

He had slept for a couple of hours and had woken up to a thundering headache and furious banging on the door. When he opened up, Waaler, Falkeid of the Special Forces and some character calling himself Harry Hole, who looked nothing like a police inspector, crashed in on him and the first thing they did was to complain about the air inside the bus. But after getting a coffee down him from one of the four thermos flasks, turning on the screens and setting the tapes to 'record', Otto felt the wonderful tingle of excitement he always got when a target was approaching.

Falkeid explained that guards wearing civilian clothes had been posted all round the student building the evening before. The dog patrol had gone through the loft and the cellar to check that no-one was hiding in the building. Only the house occupants had been coming and going, although the girl in 303 had explained to the guard at the entrance that she had her boyfriend staying. Falkeid's people were in position and awaiting orders.

Waaler nodded.

Falkeid checked the communication at regular intervals. Special Forces' own equipment, not Otto's responsibility. Otto closed his eyes and enjoyed the sounds. The brief second of atmospheric noise when they released the 'speak' button, then the mumbling incomprehensible codes, a kind of playground lingo for adults.

'Smilly dillies.' Otto shaped the words silently with his lips and remembered sitting in the apple tree one autumn evening spying on the adults behind the illuminated windows. Whispering 'smilly dillies' into a tin can with a cord hanging down over the fence, where Nils crouched waiting with the other tin can next to his ear. If he hadn't got sick of it and gone home for his supper, that is. The tin cans had never quite worked the way it said they should in the *Woodchuck Book*.

'We're ready to go on air,' Waaler said. 'Clock ready, Tangen?'

Otto nodded.

'Sixteen hundred,' Waaler said. 'Right . . . now.'

Otto started the timer on the recorder. Tenths of seconds and seconds shot past on the screen. He felt a silent joyful childlike laughter burst in his intestines. This was better than the apple tree. Better than Aud-Rita's cream buns. Better than when she groaned with a lisp and told him what he should do to her.

Show Time.

Olaug Sivertsen smiled as she opened the door to Beate, as if she had been looking forward to her visit for ages.

'Oh it's you again! Come in. You can keep your shoes on. Horrid this heat, isn't it?'

Olaug Sivertsen went down the hallway ahead of Beate.

'Don't worry, frøken Sivertsen. It looks as if this case will soon be over.'

'As long as I've got a visitor, you may take your time,' she laughed and then put her hand over her mouth in alarm: 'Dear me, what am I saying! After all, the man's taking people's lives, isn't he?'

The grandfather clock in the sitting room struck four as they entered.

'Tea, my dear?'

'Please.'

'Am I allowed to go to the kitchen on my own?'

'Yes, but if I may come along . . .'

'Come on, come on.'

Apart from a new stove and fridge, the kitchen did not seem to have changed much since wartime. Beate found a chair by the large wooden table while Olaug put the kettle on.

'It smells great in here,' Beate said.

'D'you think so?'

'Yes. I like kitchens that smell like this. To be honest, I prefer being in the kitchen. I'm not so fond of sitting rooms.'

'Aren't you?' Olaug Sivertsen put her head to one side. 'Do you know what? I don't think we're so different, you and me. I'm a kitchen person, too.'

Beate smiled.

'The sitting room shows how you want to present yourself. But in the kitchen everyone relaxes more. It's like you're allowed to be yourself. Did you notice that we relaxed with each other as soon as we came in?'

'I think you're absolutely right.'

The two women laughed.

'D'you know what?' Olaug said. 'I'm glad they sent you. I like you. And there's no need to blush, my dear. I'm just a lonely old lady. Save it for an admirer. Or perhaps you're married? You're not? No, well, that's not the end of the world.'

'Have you ever been married?'

'Me?'

She laughed as she set out the cups.

'No, I was so young when I had Sven that I never had a chance . . .'

'You didn't?'

'Well, yes, I probably did have a chance or two. But a woman in my situation had such low prestige in those days that the offers you received were generally from men no-one else wanted. It's not called "finding your match" for nothing.'

'Just because you were a single mother?'

'Because Sven was the son of a German, my dear.'

The kettle began to give a low whistle.

'Ah, I understand,' Beate said. 'He must have had a tough time growing up.'

Olaug stared into the air without sensing that the whistling was getting louder.

'The toughest you can imagine. Just thinking about it can still make me cry. Poor boy.'

'The water . . .'

'There you see. I'm getting senile.'

Olaug lifted the kettle from the stove and poured water into their cups.

'What does your son do now?' Beate asked, looking at her watch: 4.15.

'Import-Export. Various things from the old communist countries.' Olaug smiled. 'I don't know how much money he's making out of it, but I like the sound of it. "Import-Export." It's just nonsense, but I like it.'

'Anyway, it's all worked out fine. Despite the tough time he had growing up, I mean.'

'Yes, but it wasn't always like that. You've probably got him on your records.'

'There are lots of people on our records. Many who've turned out alright, too.'

'Something happened once when he went to Berlin. I don't know quite what. He's never liked talking about what he does, Sven hasn't. Always so secretive. But I think he might have been visiting his father. And I think it made him feel better about himself. Ernst Schwabe was a dashing man.'

Olaug sighed.

'But I may be wrong. Anyway, Sven changed.'

'Oh, how?'

'He became calmer. Before, he was always chasing things.'

'Such as what?'

'Everything. Money. Excitement. Women. He's like his father, you know. An incurable romantic and ladies' man. He likes young women, Sven does. And they like him. But I suspect he's found someone special. He said on the phone that he's got some news for me. He sounded excited.'

'He didn't say what it was?'

'He wanted to wait until he got here, he said.'

'Got here?'

'Yes, he's coming this evening. He has a meeting first. He's staying in Oslo until tomorrow, then he's going back.'

'To Berlin?'

'No, no. It's a long time since Sven lived there. Now he lives in the Czech Republic. Bohemia, he usually calls it, the show-off.'

'In . . . er . . . Bohemia?'

'Prague.'

Marius Veland stared out of the window of room 406. A girl was lying on a towel on the lawn in front of the student building. She was not unlike the one in 303 whom he had secretly christened Shirley, after Shirley Manson from Garbage. But it wasn't her. The sun over Oslo fjord had hidden itself behind the clouds. At last the weather had begun to warm up – a heatwave was forecast for the week. Summer in Oslo. Marius Veland was looking forward to it. The alternative had been to go home to Bøfjord, the midnight sun and a summer job at the petrol station. To Mother's meatballs and Father's endless questions about why he had begun to study Media Studies in Oslo when he had the grades to train to become a civil engineer at NTNU in Trondheim. To Saturdays at the community centre with drunken locals, screaming classmates who had never left their own neighbourhood and thought that those who had were traitors; to the dance band that called itself a 'blues band', but always managed to mangle Creedence Clearwater Revival and Lynyrd Skynyrd.

That was not the only reason for him to be in Oslo this summer, though. He had landed the dream job. He was going to listen to records, watch movies and get paid for typing up his opinions on a PC. Over the past two years he had sent his reviews to several of the established papers, without success, but last month he went to *So What!* where a friend had introduced him to Runar. Runar had told him that he had wound up the clothes business he was running to start *Zone*, a free paper whose first issue would come out in August, if everything went to plan. The friend had mentioned that Marius liked writing reviews; Runar had said that he liked his shirt and employed him there and then. As a reviewer, Marius's brief was to reflect 'new urban values by dealing with popular culture with an irony that was warm, well informed and inclusive'. Such was Runar's formulation of Marius's assignment, and for it Marius would be richly rewarded, not in cash, but in free tickets to concerts, films, new bars and access to a milieu where he could make interesting contacts with a view to his future. This was his chance and he needed to be properly prepared. Of course, he had a good general background in pop, but he had borrowed CDs from Runar's collection to do some further swotting up on the history of popular music. In recent days it had been American rock in the '80s: R.E.M., Green On Red, Dream Syndicate, Pixies. Right now Violent Femmes was on the CD player. It sounded dated, but energetic.

The girl below got up from her towel. It was probably a little cool. Marius followed her with his eyes towards the neighbouring block. On her way she passed someone walking with a bike. From his clothing he looked like a courier. Marius closed his eyes. He was going to write.

Otto Tangen rubbed his eyes with nicotine-stained fingers. A sense of unease had spread through the bus, though it may have seemed to the outside world like calm. No-one stirred and no-one uttered a word. It was 5.20 and there had not been so much as a movement on one of the screens, just tiny fragments of time spurting by in white digits in the corner. Another drop of sweat rolled down between Otto's buttocks. Sitting like this you began to have paranoid thoughts, you imagined that someone had been tampering with the equipment and that you were sitting watching a recording from the previous day or something of that kind.

He was drumming his fingers on the table beside the console. That bastard Waaler had banned smoking in the bus.

Otto leaned to the right and squeezed out a silent fart while looking at the guy with the blond shaven skull. He had been sitting in a chair without saying a word ever since he arrived. Looked like a retired bouncer.

'Doesn't seem our man's turning up for work today,' Otto said. 'Perhaps he thought it was too hot. Perhaps he postponed it till tomorrow and went for a beer in Aker Brygge instead. They said in the weather report that –'

'Shut up, Tangen.'

Waaler spoke in a low voice, but it was loud enough.

Otto gave a deep sigh and flexed his shoulders.

The clock in the corner of the screen said 5.21.

'Has anyone seen the guy in 303 leave?'

It was Waaler's voice. Otto discovered that Waaler was looking at him.

'I was asleep this morning,' he said.

'I want room 303 checked. Falkeid?'

The head of Special Forces cleared his throat.

'I don't consider the risk –'

'Now, Falkeid.'

The fans cooling the electronics buzzed as Falkeid and Waaler exchanged looks.

Falkeid cleared his throat again.

'Alpha to Charlie Two. Come in. Over.'

Atmospheric noise.

'Charlie Two.'

'Clear 303 right away.'

'Received. Clearing 303.'

Otto studied the screen. Nothing. Imagine if . . .

There they were.

Three men. Black uniforms, black balaclavas, black machine guns, black boots. It all happened quickly, but it seemed strangely undramatic. It was the sound. There was no sound.

They didn't use the smart little explosives to open the door, but an old-fashioned crowbar. Otto was disappointed. Must be the cutbacks.

The soundless men on the screen positioned themselves as if they were starting a race, one with the bar hooked under the lock, the other two one metre behind with their weapons raised. Suddenly they went into action. It was one coordinated movement, a crisp dance routine. The door flew open. The two men standing at the ready stormed in and the third man literally dived after them. Otto was already looking forward to showing the recording to Nils. The door glided back halfway where it stopped. Great shame they hadn't had the time to put cameras in the rooms.

Eight seconds.

Falkeid's radio crackled.

'303 cleared. One girl and one boy, both unarmed.'

'And alive?'

'Extremely . . . er, alive.'

'Have you searched the boy?'

'He's naked, Alpha.'

'Get him out,' Waaler said. 'Fuck!'

Otto stared at the doorway. They've been doing it. Naked. They've been doing it all night and all day. He stared at the doorway, transfixed.

'Get him dressed and take him back to your position, Charlie Two.'

Falkeid put the walkie-talkie down, looked at the others and gently shook his head.

Waaler banged the flat of his hand down hard against the arm of the chair.

'The bus is free tomorrow, too,' Otto said, casting a fleeting glance at the inspector.

He would have to tread warily now.

'I don't charge any more for Sundays, but I have to know when –'

'Hey, look at that.'

Otto automatically turned round. The bouncer had finally opened his trap. He was pointing to the middle screen.

'In the hall. He went in through the front door and straight into the lift.'

It went quiet in the bus for two seconds. Then there was the sound of Falkeid's voice on the walkie-talkie.

'Alpha to all units. Possible target has gone into the lift. Stand by.'

'No, thank you,' Beate smiled.

'Yes, well, that's probably enough cookies,' the old lady sighed, putting the biscuit tin back on the table. 'Where was I? Oh, yes. It's nice to have visits from Sven now that I'm on my own.'

'Yes, it must be lonely living in such a big house.'

'I chat quite a bit with Ina, but she went to her gentleman friend's holiday cabin today. I asked her to say hello to him, but they're so strange about things like that nowadays. It's as if they want to try out everything and at the same time they don't think anything will last. That's probably why they're so secretive.'

Beate stole a look at her watch. Harry said they would ring as soon as it was all over.

'You're thinking about something else now, aren't you?'

Beate nodded slowly.

'That's quite alright,' Olaug said. 'Let's hope they catch him.'

'You've got a good son.'

'Yes, it's true. And if he had visited me as often as he has just recently, I wouldn't complain.'

'Oh? How often's that?' Beate asked. It should be over by now. Why hadn't Harry rung? Hadn't he shown up after all?

'Once a week for the last four weeks. Well, even more frequently actually. He's been here every five days. Short stays. I really think he's got someone down there in Prague waiting for him. And, as I said, I think he's got some news for me this evening.'

'Mm.'

'Last time, he brought me a piece of jewellery. Do you want to see it?'

Beate looked at the old lady. And suddenly she felt how tired she was, tired of the job, of the Courier Killer, of Tom Waaler and Harry Hole, of Olaug Sivertsen and, most of all, of herself, the noble, dutiful Beate Lønn who thought she could achieve something, make a differ- ence, if she was a good girl, good and bright with it, bright and always doing what other people wanted her to do. It was time for a change, but she didn't know whether she could carry it through. Most of all she just wanted to go home, hide under the duvet and sleep.

'You're right,' Olaug said. 'There's not much to see, anyway. More tea?'

'Please.'

Olaug was just going to pour out the tea when she saw that Beate was holding her hand over her cup.

'Sorry,' Beate said laughing. 'What I meant was that I would like to see it.'

'What . . .'

'See the piece of jewellery your son gave you.'

Olaug brightened up and went out of the kitchen.

Good girl, Beate thought. She lifted the cup to finish her tea. She would have to ring Harry and hear how it had gone.

'Here it is,' Olaug said.

Beate Lønn's teacup, that is, Olaug Sivertsen's teacup, or to be absolutely precise, the Wehrmacht teacup, stopped in mid-air.

Beate stared at a brooch – at the precious stone that was attached to the brooch.

'Sven imports them,' Olaug said. 'I suppose they're only cut in this special way in Prague.'

It was a diamond. In the shape of a pentagram.

Beate ran her tongue round her mouth to get rid of the dryness.

'I have to ring someone,' she said.

The dryness would not go.

'Can you find me a photo of Sven in the meantime? Preferably an up-to-date one. It's quite important.'

Olaug looked confused, but nodded.

Otto was breathing through an open mouth as he stared at the screen and registered the voices around him.

'Possible target going into sector Bravo Two. Possible target stopped in front of the door. Ready, Bravo Two?'

'Bravo Two ready.'

'Target stationary. He's putting his hand in his pocket. Possible weapon. We can't see his hand.'

Waaler's voice: 'Now.'

'Into action, Bravo Two.'

'Strange,' mumbled the bouncer.

Marius Veland thought at first he was hearing things and turned down Violent Femmes to be sure. There it was again. Someone was knocking at the door. Who on earth could that be? As far as he knew, everyone in the corridor had gone home for the summer. Not Shirley, though. He had seen her on the stairs. He had stopped to ask her if she would go with him to a concert. Or a film. Or a play. Free. She could choose.

Marius got up and noticed that his hands were sweating. Why? There was no sensible reason for it to be her. He cast a sweeping glance around the room and realised that he had never actually looked at it until now. He didn't have enough things for the room to be in a real mess. The walls were bare except for a ripped poster of Iggy Pop and a sad-looking bookshelf that would soon be full of free CDs and DVDs.

It was an awful room, completely without character. There was another knock. He hastily prodded a flap from his duvet sticking out of the back of the sofa bed. He opened the door. It couldn't be her. It couldn't be . . . It wasn't her.

'Mr Veland?'

'Yes?'

Taken aback, Marius stared at the man.

'I've got a package for you.'

The man took off his rucksack, pulled out an A4 envelope and passed it over. Marius held the stamped white envelope in his hand. There was no name written on it.

'Are you sure it's for me?' he asked.

'Yes. I need a receipt . . .'

The man held out a clipboard with a sheet of paper on.

Marius looked at him enquiringly.

'Sorry. You wouldn't have a pen, would you?' the man smiled.

Marius stared at him again. Something was not right, something he couldn't quite put his finger on.

'Just a moment,' Marius said.

He took the envelope with him, put it on the shelf beside the bunch of keys with the skull on, found a pen in a drawer and turned round. Marius recoiled when he saw that the man was already standing in the dark passage behind him.

'I didn't hear you,' Marius said and heard his own laughter nervously rebound off the walls.

It wasn't that he was frightened. Where he came from people generally walked in so as not to let the heat out, or to let the cold in. There was something strange about this man, though. He had taken off his goggles and helmet and now Marius could see what it was that had made him start. He seemed too old. Bike couriers were usually in their twenties. This guy's body was slim and in good shape. It could pass for a young man's. But the face belonged to someone well into his thirties, maybe into his forties even.

Marius was about to say something when he spotted what the courier was holding in his hand. The room was bright, but the hallway was dark and Marius Veland had seen enough films to recognise the contours of a gun with a silencer on the end of it.

'Is that for me?' Marius floundered.

The man smiled and pointed the gun at him. At his face. Then Marius knew that he should be afraid.

'Sit down,' the man said. 'You've got a pen. Open the envelope.'

Marius dropped into a chair.

'You have some writing to do,' the man said.

'Well done, Bravo Two!'

Falkeid shouted, his face red and shiny.

Otto was breathing through his nose. On the screen the man was lying on his stomach on the floor in front of room 205, with his wrists handcuffed behind his back. And best of all, he was lying with his face twisted towards the camera so that you could see the surprise, see it contort in pain, see the defeat slowly sink in for the bastard. It was a scoop. No, it was more than that, it was a historic recording. The dramatic climax to the bloody summer in Oslo: the arrest of the Courier Killer on his way to committing his fourth murder. The whole world will be fighting to show it. My God, he, Otto Tangen, was a rich man. No more 7-Eleven shit, no more of that bastard Waaler, he could buy . . . he could . . . Aud-Rita and he could . . .

'It's not him,' the doorman said.

The bus went quiet.

Waaler leaned forward in his chair.

'What's that, Harry?'

'It's not him, 205 is one of the rooms we didn't have any luck with. According to the room list I have here, his name is Odd Einar Lillebostad. It's difficult to see what the guy on the floor is holding in his hand, but it looks to me as though it could be a key. Sorry, guys, but my guess is that Odd Einar Lillebostad has just returned home.'

Otto stared at the picture. He had equipment worth over a million kroner in the bus, bought and borrowed equipment that could focus on the hand and magnify it easy as wink to see if that bastard doorman was right. But he didn't need to. The branch in the apple tree was cracking. He could see the light in the windows from the garden. The tin can crackled.

'Bravo Two to Alpha. According to his bank card, this guy's name is Odd Einar Lillebostad.'

Otto slumped back in his chair.

'Relax, folks,' Waaler said. 'He may still come. Isn't that right, Harry?'

That bastard Harry didn't answer. Instead his mobile phone bleeped.

Marius Veland stared at the two blank pieces of paper he had taken out of the envelope.

'Who are your next of kin?' the man asked.

Marius gulped and wanted to answer, but his voice would not obey.

'I'm not going to kill you,' the man said. 'So long as you do what I say.'

'Mum and Dad,' Marius whispered. It sounded like a pathetic SOS.

The man told him to write his parents' names and address on the envelope. Marius put pen to paper. The names. The familiar names. And Bjøford. He stared at the writing afterwards. So crooked and shaky.

The man began to dictate a letter. Marius moved his hand compliantly across the page.

'Hi! Sudden change of plans! I'm off to Morocco with Georg, a Moroccan boy I've met here. We're going to stay with his mother and father in a little mountain village called Hassane. I'll be away for four weeks. Probably difficult to get a signal, but I'll try to write, though Georg says the post is a bit iffy. Anyway, I'll get in touch as soon as I'm back, love . . .'

'Marius,' said Marius.

'Marius.'

The man told Marius to put the letter in the envelope and then in the bag he held in front of him.

'On the other piece of paper just write "Gone abroad. Back in four weeks". Sign it with the day's date and Marius. That's it, thank you.'

Marius sat in the chair contemplating his lap. The man was standing directly behind him. A puff of wind made the curtain sway. The birds were twittering hysterically outside. The man leaned forwards and closed the window. Now there was only the low hum of the combined radio and CD player on the bookshelf.

'What's the song?' the man asked.

'"Blister In The Sun",' Marius said. He had pressed 'repeat'. He liked it. He would have given it a good review. A warmly ironic, inclusive review.

'I've heard it before,' the man said, found the volume knob and turned it up. 'I just can't remember where.'

Marius lifted his head and gazed out of the window, at the summer that had gone mute, at the birch tree that seemed to be waving farewell, at the green lawn. In the reflection he saw the man behind him raise the gun and point it at the back of his head.

'Go wild!' came the squeal from the small loudspeakers.

The man lowered the gun again.

'Sorry. Forgot to release the safety catch. That's it.'

Marius squeezed his eyes shut. Shirley. He thought about her. Where was she now?

'Now I remember,' the man said. 'It was in Prague. They're called Violent Femmes, I think. My wife took me to a concert. They're not very good, are they?'

Marius opened his mouth to answer, but at that moment the gun gave a dry cough and no-one ever found out what Marius thought about Violent Femmes.

*

Otto kept his eyes on the screens. Behind him, Falkeid was speaking the bandit lingo with Bravo Two. That bastard Harry answered the bleeping mobile phone. He didn't say a lot. Probably some ugly dame who wants to get laid, Otto thought, and pricked up his ears.

Waaler didn't say anything, just sat biting his knuckles with a blank face as he watched Odd Einar Lillebostad being led away. No handcuffs. No real cause for suspicion. No bloody nothing.

Otto kept his eyes on the screens. He had the feeling he was sitting beside a nuclear reactor. On the outside there was nothing to see, on the inside it was seething with stuff you wouldn't want to touch with a barge pole for anything in the world. Eyes on the screens.

Falkeid said 'over and out' and put the jabber thingy down. That bastard Harry was still feeding her monosyllables.

'He's not coming,' Waaler said, his eyes on the pictures showing empty corridors and stairs.

'Still early days,' Falkeid said.

Waaler slowly shook his head. 'He knows we're here. I can feel it in my bones. He's sitting somewhere laughing at us.'

In a tree in the garden, Otto thought.

Waaler got up.

'Let's just pack everything up, boys. The theory about the pentagram won't hold. We'll start from scratch again tomorrow.'

'The theory holds.'

The other three turned towards that Harry bastard who slipped his mobile phone into his pocket.

'His name is Sven Sivertsen,' he said. 'Norwegian national living in Prague, born in Oslo in 1946, but looks a lot younger, according to our colleague Beate Lønn. He's been done twice for smuggling. He gave his mother a diamond which is identical to the ones we've found on the bodies. His mother says he's been in Oslo to visit her on all the days in question. In Villa Valle.'

Otto saw Waaler's face stiffen and blanch.

'His mother,' Waaler almost whispered. 'In the house the last point of the star was pointing to?'

'Yes,' that bastard Harry said. 'And now she's waiting for a visit from him. This evening. A car with reinforcements is already on its way to Schweigaards gate. I've got my car here in the street.'

He got up from his chair. Waaler was rubbing his chin.

'We have to regroup,' Falkeid said, grabbing the walkie-talkie.

'Wait!' Waaler shouted. 'Nobody does anything until I say.'

The others looked at him expectantly. Waaler closed his eyes. Two seconds passed. Then he opened them again.

'Stop the car before it gets there, Harry. I don't want a police car within a kilometre's radius of that house. If he gets wind of the slightest danger, we've had it. I know a few things about smugglers from Eastern Europe. They always – always – make sure they have a way out. And another thing is that when you've lost them, you never find them again. Falkeid, you and your boys stay here and continue with the job until you hear otherwise.'

'But you yourself said that he wasn't –'

'Do as I say. This may be the only chance we get, and since it's my head on the block, I'd like to deal with this personally. Harry, you take charge here. OK?'

Otto saw the Harry bastard staring at Waaler, but in a vacant sort of way.

'OK?' Waaler repeated.

'Fine,' the bastard said.

28

Saturday. The Dildo.

Olaug Sivertsen watched Beate with big red eyes as Beate checked that she had bullets in all the chambers of her revolver.

'My Sven? Goodness me, they have to understand they're making a mistake! Sven wouldn't hurt a fly.'

Beate clicked the drum of her revolver into place and went over to the kitchen window with the view out onto the car park in Schweigaards gate.

'Let's hope so. But to find out, first we have to arrest him.'

Beate's heart was beating fast, but not too fast. Her fatigue vanished and was replaced by a feeling of lightness and centredness, almost as if she had been taking some kind of drug. It was her father's old service revolver. Once she had heard him say to a colleague that you should never rely on a single-shot handgun.

'He didn't say what time he was coming here?'

Olaug shook her head.

'There were a few things he had to sort out, he said.'

'Has he got a key to the front door?'

'No.'

'Good. Then –'

'I don't usually lock it if I know he's coming.'

'Isn't the door locked?'

Beate could feel the blood rushing to her head and her voice became sharp and jagged. She didn't know who she was angrier with, the old lady who had been given police protection, but left the door open so that her son could walk right in, or herself for not having checked such an elementary thing.

She breathed in to make her voice calmer.

'I want you to sit here, Olaug. Then I'll go out into the hall and –'

'Hi!'

The voice came from behind Beate and her heart beat quickly, but not too quickly, as she swung round with her right arm outstretched and her thin white finger crooked round the taut, inert trigger. A figure filled the doorway to the hall. She hadn't even heard him. There was good and good, and stupid and stupid.

'Wow,' the voice said with a chuckle.

Beate had his face in the sights. She hesitated for a fraction of a second before releasing the pressure on the trigger.

'Who's that?' Olaug asked.

'The cavalry, Fru Sivertsen,' the voice said. 'Inspector Tom Waaler.' He put out his hand and said, with a brief glance at Beate, 'I took the liberty of locking your front door, Fru Sivertsen.'

'Where are the rest?' Beate asked.

'There is no rest. It's just . . .' Beate froze as Tom Waaler added with a smile, '. . . us two, sweetie.'

It was gone 8 p.m.

On the TV the newscaster warned that a cold front was on its way across England and that the heatwave would soon be over.

In a corridor in the Post House Roger Gjendem said to a colleague that the police had been conspicuously uncommunicative the last couple of days and his guess was that something was brewing. He had heard rumours that Special Forces had been mobilised and the head, Sivert Falkeid, had not returned one single call in the last two days. His colleague thought it was wishful thinking and the editorial desk agreed. The cold front became front-page news.

Bjarne Møller was sitting on the sofa watching *Beat for Beat*. He liked Ivar Dyrhaug. He liked his songs. And he didn't care if some people at work thought it was dated and too homely. He liked the home atmosphere. And again it struck him that Norway must have so many talented singers who never made it into the spotlight. This evening, however, Møller couldn't concentrate on the lyrics and the message; he merely stared blankly as his mind went over the update he had just received from Harry on the phone.

He checked his watch and glanced over to the telephone for the fifth time in half an hour. The agreement was that Harry would ring as soon as they had something new. And the Chief Superintendent had asked for a briefing as soon as the operation was concluded. Møller wondered whether the Chief had a TV in his log cabin and whether, right now, he was sitting, like him, watching a pop quiz with the answers in his mouth but his brain elsewhere.

Otto sucked on his cigarette, closed his eyes and saw the light in the windows, heard the wind rustling in the dry leaves and felt the sinking feeling when they drew the curtains. The other tin can had been thrown in the ditch. Nils had gone home.

Otto had run out of cigarettes, but he bummed one off that police bastard called Harry. Harry pulled out a packet of Camel Light from his pocket half an hour after Waaler had gone off. A good choice, except for the Light bit. Falkeid had glowered disapprovingly when they began to smoke, but he didn't say anything. He glimpsed Sivert Falkeid's face through the blue mist of smoke, which also cast a compensatory veil over the irritatingly static pictures of corridors and stairs.

Harry had shoved his chair close up to Otto's so that he could get closer to the screen. He smoked his cigarette unhurriedly while staring intensely at the pictures and studying them one by one. As if there might be something there he hadn't noticed yet.

'What's that?' Harry asked, pointing to one of the pictures on the left-hand screen.

'There?'

'No, higher up. On the fourth floor.'

Otto stared at a picture of yet another empty corridor with pale yellow walls.

'I can't see anything special,' Otto said.

'Over the third door on the right-hand side. In the plaster.'

Otto squinted. There were some white marks. He wondered at first if they had been made while unsuccessfully trying to mount one of the cameras, but he couldn't remember making a hole in the wall in that particular spot.

Falkeid bent forwards. 'What *is* that?'

'Don't know,' Harry said. 'Otto, could you magnify just that . . . ?'

Otto dragged the cursor across the screen and drew a little square above the door. He held down two keys. The section above the door covered the whole of the 21-inch screen.

'Oh my God,' Harry mumbled.

'Yessir, this is no mean shit,' Otto boasted, patting the console with affection. He was beginning to take to this Harry character.

'The devil's star,' Harry whispered.

'Hey?'

But the policeman had already turned to Falkeid.

'Ask Delta One or whatever the fuck he's called to get ready to break into 406. Tell them to wait until they see me.'

The policeman got up and took out a gun that Otto recognised from late-night surfing on the Net. Glock 21. He didn't know what, but he knew something was going to happen, something that might mean he got his scoop after all.

The policeman was already out the door.

'Alpha to Delta One,' Falkeid said and released the button on the walkie-talkie.

Noise. Lovely, crackling atmospheric noise.

Harry stopped in front of the lift inside the entrance, dithered for a second, then grasped the handle and slid open the door. His heart skipped a beat when he saw the black grille. A sliding grille.

He let the door go as if he had been burned, let it close. It was too late anyway. This was just the pathetic final spurt towards the platform when you know the train has already gone, but you would like to catch a glimpse of it before it completely disappears.

Harry took the stairs. He tried to walk calmly. When had the man been here? Two days ago? A week ago?

He couldn't restrain himself. His shoe soles sounded like sandpaper on the stairs as he began to run. He wanted to catch a glimpse.

Just as he swung left into the corridor on the fourth floor, three black-clad figures came from the furthest end of the corridor.

Harry stood under the star carved into the wall. The whiteness shone against the yellow of the wall.

Beneath the room number – 406 – there was a name. VELAND. And beneath that a piece of paper stuck to the wall with two bits of tape.

GONE ABROAD. BACK IN FOUR WEEKS, MARIUS

He nodded to Delta One that they could go into action.

Six seconds later the door was open.

Harry told the others to wait outside and he went in alone. Empty. His eyes scanned the room. It was clean and tidy. Too tidy. It did not match the torn poster of Iggy Pop on the wall above the sofa bed. A few tatty paperbacks on the shelf above the cleared desk. Beside the books, five or six keys on a keyring in the shape of a skull. A photo of a suntanned girl smiling. Girlfriend or sister, Harry guessed.

Between a book by Bukowski and a ghettoblaster there was a wax thumb painted white and pointing upwards, giving the thumbs up. Everything ready. Everything OK. Was it?

Harry looked at Iggy Pop, the lean, bare body stripped to the waist, the self-inflicted scars, the intense gaze from the deep eye sockets, a man who must have been through a Calvary or two of his own. Harry touched the thumb on the shelf. Too soft to be plaster or plastic, it almost felt like a real finger. Cold, but real. He thought of the dildo he had seen at Barli's while sniffing the white thumb. It smelled of a mixture of formalin and paint. He held it between two fingers and squeezed. The paint cracked. Harry recoiled as he caught the pungent smell.

'Beate Lønn.'

'Harry here. How's it going with you?'

'We're still waiting. Waaler has taken up a position in the hall and chased me and Miss Sivertsen into the kitchen. So much for women's liberation.'

'I'm ringing from room 406 in the student block. He's been here.'

'Been there?'

'He carved a devil's star in the plaster above the door. The boy staying here, a Marius Veland, has gone. The other residents haven't seen him for several weeks. And there's a slip of paper hanging on the door saying he's gone away.'

'Well, perhaps he really *has* gone away.'

Harry noticed that Beate had started to take on his speech mannerisms.

'Hardly,' Harry said. 'His thumb is still in his room. In a sort of embalmed state.'

It went quiet at the other end of the line.

'I've rung your lot at Forensics. They're on their way now.'

'But I don't understand,' Beate said. 'Haven't you had the whole building under surveillance?'

'Well, yes. But not for the 20 days since this happened.'

'Twenty days. How do you know that?'

'Because I found his parents' telephone number and called them. They'd received a letter saying that he was off to Morocco. His father says that it's the first time he can remember ever receiving a letter from Marius. Usually he phones. The postmark on the letter is from 20 days ago.'

'Twenty days . . .' Beate murmured.

'Twenty days. In other words, exactly five days before the murder of Camilla Loen. In other words . . .'

He could hear Beate taking deep breaths on the phone.

'. . . five days before what we thought was the first murder,' he said.

'My God.'

'There's more. We rounded up the occupants of the house and asked if anyone could remember anything from that day and the girl in 303 says she remembers sunbathing on the grass outside the building that afternoon. On her way back she passed a bike courier. She remembers it because they don't often have couriers here and she'd joked about it with the others in the corridor when the papers had started writing about the Courier Killer a couple of weeks later.'

'He's cheated with the sequence of murders then?'

'No,' Harry said. 'It was me being stupid. Do you remember I was wondering if any of the fingers he cut off were also a kind of code? Well. It was the simplest of all. The thumb. He started with the first digit on the left hand and worked his way round. You don't need to be a genius to work out that Camilla was number two.'

'Mm.'

Now she's doing it again, Harry thought.

'And now we just need number five,' Beate said. 'The little finger.'

'You know what that means, don't you?'

'That it's our turn. That it's been our turn all along. My God, is he really planning to . . . you know?'

'Is his mother sitting beside you?'

'Yes. Tell me what he'll do, Harry.'

'I have no idea.'

'I know you have no idea, but tell me anyway.'

Harry hesitated.

'OK. Many serial killers are driven by self-contempt. And since the fifth killing is the last one, the final one, there is a great likelihood that he's planning to take the life of his progenitor. Or himself. Or both. It's got nothing to do with his relationship with his mother, but with himself. Anyway, the choice of the location for the murder is logical.'

Silence.

'Are you there, Beate?'

'Yes, indeed. He grew up as the son of a German.'

'Who?'

'The person on his way here.'

New silence.

'Why is Waaler waiting on his own in the hall?'

'Why are you asking?'

'Because the usual procedure would be for both of you to arrest him. It's safer than having you sit in the kitchen.'

'Maybe,' Beate said. 'I don't have much experience in this kind of fieldwork. He must know what he's doing.'

'Yes,' Harry said.

Some thoughts passed through his mind. Thoughts he was trying to repress.

'Is there anything wrong, Harry?'

'Yes,' Harry said. 'I've run out of cigarettes.'

29

Saturday. Drowning.

HARRY PUT HIS MOBILE PHONE BACK IN HIS JACKET POCKET AND leaned back against the sofa. Forensics would probably be hacked off, but there weren't exactly many leads here to destroy. It was obvious that the killer had done a thorough job of clearing up after himself this time as well. Harry had even detected the faint aroma of soft soap when he put his face to the floor to examine some black lumps of what seemed at first sight to be rubber burned onto the lino.

A face appeared in the doorway.

'Bjørn Holm, Forensics.'

'Good,' Harry said. 'Have you got a smoke?'

He stood up and walked to the window as Holm and his colleague got down to work. The angular evening light gilded the house fronts, the streets and the trees across Kampen and into Tøyen. Harry didn't know of a more beautiful town than Oslo on evenings like this. There had to be others, but he didn't know any.

'I'd like you to find out what these black lumps are.'

Harry pointed to the floor.

'Fine,' Holm said.

Harry was dizzy. He had chain-smoked eight cigarettes. It had kept his thirst in check. In check, but not gone completely. He stared at the thumb. Presumably it had been severed with pincers. Paint and glue. A chisel and a hammer to carve the pentagram over the door. He had brought quite a bit of equipment with him this time.

He understood the pentagram. And the finger. But why the glue?

'Looks like melted rubber,' Holm said. He squatted on the floor.

'How do you melt rubber?' Harry asked.

'You can set fire to it. Or use an electric iron. Or a heat gun.'

Holm shrugged his shoulders.

'What do you use melted rubber for?'

'Vulcanisation,' his colleague said. 'You use it for repairing things or making them watertight. Car tyres, for example. Or sealing something that has to be airtight. That kind of thing.'

'And that?'

'No idea. Sorry.'

'Thank you.'

The thumb was pointing to the ceiling. If only it could point to the solution to the code, Harry thought. Obviously it was a code. The killer had attached a ring to their noses and he was leading them like dumb animals wherever he wanted, and so this code had a solution too. Quite a simple solution if it was intended for moderately intelligent idiots like himself.

He stared at the finger. Pointing upwards. OK. Roger. Message understood.

The evening light continued to stream in.

He sucked hard on his cigarette. The nicotine travelled through his veins, through the narrow capillaries from his lungs and northwards. Poisoned, health-damaged, manipulated but primed. Shit!

Harry was racked with a bout of violent coughing.

He pointed to the ceiling. Of room 406. The ceiling on the fourth floor. Of course. Idiot. Idiot.

*

Harry turned the key, opened the door and found the light switch along the wall. He stepped inside. The loft was high and airy without any windows. Numbered storage rooms, two metres square, abutted against each other and lined the walls. Property was piled up behind the chicken wire in transit from the owner to the rubbish skip: mattresses with holes in, unfashionable furniture, cardboard boxes of clothes, electrical goods that still work and so cannot be thrown out yet.

'Hellfire,' mumbled Falkeid as he and two of the men from Special Forces came in.

Harry thought it a very accurate image. The sun outside may have been low in the sky and losing power over to the west, but it had spent all day charging the roof tiles, which now radiated with the force of storage heaters and turned the loft into a veritable sauna.

'Looks like the storage room for 406 is this way,' Harry said, heading to the right.

'Why are you so sure that he'll be in the loft?'

'Well, because the killer has himself pointed out the obvious fact that the fifth floor is above the fourth. In this case, the loft.'

'Pointed out?'

'A kind of rebus.'

'Are you aware that it's absolutely impossible for there to be a body up here?'

'Why's that?'

'We came up here yesterday with a dog. A body lying here in this heat for four weeks . . . Transfer a dog's olfactory organs to our own sense of hearing and it would have been like searching for a wailing siren inside here. It would have been impossible for a dog not to find it, even a less competent dog. And the one we had yesterday was first rate.'

'Even if the body is wrapped in something that prevents the smell escaping?'

'Molecules of air move quickly and can penetrate even microscopic openings. It is not possible for –'

'Vulcanisation,' Harry said.

'Eh?'

Harry stopped in front of one of the storage areas. Instantly the two uniformed men were on the spot with their crowbars.

'Let's try it this way first, boys.'

Harry dangled the bunch of keys with the skull on in front of them. The smallest key fitted the padlock.

'I'll go in alone,' Harry said. 'The forensics people don't like the place being trampled under foot.'

He borrowed a torch and stood in front of a tall, broad white wardrobe with double doors which took up most of the room in the storage area. He laid his fingers on the handle and steeled himself before jerking open the door. The smell of musty clothes, dust and wood met his nostrils. He switched on the torch. There were three generations of blue suits hanging in a row on the bar which Marius must have inherited. Harry shone the torch inside and ran his hand across the material. Coarse wool. One of them had a thin plastic cover over it. Inside was a grey protective bag for a suit.

Harry shut the wardrobe doors and turned towards the back wall of the storage space where there was a pair of curtains – home-made by the look of them – hanging over a clothes horse. Harry heaved them off. A set of small sharp predator teeth snarled silently at him. What was left of its coat was grey and the brown marble-like eyes needed a polish.

'A marten,' Falkeid said.

'Mm.'

Harry cast his eyes around. There weren't many places left to look. Had he really been mistaken?

Then he spotted the roll of carpet. It was Persian – at least, that was what he thought – and was lodged against the chicken wire and reached halfway up to the roof. Harry pushed a wicker chair up against the carpet, climbed onto it and shone the torch down into the carpet. The policemen standing outside stared at him with tense expressions on their faces.

'Right,' Harry said, getting down from the chair and switching off the torch.

'Well?' Falkeid said.

Harry shook his head. A sudden fury possessed him and he kicked the side of the wardrobe so that it began to stand and sway like a belly dancer. The dogs barked. A drink, one drink, a moment without torment. He turned to leave the room when he heard a scraping noise. As if something was sliding down a wall. He turned instantaneously and just saw the wardrobe door shoot open before the suit bag leapt onto him and knocked him to the ground.

Harry knew he must have been out for a second because when he opened his eyes again he was lying on his back and could feel a dull ache at the back of his head. He breathed in a cloud of dust that had risen from the dry wooden floor. The weight of the suit bag had knocked the air out of him and he felt as if he were drowning, lying underneath a big plastic bag filled with water. He hit out in panic and felt his fist strike the smooth surface and, inside, something soft that gave way.

Harry went rigid and remained totally still. Slowly he managed to focus his eyes; just as slowly the feeling that he was drowning began to wear off. And was replaced by the feeling that he had drowned.

Glazed eyes stared back at him from behind a grey plastic membrane.

They had found Marius Veland.

30

Saturday. The Arrest.

THE EXPRESS TRAIN GLIDED PAST OUTSIDE, SHINY SILVER, QUIET AS A tentative puff of air. Beate watched Olaug Sivertsen. She straightened her head and looked out of the window, blinking again and again. Her wrinkled, sinewy hands on the kitchen table resembled a bird's-eye view of the countryside. The wrinkles were long valleys, the blue-black veins rivers and the knuckles chains of mountains with the skin stretched over like a grey-white tent canvas. Beate examined her own hands. She thought about what hands can do in the course of a lifetime. And what they cannot do. Or what they don't manage to achieve.

At 21.56 Beate heard the gate open and the sound of steps on the gravel path outside.

She stood up, her heart beating as quickly and lightly as a Geiger counter.

'That's him,' Olaug said.

'Are you sure?'

Olaug gave her a distressed smile. 'I've heard his steps on the gravel path ever since he was a little boy. When he was old enough to go out in the evening I used to wake up to the second step he took. He used to take twelve steps. Just count.'

Suddenly Waaler was standing in the kitchen doorway.

'Someone's coming,' he said. 'I want you to stay there. Whatever happens. OK?'

'It's him,' Beate said, nodding in Olaug's direction.

Waaler gave a brief nod. Then he was gone again.

Beate put her hand on the old lady's.

'It'll be alright,' she said.

'You'll see that there's been a mistake,' Olaug said, without meeting her eyes.

Eleven, twelve. Beate heard the door opening in the hall.

Then she heard Waaler shout:

'Police! My ID card is on the floor in front of you. Drop the gun or I'll shoot!'

She felt Olaug's hand jerk.

'Police! Put down your gun or I'll be forced to shoot!'

Why was he shouting so loudly? They couldn't be more than five or six metres apart.

'For the last time!' Waaler shouted.

Beate got up and took her revolver out of the holster she had in the belt across her shoulder.

'Beate . . .' Olaug's voice shook.

Beate looked up and met the old lady's imploring eyes.

'Drop your weapon! You're shooting at a policeman.'

Beate took the four steps to the door, pulled it open and stepped into the hallway with her weapon raised. Tom Waaler was two metres away, with his back to her. In the doorway stood a man wearing a grey suit. He was holding a suitcase in one hand. Beate had taken a decision based on what she thought she would see. That was why her first reaction was one of confusion.

'I'll shoot!' Waaler shouted.

Beate could see the open mouth and the stunned face of the man standing in line with the front door. Waaler had already thrust his shoulder forward to take the recoil when he pulled the trigger.

'Tom . . .'

She said it in a low voice, but Tom Waaler's back went as rigid as if she had shot him from behind.

'He hasn't got a gun, Tom.'

Beate had the feeling she was watching a film. An absurd scene where someone had pressed the pause button and the picture was locked in position, frozen; the picture quivered and jerked and time stood still. She waited for the crack of the gun, but it didn't come. Tom Waaler was not crazy. Not in a clinical sense. He didn't lack control where his impulses were concerned. That was presumably what had frightened her most at that time. The cold control as he abused her.

'Since you're here, anyway . . .' Waaler said finally. His voice sounded strained. '. . . perhaps you can put the handcuffs on our prisoner.'

31

Saturday. 'Isn't it wonderful to have someone to hate?'

IT WAS ALMOST MIDNIGHT WHEN FOR THE SECOND TIME BJARNE Møller met the press outside the entrance to Police HQ. Only the brightest of stars shone through the heat-haze over Oslo, but he had to shield his eyes against the flashbulbs and the camera lights. Short, stabbing questions rained down on him.

'One at a time,' Møller said, pointing to a raised arm. 'And please introduce yourself.'

'Roger Gjendem, *Aftenposten*. Has Sven Sivertsen confessed?'

'At the present moment the suspect is being interviewed by the man leading the investigation, Inspector Tom Waaler. Until the interviews are over I cannot answer your question.'

'Is it true that you found weapons and diamonds in Sivertsen's case? And that the diamonds are identical to those you found on the victims' bodies?'

'I can confirm that this is true. Over there, yes please.'

A young woman's voice. 'Earlier this evening you said that Sven

Sivertsen lives in Prague, and in fact I have been able to find out his official address. It's a boarding house, but they say that he left there more than a year ago and no-one seems to know where he lives. Do you?'

The other journalists were taking notes before Møller answered.

'Not yet.'

'I managed to get talking to a couple of the residents there,' the woman's voice said with barely concealed pride. 'They said Sven Sivertsen had a young girlfriend. They didn't know her name, but one of them suggested she was a prostitute. Are the police aware of this?'

'We weren't until this minute,' Møller said. 'But we appreciate your help.'

'And we do, too,' shouted one voice in the crowd, followed by all-male hyena laughter. The woman smiled uncertainly.

A question in Østfold dialect: '*Dagbladet.* How's his mother taking it?'

Møller caught the journalist's eye and bit his lower lip to prevent himself from snarling in anger.

'I cannot make any judgment on that. Yes. Please.'

'*Dagsavisen.* We're wondering how it's possible that Marius Veland's body could lie for four weeks in the loft of his building, in the hottest summer ever without anyone discovering it.'

'We are as yet uncertain about the precise timing of this, but it looks as if a plastic bag was used, similar to a suit bag which was then sealed and made airtight before being . . .' Møller searched for the right words, 'hung in the wardrobe in the loft of the student block.'

A low mumble ran through the throng of journalists and Møller wondered if he had given away too much detail.

Roger Gjendem was asking another question.

Møller saw his mouth moving as he listened to the tune that was buzzing round in his head. 'I Just Called to Say I Love You.' She had sung it so well on *Beat for Beat,* her sister, the one who was taking over the main role in the musical, what was her name again?

'I apologise,' Møller said. 'Could you repeat that, please.'

*

Harry and Beate were sitting on a low wall set back from the jostling crowd of journalists, watching and smoking a cigarette. Beate had announced that she was a social smoker and took one from the packet that Harry had just bought.

Harry himself didn't feel any need to be sociable. Just to sleep.

They saw Tom Waaler coming out of the main entrance smiling into the hail of flashbulbs going off. The shadows were dancing a victory jig against the wall of Police HQ.

'He'll be a celebrity now,' Beate said. 'The man who led the investigation and single-handedly arrested the Courier Killer.'

'With two guns and stuff?' Harry smiled.

'Yes, it was just like the Wild West. And can you tell me why you would ask someone to put down a weapon they don't have?'

'Waaler probably meant the weapon Sivertsen was carrying. I would've done the same.'

'Of course, but do you know where we found his gun? In his suitcase.'

'For all Waaler knew, he could have been the fastest gun in the West from a standing suitcase.'

Beate laughed. 'You're coming afterwards for a beer, aren't you?'

Their eyes met and her smile became fixed as her blush spread over her neck and face.

'I didn't mean . . .'

'It's fine. You can celebrate for us both, Beate. I've done my bit.'

'You could come with us, anyway?'

'Don't think so. This was my last case.'

Harry flicked his cigarette away and it flew like a firefly through the night.

'Next week I won't be a policeman any more. Perhaps I ought to feel that there is something to celebrate, but I don't.'

'What will you do?'

'Something else.' Harry got up. 'Something completely different.'

*

Waaler caught up with Harry in the car park.

'Off so soon, Harry?'

'Tired. What's the taste of fame like?'

'It was just a couple of photos for the papers. You've been there yourself, so you know what it's like.'

'If you're thinking of that time in Sydney, they made me out to be trigger happy because I shot the man. You managed to catch yours alive. You're the kind of police hero a social democracy likes to have.'

'Do I detect the merest hint of sarcasm?'

'Not at all.'

'OK. I don't care who they turn into a hero. If it improves the image of the police force, as far as I am concerned, they can paint a falsely romantic picture of people like me. At the station, we still know who the real hero was this time.'

Harry pulled out his car keys and stopped in front of his white Escort.

'That was what I wanted to say, Harry. On behalf of everyone who was working with you. You solved the case, not me or anyone else.'

'I was just doing my job, wasn't I.'

'Your job, yes. That was the other thing I wanted to talk to you about. Shall we sit in the car for a second?'

There was the sweet stench of petrol in the car. A hole rusted through somewhere, Harry guessed. Waaler refused a cigarette.

'Your first task is arranged,' Waaler said. 'It isn't easy and it's not without danger, but if you carry it off, we'll agree to make you a full partner.'

'What is it?' Harry said, blowing smoke over the rear-view mirror.

Waaler ran the tips of his fingers along the wires coming out of the hole in the dashboard where the radio had once been.

'What did Marius Veland look like?' he asked.

'After four weeks in a plastic bag, what do you think?'

'He was twenty-four years old, Harry. Twenty-four years old. Can you remember what you dreamed of when you were twenty-four, what you expected from life?'

Harry remembered.

Waaler gave a rueful smile.

'The summer I turned twenty-two I went inter-railing with Geir and Solo. We ended up at the Italian Riviera, but the hotels were so expensive that we couldn't afford to stay anywhere. Even though Solo had brought with him the whole of the takings from the till in his father's kiosk the day we left. So we pitched our tent on the beach at night and spent the days walking round staring at the women, the cars and the boats. The strange thing was that we felt wealthy. Because we were twenty-two. We thought everything was for us, presents lying under the Christmas tree just waiting for us. Camilla Loen, Barbara Svendsen, Lisbeth Barli, they were all young. Perhaps they hadn't got to the stage of being disappointed yet, Harry. Perhaps they were still waiting for Christmas.'

Waaler ran his hand over the dashboard.

'I've just interrogated Sven Sivertsen, Harry. You can read the report later, but all I can tell you now is what's going to happen. He's a cold, calculating devil. He's going to play insane. He's going to fool the jury and create so much doubt for the psychologists that they won't dare to send him to prison. In short, he'll end up in a psychiatric department where he'll show such sensational progress that he'll be released after a few years. That's what it's like now, Harry. That's how we deal with the human detritus we're surrounded by. We don't clean it up, we don't throw it away; we just move it around a little. And we don't see that when the house is a stinking, rat-infested hole, it's too late. Just look at other countries where criminality has a firm foothold. Unfortunately we live in a country that is so rich at the moment that the politicians compete with each other to be the most open-handed. We've become so soft and nice that no-one dares to take the responsibility for doing unpleasant things any more. Do you understand?'

'So far.'

'That's where we come in, Harry. We take the responsibility. We see it as the sanitation job that society dare not take on.'

Harry sucked so hard that the cigarette paper crackled.

'What do you mean?' he asked, inhaling.

'Sven Sivertsen,' Waaler said, keeping a lookout through the window. 'Human detritus. You have to get rid of him.'

Harry bent double and coughed the smoke back out.

'Is that what you do? What about the other stuff? Smuggling?'

'All our activities are carried out to finance this.'

'Your cathedral?'

Waaler nodded slowly. Then he leaned across to Harry and Harry felt him put something in his jacket pocket.

'An ampoule,' Waaler said. 'It's called "Joseph's Blessing". Developed by the KGB during the Afghan War for assassinations, but best known as a means of committing suicide for captured Chechen soldiers. It stops your breathing, but unlike Prussic acid there's no taste and there's no smell. The ampoule fits nicely up the rectum or under the tongue. If he drinks the contents dissolved in water, he'll die in seconds. Have you understood the job?'

Harry straightened up. He wasn't coughing any more, but the tears stood in his eyes.

'So, it's supposed to look like suicide?'

'Witnesses in the custody block will confirm that they omitted to search the rectum when he was brought in. It's all arranged. Don't worry.'

Harry breathed in deeply. The fumes from the petrol were making him feel nauseous. The whine of a siren rose and died in the distance.

'You thought about shooting him, didn't you?'

Waaler didn't answer. Harry saw a police car roll up in front of the entrance to the custody block.

'You never intended to arrest him. You had two guns because you planned to put the other one in his hand after you had shot him to make it look as though he'd threatened you. You put Beate and the mother in the kitchen, then you shouted so that they could testify afterwards that they'd heard you shout and that you had acted in self-defence. But Beate came into the hall too early and your plan went down the drain.'

Waaler gave a deep sigh.

'We're cleaning up, Harry. The same way you got rid of the murderer in Sydney. The legal system doesn't work; it was made for a different time, a more innocent time. And until it is changed we cannot allow Oslo to be taken over by criminals. But you must know all that since you see it at close quarters every day?'

Harry studied the glow of his cigarette in the dark. Then he nodded.

'I just needed to have the whole picture,' he said.

'OK, Harry, listen. Sven Sivertsen will be in cell number nine in the custody block up to and including tomorrow night. Until Monday morning, in other words. Then he'll be moved to a secure cell in Ullersmo where we will not be able to get at him. The key to cell number nine is on the reception desk on the left. You've got until midnight tomorrow, Harry. Then I'll ring Custody to be told that the Courier Killer has received his deserved punishment. Understood?'

Harry nodded again.

Waaler smiled.

'Do you know what, Harry? Even though I'm happy that we're finally on the same team, there is a little part of me that is a tiny bit sad. Do you know why?'

Harry shrugged his shoulders. 'Because you thought there were things that money couldn't buy?'

Waaler laughed.

'Nice one, Harry. It's because I feel I've lost a good enemy. We're similar. You understand what I'm talking about, don't you?'

'"Isn't it wonderful to have someone to hate?"'

'What?'

'Michael Krohn. Raga Rockers.'

'Twenty-four hours, Harry. Good luck.'

Part Five

32

Sunday. The Swallows.

RAKEL WAS IN THE BEDROOM STUDYING HERSELF IN THE MIRROR. THE window was open so that she could listen out for the car and steps on the gravel leading up to the house. She looked at the photograph of her father on the dressing table in front of the mirror. It always struck her how young and innocent he seemed in the picture.

She had her hair held in place with a hairslide, as always. Should she do it differently? The dress was her mother's, a red muslin dress she had had altered. She hoped she wasn't overdressed. When she was small her father often used to tell her about the first time he saw her mother in this dress and Rakel never grew tired of hearing that it had been like in a fairy tale.

Rakel undid the hairslide and shook her head from side to side so that her dark hair fell over her face. The doorbell rang. She could hear Oleg's footsteps as he ran down the hall. She could hear the enthusiasm in his voice and Harry's deep laugh. Then she took a last look in the mirror. She could feel her heart beating faster. She went out the door.

'Mummy, Harry's . . .'

Oleg's shout died when Rakel appeared at the top of the stairs. She placed one foot cautiously on the top stair – her high heels suddenly felt unsteady, wobbly – but then she found her balance and looked up. Oleg was standing at the foot of the stairs and staring at her open-mouthed. Harry was standing beside him. His eyes were shining so much that she could feel the heat from them burning in her own cheeks. He was holding a bunch of roses in his hand.

'You're beautiful, Mummy,' Oleg whispered.

Rakel closed her eyes. Both side windows were rolled down and the wind brushed against her hair and skin as Harry carefully steered the Escort through the bends on the way down Holmenkollen. The faint smell of washing-up liquid lingered. Rakel moved the sun visor down to check her lipstick and noticed that even the little mirror on the inside had been buffed up.

She smiled at the thought of the first time they had met. He had offered to drive her to work and she had had to help push the car to get it started.

It was incredible really that he still had the same unroadworthy vehicle as then.

She observed him out of the corner of her eye.

And the same sharp bridge of the nose. And the same gently curved, almost feminine lips that contrasted with the other hard masculine features. And the eyes. He could hardly be called good-looking, not in the classical sense. However, he was – what was the word? – real. Real. It was his eyes. No, not his eyes. The expression in his eyes.

He turned towards her as if he could hear her thoughts.

He smiled. And there it was. The childlike softness in his eyes. The boy sitting behind them and laughing at her. There was a certain ingenuousness about the way he looked at her. An uncorrupted sincerity. Honesty. Integrity. It was a look you could rely on. Or you wanted to rely on.

Rakel smiled back.

'What are you thinking about?' he asked and had to get his eyes
back on the road.

'This and that.'

She had had plenty of time to think over the last few weeks. Time
enough to realise that Harry had never made her a promise he hadn't
kept. He had never promised that he would not go to pieces again. He
had never promised that work would not continue to be the most
important thing in his life. He had never promised that it would be
easy with him. All these were promises he had made to himself. She
could see that now.

Olav Hole and Sis were standing at the entrance waiting for them
when they arrived at the house in Oppsal. Harry had talked so much
about it that Rakel occasionally felt that it was her who had grown up
there in the small house.

'Hi, Oleg,' Sis said, looking adult and big-sister-like. 'We've made
meatballs.'

'Have you?' Oleg pushed impatiently at the back of Rakel's seat to
try to get out.

On the way back Rakel leaned her head back in her seat and said
that she thought he was good-looking, but that he shouldn't let it go
to his head. He replied that he thought she was better looking and
that she could let it go to her head as much as she liked as far he was
concerned. When they reached the slopes of Ekeberg and Oslo lay
below them, she saw black Vs intersecting the sky beneath.

'Swallows,' Harry said.

'They're flying low,' she said. 'Doesn't it mean that it's going to rain?'

'Yes, rain is forecast.'

'Oh, that'll be wonderful. Is that why they're out flying, to tell everyone?'

'No,' Harry said. 'They're doing a more useful job than that. They're
clearing the air of insects. Pests and so on.'

'But why are they so busy? They seem almost hysterical, don't they?'

'It's because they haven't got much time. The insects are out now,
but when the sun goes down the hunt for pests has to be over.'

'*Is* over, you mean?'

She turned towards him. He was staring ahead, lost in thought.

'Harry?'

'Yes. Sorry,' he said. 'I was gone there for a minute.'

The audience for the play had assembled in the now shaded square in front of the National Theatre. Celebrities were making conversation with celebrities while journalists were swarming around and cameras were whirring. Apart from rumours about some summer romance, the topic of conversation was the same for everyone: the previous day's arrest of the Courier Killer.

Harry's hand lay lightly against the small of Rakel's back as they rushed towards the entrance. She could feel the heat from the tips of his fingers through the thin material. A face appeared in front of them.

'Roger Gjendem from *Aftenposten*. Sorry, but we're conducting a survey about what people think about the capture of the man who kidnapped the woman chosen to play the lead this evening.'

They stopped and Rakel noticed that the hand on her back was suddenly no longer there.

The journalist's rictus smile was there, but his eyes were roaming.

'We've met before, Inspector Hole. I work on crime reports. We chatted a couple of times when you returned after the case in Sydney. You once said that I was the only journalist who reported what you said accurately. Do you remember me now?'

Harry studied Roger Gjendem's face thoughtfully and nodded.

'Mm. Finished with crime?'

'No, no!' The journalist shook his head energetically. 'I'm just standing in. National holidays. Could I have a comment from Harry Hole, the policeman?'

'No.'

'No? Not even a couple of words?'

'I mean, no, I'm not a policeman,' Harry said.

The journalist seemed taken aback.

'But I saw you . . .'

Harry quickly panned around him before leaning forwards.

'Have you got a business card?'

'Yes . . .'

Gjendem passed him a white card with the blue Gothic letters of *Aftenposten* on; Harry put it in his back pocket.

'The deadline's eleven o'clock.'

'We'll see,' Harry said.

Roger Gjendem stood still with a puzzled expression on his face as Rakel went up the steps with Harry's warm fingers back in position.

A man with a large beard was standing by the entrance smiling at them through tear-stained eyes. Rakel recognised the face from the newspapers. It was Wilhelm Barli.

'I'm so glad to see that you're here together,' he boomed and opened his arms. Harry hesitated, but was caught.

'You must be Rakel.'

Wilhelm Barli twinkled at her over Harry's shoulder as he hugged the tall man like a teddy bear he had lost and found again.

'What was that?' Rakel asked when they had found their seats in the fourth row.

'Male affection,' Harry said. 'He's arty.'

'Not that. All that stuff about you not being a policeman.'

'I did my last day's work as a policeman yesterday.'

She stared at him. 'Why didn't you say anything?'

'I did say something. In the garden that time.'

'And what are you going to do now?'

'Something else.'

'What then?'

'Something completely different. A friend has made me an offer and I have accepted. I hope I'm going to have better times. I can tell you more about it later.'

The curtain went up.

*

There was a roar of applause as the curtain fell and it continued with undiminished vigour for almost ten minutes.

The actors came out and went back in consistently new formations until there were no rehearsed moves left and they just stood and received the applause. Shouts of 'Bravo' reverberated around whenever Toya Harang stepped forward to bow yet again, and in the end everyone who had had any connection with the performance was called up onto the stage and Toya was embraced by Wilhelm Barli, and tears were flowing both in the cast and in the audience.

Even Rakel had to take out her handkerchief as she squeezed Harry's hand.

'You look weird,' Oleg said from the back seat. 'Is something up or what?'

Rakel and Harry twisted their heads round in unison.

'Are you friends again? Is that it?'

Rakel smiled. 'We've never fallen out, Oleg.'

'Harry?'

'Yes, boss?' Harry looked in the mirror.

'Does that mean that we can go to the cinema again soon? To see boys' films?'

'Maybe. If it's a decent boys' film.'

'Oh yes,' Rakel said. 'And what will I do?'

'You can play with Olav and Sis,' Oleg enthused. 'It's really cool, Mummy. Olav taught me how to play chess.'

Harry swung into the drive and pulled up in front of the house. He let the engine idle. Rakel gave Oleg the house key and let him out. They watched him as he sprinted across the gravel.

'My God, how he's grown,' Harry said.

Rakel rested her head against Harry's shoulder. 'Are you coming in?'

'Not now. There's one last thing I have to do at work.'

She stroked his face with her hand. 'You can come later. If you'd like.'

'Mm. Have you thought this through, Rakel?'

She sighed, closed her eyes and nestled the top of her head against his shoulder.

'No. And yes. It feels a bit like jumping out of a burning house. Falling is better than burning.'

'At least until you land.'

'I've come to realise that falling and living have certain things in common. For a start, both are very temporary states of being.'

They sat in silence looking at each other while listening to the irregular rhythm of the engine. Then Harry put a finger under Rakel's chin and kissed her. She had the feeling that she was losing her grip, losing her balance, and her composure, and there was only one thing she could cling on to, and he made her burn and fall at the same time.

She didn't know how long they had been kissing when he gently freed himself from her embrace.

'I'll leave the door open,' she whispered.

She should have known it was stupid.

She should have known it was dangerous.

But she hadn't thought for weeks. She was tired of thinking.

33

Sunday Night. Joseph's Blessing.

There were almost no cars and no people in the car park outside the custody block.

Harry switched off the ignition and the engine died with a death rattle.

He checked his watch: 23.10. Fifty minutes left.

The echo of his footsteps rebounded off Telje, Torp & Aasen's exterior brick walls.

Harry took two deep breaths before he entered.

There was no-one behind the reception desk and there was total silence in the room. He detected a movement to his right. The back of a chair rotated slowly in the duty office. Harry caught sight of half a face with a liver-coloured scar running down like a tear from an eye staring blankly at him. Then the chair returned to its former position and turned its back on him.

Groth. He was alone. Strange. Or perhaps not.

Harry found the key to cell number nine behind the reception desk to the left. Then he walked to the cells. There were voices coming from the warders' room, but conveniently enough number nine was situated so that he didn't have to pass it.

Harry put the key into the lock and turned. He waited for a second; he could hear a movement inside. Then he pulled open the door.

The man staring up at him from the bunk didn't look like a killer. Harry knew that didn't mean a thing. Sometimes they looked like what they were; sometimes they didn't.

This one was good-looking, clean cut, solidly built, short dark hair and blue eyes that may once have been like his mother's, but over the years had become his own. Harry would soon be 40, Sven Sivertsen was over 50. Harry felt sure that most people would have guessed the other way round.

Sivertsen, for one reason or another, was wearing the red prison working trousers and jacket.

'Good evening, Sivertsen. I'm Inspector Hole. Would you mind standing up and turning round.'

Sivertsen raised an eyebrow. Harry dangled the handcuffs in front of him.

'It's the rules.'

Sivertsen got up without a word, and Harry clicked the handcuffs into place and pushed him back down on the bunk.

There were no chairs to sit on in the cell. There was no personal property that could be used to harm yourself or others. In here the state had a monopoly on punishment. Harry leaned against the wall and pulled a crumpled packet of cigarettes out of his pocket.

'You'll set off the smoke alarm,' Sivertsen said. 'They're extremely sensitive.'

His voice was surprisingly high-pitched.

'That's true. You've been here before, haven't you.'

Harry lit the cigarette, stood up on tiptoes, whipped off the alarm cover and took out the batteries.

'And what do the rules say about that?' Sven Sivertsen asked acidly.

'Don't remember. Smoke?'

'What's this? The good-cop trick?'

'No.' Harry smiled. 'We've got so much on you that we don't need to do any play-acting. We don't need to clear up details. We don't need the corpse of Lisbeth Barli. We don't need a confession. We simply don't need your help, Sivertsen.'

'Why are you here then?'

'Curiosity. We deal with deep-sea creatures here and I wanted to see what kind of creature we had got on the hook this time.'

Sivertsen snorted a laugh.

'A fanciful image, but you'll be disappointed, Inspector Hole. It might feel like something big, but I'm afraid this one's just an old boot.'

'Would you mind lowering your voice a bit.'

'Are you frightened someone will hear us?'

'Just do as I say. You seem very calm for someone who's been arrested for four murders.'

'I'm innocent.'

'Mm. Let me give you a brief résumé of the situation, Sivertsen. In your briefcase, we find a red diamond that is not exactly an everyday item, but has been found on the bodies of several of the victims. Plus a Ceská Zbrojovka, a relatively rare weapon in Norway, but the same make as the gun used to murder Barbara Svendsen. According to your statement, you were in Prague on the dates the murders were committed, but we've checked with the airlines and it turns out that you were on a flying visit to Oslo on all of the five relevant dates, including yesterday. How are your alibis for five o'clock on all of the days in question, Sivertsen?'

Sven Sivertsen did not reply.

'Thought so. So don't you *innocent* me, Sivertsen.'

'As if I care what you think, Hole. Was there anything else?'

Harry, his back against the wall, slid down into a crouch position.

'Yes. Do you know Tom Waaler?'

'Who?'

It came quickly. Too quickly. Harry took his time, blew smoke up at the ceiling. The expression on Sven Sivertsen's face was one of abject boredom, but Harry had met killers with a hard shell before – and with a psyche that was like a shaking jelly inside. Nonetheless, he'd also met the deep-frozen variety who were shell right the way through. He wondered how tough this one actually was.

'You don't need to pretend that you don't remember the name of the man who arrested and questioned you, Sivertsen. I wonder if you already knew him?'

Harry noted a tiny little hesitation in his eyes.

'You've been done for smuggling before. The weapon that was found in your case has a particular mark on it made by a machine used to grind away the serial number. In recent years we have found the same marks on more and more unregistered guns in Oslo. We think there is a ring of smugglers responsible.'

'Interesting.'

'Have you been smuggling arms for Waaler, Sivertsen?'

'Jesus, do you guys do that kind of thing, too?'

Sven Sivertsen didn't even blink. However, a little bead of sweat was making its way down from his dense hairline.

'Warm, Sivertsen?'

'Comfortable.'

'Mm.'

Harry got up, went over to the basin and with his back to Sivertsen he loosened a white plastic beaker from the container and turned the tap on full.

'Do you know what, Sivertsen? It didn't occur to me until a colleague told me about the way Waaler arrested you. Then I remembered how Waaler reacted when I said that Beate Lønn had found out who you were. Normally, he's a cold sod, but he went ashen and for a while seemed almost stunned. At that time I thought it was because he realised we'd been outmanoeuvred and we might get landed with another dead body. But when Lønn told me about Waaler's two guns and said that he'd shouted out that you shouldn't shoot him, it all clicked into place. It wasn't the fear of another murder that had given him the shakes. It was my mentioning your name. He knew you. In fact, you're one of his couriers. And Waaler appreciated of course that if you were accused of murder everything would come out into the open. All about the guns you used, the reason for your frequent trips to Oslo, all your contacts. A judge might even mitigate the sentence if you were willing to work with the police. That was why he planned to shoot you.'

'Shoot . . .'

Harry filled the beaker with water, turned and went over to Sven Sivertsen. He put the beaker on the floor in front of him and unlocked his handcuffs. Sivertsen rubbed his wrists.

'Drink up,' Harry said. 'Then you can have a smoke before I put the cuffs back on.'

Sven hesitated. Harry looked at his watch. He still had half an hour left.

'Come on, Sivertsen.'

Sven took the beaker, put his head back and emptied it while keeping an eye on Harry.

Harry put a cigarette between his lips and lit it before giving it to Sivertsen.

'You don't believe me, do you?' Harry said. 'You think the opposite, that Tom Waaler is the one who's going to rescue you from this – what shall we call it? – tiresome situation, don't you? That he'll take a risk as a reward to you for long and loyal service to his wallet. With all you've got on him, the worst that can happen is that you can black-mail him into helping you.'

Harry gently shook his head. 'I thought you were smart, Sivertsen. All these puzzles you set up, the way you stage-managed everything, with you always one step ahead. All this and I imagined someone who knew exactly what we would think and what we would do. But you aren't even up to understanding how a shark like Waaler operates.'

'You're right,' Sivertsen said, blowing smoke up at the ceiling with his eyes half closed. 'I don't believe you.'

Sivertsen tapped at the cigarette. The ash fell outside the plastic beaker he was holding underneath.

Harry wondered if it was a crack he could see. But then he had seen cracks before and had been wrong.

'Did you know that colder weather is forecast?' Harry asked.

'I don't follow Norwegian news.' Sivertsen smirked. The man apparently thought that he had won.

'Rain,' Harry said. 'How was the water, by the way?'

'Like water.'

'Joseph's Blessing does what it's supposed to, then.'

'Joseph's what?'

'Blessing. No taste and no smell. You seem to know about the product. You might even have smuggled it in for him? From Chechnya to Prague to Oslo?' Harry smirked. 'That's an irony of fate.'

'What are you talking about?'

Harry threw something high in the air over to Sivertsen, which he caught and inspected.

'It's empty . . .' He sent Harry a searching look.

'*Skål.*'

'What?'

'Best wishes from our mutual boss, Tom Waaler.'

Harry blew the smoke through his nose while watching Sivertsen.

The involuntary twitch of his brow. The Adam's apple bobbing up and down. The fingers that suddenly needed to scratch his chin.

'With you under suspicion of committing four murders you should be sitting in a high-security prison, Sivertsen. Have you thought about that? Instead of that you're in a standard detention cell where anyone with a police badge can walk in and out as they like. As a detective I could have taken you out, told the guard on duty that I was taking you for questioning, signed you out with some scrawl and then given you a plane ticket to Prague. Or – as in this case – to hell. Who do you think arranged for you to be here, Sivertsen? How do you feel, by the way?'

Sivertsen gulped. Crack. Major crack.

'Why are you telling me this?' he whispered.

Harry shrugged his shoulders.

'Waaler restricts what he tells his underlings and, as you know, I'm curious by nature. Do you, like me, want to see the big picture, Sivertsen? Or are you one of those who believe that you'll get the full enlightenment when you're dead? Fine. My problem is that, in my case, that's still quite a long wait . . .'

Sivertsen went pale.

'Another smoke?' Harry asked. 'Or are you beginning to feel nauseous?'

Sivertsen opened his mouth, seemingly on cue, tossed his head to the side and the next moment yellow vomit splattered against the brick wall. He sat gasping for breath.

Harry glared at the drips that had ricocheted onto his trousers, went to the sink, tore paper off the roll, tore off another piece and gave it to Sivertsen. Sivertsen dried his mouth. Then his head slumped forward and he hid his face in his hands. His voice was tearful as he finally opened up:

'When I came into the hallway . . . I was confused, but, naturally, I understood that he was play-acting. He winked at me and twisted his head in such a way that I was meant to interpret the shouts as meant for someone else. It took me a few seconds to understand the scene. What I thought was the scene. I thought . . . I thought he wanted it to sound as if I was armed so that he had a reason for letting me get away. He had two guns. I thought the other one was for me. So that I was armed in case anyone saw us. I just stood there waiting for him to give me the gun. Then that bloody woman came and ruined everything.'

Harry had taken up his stance with his back to the wall again.

'So you admit that you knew the police were after you in connection with the courier killings?'

Sivertsen shook his head.

'No, no, I'm no murderer. I thought I'd been arrested for smuggling arms. And the diamonds. I knew that Waaler was in charge of all of this and that was why everything was going so smoothly. And that was why he was trying to let me get away. I have to . . .'

More vomit splashed on the floor, a greener colour this time.

Harry handed him more paper.

Sivertsen began to sob.

'How much time do I have left?'

'That depends,' Harry said.

'On what?'

Harry stubbed out his cigarette on the floor, put his hand into his pocket and played his trump card.

'Do you see this?'

He held up a white pill between his thumb and first finger. Sivertsen nodded.

'If you take this within ten minutes of drinking Joseph's Blessing there is a reasonable chance that you'll survive. I got this from a friend who works with pharmaceutical products. Why, I'm sure you're wondering. Well, because I want to strike a deal with you. I want you to testify against Tom Waaler and to say everything you know about his arms smuggling dealings.'

'Yes, yes. Just give me the pill.'

'But can I trust you, Sivertsen?'

'I swear.'

'I need a carefully considered answer, Sivertsen. How do I know that you won't change sides again as soon as I'm out of sight?'

'What?'

Harry put the pill back in his pocket.

'The seconds are ticking away. Why should I trust you, Sivertsen? Give me one good reason.'

'Now?'

'The Blessing stops you breathing. Extremely painful according to those who have seen people take it.'

Sivertsen blinked twice before he began to speak:

'You have to trust me because that's the logical follow-on. If I don't die this evening, Tom Waaler will know that I've uncovered his plan to kill me. And then there's no way back. He'll have to get me before I get him. I simply don't have a choice.'

'Well done, Sivertsen. Go on.'

'I haven't got a chance in here. I'll be done for long before they come to get me early tomorrow. My only chance is if Waaler is exposed and put behind bars as soon as possible. And the only person who can help me is . . . you.'

'Bullseye. Congratulations,' Harry said, getting up. 'Hands behind your back, please.'

'But . . .'

'Do as I say. We've got to get out of here.'

'Get the pill . . .'

'The pill's called Flunipam and it's only really any good for insomnia.'

Sven gawped at Harry in disbelief.

'You . . .'

Harry was ready for the attack. He stepped to the side and punched hard and low. Sivertsen made a sound like air being deflated from a beach ball and folded in the middle.

Harry held him up with one hand and secured the handcuffs with the other.

'I wouldn't be too worried, Sivertsen. I emptied the contents of Waaler's ampoule down the sink last night. Any complaints about the taste of the water you'll have to take up with Oslo Water.'

'But . . . I . . .'

They both looked down at the vomit.

'Eyes too big for your belly,' Harry said. 'I won't tell anyone.'

*

The back of the chair in the duty room rotated slowly. A half-closed eye hove into view. Then it reacted, and the loose folds of skin slid back to reveal a large, glaring eye. 'Griever' Groth shifted his fat body surprisingly quickly out of the chair.

'What's this?' he barked.

'The prisoner from cell number nine,' Harry said nodding towards Sivertsen. 'He's needed for questioning on the sixth floor. Where do I sign for him?'

'Questioning? I haven't been told about any questioning.'

The Griever had taken up a stance a short way back from the reception desk with his arms crossed and his legs wide apart.

'As far as I'm aware, we don't usually tell you about that kind of thing, Groth,' Harry said.

The Griever's eyes darted in confusion from Harry to Sivertsen and back again.

'Relax,' Harry said. 'It's just a few changes to the plans. The prisoner won't take his medicine. We'll find another way.'

'I've no idea what you're talking about.'

'Of course not, and if you want to avoid hearing any more, I suggest you put the signing-out book on the desk now, Groth. We've got a lot to do.'

The Griever stared at him with his grieving eye while rubbing the other.

Harry concentrated on breathing and hoped that his pounding heart would not be visible from the outside. All of his plans could collapse like a house of cards at this point. Handy theme for metaphors. He had a terrible hand of cards. Not one single ace. The only thing he could hope for was that Groth's addled brain would connect in the way he anticipated. An anticipation that was loosely based on Aune's fundamental principle that man's ability to think rationally when self-interest was at stake was inversely proportionate to intelligence.

The Griever grunted.

Harry hoped that meant that he had appreciated the point; that there was less risk for the Griever if Harry signed out the prisoner according to regulations. That way, later on, he could tell the detectives everything exactly as it happened. Instead of risking being caught lying when he said that no-one had come in or gone out at the time of the mysterious death in cell number nine. He hoped Groth was thinking at this very moment that Harry could take a weight off his mind at the stroke of a pen and that this was good news. No reason to double-check. After all, Waaler had said that this idiot was on their side now.

The Griever cleared his throat.

Harry scribbled his name on the dotted line.

'March,' he said, giving Sivertsen a shove.

The night air in the car park outside the custody block tasted like cold beer in his throat.

34

Sunday Night. The Ultimatum.

RAKEL WOKE UP.

She had heard the door go downstairs.

She rolled over in bed and looked at the clock: 12.45.

She stretched and lay still, listening. The feeling of sleepy well-being was replaced by the tingle of expectation. She would pretend that she was sleeping when he crept into bed. She knew it was a childish game, but she enjoyed it. He would just lie there breathing. And when she turned in her sleep and her hand happened to touch his stomach, she would hear him breathing faster and deeper. Then they would lie there without moving and see who could hold out longest, a kind of competition. And he would lose.

Maybe.

She closed her eyes.

After a while, she opened them again. A nagging fear had entered her mind.

She got up, opened the bedroom door and listened.

Not a sound.

She went over to the stairs.

'Harry?'

Her voice sounded anxious and it frightened her even more. She pulled herself together and went downstairs.

There was no-one there.

She concluded that the unlocked front door had not been properly closed and that she had woken up when it blew open.

After locking it she sat down in the kitchen with a glass of milk. She listened to the creaking of the wooden house. The old walls seemed to be talking.

At 1.30 she got up. Harry had gone back to his place. And he would never know that he could have won tonight.

On her way to the bedroom a thought occurred to her and created momentary panic. She turned back. And gave a sigh of relief when she saw from the door of Oleg's room that he was asleep in bed.

Nevertheless, she woke up an hour later with nightmares and lay tossing and turning for the rest of the night.

The white Ford Escort passed through the summer's night like a rumbling, ageing submarine.

'Økernveien,' Harry mumbled. 'Sons gate.'

'What?' Sivertsen asked.

'Just talking to myself.'

'What about?'

'About the shortest route.'

'Where to?'

'You'll soon find out.'

They parked down a small one-way street where a few detached houses had strayed into a zone of high-rise flats. Harry leaned over Sivertsen and pushed the door open on the passenger side. The car had been broken into a number of years ago and the passenger door wouldn't open from the outside. Rakel joked about it, about cars and the personality of car owners. He was not sure that he had grasped the subtext. Harry walked round the car to the passenger door, pulled Sivertsen out and told him to stand with his back to him.

'Are you a southpaw?' Harry asked while unlocking the handcuffs.

'What?'

'Do you punch best with your left hand or your right?'

'Oh, I see. I don't punch.'

'Terrific.'

Harry attached the handcuffs to Sivertsen's right wrist and to his own left. Sivertsen sent him a surprised look.

'Don't want to lose you, old chap.'

'Wouldn't it have been easier to point a gun at me?'

'Course it would, but I had to be a good boy and hand it over a couple of weeks ago. Let's go.'

They cut across a field towards the dark, heavy profiles of high-rise flats towering up against the night sky.

'Nice to be back in old familiar territory?' Harry asked when they stood in front of the entrance to the student block.

Sivertsen shrugged his shoulders.

Once inside, Harry heard something he would have preferred not to hear. Footsteps on the stairs. He shot a quick glance around. He saw the light in the porthole-shaped window in the lift door and stepped sideways into the lift, dragging Sivertsen after him. The lift rocked under their weight.

'Guess which floor we're going to!' Harry said.

Sivertsen rolled his eyes as Harry dangled a bunch of keys with a plastic skull attached in front of his face.

'Not in the mood for games? OK, take us to the fourth, Sivertsen.'

Sivertsen pressed the button with the figure four on and looked up, waiting for the lift to move. Harry scrutinised Sivertsen's face. He was a damned good actor; he had to give him that.

'The grille,' Harry said.

'What?'

'The lift won't move unless you close the grille. You know that.'

'This?'

Harry nodded. The metal rattled as Sivertsen pulled the grille door to the right. The lift still didn't budge.

Harry felt a bead of sweat forming on his brow.

'Pull it right to the end,' Harry said.

'Like this?'

'Cut out the play-acting,' Harry said, swallowing. 'It has to be pulled right over. If it doesn't touch the contact on the floor by the door frame, the lift won't work.'

Sivertsen smiled.

Harry clenched his right fist.

The lift gave a jerk and the white brick wall began to move behind the black, glistening iron grille. They passed one lift door and through the porthole Harry saw the back of someone's head, going downstairs. One of the students, he hoped. At any rate, Bjørn Holm had said that forensics had finished their work here.

'You don't like lifts, do you?'

Harry didn't answer; he just watched the wall gliding by.

'A tiny little phobia?'

The lift stopped suddenly and Harry had to take a step to the side not to lose balance. The floor rocked beneath them and the wall was visible through the porthole.

'What the fuck are you doing?' he whispered.

'You're soaked in sweat, Inspector Hole. I thought this would be a good moment to get one thing clear with you.'

'This is not a good moment for anything. Move, or else . . .'

Sivertsen had taken up a position in front of the lift buttons and didn't seem to have any intention of moving. Harry raised his right hand. It was then that he saw it. The chisel in Sivertsen's left hand. With the green handle.

'I found it at the back of the seat,' Sivertsen said with almost an apologetic smile. 'You should tidy up your car. Are you listening to me now?'

The steel flashed. Harry tried to think. Tried to keep panic at bay.
'I'm listening.'

'Good, because what I'm going to say requires a little bit of concentration. I'm innocent. That is, I did smuggle arms and diamonds. I've been doing that for years. However, I have not taken anyone's life.'

Sivertsen raised the chisel when Harry moved his hand. Harry dropped it again.

'The gun-running went through someone called Prince, who I've known for a little while now is the same person as Inspector Tom Waaler. And even more interesting, I can prove that it's Tom Waaler. Also, if I've understood the situation correctly, you're dependent on my testimony and my evidence to nail Tom Waaler. If you don't nail him, he'll nail you. Right?'

Harry's eyes were on the chisel.

'Hole?'

Harry nodded.

Sivertsen's laugh was high-pitched, like a girl's.

'Isn't that a wonderful paradox, Hole? Here we are, an arms smuggler and a flatfoot, chained together and totally dependent on one another, and still we're puzzling how to kill each other?'

'True paradoxes don't exist,' Harry said. 'What do you want?'

'I want,' said Sivertsen, raising the chisel in the air and holding it so that the handle pointed at Harry, 'you to find the person who made it look as if I'd killed four people. If you can do that, then you can have Waaler's head served on a silver platter. You scrub my back and I'll scrub yours.'

Harry gave Sivertsen an intense glare. Their handcuffs rubbed together.

'OK,' Harry said. 'But let's do things in the right order. First we put Waaler behind bars. That done, we can work undisturbed and I can help you.'

Sivertsen shook his head.

'I'm aware of the case against me. I've had an entire day to think about it, Hole. The only thing I have to bargain with is my evidence against Waaler, and the only person I have to bargain with is you. The police have already received the bouquets for their triumph and so none of them is going to look into this case with fresh eyes and risk the success of the century being turned into the blunder of the century. The maniac who murdered these women wants me to take the rap. I've been set up. And I don't have a chance in hell without help.'

'Are you aware that Tom Waaler and his colleagues are busting a gut at this very moment to find us? For every hour that passes, they'll be closer. And when – not if – they find us, we're done for, both of us?'

'Yes.'

'So why take the risk? Given that what you say about the police is correct, that they won't under any circumstances waste more time on this case, isn't twenty years in prison still better than losing your life?'

'Twenty years in prison is not a choice I have any more, Hole.'

'Why not?'

'Because I've just found out that something is about to change my life for ever.'

'And that is?'

'I'm going to be a father, Inspector Hole.'

Harry blinked twice.

'You have to find the real murderer before Waaler finds us, Hole. It's as simple as that.'

Sivertsen passed the chisel to Harry.

'Do you believe me?'

'Yes,' Harry lied, stuffing the chisel into his jacket pocket.

The steel cables screamed as the lift began to move again.

35

Sunday Night. Fascinating Nonsense.

'Hope you like Iggy Pop,' Harry said handcuffing Sven Sivertsen to the radiator under the window of room 406. 'This is the only view we're going to have for a while.'

'Could be worse,' Sven said looking up at the poster. 'I saw Iggy and the Stooges in Berlin. I suppose before the owner of the poster was born.'

Harry checked his watch: 1.10. Waaler and his people had probably already checked his flat in Sofies gate and were doing the rounds of the hotels. It was impossible to say how much time they had left. Harry sank down into the sofa and rubbed his face with both palms.

Damned Sivertsen!

The plan had been so simple. Just find a safe place, then ring Bjarne Møller and the head of *Kripos* and let them hear Sven Sivertsen's testimony over the telephone. Then tell them they had three hours to arrest Tom Waaler before Harry rang the press and dropped the bombshell. A simple choice. All he and Sivertsen had to do was sit tight until they had confirmation that Tom Waaler was in the slammer. Afterwards,

Harry would phone Roger Gjendem at *Aftenposten* and ask him to ring the head of *Kripos* for a comment about the arrest. Only then – when it was public – would Harry and Sivertsen crawl out of their hidey-hole.

But for Sivertsen and his ultimatum, it would have been relatively plain sailing.

'What if . . .'

'Don't try it, Hole.'

Sivertsen didn't even look at him.

Damn him!

Harry checked his watch again. He knew he had to stop doing it. He had to shut out the time element and collect his thoughts, regroup, improvise, see what options the situation threw up. Shit!

'OK,' Harry said, closing his eyes. 'Give me your side of things.'

The handcuffs rattled as Sven Sivertsen leaned forwards.

Harry stood by the open window smoking a cigarette while listening to Sven Sivertsen's high-pitched voice. He began with the time when he was 17 and met his father for the first time.

'My mother thought I was in Copenhagen, but I'd gone to Berlin to search him out. He lived in a huge house with guard dogs in the area around Tiergarten Park, where the embassies are. I persuaded the gardener to accompany me to the front door and I rang the bell. When he opened up it was like looking at a mirror image. We just stood there gawping at each other. I didn't even need to say who I was. In the end he began to cry and embraced me. I stayed with him for four weeks. He was married and had three children. I didn't ask him what he did and he didn't tell me. Randi, his wife, was staying at some expensive sanatorium in the Alps with an incurable heart ailment. It sounded like something out of a romance novel, and I did sometimes wonder if that was what had inspired him to send her there. There was no doubt that he loved her. Or it might be more correct to say that he was in love. When he talked about her dying, it sounded like something out of a women's weekly mag. One afternoon one of his wife's girlfriends came by. We drank tea and my father said that it was fate that had sent Randi his way, but they had loved each other so much and so shamelessly that fate had punished them by letting her wither away with her beauty still untarnished. He could say things like that without a hint of a blush. That night, when I couldn't sleep, I went downstairs to rummage around in his drinks cabinet and saw the girlfriend sneaking out of his bedroom.'

Harry nodded. Was there more of a nip in the night air, or was he imagining it? Sivertsen shifted position.

'During the day I had the house to myself. He had two daughters, one fourteen and the other sixteen. Bodil and Alice. For them, of course, I was incredibly exciting. An unheard of older half-brother who had dropped in out of the blue. Both of them fell in love with me, but I chose Bodil, the younger one. One day she came home early from school and I took her into her father's bedroom. She was removing the blood-stained sheets afterwards when I chased her out, locked the door, gave the key to the gardener and asked him to give it to my father. At breakfast the next morning Father asked me if I wanted to work for him. That was how I got into smuggling diamonds.'

Sivertsen broke off.

'Time's ticking away,' Harry said.

'I worked from Oslo. Apart from a couple of early blunders that led to two conditional sentences, I did well. My speciality was going through customs at airports. It was very easy. Just dress up as a respectable person and don't look frightened. And I wasn't frightened; I didn't give a damn. I used to wear a priest's dog collar. Of course it's such an obvious trick that it can arouse the suspicions of the customs people right away, but the thing is you also have to know how a priest walks, how he wears his hair, what shoes he likes, the way he holds his hands and the facial expression he uses. If you learn these things, you'll almost never be stopped. A customs officer may still be suspicious, but the threshold for stopping priests is higher. Any customs officer going through a priest's suitcase without finding anything while long-haired hippies stroll through is bound to be the subject of complaints. The customs set-up is like any other. They're bent on giving the public a positive – though erroneous – impression that they're doing a good job.

'My father died of cancer in 1985. Randi's incurable heart ailment was still incurable, but it was not bad enough to prevent her from flying back home and taking over the business. I don't know if she found out that I had deflowered Bodil, but I soon found myself without work. Norway was no longer an area they wanted to operate in, she said, but she didn't offer me anything else. After some years of unemployment in Oslo I moved to Prague, which was a smugglers' El Dorado after the fall of the Iron Curtain. I spoke good German and soon found my feet. I earned fast money, but spent it just as quickly. I made friends, but no strong attachments to anyone. Not to women, either. I didn't need to, because do you know what, Hole? I discovered that I had inherited a gift from my father – the power of falling in love.'

Sivertsen nodded towards the Iggy Pop poster.

'There's no greater aphrodisiac for a woman than a man who is in love. I specialised in married women – they didn't give me so much trouble afterwards. When I was strapped for cash, they could also be a welcome, though fleeting, source of income. And so the years flitted by without a twinge of worry. For more than thirty years my smile was free, the bed my stamping ground and my dick the relay baton.'

Sivertsen rested his head against the wall and closed his eyes.

'It must sound cynical, but you can take it from me that every declaration of love that came out of my mouth was just as genuine and sincere as those my stepmother received from my father. I gave them everything I had, until it was over and I showed them the door. I couldn't afford a sanatorium. It always ended like that and that was how I thought it would always be. Until one autumn day I went into the café in Grand Hotel Europa in Wenceslas Square and there she was. Eva. Yes, that was her name, and it's not true that paradoxes do not exist, Hole. The first thing that struck me was that she was no beauty; she just behaved like one. However, people who are convinced that they are beautiful are beautiful. I have a certain knack with women and I went over to her. She didn't tell me to go to hell; she just treated me with a distant courtesy that drove me wild.'

Sivertsen gave a knowing smile.

'There's no stronger aphrodisiac for a man than a woman who's not in love. She was twenty-six years younger than me, had more style than I will ever have and – most of all – she didn't need me. She could continue with her work that she thinks I know nothing about, whipping German businessmen and giving them blow jobs.'

'So why didn't she?' Harry asked, puffing smoke at Iggy.

'She didn't have a chance. I was in love, enough for two men, but I wanted her for myself, and Eva is like most women who are not in love – she values economic security. So, to acquire exclusivity I had to acquire some money. Smuggling blood diamonds from Sierre Leone was low-risk, but it did not produce enough money to make me irresistibly wealthy. Drugs was high-risk. That was how I got into smuggling arms and met Prince. We met twice in Prague to agree on procedures and conditions. The second time was in an open-air restaurant in Václav Square. I persuaded Eva to act the photo-snapping tourist, and the table where Prince and I were sitting happened to come up on the majority of the photos. People who don't settle their accounts after I've done jobs for them usually receive a photo in the post together with a reminder. It works. Prince was promptitude personified, though, and I've never had any trouble with him. I only found out that he was a policeman some time later.'

Harry closed the window and sat on the sofa bed.

'In spring I received a phone call,' Sivertsen said. 'From a Norwegian with an Østland dialect. I've no idea how he managed to get hold of my telephone number. He seemed to know all about me. It was almost creepy. No, it *was* creepy. He knew who my mother was, about the prison sentences I had had, and about the pentagram-shaped blood diamonds I had specialised in for years. Worst of all, though: he knew I had started smuggling guns. He wanted both. A diamond and a Ceská with a silencer. He offered an unimaginably high sum. I said "no" to the weapon, that it would have to go via another channel, but he insisted it had to come directly through me, no middle-man. He raised his offer. And Eva is, as I have said, a demanding woman, and I couldn't afford to lose her. So we agreed.'

'What exactly did you agree?'

'He had very specific requests regarding the delivery. It had to take place in Frogner Park, directly below the Monolith. The first delivery was just over five weeks ago. It had to be at five o'clock, in the peak period when tourists were about and people were walking in the park after work. That made it easier for him and for me to get in and out without attracting attention, he said. The chances of me being recognised were minimal anyway. Many years ago, at my local bar in Prague, I saw a Norwegian guy who used to beat me up at school. He looked right through me. He and a lady I had while she was honeymooning in Prague are the only people from Oslo I've seen since I moved away from here, you know.'

Harry nodded.

'Anyway,' Sivertsen said, 'the client didn't want us to meet and that was fine by me. I was to carry the items in a brown polythene bag and put it in the green litter bin at the centre of Frogner Park in front of the Fountain and then leave immediately. It was very important that I was on time. The agreed sum was paid up front into my account in Switzerland. He said that the simple fact that he had found me was unlikely to give me any ideas about tricking him and that was what he was counting on. He was right. Could I have a cigarette?'

Harry lit it for him.

'The day after the first handover he rang me and ordered a Glock 23 and another blood diamond for the following week. Same place, same time, same procedure. It was a Sunday, but there were just as many people there.'

'Same day and same time as the first killing, of Marius Veland.'

'What?'

'Nothing. Go on.'

'This was repeated three times. Always with five days between. But the last time was a little different. I was told about two deliveries: one on the Saturday and one on the Sunday, yesterday that is. The client asked me to stay at my mother's on Saturday night so that he could contact me should there be any changes to the plan. Fine by me. I was going to do that anyway. I was looking forward to seeing Mother. After all, I had good news for her.'

'That she was going to be a grandmother.'

Sivertsen nodded.

'And that I was going to get married.'

Harry stubbed out his cigarette.

'So what you're saying is that the diamond and the gun we found in your briefcase were for the handover on Sunday?'

'Yes.'

'Mm.'

'And now?' Sivertsen asked, after a prolonged silence.

Harry put his hands behind his head, leaned back against the sofa bed and let out a yawn.

'As an old Iggy fan you must have heard *Blah Blah Blah*? Good album. Fascinating nonsense.'

'Fascinating nonsense?'

Sven Sivertsen hit his elbow on the radiator creating a hollow and empty clang.

Harry got up. 'I need to clear my head. There's a 24-hour garage down in the street. Do you want me to bring you anything?'

Sivertsen closed his eyes.

'Listen, Hole. We're in the same boat. Sinking. OK? You're not just a mean bastard, you're stupid with it.'

Harry grinned and got up.

'I'll have a think about that.'

When Harry returned 20 minutes later, Sven was asleep with his arm attached to the top of the radiator, as if waving.

Harry put two hamburgers, chips and a large bottle of Coca-Cola on the table.

Sven rubbed the sleep out of his eyes.

'Did you have a think, Hole?'

'Yup.'

'And what did you think about?'

'About the pictures your girlfriend took of you and Waaler in Prague.'

'What's that got to do with anything?'

Harry unlocked the handcuff.

'The pictures have nothing to do with the case. I was thinking that she was pretending to be a tourist, doing what tourists do.'

'And that is?'

'What I said. Taking pictures.'

Sivertsen rubbed his wrists and scrutinised the food on the table.

'What about a glass to drink from, Hole?'

Harry pointed to the bottle.

Sven unscrewed the top while squinting through semi-closed eyes at Harry.

'So you'll risk drinking from the same bottle as a serial killer?'

Harry replied with a mouth full of hamburger: 'Same boat. Same bottle.'

Olaug Sivertsen was sitting in her living room staring vacantly ahead of her. She had not switched on the light in the hope that they would think she wasn't at home and give up. They had been ringing the phone, ringing the doorbell, shouting from the garden and throwing pebbles at the kitchen window. 'No comment,' she had said, and pulled out the telephone jack plug. In the end they stood around outside, waiting with their long, black telephoto lenses. Once she had gone to draw the curtains in front of one of the windows and she had heard the insect noises from their cameras. Zzzz, Zzzz, click. Zzzz, Zzzz, click.

Almost a day had passed and still the police had not discovered their mistake. It was the weekend. Perhaps they were waiting until Monday and their usual office hours before sorting it out.

If only she had someone to talk to. But Ina still had not returned from her holiday with this mysterious gentleman. Perhaps she should ring Beate, the policewoman? It wasn't her fault they had arrested Sven. Beate seemed to know that he wasn't the kind of person to go round killing people. She had even given her a telephone number and said that she could ring if there was anything she wanted to tell them. Anything.

Olaug gazed out of the window. The silhouette of the dead pear tree looked like fingers grasping the moon, which hung low over the garden and the station building. She had never seen a moon like it before. It resembled a dead man's face. Blue veins standing out against white skin.

What had happened to Ina? Sunday afternoon at the latest, she had said. Olaug had imagined how cosy it would be with a cup of tea, and Ina would be able to meet Sven. Ina who was so reliable as far as punctuality and so on went.

Olaug waited until the wall clock struck two.

Then she pulled out the telephone number.

There was an answer at the third ring.

'Beate,' said a sleepy voice.

'Hello, this is Olaug Sivertsen. I'm really terribly sorry for ringing so late.'

'Don't worry, Fru Sivertsen.'

'Olaug.'

'Olaug. Sorry, I'm not quite awake yet.'

'I'm ringing because I'm concerned about Ina, my lodger. She should have been home ages ago and with all the things that have happened, well, yes, I'm worried.'

When Olaug did not get an immediate response, she wondered if Beate had gone back to sleep. But then her voice was there again, and this time it was not sleepy.

'Are you telling me that you've got a lodger, Olaug?'

'Yes, indeed. Ina. She has got the maid's room. Oh, yes, I didn't show you, did I. It's because it's on the other side of the back steps. She's been away all weekend.'

'Where? Who with?'

'I wish I knew. The person is a relatively new acquaintance whom I have not yet been introduced to. She just said they were going to his holiday cabin.'

'You should have told us that before, Olaug.'

'Should I? I'm really very sorry . . . I . . .'

Olaug could feel the tears welling up, but she was powerless to prevent it.

'No, I didn't mean it like that, Olaug,' she heard Beate hasten to add. 'It's not you I'm angry with. It's my job to check these things. You couldn't have known this was relevant to our inquiry. I'll ring the police control room and they'll phone you back for personal details about Ina so that they can look into the matter. I'm sure nothing has happened to her, but it's better to be on the safe side, isn't it. After that, I think you should try to get a little sleep. I'll ring you back early in the morning. Shall we say that, Olaug?'

'Yes,' Olaug said, trying to put a smile into her voice. She really wanted to ask Beate if she knew how things were going with Sven, but she couldn't bring herself to ask.

'Yes, let's say that. Bye, Beate.'

She replaced the handset with tears running down her cheeks.

Beate settled down and tried to sleep. She listened to the house. It was talking. Mother had switched off the television at 11.00 and now it was quite still on the floor below. Beate wondered if her mother was also thinking about him, about her father. They seldom spoke of him.

It took too much out of them. She had started looking for a flat in the city centre. Last year she had begun to feel confined living on one floor in her mother's house. Especially since she had started seeing Halvorsen, the rock-steady officer from Steinkjer whom she called by his surname and who treated her with a kind of respect and trepidation that she unaccountably set great store by. She would not have so much room in Oslo. And she would miss the sounds of this house, the wordless monologues she had gone to sleep to all her life.

The telephone rang again. Beate sighed and reached out her arm.

'Yes, Olaug?'

'It's Harry. You seem to be awake already.'

She sat up in bed.

'Yes, the phone's been going non-stop tonight. What's up?'

'I need some help. And you're the only person I dare trust.'

'Right. Knowing you, I suppose that means hassle for me.'

'Loads of hassle. Are you with me?'

'What if I say "no"?'

'Listen to what I have to say first, and then you can say "no" afterwards.'

36

Monday. The Photograph.

AT 5.45 ON MONDAY MORNING THE SUN WAS SHINING DOWN FROM Ekeberg Ridge. The Securitas guard on duty in reception at Police HQ yawned loudly and raised his eyes from his *Aftenposten* as the first arrival signed in with his ID card.

'Rain on the way according to the paper,' he said, happy to see another human being.

The tall, sombre-looking man cast a brief glance at him, but he didn't respond.

During the next two minutes three other men followed him in, all equally uncommunicative and sombre.

At 6.00 the four men were sitting in the Divisional Commander's office on the sixth floor.

'Well,' the Divisional Commander said, 'one of our police inspectors has taken a possible killer from the custody block and nobody knows where they are.'

One of the things that made the Divisional Commander relatively well suited to his position was his ability to sum up a problem. Another was his ability to formulate what had to be done concisely:

'So I propose we find them quick as fuck. What's happened so far?'

The head of *Kripos* stole a furtive glance at Møller and Waaler before clearing his throat and answering:

'We've put a small but experienced group of detectives on the case. Handpicked by Inspector Waaler, who is leading the search. Three from POT. Two from Crime Squad. They began last night only an hour after the officers in the custody block reported that Sivertsen had not been returned.'

'Snappy work. But why haven't the uniformed police been informed? And the patrol cars?'

'We wanted to await developments and make a decision at this meeting, Lars. Hear what you thought.'

'What I thought?'

The head of *Kripos* ran his finger along his top lip.

'Inspector Waaler has promised that he'll catch Hole and Sivertsen before the day is out. We've managed to confine the spread of information so far. We four and Groth in the custody block are the only ones who know that Sivertsen is out. In addition, we've phoned Ullersmo and cancelled Sivertsen's cell and transport. We told them that we'd received information which gave us reason to believe that Sivertsen might not be safe there and therefore he would be transferred to a, for the moment, secret destination. To cut a long story short, we're in a position to keep the lid on this until Waaler and his group have resolved the situation for us. Naturally, it is your decision, though, Lars.'

The Divisional Commander placed the tips of his fingers together and nodded thoughtfully. Then he got up and went to the window, where he remained with his back to them.

'Last week I took a taxi. The driver had a paper lying open on the seat next to me. I asked him what he thought about the Courier Killer. It's always interesting to hear what people at grass-roots level think.

He said it was the same problem with the Courier Killer as with the World Trade Center: questions were being asked in the wrong order. Everyone was asking "who" and "how". But to solve a riddle you first have to ask another question. And do you know what that question is? Torleif?'

The head of *Kripos* didn't answer.

'It's "why", Torleif. This taxi driver was no dummy. Has anyone here asked themselves that question, gentlemen?'

The Divisional Commander rocked on his heels and waited.

'With all respect to the taxi driver,' the head of *Kripos* said finally, 'I'm not so sure there is a "why" in this case. At least, not a rational "why". All of us here know that Hole is psychologically unstable and an alcoholic. That's why he's being dismissed.'

'Even crazy people have motives, Torleif.'

There was the sound of someone discreetly clearing their throat.

'Yes, Waaler.'

'Batouti.'

'Batouti?'

'The Egyptian pilot who deliberately crashed a full passenger plane to avenge himself on the airline who had demoted him.'

'What are you getting at, Waaler?'

'I ran after Harry and talked to him in the car park after we'd arrested Sivertsen on Saturday evening. It was obvious that he was bitter, both for being dismissed and because he thought we'd cheated him out of the credit he was due for arresting the Courier Killer.'

'Batouti . . .'

The Divisional Commander shaded his eyes from the first rays of sun to hit his window.

'You haven't said anything yet, Bjarne. What do you think?'

Bjarne Møller stared up at the silhouette in front of the window. He had such pains in his stomach that he not only felt that he was going to explode, he hoped he would. From the moment he was woken up in the night and informed about the kidnapping he had waited for someone to give him a good shake and tell him he was having a nightmare.

'I don't know,' he sighed. 'Quite frankly, I don't understand what's going on.'

The Divisional Commander nodded slowly.

'If it leaks out that we've kept this under wraps we'll be crucified,' he said.

'A concise summary, Lars,' the head of *Kripos* said. 'But if it leaks out that we've let a serial killer go, we'll also be crucified. Even if we find him again. There's still one way of resolving this problem on the quiet. Waaler has, I'm led to understand, a plan.'

'And what is it, Waaler?'

Tom Waaler put his left hand round his clenched fist.

'Let's put it this way,' he said. 'It's absolutely clear to me that we cannot afford to fail, so I may have to use some unconventional methods. Bearing possible repercussions in mind, I'm going to suggest that you know nothing about the plan.'

The Divisional Commander swivelled round with a mildly astonished expression on his face.

'That's very generous of you, Waaler, but I'm afraid we cannot agree to –'

'I insist.'

The Divisional Commander frowned.

'You insist? Are you aware of the risks, Waaler?'

Waaler opened the palms of his hands and examined them.

'Yes, but it's my responsibility. I ran the investigation and worked closely with Hole. As the person in charge I ought to have seen the signs before and done something. At any rate, after the conversation in the car park.'

The Divisional Commander gave Waaler a searching look. He turned back to the window and stayed there as a rectangle of light crept across the floor. Then he raised his shoulders and shook himself as if he were freezing cold.

'You've got until midnight,' he said to the window pane. 'Then the news of the disappearance will be announced to the press. And this meeting never took place.'

On the way out Møller noticed the head of *Kripos* squeeze Waaler's hand and flash him a warm smile of gratitude. The way you thank a colleague for loyalty, Møller mused. The way you tacitly appoint a Crown Prince.

Police Officer Bjørn Holm from Forensics felt a complete fool standing there with a microphone in his hand looking at the Japanese faces staring expectantly back at him. His palms were sweaty, and not just from the heat. Quite the contrary, the temperature in the air-conditioned luxury bus standing outside Hotel Bristol was several degrees lower than the temperature in the morning sun outside. It was from having to speak into a microphone. In English.

He had been introduced by the guide as a Norwegian police officer and an old man with a smile on his face had pulled out his camera as if Bjørn Holm was an integral part of the sightseeing tour. He looked at his watch: 7.00. He had more groups to see, so it was simply a question of pressing on. He took a deep breath and started the sentence he had rehearsed on the way:

'We have checked the schedules with all the tour operators here in Oslo,' Holm said. 'And this is one of the groups that visited Frogner Park around five o'clock on Saturday. What I want to know is: how many of you took pictures there?'

No reaction.

Holm was disconcerted and glanced over to the guide.

He bowed with a smile, relieved him of the microphone and gave the passengers what Holm could only assume was roughly the same message he had given, in Japanese. He concluded with a small bow. Holm surveyed all the outstretched arms. They were going to have a busy day at the photo lab.

*

Roger Gjendem was humming a song about 'turning Japanese' as he locked his car. The distance from the car park to *Aftenposten*'s new offices in the Post House was short, but still he knew he would jog in, not because he was late, quite the opposite. The reason was that Roger Gjendem was one of the lucky few who looked forward to going to work every day, who could not wait until he had all the familiar things around him that reminded him of work: the office with the telephone and the computer, a pile of the day's newspapers, the hum of colleagues' voices, the gurgling coffee machine, the gossip in the smokers' room, the alert atmosphere at the morning meeting. He had spent the previous day outside Olaug Sivertsen's house with nothing more than a picture of her in the window to show for it. But it was good. He liked difficult tasks. And there were more than enough of those in the crime section. A crime junkie. That was what Devi had called him. He didn't like her using those words. Thomas, his little brother, was a junkie. Roger was a hard worker who had studied political science and happened to like working as a crime reporter. That apart, she had a point of course, in that there were aspects of the job that were reminiscent of an addiction. After working with politics he had subbed in the crime section of the paper and it was not long before he felt the rush that only the daily adrenalin kick of stories about life and death can give. The same day he talked to the chief editor and was immediately transferred on a permanent basis. The editor had obviously seen it happen to others before him. And from that day on Roger jogged from his car to work.

On this day, however, he was pulled up before he got into his stride.

'Good morning,' said the man who had appeared from nowhere and who now stood in front of him. He was wearing a short, black leather jacket and aviator sunglasses even though it was fairly dark in the multistorey car park. Roger knew a policeman when he saw one.

'Good morning,' Roger said.

'I've got a message for you, Gjendem.'

The man's arms hung straight down. His hands were covered in black hair. Roger thought that he would have appeared more natural if he had kept them in the pockets of his leather jacket. Or behind his back. Or folded in front of him. As it was, you had the impression he was about to use his hands for something, but it was impossible to guess what.

'Yeah?' Roger asked. He heard the echo of his own 'e' vibrate briefly between the walls, the sound of a question mark.

The man leaned forward.

'Your brother's doing time in Ullersmo,' the man said.

'So what?'

Roger knew that the morning sun was shining outside in Oslo, but down in the car catacombs it had suddenly turned ice cold.

'If you care about what happens to him, you need to do us a favour. Are you listening, Gjendem?'

Roger nodded in amazement.

'If Inspector Harry Hole rings you, we want you to do the following. Ask where he is. If he won't tell you, arrange to meet him. Say that you won't risk printing his story until you've met him face to face. The meeting must be arranged before midnight tonight.'

'What story?'

'He might make unfounded allegations against a police inspector whose name I cannot reveal, but you needn't bother about that. It'll never get into print anyway.'

'But –'

'Are you listening? After he rings, I want you to phone this number and tell us where Hole is or where and when you've arranged to meet him. Is that clear?'

He put his left hand in his pocket and passed Roger a slip of paper.

Roger read the number and shook his head. As frightened as he was, he could feel laughter bubbling up inside him. Or maybe his fear was precisely the reason.

'I know you're a policeman,' Roger said, repressing his smile. 'You must know that this won't wash. I'm a journalist, I can't –'

'Gjendem.'

The man took off his sunglasses. Even though it was dark, the pupils were just small dots in the grey irises.

'Your little brother's in cell A107. Every Tuesday – like most of the other old lags – he has his junk smuggled in. He injects it straight-away, never checks it. That's been fine so far. Do you see what I mean?'

Roger wondered if his ears had deceived him. He knew they had not.

'Good,' the man said. 'Any questions?'

Roger had to moisten his lips before he could answer.

'Why do you think that Harry Hole will call me?'

'Because he's desperate,' said the man, putting his sunglasses back on. 'And because you gave him a business card in front of the National Theatre yesterday. Have a good day, Gjendem.'

Roger did not move until the man had gone. He breathed in the clammy, dusty underground air of the car park. And he walked the short distance to the Post House with slow, reluctant steps.

The telephone numbers hopped and danced on the screen in front of Klaus Torkildsen in the control room at Telenor Operations Centre, Oslo region. He had told his colleagues that he was not to be disturbed and had locked the door.

His shirt was drenched with sweat. Not because he had been jogging to work. He had walked – neither particularly quickly nor slowly – and he had been heading for his office when the receptionist had called his name and stopped him. His surname. He preferred that.

'Visitor,' she had said, pointing to a man sitting on the sofa in reception.

Klaus Torkildsen was stunned. Stunned because he had a job that did not include receiving visitors. This was not by chance; his choice of profession and private life were controlled by a desire to avoid all direct contact with human beings other than was absolutely necessary.

The man on the sofa had got up, told him he was from the police and then asked him to sit down. Klaus had sunk into a chair, sunk further and further down as he felt the sweat breaking out over his whole body. The police. He had not had anything to do with them for 15 years and, even though he had only received a fine, he still reacted with immediate paranoia whenever he saw a uniform in the street. From the moment the man had opened his mouth, his pores had flowed.

The man went straight to the heart of the matter and told him they needed him to trace a mobile phone for them. Klaus had done a similar job for them before. It was relatively simple. A mobile phone, when it is switched on, transmits a signal every half-hour, and this is registered by the phone masts scattered around town. In addition, the phone masts pick up and register all the conversations of subscribers, calls both in and out. From the coverage of individual phone masts they could take cross-bearings to pinpoint the location of a mobile phone to within a square kilometre. That was what had caused such a stink the one time he had been involved, in the nature reserve near Kristiansand.

Klaus had said that wire tapping had to be ratified by the boss, but the man had said it was urgent, that they didn't have time to go through official channels. In addition to monitoring a particular mobile phone number (which Klaus had discovered belonged to a certain Harry Hole) the man also wanted him to monitor the lines belonging to a number of people whom the wanted man might conceivably contact. He had also given Klaus a list of telephone numbers and e-mail addresses.

Klaus asked him why they had specifically come to him. After all, there were other people who had more experience of this than he. The sweat froze on his back and he began to shiver a little in the air-conditioned reception area.

'Because we know that you'll keep your mouth shut about this, Torkildsen. Just as we will keep our mouths shut to your superiors and colleagues about the time you were literally caught with your trousers down in Stens Park in January 1987. The undercover policewoman said you were stark naked under the coat. Must have been damned cold . . .'

Torkildsen swallowed hard. They had said that it would be taken off public records after a few years.

He swallowed again.

It seemed absolutely impossible to trace the mobile phone. It was switched on; he knew that as he received a signal every half-hour, but it came from a different place every time, as if it were trying to tease him.

He concentrated on the addresses on the list. One was an internal number at Kjølberggata 21. He checked the number. It was *Krimteknisk*, the Forensics department.

Beate picked up the phone as soon as it rang.

'Well?' said a voice at the other end.

'Not looking good so far,' she said.

'Mm.'

'I have two men developing the photographs and they'll land on my desk the second they're finished.'

'And no Sven Sivertsen.'

'If he was by the Fountain in Frogner Park when Barbara Svendsen was killed, he was unlucky. He's definitely not in any of the photographs I've seen and we're talking close on a hundred so far.'

'White, short-sleeved shirt and blue –'

'You've said all that before, Harry.'

'No faces even similar?'

'I've got a good eye for faces, Harry. He isn't in any of the photos.'

'Mm.'

She waved in Bjørn Holm with a new stack of photographs stinking of developer reagent. He dumped them down on her desk, pointed to one, gave a thumbs-up and disappeared.

'Wait,' she said. 'I've just got some new ones in. They're from the group who were there on Saturday at five o'clock. Now let me see . . .'

'Come on.'

'Yes indeed. Gosh . . . Guess who I'm sitting looking at now?'

'Really?'

'Yep. Sven Sivertsen as large as life, as tall as ever. In profile in front of Vigeland's six giants. Looks as if he's walking past.'

'Has he got a brown polythene bag in his hand?'

'The picture is cut off too high to see.'

'OK, but at least he was there.'

'Yes, but no-one was killed on a Saturday, Harry. So that's no alibi for anything.'

'It means that at least something of what he said is true.'

'Well, the best lies are ninety per cent truth.'

Beate could feel the lobes of her ears getting warm as she realised that that was a direct quote from The Gospel According to Harry. She had even used his intonation.

'Where are you?' she added quickly.

'As I said, it's best for us both that you don't know.'

'Sorry, slipped up there.'

Pause.

'We . . . er, we'll keep checking the photos,' Beate said. 'Bjørn's got hold of a list of tourist groups who were in Frogner Park at the times of the other murders.'

Harry rang off with a grunt, which Beate interpreted as a 'thank you'.

Harry put his thumb and first finger in the corners of his eyes on each side of the ridge of his nose and squeezed his eyes shut. Including the two hours he had slept this morning, he had had six hours' sleep in the last three days. And he knew it might be a long time before he had any more. He had dreamed about streets. He had seen the map slide into his view and he had dreamed about street names in Oslo. Sons gate, Nittedalgata, Sørumgata, Skedsmogata, all the twisting little streets in Kampen. And then he had dreamed it was night, snow was falling and he was walking along a street in Grünerløkka (Markveien?

Toftes gate?) and a red sports car was parked there with two people in it. As he drew closer, he saw that one person was a woman with the head of a pig, wearing an old-fashioned dress. He called her name, he called out 'Ellen', but when she turned round and opened her mouth to answer, it was full of gravel and the gravel spilled out.

Harry stretched his stiff neck from side to side. 'Listen,' he said, attempting to focus on Sven Sivertsen, who was lying on a mattress on the floor. 'The person I just talked to on the phone has set some machinery in motion for your and my sake that could lead to her not only losing her job, but also being imprisoned for acting as an accomplice. I need something that can give her peace of mind.'

'What do you mean?'

'I want her to see a copy of one of the pictures you have of you and Waaler in Prague.'

Sivertsen laughed.

'Are you hard of hearing, Harry? This is the only card I have to bargain with, I'm telling you. If I play it now, you can just cancel Operation Save Sivertsen.'

'We may do that sooner than you imagine. They've found a picture which proves you were in Frogner Park on Saturday. But nothing for the day Barbara Svendsen was killed. Rather odd considering that the Japanese have had the Fountain under flash attack all summer, don't you think? It's bad news for your story anyway. That's why I want you to ring your girl and get her to mail or fax the picture to Beate Lønn in Forensics. She can censor Waaler's face if you think you have to keep what you claim is your trump card, but I want to see a picture of you and someone else in that square, someone who *could* be Tom Waaler.'

'Václav Square.'

'Whatever. She's got an hour to do it, starting now. If not, our agreement is history. Understand?'

Sivertsen fixed Harry with a long stare before he answered.

'I don't know if she'll be at home.'

'She doesn't work,' Harry said. 'Worried, pregnant girlfriend. How is she not going to be at home waiting for a telephone call from you? Let's hope so anyway, for your sake. Fifty-nine minutes left.'

Sivertsen's gaze took in a whistle-stop tour of the room, but rested on Harry again in the end. He shook his head.

'I can't, Hole. I can't drag her into this. She's innocent. For the moment, Waaler knows nothing about her or where we live, but if this fails I know he'll find out. And then he'll go after her as well.'

'And what will she think about being left alone to bring up a child while the father's serving a life sentence for four murders? You're caught between the devil and the deep blue sea, Sivertsen. Fifty-eight.'

Sivertsen put his face in his hands.

'Fuck . . .'

When he looked up again Harry was holding out the mobile phone.

He bit his bottom lip. Then he took the phone, punched in the number and pressed the red phone against his ear. Harry checked his watch. The second hand was stuttering its way round. Sivertsen shifted with unease. Harry counted 20 seconds.

'Well?'

'She may have gone to her mother's in Brno,' Sivertsen said.

'Pity. For you,' Harry said with his eyes still on his watch. 'Fifty-seven.'

He heard the phone fall to the floor. He glanced up and caught a glimpse of Sivertsen's contorted face before feeling a hand close around his neck. Harry brought both arms up quickly. He hit Sivertsen's wrists and Sivertsen lost his grip. Then Harry lunged at the face ahead of him and hit something; he felt it give way. He struck again and felt warm sticky blood running between his fingers and made a bizarre association: that the blood was like freshly stirred strawberry jam off slices of bread at his grandmother's house. He raised his hand to strike again. He saw the handcuffed, defenceless man try to cover his body, but it only made him even more furious. Tired, frightened and furious.

'*Wer ist da?*'

Harry froze. He and Sivertsen stared at each other. Neither of them said anything. The nasal sound came from the mobile phone on the floor.

'*Sven? Bist du es, Sven?*'

Harry grabbed the phone and held it to his ear.

'Sven is here,' he said slowly. 'Who are you?'

'*Eva*,' said the indignant woman's voice. '*Bitte, was ist passiert?*'

'Beate Lønn.'

'Harry. I –'

'Hang up and call my mobile.' She rang off.

Ten seconds later he had her on what he would insist on calling 'the line'.

'What's up?'

'We're being monitored.'

'How?'

'We've got an anti-hacking software package and it shows that all our phone calls and e-mails are being monitored by a third party. It's meant to protect us against criminals, but Bjørn says it looks like the ISP is doing it.'

'Listening in?'

'Hardly. But all our conversations and e-mails are being recorded.'

'That's Waaler and his boys.'

'I know. So now they know that you're ringing me, which in turn means that I cannot help you any more, Harry.'

'Sivertsen's girl is sending you a picture of a meeting Sivertsen and Waaler had in Prague. The picture shows Waaler from the back and can't be used as evidence of any kind, but I want you to look at it and tell me if it seems genuine. She has the photo on her computer, so she can mail it to you. What's the e-mail address?'

'Didn't you hear what I said, Harry? They check all incoming e-mails and calls. What do you think will happen if we get an e-mail or a fax from Prague right now? I can't do it, Harry. And I'll have to find a plausible explanation for why you phoned me and I'm not as quick-thinking as you. My God, what will I say to them?'

'Relax, Beate. You don't need to say anything. I haven't rung you.'

'What are you saying? You've rung me three times in all.'

'Yes, but they don't know that. I'm using a mobile I exchanged with a pal.'

'So, you anticipated all this?'

'No, not this. I did it because mobile phones send signals to phone masts that pinpoint which part of the town the phone is in. If Waaler has got people working on the mobile phone network trying to trace me with the help of my mobile they'll have something to sharpen their wits on because it is more or less in constant motion all over Oslo.'

'I want to know as little about this as possible, Harry. But don't send me anything here. OK?'

'OK.'

'I'm sorry, Harry.'

'You've given me your right arm, Beate. You don't need to apologise for holding on to your left.'

He knocked at the door. Five short knocks at room number 303. He hoped it was loud enough to be heard over the music. He waited. He was going to knock once more when he heard the music being turned down and the padding of bare feet on the floor. The door opened. She looked as if she had been asleep.

'Yes?'

He flashed his ID card which, strictly speaking, was false since he was no longer a police officer.

'Apologies again for what happened on Saturday,' Harry said. 'Hope you weren't too frightened when they burst in.'

'That's OK,' she said with a grimace. 'I suppose you were only doing your job.'

'Yes.' Harry rocked on his heels while casting quick glances up and down the corridor. 'A colleague from Forensics and I are checking Marius Veland's room for clues. We have to send off a document right this minute but my laptop has gone on strike. It's pretty important. I remembered that you were surfing the Net on Saturday and so I wondered . . .'

She gestured that any further explanation was superfluous and switched on the computer.

'The computer's on. I suppose I ought to apologise for the mess or something like that. Hope you don't mind if I don't give a damn.'

He sat down in front of the screen, got the e-mail program up, pulled out a slip of paper and banged Eva Marvanova's address in with the greasy keys. The message was brief. *Ready. This address.* Send.

He swung round on the chair and watched the girl, who was sitting on the sofa, pulling on a tight pair of jeans. He hadn't even noticed that she was only wearing a pair of knickers, presumably because of the baggy T-shirt with a picture of a hemp leaf on.

'On your own today?' he asked, mostly to say something while waiting for Eva. He could tell by the expression on her face that it was not a particularly successful attempt at conversation.

'I only screw at weekends,' she said, sniffing a sock before she put it on. And she beamed with pleasure when it was apparent that Harry had no intention of following up her comment. It was apparent to Harry that she could have done with a trip to the dentist.

'You've got an e-mail,' she said.

He turned round to the screen. It was from Eva. No text, just an attachment. He double-clicked on it. The screen went black.

'He's old and sluggish,' the girl said with an even broader grin. 'He'll get it up eventually. You'll just have to wait a bit.'

In front of Harry the picture had begun to appear on the screen, first as a blue glaze, and then, when there was no more sky, a grey wall and a black and green monument. Then the square. And the tables. Sven Sivertsen. And a man in a leather jacket with his back to the camera. Dark hair. Powerful neck. It was no good as evidence, of course, but Harry was in no doubt at all that it was Tom Waaler. Nevertheless, that was not what made him sit and stare at the picture.

'Er, you, I have to go to the loo,' the girl said. Harry had no idea how long he had been sitting there. 'And the bloody sound carries, so I get very embarrassed, don't I? So if you could . . .'

Harry stood up, mumbled his thanks and left.

On the stairs between the third and the fourth floor he stopped.

The picture.

It couldn't be chance. It was theoretically impossible.

Or was it?

Anyway, it couldn't be true. No-one did that kind of thing.

No-one.

37

Monday. Confession.

THE TWO MEN STANDING OPPOSITE EACH OTHER IN THE CHURCH OF the Holy Apostolic Princess Olga were the same height. The warm, clammy air smelled of sweet smoke and acrid tobacco. The sun had shone on Oslo every day now for almost five weeks, and the sweat was running in streams down Nikolai Loeb's thick woollen tunic as he was reading the prayer to take confession:

'Lo, you have come to the place of healing. The invisible spirit of Jesus Christ is here and will receive your confession.'

He had tried to find a lighter, more modern tunic in Welhavens gate, but they didn't have any for Russian Orthodox priests, they said. The prayer over, he placed the book beside the cross on the table between them. The man standing in front of him would soon clear his throat. They always cleared their throats before confessing, as if their sins were encapsulated in mucus and saliva. Nikolai had a vague sensation that he had seen the man before, but he could not remember where. And the name meant nothing to him. The man had seemed a little taken aback when he realised that the confession would be face to face and that he would even have to give his name. To tell the truth, Nikolai had had a feeling that the man had not given his real name, either. He may have come from a different congregation. Occasionally they came here with their secrets because this was a small anonymous church where they didn't know anyone. Nikolai had often pardoned the sins of members of the established Church of Norway. If they asked for it, they got it; the mercy of the Lord was infinite.

The man cleared his throat. Nikolai closed his eyes and promised himself that he would cleanse his body with a bath and his ears with Tchaikovsky as soon as he arrived home.

'It is said that lust – exactly like water – will find the lowest level, Father. If there is an opening, a crack or a flaw in your character, lust will find it.'

'We are all sinners, my son. Have you any sins to confess?'

'Yes. I have been unfaithful to the woman I love. I have been together with a wanton woman. Even though I do not love her, I have not been able to resist going back to her.'

Nikolai suppressed a yawn. 'Continue.'

'I . . . she became an obsession.'

'Became, you say. Does that mean that you have stopped meeting her?'

'They died.'

It was not just what he said; there was also something in his voice that startled Nikolai.

'They?'

'She was pregnant. I believe.'

'I am sorry to hear of your loss, my son. Does your wife know this?'

'No-one knows anything.'

'What did she die of?'

'A bullet through the head, Father.'

The sweat on Nikolai Loeb's skin suddenly went ice cold. He swallowed.

'Are there any other sins you would like to confess, my son.'

'Yes. There is a person. A policeman. I have seen the woman I love go to him. I have thoughts about . . .'

'Yes?'

'Sinning. That is all, Father. Can you read the prayer of absolution now?'

A silence fell over the church.

'I . . .' Nikolai began.

'I have to go now, Father. Would you be so kind?'

Nikolai closed his eyes again. Then he began to read and did not open his eyes until he came to 'I absolve you of your sins in the name of the Father, the Son and the Holy Ghost'.

He crossed himself over the man's bowed head.

'Thank you,' the man whispered. He turned and scurried out of the church.

Nikolai did not move from the spot and listened to the echo of the words still hanging between the walls. He thought he could remember where he had seen him now. In Gamle Aker assembly house. He had brought a new Star of Bethlehem to replace the ruined one.

As a priest Nikolai was bound by his oath of secrecy and he had no intention of breaking it as a result of what he had heard. Yet there was something about the man's voice, the way he had said he had thoughts about . . . about what?

Nikolai gazed out of the window. Where were the clouds? It was so sultry now that something had to happen soon. Rain. First of all though, thunder and lightning.

He closed the door, knelt in front of the small altar and prayed. He prayed with an intensity that he had not felt for many years. For guidance and strength. And for forgiveness.

At 2.00 Bjørn Holm stood in the doorway to Beate's office and told her they had something she should have a look at.

She got up and followed him into the photo lab, where he pointed to a photograph that was still hanging on a piece of cord to dry.

'That's from last Monday,' Bjørn said. 'Taken at about half past five, so roughly half an hour after Barbara Svendsen was shot in Carl Berners plass. You can easily cycle to Frogner Park in that time.'

The picture showed a girl smiling in front of the Fountain. Beside her you could see part of a sculpture. Beate knew which one it was. One of the 'tree groups', the carving of a girl diving. She had always stood in front of the sculpture when she and her mother and father had driven to Oslo to go for a Sunday walk in Frogner Park. Her father had explained that Gustav Vigeland had intended the diving girl to symbolise the young girl's fear of adult life and becoming a mother.

However, today it was not the girl Beate was looking at. It was the back of a man on the margin of the picture. He was standing in front of a green litter bin. In his hand he was holding a brown polythene bag. He was wearing a tight yellow top and black cycling pants. On his head he wore a black helmet, sunglasses and there was a cloth over his mouth.

'The courier,' Beate whispered.

'Maybe,' Bjørn Holm said. 'Unfortunately, he is still masked.'

'Maybe.' It sounded like an echo. Beate stretched out her hand without taking her eyes off the photo. 'The magnifying glass.'

Holm found it on the table between the bags of chemical reagents and passed it to her.

She squeezed one eye shut as she moved the magnifying glass across the photograph.

Bjørn Holm watched his boss. Of course he had heard the stories about Beate Lønn when she was working on bank robbery cases. About how she had sat for days on end in the 'House of Pain' – the hermetically sealed video room – playing the videos of the robbery, frame by frame, while she checked every detail of build, body language, contours of faces behind the masks. In the end she discovered the identity of the bank robber because she had seen him in another recording, from some post office robbery 15 years before, when she had still been pre-pubescent, a recording that had been stored on the hard disk containing a million faces and every bank robbery committed in Norway since video surveillance began. Some people had maintained it was down to Beate's unusual fusiform gyrus – the part of the brain that recognises faces – and that it must have been a talent she was born with. That was why Bjørn Holm didn't look at the photo, just at Beate Lønn's eyes scrutinising the picture in front of her, examining it in minute detail in a way that would be impossible to learn.

That was how he noticed that it was not the face of the man she was studying through the magnifying glass.

'The knee,' she said. 'Can you see it?'

Bjørn went closer.

'What about it?' he said.

'On the left knee. Looks like a plaster.'

'You mean we should keep an eye open for people with plasters on their left knee?'

'Very funny, Holm. Before we can find out who it is in the photo we have to find out if he could be the Courier Killer.'

'And how do we do that?'

'We visit the only man we know of who has seen the Courier Killer close up. Make a copy of the photo while I fetch the car.'

Sven Sivertsen stared at Harry, thunderstruck. Harry had just explained his theory to him, his impossible theory.

'I really had no idea,' Sivertsen whispered. 'I never saw any of the pictures of the victims in the papers. They mentioned names when they questioned me, but none of them meant a thing.'

'For the moment it's simply a theory,' Harry said. 'We don't know it's the Courier Killer. We need concrete proof.'

Sivertsen smiled and said, 'You'd better convince me first that you've got enough to get me off the hook already. Then I'll agree to our giving ourselves up and you can have the use of my evidence to incriminate Waaler.'

Harry shrugged.

'I can ring the head of my section, Bjarne Møller, and ask him to come in a patrol car and get us out of here safely.'

Sivertsen shook his head firmly.

'There have got to be others involved in this, in higher positions in the police force than Waaler. I don't trust anyone. You'll have to find the proof first.'

Harry opened and closed his fist. 'We have an alternative. One that would protect both of us.'

'And that is?'

'Go to the papers and tell them what we know. About the Courier Killer and Waaler. Then it would be too late for anyone to do anything.'

Sivertsen wore a sceptical expression.

'Time's running out for us,' Harry said. 'He's getting closer. Can't you feel it?'

Sivertsen rubbed his wrist.

'OK,' he said. 'Do it.'

Harry shoved his hand in his back pocket and pulled out a crumpled business card. He hesitated for a second. Possibly because he anticipated the consequences of what he was about to do. Or perhaps because he didn't anticipate them. He tapped in the work number. The reply came surprisingly quickly.

'Roger Gjendem.'

Harry could hear the hum of voices, the clatter of computer keyboards and telephones ringing in the background.

'This is Harry Hole. I want you to listen very carefully, Gjendem. I have some information about the Courier Killer. And arms smuggling. One of my colleagues in the police is involved. Do you understand?'

'I believe so.'

'Good. The story's yours exclusively so long as you publish it on *Aftenposten*'s web pages as quickly as possible.'

'Of course. Where are you ringing from, Inspector Hole?'

Gjendem sounded less surprised than Harry had expected.

'It's not important where I am. I have information which proves

Sven Sivertsen cannot be the Courier Killer and that a leading policeman is involved in a network of arms smuggling that has been operating in Norway for several years.'

'That's fantastic. But I'm sure you're aware that I cannot write that on the basis of one telephone conversation.'

'What do you mean?'

'No serious newspaper would print an allegation about a named police inspector smuggling arms without checking that the sources are reliable. I don't doubt for a minute that you're the person you say you are, but how do I know that you aren't drunk or crazy or both? If I don't check this out properly, the paper can be sued. Let's meet, shall we, Inspector Hole. Then I'll write everything you tell me. I promise.'

In the pause that followed Harry could hear someone laughing in the background. A carefree ripple of laughter.

'Don't even think about ringing other papers – they'll give you the same answer. Trust me, Inspector.'

Harry took a deep breath.

'OK,' he said. 'At Underwater in Dalsbergstien. At five o'clock. Come on your own or I won't turn up. And not a single word about this to a living soul, understood?'

'Understood.'

'See you.'

Harry pressed the 'off' button and chewed his bottom lip.

'I hope that was wise,' said Sven.

Bjørn Holm and Beate turned off busy Bygdøy allé and one moment later they found themselves in a silent road with misshapen detached timber houses on one side and fashionable brick apartment buildings on the other. The kerbsides came complete with rows of German makes of car.

'Nobsville,' Bjørn said.

They pulled up outside a doll's-house-yellow building.

A voice answered the intercom after the second buzz.

'Yes?'

'André Clausen?'

'I believe so, yes.'

'Beate Lønn, police. May we come in?'

André Clausen was waiting for them in the doorway, dressed in a thigh-length dressing gown. He was scratching at the scab of a cut on his cheek as he made a half-hearted attempt at suppressing a yawn.

'Apologies,' he said. 'I got home late last night.'

'From Switzerland perhaps?'

'No, I've just been up in the mountains. Come in.'

Clausen's sitting room was a little on the small side for the collection of objets d'art he had, and Bjørn Holm was quick to establish that Clausen's taste tended more towards Liberace than minimalism. Water trickled through a fountain in the corner where a naked goddess stretched up towards the Sistine paintings on the vaulted ceiling.

'I'd like you to concentrate first and think about the time you saw the Courier Killer in the reception area at the solicitors' office,' Beate said. 'And then look at this.'

Clausen took hold of the picture and studied it while running a finger across the cut on his cheek. Bjørn Holm examined the sitting-room area. He heard a shuffling noise behind a door and the sound of paws scratching against the other side.

'Maybe,' Clausen said.

'Maybe?' Beate was perched on the edge of the chair.

'Very possible. The clothes are the same. The cycling helmet and the sunglasses too.'

'Good. And the plaster on his knee. Did he have that?'

Clausen laughed softly.

'As I told you, it is not my habit to study men's bodies in such detail. But if it makes you happier, I can say that my immediate reaction is that this is the man I saw. Beyond that . . .'

He made a gesture with outstretched arms.

'Thank you,' Beate said getting up.

'My pleasure,' Clausen said, following them to the door where he proffered his hand. That was a strange thing to do, Holm thought, but he took it. But when Clausen proffered his hand to Beate, she shook her head with a little smile:

'Sorry, but . . . you have blood on your fingers. And your chin's bleeding.'

Clausen put a hand up to his face.

'Indeed,' he said smiling. 'That's Truls. My dog. Our games at the weekend got a little out of hand.'

He looked Beate in the eyes and his smile became broader and broader.

'Goodbye,' Beate said.

Bjørn Holm was not quite sure why he shuddered when he emerged into the heat again.

Klaus Torkildsen had pointed both fans in the room towards his face, but it felt as if they were only blowing the hot air from the machine back at him. He tapped his finger against the thick glass of the screen. Under the internal number in Kjølberggata. The subscriber had just rung off. That was the fourth time today that the person in question had spoken to precisely that mobile phone number. Brief conversations.

He double-clicked on the mobile phone number to find the subscriber's name. A name appeared on the screen. He double-clicked to find an address and a profession. When it came up, Klaus sat looking at the information for a moment. Then he dialled the number he had been told to call when he had something to report.

A phone was picked up.

'Hello?'

'This is Torkildsen at Telenor. Who am I talking to?'

'Never mind about that, Torkildsen. What have you got for us?'

Torkildsen could feel his sweaty upper arms sticking to his chest.

'I've done a bit of checking around,' he said. 'Hole's mobile is constantly on the move and impossible to trace. But there is another mobile which has rung the internal number in Kjølberggata several times.'

'Right. Whose is it?'

'The subscription is under the name of Øystein Eikeland. His profession is given as taxi driver.'

'So?'

Torkildsen pushed out his lower lip and tried to blow hot air upwards to clear his glasses, which were wet with condensation.

'I was just thinking that there could be a connection between a telephone that is continually on the move all over town and a taxi driver.'

The line went quiet at the other end.

'Hello?' Torkildsen said.

'Received and understood,' the voice said. 'Keep tracing the numbers, Torkildsen.'

As Bjørn Holm and Beate wandered into reception in Kjølberggata, Beate's mobile phone bleeped.

She whipped it out of her belt, read the display and placed it against her ear in one sweeping movement.

'Harry? Ask Sivertsen to roll up his left trouser leg. We've got a picture of a masked cyclist in front of the Fountain at half past five last Monday with a plaster on his knee. And he's holding a brown polythene bag.'

Bjørn had to take longer strides to keep up with his diminutive female colleague as she made her way down the corridor. He heard a voice crackling on the phone.

Beate swung into her office.

'No plaster and no wound? No, I know that doesn't prove anything, but for your information André Clausen has more or less identified the cyclist in the picture as the same person he saw at Halle, Thune and Wetterlid.'

She sat down behind her desk.

'What?'

Bjørn Holm saw three deep sergeant's chevrons appear on her forehead.

'Right.'

She put down the phone and stared at it as if she didn't know whether to believe what she had just heard.

'Harry thinks he knows who the Courier Killer is,' she said.

Bjørn didn't answer.

'Check to see if the lab is free,' she said. 'He's given us a new job.'

'What kind of job?' Bjørn asked.

'A real shit job.'

Øystein Eikeland was sitting in a taxi in the parking area below St Hanshaugen with his eyes half closed, peering down the street at a girl with long legs, imbibing caffeine on a seat on the pavement outside Java. The hum of the air conditioning was drowned out by the sounds of music the loudspeakers were emitting.

Malicious rumour had it that the song was a Gram Parsons number and that Keith and the Stones had nicked it for the *Sticky Fingers* album while they were down in France. The '60s were over and they were trying to drug themselves into creativity: 'Wild Horses'.

One of the back doors opened. Øystein was startled. Whoever it was must have come from behind, from the park. In the mirror he saw a tanned face with a powerful jaw and reflector sunglasses.

'Lake Maridal, driver.' The voice was soft, but the command intonation was unmistakable. 'If it isn't too much trouble . . .'

'Not at all,' Øystein mumbled as he turned down the music and took a last deep drag of his cigarette before he tossed it out of the open window.

'Whereabouts by Lake Maridal?'

'Just drive. I'll tell you.'

They drove down Ullevålsveien.

'Rain is forecast,' Øystein said.

'I'll tell you,' the voice repeated.

No tip then, Øystein thought.

After a ten-minute drive they had left the residential quarter behind them and suddenly it was all fields, farms and Lake Maridal. It was such a wonderful transition that an American passenger had once asked Øystein if they were in a theme park.

'You can take the turning up there to the left,' the voice said.

'Up into the woods?' Øystein asked.

'Right. Does that make you nervous?'

The thought had never occurred to Øystein. Until now. He looked into the mirror again, but the man had moved across to the window so that he could only see half of his face.

Øystein slowed down, indicated he was turning left and swung into the turning. The gravel track in front of them was narrow and bumpy with grass growing in the middle.

Øystein hesitated.

Branches with green leaves that reflected in the light hung over the track on each side and seemed to be waving them on. Øystein put his foot on the brake. The gravel crunched under the tyres and the car came to a halt.

'Sorry,' he said to the mirror. 'Just had the chassis fixed for 40 thousand and we are under no obligation to drive on tracks like these. I can ring for another car if you like.'

The man in the back seat appeared to be smiling, at least the half he could see.

'And which telephone were you thinking of using, Eikeland?'

Øystein felt the hairs on the back of his neck rising.

'Your own telephone?' the voice whispered. 'Or Harry Hole's?'

'I'm not exactly sure what you're talking about, but the trip stops here, mister.'

The man laughed.

'*Mister*? I don't think so, Eikeland.'

Øystein felt an urge to swallow, but resisted the temptation.

'Listen, you don't have to pay since I couldn't drive you to your destination. Get out and wait here and I'll organise another car for you.'

'Your record says that you're smart, Eikeland. So I assume you know what I'm after. I hate to have to use this cliché, but it is up to you whether we do this the easy way or the hard way.'

'I really don't know what . . . Ow!'

The man had slapped the back of Øystein's head, just above the headrest, and as Øystein was automatically thrust forwards, he could feel, to his surprise, his eyes filling with tears. It wasn't that it hurt particularly. The blow had been of the type they handed out at junior school: light, a sort of introductory humiliation. The tear ducts were, however, already aware of what his brain still refused to accept. That he was in serious trouble.

'Where's Harry's phone, Eikeland? In the glove compartment? In the boot? In your pocket perhaps?'

Øystein didn't answer. He sat still as his eyes fed his brain. Forest on both sides. Something told him that the man in the back seat was fit and that he would catch Øystein in a matter of seconds. Was the man alone? Should he set off the alarm that was connected to the other cars? Was it a good idea to get other people involved?

'I see,' the man said. 'The hard way then. And do you know what?' Øystein was unable to react before he felt an arm around his neck pulling him back against the headrest. 'Deep down, that's what I'd hoped.'

Øystein lost his glasses. He stretched his hand out towards the steering column, but couldn't reach.

'Press the alarm and I'll kill you,' the man whispered into his ear. 'And I'm not speaking metaphorically, Eikeland, but in the sense that I will literally take your life.'

Despite the fact that his brain was not getting oxygen, Øystein Eikeland could hear, see and smell unusually well. He could see the network of veins on the inside of his own eyelids, smell the aroma of the man's aftershave and hear the slightly whining overtone of glee – like a kind of drivebelt – in the man's voice.

'Where is he, Eikeland? Where is Harry Hole?'

Øystein opened his mouth and the man released his grip.

'I have no idea what it is you –'

Then the arm was back, squeezing.

'Last try, Eikeland. Where's your piss-artist pal?'

Øystein felt the pains, the irritating will to live, but he also knew that it would soon be over. He had experienced similar things before. It was just a phase, a stage before the much more pleasurable sense of indifference kicked in. The seconds passed. The brain was beginning to shut down branch lines. First his sight went.

Then the man let go again and the oxygen streamed into his brain. Sight returned. And the pain.

'We'll find him anyway,' the voice said. 'You can choose whether it's before or after you've left us.'

Øystein felt something cold and hard move across his temples. Then across the bridge of his nose. Øystein had seen his share of Westerns, but he had never seen a .45-calibre revolver close up before.

'Open up.'

Let alone tasted one.

'I'm going to count to five. Then I'll shoot. Nod if there's something you want to say to me. Preferably before I count to five. One . . .'

Øystein tried to combat his fear of death. Tried telling himself that mankind is rational and that the man behind him would not gain anything by taking his life.

'Two . . .'

Logic is with me, Øystein thought. The barrel had a nauseous smell of metal and blood.

'Three. And don't worry about the seat covers, Eikeland. I'll tidy up and wash everything down thoroughly after me.'

Øystein could feel his body beginning to shake, an uncontrollable reaction he could only view as a spectator, and he was reminded of a rocket he had seen on TV that had shaken in the same way, seconds before it was fired into the cold, empty void of outer space.

'Four.'

Øystein nodded. Repeatedly and with vigour.

The gun disappeared.

'It's in the glove compartment,' he gasped. 'He said I should keep it switched on and I wasn't to touch it if it rang. He took mine.'

'I'm not interested in the phones,' the voice said. 'I want to know where Hole is.'

'I don't know. He didn't say anything. Yes, he did. He said it was best for both of us if I knew nothing.'

'He was lying,' the man said.

The words came slowly and calmly, and Øystein could not make out whether the man was angry or enjoying himself.

'Just best for him, Eikeland. Not for you.'

The cold gun barrel on Øystein's cheek felt like a glowing iron.

'Wait! Harry did say something. I remember now. He said that he was going to lie low at his place.'

The words streamed out of Øystein's mouth; he had the impression that he was pumping them out half formed.

'We've been there, you numbskull,' the voice said.

'I don't mean the place where he lives. His place in Oppsal. The place where he grew up.'

The man laughed and Øystein smarted with pain as the gun barrel was thrust up his nostril.

'We've been tracking your phone for the last few hours, Eikeland. We know which part of town he's in. And it isn't in Oppsal. You're lying: fact. Or to put it another way: five.'

A bleep. Øystein squeezed his eyes shut. The bleeping would not stop. Was he dead already? The bleeps formed a tune. *Purple Rain.* Prince. It was the digital ringtone of a mobile phone.

'Yes, what's up?' the voice behind him said.

Øystein didn't dare open his eyes.

'At Underwater? Five o'clock? OK, get all the guys together immediately. I'm on my way.'

Øystein heard the rustle of clothing behind him. His hour had come. He heard a bird singing outside. A beautiful high trill. He didn't even know what kind of bird it was. He should have known. Now he would never know. Then he felt a hand on his shoulder.

Øystein tentatively opened his eyes and peered in the mirror.

A flash of white teeth and then the voice with the same undertone of glee: 'City centre, driver. Step on it.'

38

Monday. The Cloud.

RAKEL OPENED HER EYES WITH A START. HER HEART WAS POUNDING fiercely. She had slept. She listened to the unrelenting din of children swimming in the open-air Frogner swimming pool. A faintly bitter taste of grass lingered in her mucous linings and the heat lay like a warm duvet on her back. Had she been dreaming? Was that what had woken her?

A sudden gust of wind blew the duvet away and gave her goosepimples.

Odd how dreams sometimes just slide away from you, like slippery soap, she thought as she rolled over. Oleg was gone. She raised herself on her elbows and looked around her.

The next second she was on her feet.

'Oleg!'

She began to run.

She found him by the diving pool. He was sitting on the edge talking to a boy she thought she had seen before. Could have been a boy in his class.

'Hi, Mummy.' He squinted up at her and smiled.

Rakel grabbed his arm, harder than she had intended.

'I told you not to clear off without saying a word.'

Oleg was taken aback and a little embarrassed. His friend fell back a couple of paces.

She let go. Sighed and stared at the horizon. The sky was blue apart from one single white cloud that seemed to be pointing upwards as if someone had just fired a rocket.

'It's nearly five. We're going home now,' she said. Her voice was a long way off. 'Time to eat.'

In the car on the way home Oleg asked if Harry was coming.

Rakel shook her head.

While they were waiting for the lights to change on the Smestad crossing she bent forwards to look up and find the cloud again. It had not moved, but it was a bit higher now and there was a tinge of grey at the bottom.

She remembered to lock the door when they arrived home.

39

Monday. Meetings.

ROGER GJENDEM STOPPED AT THE WINDOW OF UNDERWATER TO STARE at the water bubbling in the aquarium. An image flickered past. A seven-year-old boy swimming towards him with hurried, frantic strokes and the panic visible on his face, as if he, Roger, his big brother, was the only person in the world who could save him. Roger had called out to him with a laugh, but Thomas had not realised that he was already in shallow water and all he had to do was put his feet on the bottom. Now and then Roger mused that he had managed to teach his brother how to swim in water; it was on land that he had gone under.

He stood in the doorway to Underwater for a few seconds to let his eyes grow accustomed to the dark. Apart from the barman he could only see one single person in the room, a red-haired woman sitting with her back half turned towards him with half a glass of beer in front of her and a cigarette between her fingers. Roger went down the steps to the lower floor and peered in. Not a soul. He decided to wait by the bar on the ground floor. The wooden planks creaked under his feet and the red-haired woman looked up. Shadows fell across her face, but there was something about the way she was sitting, her bearing, that made him think that she was nice-looking. Or had been. He noticed that she had a bag beside the table. Perhaps she was waiting for someone too.

He ordered a beer and checked the time on his watch.

He had walked round the block a few times so that he would not arrive before 5.00, as arranged. He didn't want to give the impression he was too keen – that would arouse suspicion. Though who could mistrust a journalist for being too keen when it was information that might lead to the biggest case of the summer being turned on its head? If indeed that was what this was all about.

Roger had kept an eye open while trudging up and down the streets. For a car parked where it shouldn't be, someone standing and reading a paper at the corner of the street, a tramp sleeping on a bench, perhaps. He hadn't spotted anything though. They were professionals of course. That was what frightened him most. The certainty that they could carry out their threat and get away with it. He had heard a colleague mumbling in his cups that there were some things going on at Police HQ that the public would not believe, even if it had been reported in the papers, but Roger shared the public's view.

He looked at his watch again. Seven minutes past.

Would they storm in the minute Harry Hole arrived? They hadn't told him a thing, they just said that he should turn up as arranged and behave as he normally would when working on a job. Roger took another large gulp in the hope that the alcohol would settle his nerves.

Ten minutes past. The barman was sitting in the corner of the bar reading a holiday brochure.

'Excuse me,' Roger said.

The barman scarcely raised his eyes.

'A guy hasn't just been in here, has he? Tall, blond hair with . . .'

'Sorry,' the barman said, licking his thumb and flipping the page. 'I just started my shift before you came in. Ask her over there.'

Roger hesitated. He drank down as far as the Ringnes logo on the glass and got up.

'Excuse me . . .'

The woman looked up at him with a strained smile.

'Yes?'

It was then that he saw. It wasn't shadows he had seen across her face. It was bruises. On the forehead. On the cheekbones. And on her neck.

'I was supposed to meet a guy here, but I'm afraid he must have gone again. About one ninety with short cropped blond hair.'

'Oh? Young?'

'Well. About thirty-five, I think. Looks a bit ravaged.'

'Red nose and blue eyes that seem both old and young at the same time?'

She was still smiling, but in such an introverted way that he sensed the smile was not for him.

'That could be him, yes,' Roger dithered. 'Has he . . .'

'No, I'm sitting waiting for him myself.'

Roger looked her over. Was she with the others? A battered, fairly attractive woman in her mid-thirties? It seemed unlikely.

'Do you think he's going to come?' Roger asked.

'No.' She raised her glass. 'The ones you want to come, never do. It's the others who come.'

Roger went back to the bar. His glass had been removed. He ordered another beer.

The barman put on some music. Gluecifer did their best to lighten the gloom.

'I got a war, baby. I got a war with you.'

He wasn't coming. Harry Hole was not coming. What did it mean? It sure as shit wasn't his fault.

At 5.30 the door opened.

Roger looked up hopefully.

A man in a leather jacket stood and eyeballed him.

Roger shook his head.

The man cast a quick glance around the bar. He ran a flat hand across his throat. Then he was gone again.

Roger's first thought was to run after him. Ask him what he meant by his gesture. That they were suspending operations. Or that Thomas . . . His mobile phone rang. He took it out of his pocket.

'No show?' a voice said.

It was not the man wearing the leather jacket, and it was definitely not Harry. There was something familiar about the voice though.

'What shall I do?' Roger asked quietly.

'Stay there until eight o'clock,' the voice said. 'And ring the number you were given if he turns up. We have to push on.'

'Thomas . . .'

'Nothing will happen to your little brother as long as you do what we tell you. And none of this will come out.'

'Of course not. I . . .'

'Have a good evening, Gjendem.'

Roger put the phone back in his pocket and plunged into his beer. He was gasping for air when he came up again. Eight o'clock. Two and a half hours.

'What did I tell you?'

Roger turned his head. She was standing right behind him holding up her index finger to the barman, who reluctantly dragged himself to his feet.

'What did you mean by "the others"?' he asked.

'Which others?'

'You said that the others come instead of the ones you want to come.'

'The ones you have to make do with, my dear.'

'Yes?'

'People like you and me.'

Roger turned right round. There was something about the way she had said that. No drama, no earnest tone, but with a slight resigna-tion in her voice. There was something there he recognised, a sort of affinity. And now he could see more too. Her eyes. The red lips. She had certainly been good-looking at one time.

'Did your partner beat you up?' he asked.

She raised her head and thrust out her chin. She looked at the barman who was pouring her beer.

'I really don't think it's any of your business, young man.'

Roger closed his eyes for a second. It had been a strange day. One of the strangest. No reason for it to stop here.

'It could be,' he said.

She turned and gave him a sharp look.

He nodded towards her table.

'Judging from the size of the bag you've got with you, he's an ex-partner now. If you need somewhere to crash tonight, I have a huge flat with a spare bedroom.'

'Oh really?'

The intonation was dismissive, but he noticed her facial expression change. It became inquisitive, curious.

'It suddenly became larger last winter,' he said. 'I would very happily pay for your beer if you would keep me company. I have to stay here for a while.'

'Well,' she said. 'We can always wait a little together.'

'For someone who won't come?'

Her laughter sounded sad, but at least it was laughter.

Sven was sitting on the chair staring out of the window at the field outside.

'Perhaps you should have gone after all,' he said. 'It might have been subconscious on the journalist's part.'

'I don't think so,' Harry said.

He was lying on the sofa contemplating the cigarette smoke as it spiralled up into the grey ceiling above them.

'It's my belief that, subconsciously, he was giving me a warning.'

'Simply because you referred to Waaler as "a leading policeman" and the journalist referred to him as "an inspector" does not necessarily mean that he already knew it was Waaler. He might have been guessing.'

'He slipped up. Unless his phone was being tapped and he was trying to warn me.'

'You're paranoid, Harry.'

'Maybe, but that doesn't mean–'

'– that they aren't after you. You're right there. There must be other journalists you can call on, aren't there?'

'None I trust. And, besides, I don't think we should make many more calls with this mobile. In fact, I think I'll switch it off. The signals can be used to trace us.'

'What? Waaler can't know which phone you're using.'

The green display light on the Ericsson went out and Harry dropped it into his jacket pocket.

'You're clearly not quite in the picture with respect to what Tom Waaler can or can't do, Sivertsen. The agreement with my taxi-driving pal was that he was to ring between five and six if everything was OK. It's now ten past six. Did you hear the phone ring?'

'No.'

'That may mean that they know all about this phone. He's getting closer.'

Sven groaned.

'Has anyone told you that you have a tendency to repeat yourself, Harry? And, by the way, it's struck me that you're not doing a helluva lot to get us out of this mess.'

Harry blew a fat zero towards the ceiling by way of answer.

'I'm sort of getting the feeling that you *want* him to find us. And that all this other stuff is just playing to the gallery. It has to look as if we're trying bloody hard to hide so that you can be sure that he will be tricked into coming after us.'

'Interesting theory,' Harry mumbled.

*

'The expert at Norske Møller has confirmed what you suspected,' Beate said on the phone, waving Bjørn Holm out of the office.

She could tell from the clicks that Harry was phoning from a public call box.

'Thanks for your help,' he answered. 'That was exactly what I needed.'

'Was it?'

'I hope so.'

'I've just rung Olaug Sivertsen, Harry. She's beside herself with worry.'

'Mm.'

'It's not just her son. She's frightened for her lodger who was in the mountains over the weekend and hasn't returned. I don't know what to say to her.'

'As little as possible. It'll soon be over.'

'Can you promise that?'

Harry's laughter sounded like the dry cough of a machine gun: 'Precisely that I can promise, yes.'

There was a crackle on the intercom.

'Visitor for you,' the nasal voice of a receptionist announced. In fact, since it was past 4.00, it would have been one of the female Securitas guards, but Beate had noticed that even the Securitas personnel acquired a nasal twang after a stint behind the reception desk.

Beate pressed a button on the rather antiquated box in front of her.

'You'll have to ask whoever it is to wait a moment. I'm busy.'

'Yes, but he –'

Beate switched off the intercom.

'Just hassle,' she said.

Beyond the crackle of Harry's breathing on the phone Beate could hear a car stopping and the engine being switched off. At that moment she noticed a change in the way the light fell in her room.

'I'll have to be off,' he said. 'Time's getting short. I may ring you afterwards. If it went as I hoped. OK? Beate?'

Beate put down the phone. Her eyes went to the doorway.

'Well?' Tom Waaler said. 'Don't you say goodbye to good friends?'

'Didn't the receptionist say that you were to wait?'

'Yes, she did.'

Tom Waaler closed the door and pulled the cord so the white blinds slid down in front of the window looking out onto the open-plan office. Then he walked round her desk, stood beside her chair and looked at the desk.

'What's that?' he asked, pointing to the two glass specimen slides stuck together.

Beate began to hyperventilate.

'According to the laboratory it's a seed.'

He placed a hand lightly on her neck. She tensed up.

'Was that Harry you were talking to?'

He stroked her skin with his finger.

'Stop that,' she said with fiercely contained restraint. 'Take your hand away.'

'Dearie me. Did I do something wrong?' Waaler smiled and raised both hands in surrender. 'You used to like that, Lønn.'

'What do you want?'

'To give you a chance. I think I owe you that.'

'Do you? What for?'

She tilted her head to the side and stared at him. He moistened his lips and leaned down towards her.

'For your services. And your submission. And a cold, tight cunt.'

She struck out, but he caught her wrist in the air and twisted her arm behind her back and forced it upwards in one movement. She gasped, fell forwards off her chair and hit her forehead on the table. His voice wheezed in her ear:

'I'll give you a chance to keep your job, Lønn. We know Harry's been ringing from his taxi driver friend's phone. Where is he?'

She groaned. Waaler pushed her arm up higher.

'I know it hurts,' he said. 'And I know that you'll tell me sweet FA however much I hurt you. So this is for my own personal pleasure. And yours.'

He pushed his groin into her ribs. The blood was rushing in her ears. Beate aimed and lunged forwards. Her head hit the plastic intercom box with a crack.

'Yes?' said a nasal voice.

'Send Holm in immediately,' Beate groaned with her cheek against the blotting pad.

'Right.'

Waaler hesitated, then let go of her arm. Beate straightened up.

'You bastard,' she said. 'I don't know where he is. He would never even have dreamed of putting me in such an impossible situation.'

Tom Waaler stared at her. Observed her. While he was doing this, Beate discovered something strange. She was not frightened of him any more. Her reason told her that he was more dangerous than ever, but there was something in his eyes, an anxiety she had never seen before. And he had just lost control. Only for a few seconds, but it was the first time she had seen him lose his grip.

'I'll be back for you,' he whispered. 'That's a promise. And you know I keep promises.'

'What's this . . . ?' Bjørn Holm began, stepping quickly to the side as Tom Waaler shot past him through the door.

40

Monday. Rain.

It was 7.30. The sun was moving towards Ullern Ridge and from her veranda in Thomas Heftyes gate, widowed Fru Danielsen saw that several white clouds had floated in over Oslo fjord. Beneath her, in the street, André Clausen and Truls passed by. She didn't know either the man or his golden retriever by name, but she had often seen them coming down Gimle terrasse. They stopped at the lights by the cross-roads near the taxi rank in Bygdøy allé. Fru Danielsen assumed that they were intending to go up to Frogner Park.

They both looked a bit the worse for wear, she thought. What's more, the dog was in need of a good wash.

She wrinkled her nose when she saw the dog, half a step behind its owner, raise its backside and do its business on the pavement. And when the owner made no attempt to pick up the dog dirt – in fact, he just dragged the dog over the crossing as soon as the lights went green – Fru Danielsen became indignant and a little elated at the same time. She was indignant because she had always been concerned for the good of the town – well, at least for the good of this part of the town – and she was elated because now she had some material for another reader's letter in *Aftenposten*, and she had not had a letter accepted of late.

She stood glaring at the scene of the crime while dog and dog owner, clearly guilt-ridden, scurried up Frognerveien. And so she became an unwilling witness to a woman rushing from the opposite direction to cross the lights before they turned red and falling victim to another person's total disregard of their civic responsibilities. The woman was obviously trying to hail a taxi and was not looking where she was treading.

Fru Danielsen emitted a loud sniff, cast a final glance at the armada of clouds and went in to begin her reader's letter.

A train passed like a long, gentle breath of air. Olaug opened her eyes and discovered that she was standing in the garden.

Odd. She couldn't remember leaving the house. But there she was, standing between the railway lines with the smell of roses and lilacs in her nostrils. The pressure on her temples had not eased, quite the contrary. She looked up. It had clouded over – that was why it was so dark. Olaug looked down at her bare feet. White skin, blue veins, the feet of an old lady. She knew why she was standing on this exact spot. They had stood here. Ernst and Randi. She had been standing by the window in the maid's room, watching them in the twilight by the rhododendron bushes, which were no longer there. The sun had been going down and he had been murmuring something in German and had plucked a rose which he put behind his wife's ear. She had laughed and nuzzled his neck. Then they turned to face west, they put their arms round each other and stood still. She rested her head on her husband's shoulder while they watched the sun setting, all three of them. Olaug did not know what they were thinking, but for her part she had been thinking that the sun would be up again another day. So young.

Olaug instinctively peered up at the window of the maid's room.

No Ina, no young Olaug, merely a black surface reflecting the popcorn-shaped clouds.

She would weep until the summer was over. Perhaps a little longer. And then the rest of life would begin again as it always did. It was a plan. You needed a plan.

There was a movement behind her. Olaug turned round cautiously. She could feel the cool grass being torn away as she twisted round on the balls of her feet. Then – in the middle of the movement – she froze.

It was a dog.

It gazed up at her with eyes that seemed to be begging forgiveness for something that as yet had not happened. At that moment something slid soundlessly from out under the fruit trees and towards the side of the dog. It was a man. His eyes were large and black, just like the dog's. She felt as if someone had thrust a little animal down her throat and she couldn't breathe.

'We were inside, but you weren't there,' the man said, tilting his head and looking at her the way you would study an interesting insect.

'You don't know who I am, Fru Sivertsen, but I've been looking forward to meeting you.'

Olaug opened her mouth and then closed it again. The man came closer. Olaug was looking over his shoulder, beyond him.

'My God,' she whispered, stretching out her arms.

She came down the steps, ran over the gravel laughing and into Olaug's embrace.

'I was so worried about you,' Olaug said.

'Oh?' Ina said with surprise in her voice. 'We just stayed in the log cabin a little longer than we'd planned. It *is* a holiday, you know.'

'Yes, yes, of course,' Olaug said, squeezing her tight.

The dog, an English setter, let itself get carried away by the pleasure of being reunited and it jumped up and put its paws on Olaug's back.

'Thea!' the man said. 'Sit!'

Thea sat.

'And who's this?' Olaug asked, finally releasing Ina.

'This is Terje Rye.' Ina's cheeks glowed in the dusk. 'My fiancé.'

'Goodness me,' Olaug said, clapping her hands together.

The man put his hand forward with a broad smile. He was no picture. Snub nose, wispy hair and close-set eyes. But he had an open, direct look that Olaug liked.

'Nice to meet you,' he said.

'Nice to meet you, too,' Olaug said, hoping the darkness would conceal her tears.

Toya Harang didn't notice the smell until they were well up Josefines gate.

She examined the taxi driver suspiciously. He was dark-skinned, but he certainly wasn't an African or she wouldn't have dared enter the taxi. It wasn't that she was a racist; it was just all the talk about statistics.

What was the smell though?

She caught the driver's glance in the mirror. Had she dressed too provocatively? Was the red blouse cut too low? The skirt with the slit up the side over her cowboy boots too short? She pursued another, more pleasant, thought. He had recognised her from the splash in today's papers with all the big pictures of her. 'TOYA HARANG: NEW QUEEN OF MUSICALS,' the headline read. True, the reviewer in *Dagbladet* had called her 'gauche but charming' and said that she was more convincing as Eliza the flowerseller than as the society lady that Professor Higgins had turned her into, but the reviewers were all agreed that she could sing and dance the braids off anyone around. There. What would Lisbeth have said to that?

'Party?' the driver asked.

'Sort of,' Toya said.

A party for two, she thought. A party to Venus and . . . What was it again, what was the other name he had said? Well, Venus was her, anyway. He had come up to her during the celebrations after opening night was over and whispered in her ear that he was one of her secret admirers. Then he invited her back to his place tonight. He had not bothered to disguise his intentions and she ought to have said no. For decency's sake she ought to have said no.

'That'll be nice,' the driver said.

Decency and no. She could still smell the silo and the dust from the straw, and see her father's belt cutting through the stripes of light which fell through cracks between the slats in the barn as he tried to beat it into her. Decency and no. And she could still feel her mother's hand stroking her hair in the kitchen afterwards as she asked her why she could not be like Lisbeth. Quiet and clever. One day Toya had torn herself away and said that she was the way she was and she must have inherited it from her father and hadn't she seen him mounting Lisbeth like a sow in the sty, or didn't Mother know about that? Toya had watched her mother's face change, not because her mother didn't know that it was lies, but because she knew now that Toya would not shy away from using any weapon at her disposal to harm them. Then Toya had screamed as loudly as she could that she hated them all and her father had come in from the sitting room with the newspaper in his hand and she could see on their faces that they knew that she was not lying now. Did she still hate them now that they had gone? She didn't know. No. Nowadays she didn't hate anyone. That wasn't why she was doing what she was doing. She was doing it for the fun of it. For indecency and yes. And because it was so irresistibly forbidden.

She gave the driver 200 kroner and a smile and told him to keep the change, despite the smell in the car. It was only when the taxi had driven away that she realised why the driver had been staring in his mirror. The smell had not come from him, but from her.

'Bloody hell!'

She scraped the leather sole of her high-heeled cowboy boot against the pavement, making brown stripes. She searched around for a puddle, but there had not been one in Oslo for close to five weeks. She gave up and went to the door and rang the bell.

'Yes?'

'This is Venus,' she cooed.

She smiled to herself.

'And this is Pygmalion,' the voice said.

That was the one!

There was a buzz in the door lock. She hesitated for a second. Last chance to retreat. She flicked back her hair and pulled open the door.

He was standing in the doorway with a drink in one hand waiting for her.

'Did you do as I said?' he asked. 'You didn't tell anyone where you were going?'

'No, are you crazy?'

She rolled her eyes.

'Maybe,' he said opening the door wide. 'Come in and say hello to Galatea.'

She laughed even though she hadn't a clue what he was talking about. She laughed even though she knew something awful was about to happen.

Harry found a place to park some way down Markveien, switched off the engine and got out of the car. He lit up and had a quick recce. The streets were deserted. It seemed as if people had retired indoors. The innocent white clouds from the afternoon had spread out to form a blue-grey wall-to-wall carpet in the sky.

He followed the graffiti-covered house fronts until he stood outside the door. Just the filter remained on his cigarette and he threw it away. He rang and waited. It was so muggy that the palms of his hands were sweating. Or was it terror? He looked at his watch and took note of the time.

'Yes?' The voice sounded irritated.

'Good evening. It's Harry Hole.'

No answer.

'From the police,' he added.

'Of course. Sorry, my mind was on something else. Come in.'

The door buzzed.

Harry took the steps slowly.

They stood waiting in the door for him, both of them.

'Oh no,' Ruth said. 'All hell's about to break loose.'

Harry stood on the landing in front of them.

'The rain,' the Trondheim Eagle added by way of explanation.

'Oh, I see.' Harry dried his palms on his trousers.

'How can we help you, Inspector?'

'You can help me to catch the Courier Killer,' Harry said.

Toya lay in a foetal position in the middle of the bed staring at herself in the mirror on the wardrobe door, which hung open against the wall. She listened to the shower from the lower floor. He was washing the smell of her off him. She rolled over. The waterbed gently moulded itself to her body. She looked at the photo. They were smiling at the camera. They were on holiday. In France maybe. She ran her fingers over the cool duvet cover. His body had also been cold. Cold and hard and muscular for someone so old. Particularly his backside and thighs. It was because he had been a dancer, he said. He had trained his muscles every day for 15 years. They would never disappear.

Toya's attention was caught by the black belt in his trousers lying on the floor.

Fifteen years. They would never disappear.

She rolled over onto her back, pushed herself up higher in the bed and heard the water gurgle on the inside of the rubber mattress. But now everything would be different. Toya was clever now. A good girl. Just the way Daddy and Mummy wanted. She was Lisbeth now.

Toya rested her head against the wall and sank deeper. Something was tickling her between the shoulder blades. It was like lying in a boat on the river. She lay there thinking.

Wilhelm had asked her if she would use a dildo while he watched. She had gone along with it. Good girl. He opened his toolbox. She closed her eyes, but still she had seen the stripes of light – the light through the cracks between the slats in the barn – on the inside of her eyelids. Then when he came in her mouth, it tasted of silo, but she didn't say anything. Clever girl.

Clever is how she was when Wilhelm was training her to speak and sing like her sister. Try to smile like her. Wilhelm had given make-up a photograph of Lisbeth and told them that that was how Toya was to look. The only thing she had not been able to do was laugh like Lisbeth, so Wilhelm had asked her not to try. Now and then she had been unsure how much was about playing Eliza Doolittle and how much was about Wilhelm's desperate yearning for Lisbeth. And now she was here in his bed. And perhaps this, too, was about Lisbeth, both for him and for her. What was it that Wilhelm had said? Lust found the lowest level?

Something was sticking into her back again and she twitched angrily.

For herself, Toya had not particularly missed Lisbeth much, if she were to be absolutely honest. Not that she wasn't shocked like everyone else when she had heard the news about her disappearance. But it had opened quite a lot of new doors. Toya was interviewed and Spinnin' Wheel had just received an offer for a series of well-paid concerts in memory of Lisbeth. And now the main role in *My Fair Lady*. Which on top of all this was well on the way to becoming a hit. Wilhelm had told her at the opening-night party that she would have to prepare herself for becoming a celebrity. A star. A diva. She put her hand under her back. What was digging into her? A lump. Under the sheet. It disappeared when she pressed it down. There it was again. She would have to find out.

'Wilhelm?'

She was going to shout louder to drown out the noise of the shower below, but remembered that Wilhelm had given strict instructions that she was to rest her voice. After a day off today they would have to perform every night until the end of the week. When she arrived he had asked her not to speak at all, not under any circumstances. Even though he had told her before that he wanted to rehearse a few snatches of dialogue with her that were not quite right, and he had asked her to make herself up as Eliza, for the sake of realism.

Toya undid the stretch undersheet from one side of the water bed and pulled it to the side. There was no other bedding, just the blue translucent rubber mattress. But what was sticking out over there? She laid her hand against the mattress. It was there, under the rubber. There was nothing to see. She stretched over to the side, switched on the bedside table lamp and twisted it over so that it pointed to the right spot. The bulge had gone again. She placed her hand over the rubber and waited. It came back, slowly, and she realised that whatever it was sank when she poked it and then came up again. She moved her hand.

At first she saw the contours outlined against the rubber. Like a profile. No, it wasn't *like* a profile. It was a profile. Toya lay down flat. She had stopped breathing. She could feel it now. Down from her stomach to her toes. There was a complete body on the inside. A body that was forced up by the buoyancy of the water and forced down by the weight of Toya as if two people were trying to be one. And perhaps they were. Because it was like looking in a mirror.

She wanted to scream now. Wanted to ruin her voice. Didn't want to be a good girl. Or clever. She wanted to be Toya again. But she couldn't be. She could only stare at the pallid, blue face of her sister, staring back at her with pupil-less eyes. And listen to the *ssshh* sounds of the shower, so like the TV set after transmission had finished. And then the sound of dripping water on the parquet floor by the foot of the bed behind her, telling her that Wilhelm was no longer in the shower.

'It can't be him,' Ruth said. 'It's . . . it's . . . not possible.'

'The last time I was here you said you were thinking about going over the roof to Barli's to do a bit of spying,' Harry said. 'And that his terrace door was left open all summer. Are you sure about that?'

'Absolutely, but can't you just phone?' the Trondheim Eagle asked.

Harry shook his head.

'He'll become suspicious and we cannot risk him getting away. I have to catch him this evening, if it's not too late already.'

'Too late for what?' the Trondheim Eagle asked, scrunching up one eye.

'Listen, all I'm asking is that you let me use your balcony to get up onto the roof.'

'Is there really no-one else with you?' the Trondheim Eagle asked. 'Haven't you got a search warrant or something like that?'

Harry shook his head.

'Justified grounds for suspicion,' he said. 'You don't need one.'

A rumble of thunder boomed low and menacingly over Harry's head. The gutter above the balcony had been painted yellow, but most of it had flaked off revealing large patches of red rust. Harry grabbed hold with both hands and pulled gently to see if it was properly attached. The gutter gave way with a groan and a screw detached itself from the plaster and hit the ground in the yard with a tinkle. Harry released his grip and swore. There was no alternative, however, so he put a foot on the railing and hauled himself up. He peered over the edge. An automatic sharp intake of breath. The sheet on the rotary dryer down below was like a white stamp blowing in the wind.

He forced one leg onto the gutter and scrambled over. Even though the roof was steep, the grip his robust Doc Martens had on the tiles was good enough for him to take the two steps to the drainpipe and clutch it to his chest as if it were a long-lost friend. He straightened and looked around. There was a flash of lightning over Nesodden. The air, which had not stirred when he arrived, was softly plucking at his jacket. Harry gave a start as a black shadow suddenly raced past his face. The shadow intersected the space above the central yard. A swallow. Harry just caught sight of it as it sought shelter under the eaves.

Harry scrabbled his way to the top of the roof, aimed for a black weathervane 15 metres away, took a deep breath and began to walk along the ridge of the roof with his arms held out like a line dancer.

He had reached the halfway point when it happened.

Harry heard a whoosh, which he first thought came from the tops of the trees beneath him. The sound rose in volume at the same time as the rotary dryer down in the yard began to rotate and shriek. He couldn't feel any wind, not yet. Then it hit him. The drought was over. The wind struck him in the chest like an avalanche of air set in motion by a plunging mass of water. He tottered back a step and stood swaying on the ridge. He heard it advancing towards him over the clattering roof tiles. The rain. The deluge. It beat down against the roof and in less than a second everything was wet. Harry tried to keep his balance, but there was nothing to grip; it was like walking on soap. One shoe slipped and he made a desperate dive for the weathervane. His arms were stretched out in front of him, his fingers splayed. His right hand scrabbled at the surface of a tile, searching for something to hold on to, but there was nothing. Gravity was pulling at him. The scratching of his nails made the same rasping noise as a scythe blade on a whetstone as he slid downwards. He heard the shriek of the rotary dryer abating, felt the gutter against his knees and knew he was on his way over the edge. He stretched his body out in a last-ditch attempt, tried to make himself longer, turn himself into an aerial. An aerial. His left hand grabbed hold of it, held on tight. The metal softened, bowed and bent. It threatened to follow him down into the yard. But it held.

Harry took hold of it with both hands and pulled himself up. He managed to get his rubber soles back underneath him and pushed as hard as he could against the surface and gained a foothold. With the rain furiously whipping into his face he crawled up to the ridge, sat astride it and breathed a deep sigh of relief. The contorted metal aerial beneath him was pointing downwards. Someone was going to have a reception problem with tonight's repeat showing of *Beat for Beat*.

Harry waited until his pulse had calmed down a little. Then he stood up and continued the tightrope walk. The weathervane received a kiss.

Barli's terrace was inset in the roof, so he could easily swing his legs down onto the red terracotta tiles. His feet made a splash as he landed, but the sound was drowned out by the roaring and gurgling of the flooded roof gutters.

The chairs had been taken in, the barbecue lay black and dead in a corner, but the terrace door was ajar.

At first, all he could hear was the drumming of the rain on the tiles, but as he cautiously crossed the threshold and entered the room he could discern another sound, also made by water. It came from the bathroom downstairs. The shower. Finally a bit of luck. Harry patted the pockets of his drenched jacket to find his chisel. An undressed and unarmed Barli was the best he could hope for, especially if Wilhelm still had the gun that Sven handed over in Frogner Park on Saturday.

Harry saw that the bedroom door was open. There was a Sami knife in the toolbox beside the bed. He tiptoed over to the door and crept into the bedroom.

The room was dark, barely lit by the reading lamp on the bedside table. Harry stood at the foot of the bed; his gaze fell on the wall and the picture of Lisbeth and Wilhelm on their honeymoon in front of an old majestic building and the statue of a horse and rider. Harry knew now that this picture had not been taken in France. In Sven's opinion, any half-educated person should be able to recognise this statue of the Czech national hero, Václav, in front of the National Museum in Václav Square in Prague.

Harry's eyes were used to the dark now. He shifted his attention to the double bed and froze: he held his breath and stood as rigid as a snowman. The duvet had been thrown to the floor and the sheet had been half removed so that blue rubber was revealed. On top, a naked person was lying stomach down, the upper body supported by its elbows. The eyes were directed towards the area where the cone of light from the reading lamp met the blue mattress.

The rain on the roof played its last drum roll before it abruptly stopped. The person had clearly not heard Harry coming into the room, but Harry had the same problem as most snowmen in July.

Water was running off him. Water was dripping from his jacket and onto the parquet floor with what, to Harry's ears, sounded like a thundering roar.

The body on the bed tensed up. And turned over. First of all his head. Then his entire, naked body.

What Harry first noticed was the erect penis oscillating to and fro like a metronome.

'My God! Harry?'

Wilhelm Barli's voice sounded at once frightened and relieved.

41

Monday. Happy Ending.

'GOODNIGHT.'

Rakel kissed Oleg on the forehead and tucked him in around his body. Then she went downstairs and sat in the kitchen watching the rain falling.

She liked rain. It cleaned the air and washed away the past. A new start. That was what was needed. A new start.

She walked over to the front door and felt to see if it was locked. It was the third time she had done so this evening. What was she really so frightened about?

Then she switched on the TV.

There was a kind of music programme. Three people sitting on the same piano stool. They were smiling at each other. Like a little family, Rakel thought.

She jumped as a clap of thunder rent the air.

'You have no idea what a fright you gave me just now.'

Wilhelm Barli shook his head and his detumescent penis shook with it.

'I can probably more or less imagine,' Harry said. 'Since I came in through the terrace door, I mean.'

'No, Harry, you really can't.'

Wilhelm stretched down over the edge of the bed to pick up the duvet off the floor and put it round him.

'Sounds like you're having a shower,' Harry said.

Wilhelm shook his head and pulled a face.

'Not me,' he said.

'Who then?'

'I've got a visitor. A . . . woman.'

He smirked and pointed to a chair, which had a suede skirt, a black bra and one single black stocking with an elasticated top thrown over it.

'Loneliness makes us men weak. Doesn't it, Harry? We look for solace where we can find it. Some do it with a bottle. Others . . .'

Wilhelm shrugged his shoulders.

'We willingly accept that we can make mistakes, don't we, Harry? And, yes, I do have a guilty conscience.'

Harry's eyes had focused and he could see them now, the trail of tears on Wilhelm's cheeks.

'Will you promise not to tell anyone, Harry? It was a lapse.'

Harry went over to the chair, hung the solitary stocking over the back of the chair and sat down.

'Who should I tell, Wilhelm? Your wife?'

The room was suddenly lit up by a flash followed by the crack of thunder.

'It'll be right over us soon,' Wilhelm said.

'Yes.' Harry ran his hand across his wet forehead.

'So what do you want?'

'I think you know that, Wilhelm.'

'Say it anyway.'

'We've come to take you away.'

'Not we. You're on your own, aren't you. Completely on your own.'

'What makes you think that?'

'Your eyes. Body language. I can read people, Harry. You sneak in here and you're dependent on the element of surprise. That's not how you attack when you hunt in herds, Harry. Why are you on your own? Where are the others? Does anyone know you're here?'

'That's not important. Let's say I am on my own. You still have to answer for the murder of four people.'

Wilhelm placed a finger to his lips and seemed to be reflecting as Harry rolled off the names:

'Marius Veland. Camilla Loen. Lisbeth Barli. Barbara Svendsen.'

Wilhelm stared vacantly in the air for a while. Then he slowly nodded and took his finger away from his mouth.

'How did you find out, Harry?'

'When I knew why. Jealousy. You wanted to take your revenge on them both, didn't you. When you found out that Lisbeth had met Sven Sivertsen and they had been together during your honeymoon in Prague.'

Wilhelm closed his eyes and laid back his head. The waterbed gurgled.

'I didn't know that photograph of you and Lisbeth was taken in Prague until I saw the same statue in a photo I was e-mailed from Prague earlier today.'

'And then you knew everything?'

'Well, when the thought first occurred to me I rejected it as an absurd idea, but then gradually it seemed to make sense. As much sense as insanity can. It made sense that the Courier Killer was not a sexually fixated serial killer, but someone who stage-managed the murders to make them appear to be sexual crimes. To make the whole thing look as if Sven Sivertsen was the killer. The only one person who could stage-manage something like that was a professional, someone whose job and whose passion it was.'

Wilhelm opened one eye.

'If I understand you correctly, you're saying that this person planned to kill four people to take revenge on only one person?'

'Of the five appointed victims only three were randomly chosen. You made the crime scenes look as if they had been determined by a randomly placed devil's star, but in reality you designed the star from two of the points: your own address and the house belonging to Sven Sivertsen's mother. Cunning, but simple geometry.'

'Do you really believe this theory of yours, Harry?'

'Sven Sivertsen had never heard of any Lisbeth Barli. But do you know what, Wilhelm? He remembered her well enough when I told him what her maiden name was: Lisbeth Harang.'

Wilhelm didn't answer.

'The only thing I don't understand,' Harry said, 'is why you waited so many years to take your revenge.'

Wilhelm wriggled up the bed.

'Let's assume that I don't understand what you're trying to insinuate, Harry. I'm reluctant to make a confession and put both of us in a difficult spot. However, since I'm in the fortunate position of knowing that you cannot prove a thing, I don't mind chatting for a bit. You know that I approve of people who can listen.'

Harry shifted uncomfortably in his chair.

'Yes, Harry, it is correct that I knew Lisbeth was having an affair with this man, but I didn't find out until this summer.'

It began to drizzle again. Raindrops spattered against the window.

'Did she tell you that?'

Wilhelm shook his head. 'She would never have done that. She came from a family where things were not talked about. It would never have come out if we hadn't been doing up the flat. I found a letter.'

'Yes?'

'The external wall in her study is just bare brick. It's the original wall from when the building work was done at the turn of the century. Solid, but it gets absolutely freezing in winter. I wanted to clad it with panelling and insulate it on the inside. Lisbeth objected. I thought that was weird, because she was a practical girl, brought up on a farm, not the type to become sentimental about an old brick wall. So one day, when she was out, I examined the wall. I didn't find anything until I shoved her desk to one side. I still couldn't see anything out of the ordinary, but I poked at each of the bricks. One moved just a little. I pulled, and it came away. She had camouflaged the cracks round it with grey building mortar. Inside I found two letters. The name of Lisbeth Harang was on the envelope and a *poste restante* address I had no idea she had. My first reaction was to put the letters back unread and convince myself that I had never seen them. But I'm a weak man. I wasn't capable of it. "*Liebling,* you are always in my thoughts. I can still feel your lips against mine, your skin against mine" – that's how the letter begins.'

The bed made a rippling noise.

'The words smarted like lashes from a whip, but I kept on reading. It was eerie because every word that was written could have been written by me. When he finished saying how much he loved her, he went on to describe what they had done together in the hotel room in Prague in some detail. It wasn't the description of their lovemaking that hurt me most, though. It was when he quoted what she had obviously said about our relationship. That for her it was just "a practical solution to a loveless life". Can you imagine how something like that feels, Harry? When it turns out that the woman you love has not only deceived you, but she has never loved you. Not to be loved – isn't that the essential definition of a failed life?'

'No,' Harry said.

'No?'

'Carry on, if you wouldn't mind.'

Wilhelm gave Harry a searching look.

'He'd enclosed a photo of himself. I presume she had begged him to send it. I recognised him. He was the Norwegian we met at a cafe in Perlova, a rather shady area of Prague with prostitutes and what were, to all intents and purposes, brothels. He was sitting in the bar when we came in. I noticed him because he was just like one of those mature, distinguished gentlemen that Boss uses as models. Elegantly dressed and old, actually. But with such young, playful eyes that men need to keep an extra careful eye on their wives. So I was not particularly surprised when the man came over to our table after a little while, introduced himself in Norwegian and asked us if we would like to buy a necklace. I thanked him politely and said no, but when he took it out of his pocket anyway and showed it to Lisbeth, she was swooning of course and said that she loved it. The pendant was a red diamond in the shape of a five-pointed star. I asked him what he wanted for the star and when he gave me a price that was so ridiculously over the top that it could only be interpreted as provocation, I asked him to leave us. He smiled at me as if he'd just won a victory, wrote down the address of another café on a slip of paper and said that we could find him there at the same time the following day if we changed our minds. Naturally he gave the piece of paper to Lisbeth. I can remember that I was in a bad mood for the rest of the morning. But then I forgot everything. Lisbeth is clever at making you forget. On occasion she manages . . .' Wilhelm ran his finger under his eye, '. . . to do that with her mere presence.'

'Mm. What was in the other letter?'

'It was a letter she had written and obviously tried to send to him. The envelope was stamped with "Return to sender". She wrote that she'd tried to get in touch with him in all sorts of ways, but no-one answered at the telephone number he'd given her and neither directory enquiries nor the Post Office had been able to trace him. She wrote that she hoped the letter would find him somehow and asked if he'd had to flee from Prague. Perhaps he was still beset by the same economic problems he'd had when he'd borrowed money from her?'

Wilhelm gave a hollow laugh.

'If so, he should contact her, she wrote. And she would help him again. Because she loved him. She couldn't think of anything else – the separation was driving her mad. She'd hoped it would pass with time, but instead it had spread like a disease and every centimetre of her body ached. And some centimetres obviously ached more than others because she wrote to him that when she let her husband – me, in other words – make love to her she closed her eyes and pretended it was him. I was shocked, of course. Yes, stunned. But I died when I saw the date stamp on the envelope.'

Wilhelm squeezed his eyes shut hard again.

'The letter was sent in February. This year.'

A new flash of lightning cast shadows on the wall. The shadows remained there like spectres of light.

'What do you do?' Wilhelm asked.

'Yes, what did you do?'

Wilhelm smiled weakly.

'My solution was to serve foie gras with white wine. I covered the bed with roses and we made love all night. As she slept through in the early morning I lay watching her. I knew that I could not live without her, but I also knew that to make her mine, first of all I would have to lose her.'

'And so you planned the whole thing. Stage-managed how you were going to take the life of your wife and at the same time ensure that the man she loved would be blamed.'

Wilhelm shrugged his shoulders.

'I went to work in the same way that I did with any stage produc- tion. Like all men of the theatre, I know that the most important thing is the illusion. The deceit must be presented as so credible that the truth would seem extremely unlikely. That may sound as if it is tricky to achieve, but in my profession you quickly discover that it is gener- ally easier than the alternative. People are much more used to hearing lies than the truth.'

'Mm. Tell me how you did it.'

'Why should I risk that?'

'I can't use any of what you say in a court of law anyway. I have no witnesses and I entered your flat illegally.'

'No, but you're a smart fellow, Harry. I might give something away that you can use in the investigation.'

'Maybe, but I think you're willing to take that risk.'

'Why?'

'Because you really want to tell me. You're burning to tell me. To hear yourself say it.'

Wilhelm Barli laughed out loud.

'So you think you know me, do you, Harry?'

Harry shook his head as he searched for his packet of cigarettes. In vain. He may have lost them when he fell from the roof.

'I don't know you, Wilhelm. Or any others like you. I've worked with killers for fifteen years and I still know only one thing: that they're searching for someone to reveal their secrets to. Do you remember what you made me promise in the theatre? To find the killer. Well, I've kept my promise. So let's make a deal. You tell me how you did it and I'll tell you the proof we've got.'

Wilhelm studied Harry's face. One hand stroked the mattress.

'You're right, Harry. I want to tell you. Or to be more precise, I want you to understand. From what I know of you, I think you can take it. You see, I've been following your progress ever since this case started.'

Wilhelm laughed when he saw Harry's face.

'You didn't know, did you.

'It took me longer than I thought it would to find Sven Sivertsen,' Wilhelm said. 'I made a copy of the photo Lisbeth was sent and travelled to Prague. I trawled through the cafés and bars in Mustek and Perlova showing the photo and asking if anyone knew a Norwegian called Sven Sivertsen. Nothing. But it was obvious that some of them knew more than they were willing to divulge. So, after a few days I changed my tactics. I began to ask if there was someone who could procure some red diamonds for me. I knew that it was possible to get hold of some in Prague. I took on the identity of a Danish diamond collector by the name of Peter Sandmann and I made it apparent that I was prepared to pay very well for a special diamond that had been cut into the shape of a five-pointed star. I said where I was staying and after two days the telephone in my room rang. I knew it was him as soon as I heard the voice. I disguised my voice and spoke in English. I told him I was in the middle of negotiations for another diamond and asked if I could phone him later that evening. Did he have a number where I could be sure to get hold of him? I could hear how he was trying not to sound keen and thought how easy it would be to meet him in some dark back street that evening. I controlled myself, though, like the hunter who has to control himself when he has the prey in his sights, but must still wait until everything is perfect. Do you understand?'

Harry nodded slowly. 'I understand.'

'He gave me his mobile phone number. The next day I returned to Oslo. It took me a week to find out what I needed about Sven Sivertsen. Identifying him was the easiest. There were twenty-nine Sven Sivertsens on the national register, nine of them the right age and only one without fixed residence in Norway. I noted down his last known address, got the telephone number from directory enquiries and rang.

'An old lady answered the phone. She said that Sven was her son, but that he hadn't lived at home for many years. I told her that myself and a couple of others from his old school class were trying to get everyone together for an anniversary reunion. She said he lived in Prague, but that he travelled a lot and didn't have a fixed address or telephone number. On top of which, she said, he wouldn't be very interested in meeting any of his old classmates. What did I say my name was? I said that I'd only been in his class for six months, so it was doubtful whether he would remember my name. And if he did, it was probably because I'd landed myself in a spot of bother with the police at the time. Was the rumour true that Sven had, too? His mother's tone became a bit sharp then and she said it was all a long time ago, and it was not so strange that Sven became a bit rebellious, considering the way we treated him. I apologised on behalf of the class, put down the phone and called the Law Courts. I said I was a journalist and asked if they could tell me what sentences Sven Sivertsen had received. An hour later I had a pretty good idea what he was up to in Prague. Smuggling diamonds and weapons. A plan began to take shape in my mind, based on what I now knew: that he made his money through smuggling; the five-pointed diamonds; weapons; his mother's address. Do you begin to see the links now?'

Harry didn't answer.

'When next I rang Sven Sivertsen, three weeks had gone by since my trip to Prague. I spoke Norwegian in my normal voice, went straight to the point and told him that I'd been looking for someone to procure weapons and diamonds for me for a long time and I didn't want any middle-men involved. I said I thought I had found someone: him, Sven Sivertsen. He asked me how I'd got hold of his name and number and I answered that my discretion could also benefit him. I suggested that we didn't ask each other any further unnecessary questions. That wasn't particularly well received and the conversation almost came to a halt there and then. Until I mentioned the sum of money I was willing to pay for the goods, up front and into a Swiss bank account if required. We even had the classic film dialogue where he asked me if I meant kroner and I answered in a somewhat surprised tone that of course we were talking euros. I knew that the sum of money alone would dispel any lingering suspicion that I might be a policeman. You don't need an almighty sledgehammer to crack a nut like Sivertsen. He said everything could be arranged. I said I'd get back to him presently.

'So while the rehearsals for *My Fair Lady* were in full swing, I put the finishing touches to my plan. Will that do, Harry?'

Harry shook his head. The sound of the shower. How long was she planning to stay in there?

'I want details.'

'They're mostly technical things,' Wilhelm said. 'Aren't they tedious?'

'Not to me.'

'Very well. The first thing I had to do was to give Sven Sivertsen a personality. The most important thing you have to do when unveiling a character to an audience is to show what motivates the person, what the character's innermost wishes and dreams are: in a nutshell, what makes this person tick. I decided that I would present him as a murderer without any rational motive, but with a sexual need for ritual killings. A little commonplace maybe, but the vital ingredient was that all the victims except Sivertsen's mother had to appear to have been chosen at random. I read up about serial killers and found a couple of amusing details I elected to use. For example, the stuff about mother fixation and Jack the Ripper's choice of murder locations, which investigators took to be a code. So I went to the City Planning Department where I bought a detailed map of Oslo city centre. When I returned home I drew a line from our own apartment building in Sannergata to the house where Sven Sivertsen's mother lives. From this one line I then drew a precise pentagram and found the addresses closest to the tips of the other star points. And I admit that it did give me an adrenaline rush when I put the point of the pencil down on the map and I knew that there – right there – lived someone whose fate had just been sealed that very second.

'For the first few nights I fantasised about who it could be, what they might look like and how their lives had been so far. I soon forgot them though. They weren't important – they were the scenery, the extras, the non-speaking parts.'

'Building materials.'

'Pardon?'

'Nothing. Go on.'

'I knew that the blood diamonds and the murder weapons would be traced back to Sven Sivertsen when he'd been arrested. To strengthen the illusion of ritual deaths I threw in a few clues: the severed fingers, five days between each murder, five o'clock and the fifth floor.'

Wilhelm smiled.

'I didn't want to make it too easy, but not too difficult either. And I wanted a little humour. Good tragedies always have a little humour, Harry.'

Harry told himself to sit completely still.

'You received the first gun a few days before you killed Marius Veland. Is that right?'

'Yes. The gun was in the litter bin in Frogner Park, as arranged.'

Harry took a deep breath: 'And how was that, Wilhelm? What was it like to kill?'

Wilhelm pressed his lower lip forward and appeared to be considering the question.

'They're right, the people who say the first time is the most difficult. I slipped into the student block without a problem, but it took much more time than I had ever imagined to seal the rubber bag I put him in with the heat gun. And despite having spent half of my life lifting up well-nourished Norwegian ballerinas, it was a tough job carrying the boy up into the loft.'

Pause. Harry cleared his throat.

'And afterwards?'

'Afterwards I cycled to Frogner Park to pick up the second gun and the diamond. The German half-breed Sven Sivertsen proved to be as punctual and greedy as I'd hoped. The technique of placing him in Frogner Park at the time every murder was committed was a good touch, don't you think? After all, he was committing a crime himself, so he would take care not to be recognised and make sure no-one knew where he'd been. I simply made sure that he would not have an alibi.'

'Bravo,' Harry said and ran his finger across wet eyebrows.

He felt as if there was damp and condensation everywhere, as if the water was driving in through the walls, through the roof from the terrace, and then there was the shower.

'But everything you've told me up to now I'd worked out for myself, Wilhelm. Tell me something I don't know. Tell me about your wife. What did you do with her? The neighbours saw you on the terrace at regular intervals, so how did you manage to get her out of the flat and hide her before we came?'

Wilhelm smiled.

'You're not saying anything,' Harry said.

'For a play to retain some of its mystique the author should refrain from explaining too much.'

Harry sighed.

'OK, but be so kind as to explain this much to me. Why did you make it so complicated? Why couldn't you have simply killed Sven Sivertsen? You had the chance in Prague. It would've been less bother and much safer than killing three innocent people in addition to your wife.'

'First of all, I needed a scapegoat. If Lisbeth had disappeared and the case was never cleared up, everyone would have thought it was me. Because it's always the husband, isn't it, Harry? But primarily I did it this way because love is a thirst, Harry. It needs to drink. Water. A thirst for revenge. It's a good expression, isn't it? You know what I'm talking about, Harry. Death is no revenge. Death is a delivery, a happy ending. What I wanted to make for Sven Sivertsen was a true tragedy, suffering without end. And I've achieved that. Sven Sivertsen has become one of the restless spirits wandering along the banks of the River Styx and I'm the ferryman, Charon, who refuses to ferry him across to the kingdom of the dead. Is that all Greek to you? I sentenced him to life, Harry. He'll be consumed by hatred as it consumed me. Hating without knowing whom you hate makes you turn your hatred onto yourself, onto your own miserable fate. That's what happens when you're betrayed by the one you love. Sitting behind lock and key, sentenced for something you don't know you did. Can you imagine a better revenge, Harry?'

Harry rummaged in his pocket to see if the chisel was still there.

Wilhelm chuckled. The next thing he said gave Harry a sense of déjà vu.

'You don't need to answer, Harry. I can see it in your face.'

Harry closed his eyes and listened to Wilhelm's voice rumbling on.

'You're no different from me. It's passion that drives you, too. And passion, like lust, always finds . . .'

413

'. . . the lowest level.'

'The lowest level. But now I think it's your turn, Harry. What's this proof you were talking about? Is it anything I should be concerned about?'

Harry opened his eyes again.

'First you'll have to tell me where she is, Wilhelm.'

Wilhelm gave a low laugh and placed a hand against his heart.

'She's here.'

'You're blathering,' Harry said.

'If Pygmalion was capable of loving Galatea, the statue of a woman he had never met, why could I not love a statue of my wife?'

'I don't follow you, Wilhelm.'

'You don't have to, Harry. I know it isn't easy for others to understand.'

In the silence which followed, Harry could hear the water beating down in the shower downstairs with undiminished force. How would he get this woman out of the flat without losing control of the situation?

Wilhelm's deep voice blended into a blur of sounds.

'The mistake was that I thought it was possible to bring the statue back to life again. But the person who was to do that refused to understand. That illusion is stronger than what we call reality.'

'Who are you talking about now?'

'The other one. The living Galatea, the new Lisbeth. She panicked and threatened to ruin everything. Now I can see that I'll have to be content with living with the statue. But that's fine.'

Harry could feel something was on its way up. It was cold and came from his stomach.

'Have you ever felt a statue, Harry? It's quite remarkable how the skin of a dead person feels. It's not really warm, and it's not really cold.'

Wilhelm stroked the blue mattress.

Harry could feel the cold freezing his insides, as if someone had given him an injection of ice water. He felt his throat constrict when he said: 'You know you're finished, don't you?'

Wilhelm stretched out across the bed.

'Why should I be, Harry? I'm just a storyteller who's told you a story. You can't prove a thing.'

He stretched over for something on the bedside table. There was a flash of metal and Harry's muscles went taut. Wilhelm raised it in the air. A wristwatch.

'It's late, Harry. Shall we say visiting time is over? It doesn't matter if you go before she's out of the shower.'

Harry didn't move. 'Finding the killer was only half the promise you made me make, Wilhelm. The other half was that I should punish him. Severely. And I think you meant it. Part of you is longing to be punished, isn't that right?'

'Freud has passed its sell-by date, Harry. Just like this visit.'

'Don't you want to hear the proof first?'

Wilhelm sighed with irritation.

'If it'll make you leave, go on.'

'I really should have known everything when we received Lisbeth's finger with the diamond ring in the post. Third finger on the left hand. *Vena amoris.* She was the one the murderer wanted to love him. Paradoxically enough, it was also this finger that gave him away.'

'Gave away . . .'

'To be precise, the excrement under the nail . . .'

'With my blood. Yes, but that's old news, Harry. And I've already explained that we liked to . . .'

'Yes, and when we found that out, the excrement was investigated more carefully. Usually this does not reveal a great deal. The food we eat takes twelve to twenty-four hours to travel from mouth to rectum and in the course of this time the stomach and the network of intestines has turned the food into an unrecognisable waste product. So unrecognisable that even under the microscope it is difficult to determine what a person has eaten. Nevertheless, there are still some things that manage to pass through the digestive tract unscathed. Grape pips and –'

'Can you skip the lecture, Harry?'

'Seeds. We found two seeds. Nothing special about that. So it was only today, when I realised who the killer might be, that I asked the laboratory to examine the seeds closer. And do you know what they found?'

'No idea.'

'There was a complete fennel seed.'

'So what?'

'I had a chat with the chef at the Theatre Café. You were right when you told me that it was the only place in Norway where they make fennel bread with complete seeds. It goes so well with –'

'Herring,' Wilhelm said. 'You know I eat there. What are you getting at?'

'Earlier you said that the Wednesday Lisbeth disappeared you had herring for breakfast at the Theatre Café as usual. Somewhere between nine and ten o'clock in the morning. What I'm wondering is how the seed got from your stomach to under Lisbeth's nail.'

Harry waited to be sure that Wilhelm was taking everything in.

'You said that Lisbeth had left the flat at about five o'clock. So, around eight hours after you ate herring for breakfast. Suppose that the last thing you did before she went out was to make love and she penetrated you with her finger. However efficiently your intestines worked they would not have been able to shift the fennel seed to your rectum within eight hours. It's a medical impossibility.'

Harry noticed a slight twitch in Wilhelm's open-mouthed face as he enunciated the word 'impossibility'.

'The earliest the fennel seed could have reached the rectum is at nine o'clock. So you must have had Lisbeth's finger inside you at some point in the evening, the night or the following day. All after you had reported her missing. Do you understand what I'm saying, Wilhelm?'

Wilhelm stared at Harry. That is, he was staring in Harry's direction, but his eyes were fixed on a point a lot further away.

'That's what we call forensic evidence,' Harry said.

'I understand.' Wilhelm nodded slowly. 'Forensic evidence.'

'Yes.'

'A specific, irrefutable fact?'

'That's right.'

'Judges and juries love that sort of thing, don't they. It's better than a confession, isn't it, Harry.'

The policeman nodded.

'A farce, Harry. I thought it was all a farce. People rushing on stage and then off again. I made sure we stayed on the terrace so that the neighbours over the way would see us before I asked Lisbeth to come into the bedroom with me where I took a gun out of the toolbox and she stared – yes, just like in a farce – with widening eyes at the long barrel with the silencer.'

Wilhelm took his hand out from underneath the duvet. Harry stared at the gun with the black lump round the barrel, which was now pointed at him.

'Sit down, Harry.'

Harry felt the chisel sticking into his side as he dropped down onto the chair again.

'She misunderstood me in the most amusing way. It would have been such poetic justice. To have her riding on my hand as I ejaculated hot lead into where she'd let him come.'

Wilhelm got up from the bed, which rippled and gurgled behind him.

'But the essence of farce is speed, speed, so I was forced to arrange a hasty departure.'

He stood up naked in front of Harry and raised the gun.

'I placed the mouth of the gun against her forehead. She frowned in surprise as she always did when she thought the world was unjust or simply confusing. Like the evening I told her about Bernard Shaw's *Pygmalion* on which *My Fair Lady* is based. In it, Eliza Doolittle does not marry Professor Higgins, the man who trained her and transformed her from a market girl into a well-mannered young woman. Instead she runs off with young Freddy. Lisbeth was furious and said that Eliza owed that much to the professor, and that Freddy was a dull person of no consequence. Do you know what, Harry? I started crying.'

'You're crazy,' Harry whispered.

'Apparently,' Wilhelm said gravely. 'What I've done is monstrous. There's none of the control you find in people motivated by hatred. I'm just a simple man who has followed the dictates of his heart. And it dictates love, the love that is given to us by God and makes us God's instrument. Weren't the prophets and Jesus thought to be crazy, too, perhaps? Of course we're crazy, Harry. Crazy, and yet the sanest on this earth. When people say that what I've done is insane, that my heart must be crippled inside, then I say: Whose heart is more crippled, the heart that cannot stop loving or the one that is loved but cannot return that love?'

A long silence ensued. Harry cleared his throat.

'And so you shot her?'

Wilhelm nodded slowly.

'There was a little lump in her forehead,' he said with surprise in his voice. 'And a little black hole. Just as when you hammer a nail into sheet metal.'

'And then you concealed her. In the only place even a police dog would not find her.'

'It was hot in the flat.' Wilhelm had fixed his gaze somewhere above Harry's head. 'A fly was buzzing by the window, and I took all my clothes off so that I wouldn't get any blood on them. Everything was carefully laid out in the toolbox. I used the pincers to cut off the middle finger of her left hand. Then I undressed her, took out the silicon foam spray and quickly sealed the bullet hole, the wound on her finger and all the other orifices of her body. I had let some water out of the bed earlier in the day so that it was only half full. I hardly spilled a drop as I stuffed her in through the hole I'd cut in the mattress. Then I sealed it again with glue, rubber and a heat gun. It went a lot better than the first time.'

'And she's been there ever since? Buried in her own waterbed?'

'No, no,' Wilhelm said, staring thoughtfully at the point above

Harry's head. 'I didn't bury her. On the contrary, I put her back in a womb. That was the start of her rebirth.'

Harry knew that he ought to be frightened. That it would be dangerous not to be frightened now, that his mouth should be dry and he should feel his heart thumping. He ought not to be feeling this exhaustion creeping up on him.

'And you shoved the severed finger up your anus,' Harry said.

'Hm,' Wilhelm said. 'The perfect hiding place. As I said, I thought you would use dogs.'

'There are other places that don't give off a smell, but perhaps that gave you a perverse thrill? What did you do with Camilla Loen's finger, by the way? The one you cut off before you killed her.'

'Camilla, yes . . .' Wilhelm nodded with a smile as if it were a happy memory Harry had revived. 'That will have to remain a secret between her and me, Harry.'

Wilhelm released the safety catch. Harry swallowed.

'Give me the gun, Wilhelm. It's all over. There's no point.'

'Of course there's a point.'

'And what might that be?'

'The same as always, Harry. The performance has to have a decent ending. You don't think that the audience will be fobbed off with me going quietly, do you? We need a grand finale, Harry. A happy ending. If there isn't a happy ending, I make one. That's my . . .'

'Motto in life,' Harry whispered.

Wilhelm smiled and put the gun to Harry's temple. 'I was going to say, my motto in death.'

Harry closed his eyes. All he wanted was to sleep. To be carried down to a gently flowing river. And over to the other side.

Rakel twitched and thrust open her eyes.

She had been dreaming about Harry. They had been aboard a boat.

The bedroom was in the dark. Had she heard something? Had something happened?

She listened to the rain drumming reassuringly onto the roof. For safety's sake she checked that her mobile phone, which lay on the bedside table, was switched on. In case he phoned.

She closed her eyes. Flowed gently onwards.

Harry had lost track of time. When he opened his eyes he had the impression the light was different in the empty room, and he had no idea whether a second or a minute had passed.

The bed was empty. Wilhelm was gone.

The sounds of water returned. The rain. The shower.

Harry struggled to his feet and stared at the blue mattress. He felt as if something was crawling inside his clothes. In the light from the bedside table he could see the contours of a human body inside the waterbed. The face had floated up and formed a mould like a plaster cast.

He left the bedroom. The door to the terrace was wide open. He glanced over the railing and down into the yard. He trod wet footprints on the white staircase as he walked down to the lower floor. He opened the bathroom door. The silhouette of a woman's body was outlined against the window behind the grey shower curtain. Harry drew it to the side. Toya Harang's neck was bent towards the stream of water, her chin almost touching her chest. A black stocking was tied round her neck and the top of the shower tap. Her eyes were closed and drops of water hung from the long, black lashes. Her mouth was half open and filled with a yellow mass, like hardened foam. The same material filled her nostrils, ears and the small hole in her temple.

He turned off the shower before he left.

There was no-one around on the stairs.

Harry put one foot carefully in front of the other. He felt numb, as if his body were turning to stone.

Bjarne Møller.

He had to ring Bjarne Møller.

Harry went through the entrance hall and into the yard. The rain settled on his head, but he didn't feel it. Soon he would be totally paralysed. The rotary dryer was not screeching any longer. He avoided looking at it. He caught sight of a yellow packet on the tarmac and went over to it. He opened it, pulled out a cigarette and shoved it into his mouth. He tried to light it with his lighter but discovered that the end of the cigarette was wet. Water must have got into the packet.

Ring Bjarne Møller. Get them to come here. Go with Møller over to the students' house. Question Sven Sivertsen there. Record his testimony against Tom Waaler immediately. Listen to Møller giving the order for Inspector Waaler's arrest. Then go home. Home to Rakel.

He could see the rotary dryer in his peripheral vision.

He swore, tore the cigarette in half, put the filter between his lips and lit it at the second attempt. Why was he so stressed? There was nothing left to do. It was finished, over.

He turned towards the rotary dryer.

It stooped a little to one side, but the post set in the tarmac had obviously taken the brunt of it. Only one of the strings that Wilhelm Barli was hanging on had broken. His arms hung to both sides, his wet hair clung to his face and his eyes were wrenched upwards, as if in prayer. It struck Harry that it was a strangely beautiful sight. With his naked body partly shrouded by the wet sheet he resembled a figure-head set up on the bows of a galleon. Wilhelm had got what he wanted. A grand finale.

Harry picked up his mobile phone and pressed in his PIN code. His fingers would hardly obey him. They would soon be stone. He keyed in Bjarne Møller's number. He was about to press the call button when the telephone gave a warning shriek. The display showed that there was a message on his answerphone. So what? It wasn't Harry's phone. He hesitated. Instinct told him that he should phone Møller first. He closed his eyes. And pressed.

A woman announced that he had one message. There was a bleep followed by a few seconds' silence. Then a voice whispered:

'Hi, Harry. It's me.'

It was Tom Waaler.

'You turned your phone off, Harry. That wasn't wise. Because I have to talk to you, you know.'

Tom's mouth was so close to the receiver that Harry felt he was standing right next to him.

'Apologies for having to whisper, but we don't want to wake him, do we. Can you guess where I am? I think perhaps you can. Perhaps you ought to have anticipated it even.'

Harry sucked on his cigarette without realising that it had gone out.

'It's a bit dark in here, but there's a picture of a football team over the bed. Let's see. Tottenham Hotspur? There's a little machine on his bedside table. GameBoy. Listen now. I'm holding the phone over his bed.'

He heard the calm, regular breathing of a little boy sleeping soundly in a black timber-clad house in Holmenkollveien.

'We have our eyes and ears everywhere, Harry, so don't try to phone or talk to anyone. Just do exactly as I say. Ring this number and talk to me. Do anything else and the boy is dead. Do you understand?'

Harry's heart began pumping blood round his paralysed body and slowly the numbness was replaced by almost unbearable pain.

42

Monday. The Devil's Star.

THE WINDSCREEN WIPERS WHISPERED AND THE TYRES HISSED.

The Escort aquaplaned through the crossing. Harry drove as fast as he dared, but the rain was coming down like stair-rods onto the tarmac in front of him and he knew that the remaining tread on the tyres was only really of a cosmetic nature.

He accelerated and took the next crossing on amber. Fortunately there were no cars on the streets. He snatched a glance at his watch.

Twelve minutes left. It was eight minutes since he had been standing in the central yard in Sannergata, mobile in hand, and dialling the number he was forced to dial. Eight minutes since the voice had whispered in his ear:

'At last.'

Harry said all he wanted to, but couldn't stop himself adding: 'If you lay a hand on him, I'll kill you.'

'Well, well. Where are you and Sivertsen?'

'No idea,' Harry had said staring at the rotary dryer. 'What do you want?'

'I just want to meet you. Find out why you want to break the deal we made. Find out if you're unhappy about something that we can put right. It's not too late, Harry. I'm willing to stick my neck right out to get you in the team.'

'OK,' Harry said. 'Let's meet. I'll come to you.'

Tom Waaler gave a low laugh.

'I want to meet Sven Sivertsen as well. And I think it's a better idea if I come to you. So give me the address. Now.'

Harry hesitated.

'Have you heard what it sounds like when you cut someone's throat, Harry? First of all there's the squeak as the steel cuts into the skin and cartilage, then a wheezing sound like the saliva sucker at the dentist's. It comes from the severed trachea. Or is it the oesophagus? I can never tell the difference.'

'Student block. Room 406.'

'Christ. The crime scene? I should've thought of that.'

'You should've.'

'OK, but if you're thinking of calling anyone or setting up a trap, forget it, Harry. I'm bringing the boy with me.'

'No! Don't . . . Tom . . . please.'

'Please? Did you say "please"?'

Harry didn't answer.

'I picked you up from the gutter and gave you a chance. And you stabbed me in the back, please. It's not my fault I have to do what I'm doing. It's yours. Remember that, Harry.'

'Listen –'

'In twenty minutes. Leave the door open and sit on the floor where I can see you with your hands over your heads.'

'Tom!'

Waaler had rung off.

Harry tore at the wheel and felt the tyres lose their grip. They floated on the water, sideways on. For a moment it was as if he and the car were hovering in a dream where all the laws of physics were suspended.

It only lasted for the one second, but it was enough for Harry to have the liberating sensation that everything was over, that it was too late to do anything. Then the tyres regained their grip and he was back.

The car swerved outside the student building and pulled up in front of the exit door. Harry switched off the ignition. Nine minutes left. He got out and walked round the car. He opened the boot and threw away half-empty bottles of windscreen wash and filthy rags. Grabbed a roll of black insulation tape. As he went up the stairs he pulled the gun out from the waistband of his trousers and unscrewed the silencer. He hadn't checked the weapon, but assumed that a Czech gun would stand the occasional 15-metre fall from a roof terrace. He stopped outside the lift door on the fourth floor. The handle was as he remembered: metal with a round solid wooden cap over the end. Just large enough to hide a gun minus silencer, if one was taped to the inside. He loaded the weapon and secured it with two strips of tape. If things went as planned from the beginning, he would need it. The hinges creaked as he opened the lid to the disposal chute beside the lift, but the silencer fell into the dark without a sound. Four minutes left.

He unlocked the door to room 406.

There was a clank of iron against the radiator.

'Good news?'

Sven had an almost imploring tone. His breath smelled bad as Harry unlocked the handcuffs.

'No,' Harry answered.

'No?'

'He's coming with Oleg.'

Harry and Sven sat on the floor in the corridor, waiting.

'He's late,' Sven said.

'Yes.'

Silence.

'Iggy Pop songs beginning with C,' Sven said. 'You start.'

'Pack it in.'

'"China Girl".'

'Not now.'

'It helps. "Candy".'

'"Cry For Love".'

'"China Girl".'

'You've already said that one, Sivertsen.'

'There are two versions.'

'"Cold Metal".'

'Are you scared, Harry?'

'Scared to death.'

'Me too.'

'Good. That increases our chances of survival.'

'By how much? Ten per cent? Twenty . . .'

'Shh.'

'Is that the lift . . . ?' Sivertsen whispered.

'It's on its way up. Take slow, deep breaths.'

They heard the lift come to a halt with a low groan. Two seconds passed. Then the rattle of the grille door. A long drawn-out creak told Harry that Waaler was opening the lift door with caution. Low mumbling. The sound of the disposal chute lid being opened. Sven cast Harry a questioning glance.

'Raise your hands so that he can see them,' Harry whispered.

The handcuffs rattled as they raised their hands in one synchronised movement. Then the glass front door leading into the corridor opened.

Oleg was wearing slippers and a tracksuit jacket over his pyjamas, and images flashed through Harry's brain. The corridor. Night clothes. The sound of shuffling slippers. Mummy. The hospital.

Tom Waaler was walking right behind Oleg. He had his hands in the pockets of his short jacket, but Harry could see the barrel of the gun pressing against the black leather.

'Stop,' Waaler said when there were five metres between them and Harry and Sven.

Oleg stared at Harry with black-rimmed, red eyes. Harry gave him what he hoped was a firm, reassuring look.

'Why are you cuffed together, boys? Grown inseparable already?'

Waaler's voice resounded sharply in the corridor and Harry realised that he had gone through the list they had put together before the whole operation started and found out what Harry already knew. There was no-one at home on the fourth floor.

'We've come to the conclusion that we're both sitting in the same boat,' Harry said.

'And why aren't you sitting inside the room as I told you?'

Waaler made sure that Oleg was standing between them.

'Why do you want us to sit inside?' Harry asked.

'You're not asking the questions now, Hole. Get into the room. Now.'

'Sorry, Tom.'

Harry turned over the hand that was not joined to Sven's. Two keys lay on his fingers. A Yale key and another one, smaller.

'To the room and to the handcuffs,' he said.

Then Harry opened his mouth wide, put the two keys on his tongue and closed his mouth. He winked at Oleg and swallowed.

Tom Waaler gaped in disbelief at Harry's Adam's apple rising and falling.

'You'll have to change the plan, Tom,' Harry panted.

'And what plan is that?'

Harry tucked his legs beneath him and, with his back against the wall, pushed himself up into an almost standing position. Waaler took his hand out of his jacket pocket. The gun was pointing at Harry. Harry grimaced and patted his chest twice before speaking.

'Remember, I've followed you for some years now, Tom. Bit by bit I've learned a little about how you operate. How you killed Sverre Olsen in a room in his house and made it look like self-defence. And how you did the same that time by the harbour warehouses. So my guess is that your plan was to shoot both me and Sivertsen in the room, then you would make it look as if I had shot him and then myself. You would disappear from the scene of the crime and leave it to colleagues to find me. An anonymous tip-off that someone had heard shots coming from the student block perhaps?'

Tom Waaler shot an impatient glance up and down the corridor.

Harry went on: 'And the explanation would be obvious, wouldn't it? In the end it became too much for Harry Hole, the psychotic alcoholic policeman. Abandoned by his girlfriend, kicked out of the force, he kidnaps a prisoner. Self-destructive fury ending in disaster. A personal tragedy. Almost – but only almost – incomprehensible. Wasn't that what you were thinking?'

Waaler gave a faint smile.

'Not bad, but you forgot the bit about you, grief-stricken at being rejected by your lover, driving to your ex-lover's house in the middle of the night, creeping into her house and kidnapping her son. Who is found dead alongside you.'

Harry concentrated on breathing normally.

'Do you really think they would swallow that story? Møller? Head of *Kripos*? The media?'

'Of course,' Waaler said. 'Don't you read the newspapers? Don't you watch TV? This story would circulate for a few days, a week at most. If nothing else happens in the meantime. Something really sensational.'

Harry didn't answer.

Waaler smiled. 'The only sensational thing here is that you thought I wouldn't find you.'

'Are you sure about that?'

'About what?'

'That I didn't know you would find your way here.'

'If so, had I been in your shoes, I would have done a runner. There's no way out now, Hole.'

'That's right,' Harry said, putting a hand in his jacket pocket.

Waaler raised his gun. Harry took out a wet packet of cigarettes.

'I'm sitting in a trap. The question is: Who is the trap for?'

He took a cigarette out of the packet.

Waaler's eyes narrowed. 'What do you mean?'

'Well,' Harry said, tearing the cigarette in half and putting the filter between his lips, 'national holidays are a pain, aren't they? There are never enough people on duty to get things put away, so everything's delayed. Such as, for example, putting up surveillance cameras in a student block. Or taking them down again.'

Harry noticed a small twitch in his colleague's eyelid. He pointed with his thumb back over his shoulder. 'Look up in the right-hand corner, Tom. Do you see it?'

Waaler's eyes leapt over to where Harry was pointing and then back again.

'As I said, I know what makes you tick, Tom. I knew that you would find us here sooner or later. I just had to make it difficult enough that you wouldn't think you were being lured into a trap. On Sunday morning I had a long chat with a person you know. He's been sitting in his bus since then waiting to record this scene. Wave to Otto Tangen.'

'You're bluffing, Harry. I know Tangen, and he would never have dared do anything like this.'

'I said he could have all the sales rights for the recording. Just think about it, Tom. A recording of the big showdown, starring the alleged Courier Killer, the crazy detective and the corrupt police inspector. Television companies the world over will be queuing for it.'

Harry took a pace forwards.

'Perhaps you'd better give me the gun now before you make things worse than they already are, Tom.'

'Stay right there, Harry,' Waaler whispered, and Harry saw that the gun barrel had swung round into Oleg's back. He stopped. Tom Waaler had stopped blinking. His jaw muscles were working hard with the concentration. No-one moved. It was so quiet in the building that Harry thought he could hear the sound of the walls: a long-wave, almost inaudible vibration that the ear registered as tiny changes in the air pressure. While the walls sang, ten seconds passed. Ten unending seconds in which Waaler did not blink. Øystein had once told Harry how much data a human brain could handle in one second. He couldn't remember the figure, but Øystein had explained that it meant a human could easily scan through the contents of the average town library in ten of these seconds.

Waaler finally blinked and Harry noticed a kind of calm descend over him. He didn't know what it meant, only that it was probably bad news.

'The interesting thing about murder cases,' Waaler said, 'is that you're innocent until proven guilty. And for the time being I cannot see how any cameras here have filmed me doing anything illegal.'

He went over to Harry and Sven and jerked hard at the handcuffs so that Sven got to his feet. Waaler searched them by running his free hand over the outside of their jackets and trousers while keeping his eyes on Harry.

'On the contrary, I'm just doing my job as a policeman. Arresting a policeman who kidnapped a prisoner from the custody block.'

'You've just confessed in front of a camera,' Harry said.

'To you, yes,' Waaler smiled. 'As far as I remember these cameras only record image, not sound. This is a normal arrest. Start moving towards the lift.'

'What about kidnapping a ten-year-old?' Harry said. 'Tangen has got pictures of you pointing a gun at a boy?'

'Oh, him,' Waaler said, shoving Harry so hard that he staggered forwards taking Sven with him.

'He obviously got up in the middle of the night and went down to the police station without saying anything to his mother. He's done it before, hasn't he? Let's just say that I met the boy outside when I was on my way out to find you and Sven. The boy obviously knew something was up. When I explained the situation he said he wanted to help. In fact, it was him who suggested that I use him as a hostage so that you wouldn't do anything stupid and get hurt, Harry.'

'A ten-year-old?' Harry groaned. 'Do you really think that anyone will believe that?'

'We'll see,' Waaler said. 'OK, everyone, we go out through here and stop in front of the lift. The first person to try anything gets the first bullet.'

Waaler went over to the lift and pressed the button. A rumbling sound came from the depths of the shaft.

'Strange how quiet it is in a student block during the holidays, isn't it?'

He gave Sven a smile.

'Like a haunted house.'

'Give up, Tom.'

Harry had to concentrate to articulate the words, his mouth seemed to be full of sand.

'It's too late. You must know that no-one will believe you.'

'You're beginning to repeat yourself, my dear colleague,' Waaler said casting a glance at the slanting needle as it rotated, slowly like a compass, behind the glass cover.

'They'll believe me, Harry. For the simple reason . . .' He ran a finger across his top lip. '. . . that no-one will be able to contradict me.'

Harry knew what the plan was now. The lift. There was no camera in the lift. That's where it was going to happen. He didn't know how Waaler had imagined he would present it afterwards – a scuffle had broken out and Harry had grabbed the gun – but he was in no doubt: they were all going to die there, in the lift.

'Daddy . . .' Oleg began to say.

'Everything'll be OK, son,' Harry said, trying to smile.

'Yes,' Waaler said. 'Everything'll be OK.'

They heard a clicking noise, a metallic smacking sound. The lift was getting closer. Harry looked at the round wooden handle on the lift door. He had secured the gun in such a way that he could place his hand around the handle of the gun, put his finger on the trigger and pull it off all in one movement.

The lift stopped in front of them with a thud and swayed a little.

Harry breathed in and stretched out his hand. His fingers closed around and underneath the tiled wooden surface. He expected to feel the cold, hard steel against his fingertips. Nothing. Absolutely nothing. Only more wood. And a loose bit of tape.

Tom Waaler sighed.

'I'm afraid I threw it down the disposal chute, Harry. Did you really think I wouldn't search for planted weapons?'

Waaler pulled open the iron door with one hand while pointing the gun at them.

'The boy goes in first.'

Harry averted his eyes when Oleg looked up at him. He couldn't meet Oleg's questioning gaze searching for further assurances. Instead Harry nodded mutely towards the door. Oleg went in and stood at the back of the lift. A dim light from the ceiling fell onto the brown walls of imitation rosewood and a collage of declarations of love, slogans, sexual organs and greetings carved into its surface.

SCREW U was etched above Oleg's head.

A burial chamber, Harry thought. It was a burial chamber.

He stuffed his free hand inside his jacket pocket. As he had demonstrated before, he didn't like lifts. Harry jerked his left hand and the sudden movement sent Sven sprawling against Waaler. Waaler turned towards Sven as Harry raised his right hand over his head. He took aim like a matador with a sword. He knew he would get only one stab, and accuracy was more important than power.

He brought down his hand.

The point of the chisel went through the leather jacket with a tearing sound. The metal end sank into the soft tissue over the right collarbone, perforated the jugular vein and penetrated the network of nerves in the plexus brachialis and paralysed the motor neurones leading to the arm. There was a clunk as the gun hit the stone floor and clattered down the stairs. Waaler looked down at his right shoulder with an expression of surprise. Beneath the protruding short green handle his arm hung limply by his side.

*

It had been a long, shitty day for Tom Waaler. The shit had started when he was woken up and told that Harry had taken Sivertsen and cleared off. And it continued when it proved to be much harder to find Harry than he had anticipated. Tom had explained to the others in the association that they would have to use the boy. They had refused; it was too risky, they said. In his heart of hearts he had always known that he would have to take the last few steps on his own. It was always like that. No-one would stop him and no-one would help him. Loyalty was a question of how much something was worth; charity began at home. And the shit just kept coming. He couldn't feel his arm any longer. The only thing he felt was the warm stream down his chest telling him that something with a lot of blood in it had been punctured.

He turned towards Harry again, just in time to see his face grow in size, and the next moment his head was filled with a crunching sound as Harry's spring-loaded skull hit him over the bridge of his nose. Harry took a swing at him with his right arm, but Waaler managed to move out of the way. Harry went after him, but was pulled back by Sven Sivertsen's left arm. Tom inhaled greedily through his mouth as he felt the pain unleash the blind, life-giving rage into his veins. He regained his balance. In all senses. He estimated the distance, went into a crouch position, kicked out and whirled round on one foot with the other held high. It was a perfect *O'ou tek* and hit Harry in the temple. He fell sideways and dragged Sven Sivertsen down with him.

Tom turned and looked for the gun. It was on the landing below them. He held onto the railing and was down there in two bounds. His right arm still wouldn't obey him. He swore, picked up the gun with his left hand and sprinted back.

Harry and Sven had disappeared.

He turned, just in time to see the lift door close. He clenched the gun between his teeth, grabbed hold of the door handle with his left hand and yanked. It felt as if his arm was coming out of its socket. Locked. Tom put his face against the round window in the door. They had pulled the grille shut and he could hear the excited voices inside.

An absolutely shit day. But now it was going to come to an end. Now it would be perfect. Tom raised his gun.

Out of breath, Harry leaned against the back wall and waited for the lift to move. He had just managed to close the grille and press the BASEMENT button when the door began to shake and they heard Waaler swearing on the other side.

'The bloody lift won't start!' wheezed Sven. He had sunk down to his knees beside Harry.

The lift gave a jerk, like a massive hiccup, but it didn't move.

'If the bloody lift is that slow, he can just run down the stairs and then say "welcome back" when we get there!'

'Hell,' Harry muttered. 'The door between the entrance and the basement is locked.'

Harry saw a shadow flit across the round window.

'Look out!' he screamed, pushing Oleg over towards the grille.

The sound was like a cork being drawn out of a wine bottle as the bullet bored its way into the pseudo-rosewood panel above Harry's head. He pulled Sven over towards Oleg.

At that moment the lift jerked again and, with a lot of creaking noises, started to move.

'Fuck,' Sven whispered.

'Harry . . .' Oleg began.

There was a crash. Harry caught a fleeting glimpse of a clenched fist between the latticework of the grille and above Oleg's head before he instinctively closed his eyes as the glass fragments showered over him.

'Harry!'

Oleg's scream went right through Harry. Through his ears, his nose, his mouth, his throat, he drowned in it. Harry opened his eyes again and looked straight into Oleg's wide-open eyes; his gaping mouth distorted with pain and panic; his long, black hair caught by a large white hand. Oleg was being lifted off the floor.

'Harry!'

Harry went blind. He thrust open his eyes, but couldn't see anything. Only a white sheet of panic. But he could hear. Hear Sis screaming.

'Harry!'

He could hear Ellen screaming. Rakel screaming. Everyone was screaming his name.

'Harry!'

He stared into the white void as it slowly transformed itself into black. Had he passed out? The screams subsided, like fading echoes. He floated away. They were right. He was never there when it mattered. He made sure he was elsewhere. Packed his case. Opened a bottle. Locked the door. Became scared. Went blind. They were always right. And if they weren't, they would be.

'Daddy!'

A foot struck him in the chest. He could see again. Oleg was dangling in front of him, his legs kicking out; his head held tight in Waaler's hand. But the lift had stopped. He instantly saw why. The grille had been knocked out of position. Harry looked at Sven, who was sitting on the floor beside him, his eyes fixed into a frozen stare.

'Harry!' Waaler's voice from outside. 'Bring the lift up or I'll shoot the boy.'

Harry stood up and then ducked again immediately. He had seen what he needed to see. The door to the fourth floor was half a metre higher than the lift.

'If you shoot from there, Tangen will have the murder on film,' Harry said.

He heard Waaler's deep laugh.

'Tell me, Harry. If this cavalry of yours really exists, shouldn't it have ridden in before now?'

'Daddy . . .' Oleg moaned.

Harry closed his eyes.

'Listen, Tom. The lift won't move as long as the grille isn't properly shut. Your arm is between the bars, so you had better let Oleg go so that we can get it into position.'

Waaler laughed again.

'Do you think I'm stupid, Harry? The grille only needs to move a few centimetres. You can manage that without me letting go of the boy.'

Harry looked at Sven, but only received an unfocused, faraway look in return.

'OK,' Harry said. 'But I've got cuffs on, so I'll need Sven's help. And at this moment it looks as if he's freaked out.'

'Sven!' Waaler shouted. 'Can you hear?'

Sven barely raised his head.

'Do you remember Lodin, Sven? Your predecessor in Prague?'

The echo rumbled down to the entrance. Sven swallowed.

'Head fell in a lathe, Sven. Fancy trying that?'

Sven staggered to his feet. Harry grabbed his collar and pulled him up close.

'Do you know what you've got to do, Sven?' he shouted into wan, trance-like features as he put his hand into his back pocket and brought out a key.

'Make sure the grille stays in position. Do you hear? Hold the grille tight when we start.'

Harry pointed to one of the worn, round, black buttons on the panel.

Sven gazed intently at Harry as he put the key in the lock for the handcuffs and twisted. Then he nodded.

'OK,' Harry shouted. 'We're ready. We're putting the grille in position.'

Sven stood with his back to the grille. He took hold with both hands and pushed to the right. Waaler groaned as the latticework pulled his arm the same way. There was a gentle click as the contact points on the floor and the grille met.

'There!' Harry shouted.

They waited. Harry took a step across the lift and stared up. In a small crack between the round window and Waaler's shoulder two eyes glared down at him. One, Waaler's enraged, wide-open eye; the other, the black, unseeing eye of the gun.

'Come back up,' Waaler said.

'If you spare the boy,' Harry said.

'It's a deal.'

Harry nodded slowly. Then he pressed the button.

'I knew you would do the right thing in the end, Harry.'

'One usually does,' Harry said.

He saw Waaler's one eyebrow suddenly darken. Maybe it was because he had just discovered that the handcuffs were hanging from one of Harry's wrists. Maybe it was something in Harry's intonation. Or maybe he felt it too. That the moment had come.

There was an ominous scream in the steel wires as the lift jerked into action. At the same moment Harry took a quick pace forward and stretched up on his toes. There was a dry click as the handcuff locked into place around Waaler's wrist.

'Bloody h –' Waaler began.

Harry lifted one leg. The handcuffs were biting into both of their wrists as Hole's 95 kilos dragged Waaler down. Waaler tried to take the strain, but his arm was pulled through the window until it was blocked by his shoulder.

A shit day.

'Let me go, for fuck's sake!' Tom screamed, as his chin pressed against the iron door. He tried to pull his arm back, but it was too heavy. He bellowed with rage and slammed his gun against the iron door. It wasn't supposed to be like this. They were ruining everything for him. They'd destroyed the sandcastle, kicked it to pieces and now stood there laughing. But they would see, one day they would see. That was when he noticed. That the bars of the grille were touching his lower arm, that the lift was moving. But the wrong way. Downwards. He felt his throat tighten when he realised. That he was going to be crushed. That the lift was now a slow-motion guillotine. That he too was about to meet his fate.

'Hold the grille tight, Sven!' Harry shouted.

Tom let go of Oleg and tried to pull his arm away. But Harry was too heavy. Tom panicked. He made another desperate attempt to free himself. And another. His feet skidded on the slippery floor. He felt the inside of the lift roof against his shoulder. All reasoning deserted him.

'Don't, Harry. Stop.'

He meant to shout, but sobs stifled his words.

'Mercy . . .'

43

Monday Night. Rolex.

TICK, TICK, TICK.

Harry sat listening to the second hand with his eyes closed while he counted. He mused that the time would have to be pretty accurate since the ticking was coming from a gold Rolex watch.

Tick, tick, tick.

If he had counted correctly he had been sitting in the lift for a quarter of an hour now. Fifteen minutes. Nine hundred seconds since he had pressed the stop button between the ground floor and the basement and announced that now they were safe and would have to wait. For nine hundred seconds they had sat as quiet as mice, listening. For footsteps. Voices. Doors being opened and closed. While Harry, his eyes closed, had counted the nine hundred ticks from the Rolex watch on the wrist of the blood-covered arm on the lift floor, and still attached to his handcuffs.

Tick, tick, tick.

Harry opened his eyes. He unlocked the handcuffs and wondered

how he was going to get into the boot of the car now that he had
swallowed the key.

'Oleg,' he whispered and gently shook the sleeping boy's shoulder.
'I need you to help me.'

Oleg got to his feet.

'What's the point?' Sven asked, looking up at Oleg who was standing
on Harry's shoulders and detaching the strip lighting from the roof of
the lift.

'Take it,' Harry said.

Sven reached up to Oleg and took one of the two tubes.

'Firstly, so that my eyes get used to the dark before I go out into
the basement,' Harry said. 'Secondly, so that we don't stand here in the
light blinking when the lift door opens.'

'Waaler? In the basement?' Sven's voice was full of disbelief. 'Come
on, no-one can survive that.'

He pointed with the light tube to the already pale, wax-like arm on
the floor.

'Imagine how much blood he lost. And the shock.'

'I'm trying to anticipate every eventuality,' Harry said.

Then it went dark.

Tick, tick, tick.

Harry stepped out of the lift, moved quickly to the side and crouched
down. He heard the door close softly behind him. He waited until he
heard the lift start. The arrangement had been that they should stop
the lift between the basement and the ground floor where they would
be safe.

Harry listened with bated breath. So far, no sign of ghosts. He stood
up. Faint light shone through a door window at the other end of the
basement. He made out the shapes of garden furniture, old chests of
drawers and the tips of skis behind the wire netting. Harry groped his
way along the wall. He found a door and opened it. There was the
sweet smell of refuse. He had come to the right place. He trod on torn

rubbish bags, eggshells and empty milk cartons as he fumbled his way through the sticky heat generated by the decomposing waste. The gun was over by the wall. One of the bits of tape was still attached. He made sure that it was still loaded before he went out again.

He moved in a crouch towards the door where the light was coming from.

It was only when he was close up that he saw the dark outline against the window. It was a face. Harry automatically dropped onto his haunches before he realised that the person could not see him in the dark. He held the gun in front of him with both hands as he crept two steps forward. The face was pressed up tight against the glass so that all the features were distorted. Harry had the face in the sights of his gun. It was Tom. His wide-open eyes stared beyond him and into the dark.

Harry's heart thumped so hard he could not keep the sights on the gun still.

He waited. The seconds came and went. Nothing happened.

Then he lowered his gun and straightened up.

He went to the window and looked into Tom's glazed eyes. They were covered over with a bluish-white film. Harry turned round and tried to penetrate the dark. Whatever Tom had been staring at, it was gone now.

Harry stood still, feeling the dogged, insistent throb of his pulse. Tick, tick, tick, it went. He didn't quite know what it meant. Except that he was alive, because the man on the other side of the door was dead. And that he could unlock the door, put a hand against that man's skin and feel the body heat leaving him, feel the skin changing texture, losing the substance of life and becoming packaging.

Harry rested his forehead against Tom Waaler's. The cold glass of the window burned like ice against his skin.

44

Monday Night. The Mumbling.

THEY WAITED AT THE RED LIGHTS IN ALEXANDER KIELLANDS PLASS.
The windscreen wipers beat to the left and right. In one and a half
hours the first flashes of dawn would appear, but for the moment it
was night and the clouds lay like a grey-black tarpaulin over the town.

Harry was sitting in the back seat with his arm round Oleg.

A woman and a man came staggering down the deserted pavement
in Waldemar Thranes gate towards them.

An hour had passed since Harry, Sven and Oleg had got out of the
lift, into the rain and onto solid ground. They found a tall birch tree
Harry had seen from Marius's window and threw themselves onto the
dry grass. From there Harry had phoned the editor's desk at *Dagbladet*
first of all and spoken to the journalist on duty. Then he rang Bjarne
Møller, told him what had happened and asked him to run a trace on
Øystein Eikeland. Finally, he rang Rakel and woke her up. Twenty
minutes later the area in front of the student building was lit up by
the flashes of cameras and blue lights with press and police in the
same wonderful combination as always.

Harry, Oleg and Sven had sat under the birch tree watching them run in and out of the student block.

Then Harry stubbed out his cigarette.

'Oh well,' Sven said.

'"Character",' Harry said.

Sven nodded and said: 'I forgot that one.'

Then they strolled down to the square and Bjarne Møller sprinted out and ushered them into one of the police cars.

First of all they went to Police HQ to be briefly interviewed by the police, or for a 'debriefing', as Møller had considerately called it. When Sven was taken into custody, Harry insisted that two front-line officers should stand guard outside his cell 24 hours a day. Møller, somewhat surprised, asked Harry if he really thought that the risk of him escaping was that great. Harry answered with a shake of his head and Møller complied with his wishes without saying another word.

Then they contacted the regular uniformed police and got hold of a patrol car to drive Oleg home.

The bleeping noise accompanying the traffic lights cut into the still night air as the couple crossed Uelands gate. The woman had obviously borrowed the man's jacket and held it over her head. The man's shirt was stuck to his body and he was laughing out loud. Harry thought there was something familiar about him.

The lights changed to green.

He caught a glimpse of red hair under the woman's jacket before the couple passed out of sight.

When they passed Vinderen, it suddenly stopped raining. Like curtains on the stage, the clouds slid away and a new moon shone on them from a black sky over Oslo fjord.

'At last,' Møller said, turning round in the front passenger seat with a smile.

Harry assumed he was referring to the rain.

'At last,' he answered, without taking his eyes off the moon.

'You're a very brave boy,' Møller said, patting the boy's knee. Oleg gave a wan smile and looked up at Harry.

Møller turned round again and kept his eyes forward on the road ahead.

'My stomach pains have gone,' he said. 'Vanished into thin air.'

They had found Øystein Eikeland in the same place that they took Sven Sivertsen. In the custody block. According to 'Griever' Groth's papers, Øystein had been brought in by Tom Waaler on suspicion of driving a taxi while drunk. The blood sample he had given had in fact also shown some evidence of alcohol. When Møller ordered that Eikeland was to be released and that all formalities were to be dropped, 'Griever' Groth, surprisingly enough, had no objections. On the contrary, he was unusually obliging.

Rakel was standing in the doorway as the police car swung onto the crunching gravel of the drive in front of her house.

Harry leaned across Oleg and opened the door. Oleg jumped out and ran towards Rakel.

Møller and Harry stayed in the car and watched the two of them silently hugging each other on the steps.

Møller's mobile phone rang and he raised it to his ear. He said 'Yes' twice and 'Right' once and rang off.

'That was Beate. They've found a bag full of cycling equipment in the refuse bin in the yard at Barli's place.'

'Mm.'

'It's going to be hell,' Møller said. 'They're all going to want a chunk of you, Harry. Akersgata, NRK, TV2. Foreign press as well. Just imagine, they've heard about the Courier Killer in Spain. Well, you've done all that stuff before, so you know how it goes.'

'I'll survive.'

'I suppose you will. We've got some footage of what happened in the student place last night, too. I just wonder how Tangen managed to set up the recording in his bus on Sunday afternoon and then forget to switch it off and catch the train home to Hønefoss.'

Møller studied Harry's face, but Harry remained impassive.

'And, on top of that, what a stroke of luck that he'd just wiped the hard disk so that there was enough space for several days' recording. Incredible actually. You could almost think that it had been planned beforehand.'

'Almost,' Harry mumbled.

'There's going to be an internal inquiry. I have contacted SEFO and informed them about Waaler's activities. We are not discounting the possibility that this case may have ramifications for the Force. I have the first meeting with them tomorrow. We'll get to the bottom of this, Harry.'

'Fine, boss.'

'Fine? You don't sound very convinced.'

'Well, are you?'

'Why shouldn't I be?'

'Because you don't know who you can trust, not even you.'

Møller blinked twice, but failed to get an answer out; he flashed a glance across to the policeman sitting behind the wheel.

'Can you wait for a second, boss?'

Harry got out of the car. Rakel let go of Oleg and he disappeared through the door.

She had her arms crossed in front of her chest and her eyes fixed on his shirt as he stood before her.

'You're wet,' she said.

'Well, when it rains . . .'

'. . . I get wet.' She smiled sadly and laid the palm of her hand against his cheek.

'Is it over now?' she whispered.

'It's over for now.'

She closed her eyes and leaned forwards. He took her in his arms.

'He'll manage OK,' he said.

'I know. He said he wasn't afraid. Because you were there.'

'Mm.'

'How are you?'

'Fine.'

'And it's true? It's all over?'

'Over.' He mumbled into her hair. 'Last day at work.'

'Good,' she said.

He could feel her body coming closer, filling all the small spaces between them.

'Next week I start the new one. That'll be good.'

'The one you got via a pal?' she asked, putting her hand on his neck.

'Yes.' The smell of her filled his head. 'Øystein. Do you remember Øystein?'

'The taxi driver?'

'Yes. The exam for the taxi driver's licence is on Tuesday. I've been mugging up street names in Oslo every single day.'

She laughed and kissed him on the mouth.

'What do you think?' he asked.

'I think you're crazy.'

Her laughter rippled like a little brook in his ears. He wiped a tear off her cheek.

'I have to go now,' he said.

She tried to smile, but Harry saw that she wouldn't be able to.

'I won't manage,' she blurted out before the sobs shook her voice.

'You'll manage,' Harry said.

'I can't manage . . . without you.'

'That's not true,' Harry said, pulling her close. 'You can manage very well without me. The question is: Can you manage with me?'

'Is that the question?' she whispered.

'I know you'll have to think about it.'

'You don't know anything.'

'Have a think first, Rakel.'

She tilted back her head and he held the arch of her spine. She contemplated his face. Looking for changes, Harry thought.

'Don't go, Harry.'

'I've got a meeting. If you like, I'll drop by early tomorrow morning. We could . . .'

'Yes?'

'I don't know. I have no plans. Or ideas. Does that sound OK?'

She smiled.

'That sounds perfect.'

He looked at her lips. Hesitated. Then he kissed her and left.

'Here?' the policeman behind the wheel asked, looking in the mirror. 'Isn't it closed?'

'Twelve till three in the morning on workdays,' Harry said.

The driver pulled into the kerb outside the Boxer.

'Are you coming too, boss?'

Møller shook his head.

'He wants to talk to you on his own.'

Serving had long since finished and the last guests were in the process of leaving the bar.

The head of *Kripos* was sitting at the same table as on the previous occasion. His deep eye sockets lay in shadow. The beer in front of him was almost finished. A crack opened in his face.

'Congratulations, Harry.'

Harry squeezed his way in between the bench and the table.

'Really good work. But you must tell me how you worked out that Sven Sivertsen was not the Courier Killer.'

'I saw a photo of Sivertsen in Prague and remembered that I'd seen a photo of Wilhelm and Lisbeth in the same place. On top of that, forensics examined the remains of the excrement under . . .'

The Chief Superintendent leaned across the table and placed his hand on Harry's arm. His breath smelled of beer and tobacco.

'I don't mean proof, Harry. I mean the idea. The suspicion. Whatever made you link the clues with the right man. What was the moment of inspiration? What was it that made you formulate the thought?'

Harry shrugged his shoulders. 'You think all sorts of thoughts all the time. But . . .'

'Yes?'

'It all fitted too well.'

'What do you mean?'

Harry scratched his chin. 'Did you know that Duke Ellington used to ask the piano tuners not to tune the piano to perfect pitch?'

'No.'

'When a piano is tuned to perfection, it doesn't sound good. There's nothing wrong, it just loses some of the warmth, the feeling of genuineness.'

Harry poked at a piece of varnish on the table that was coming loose.

'The Courier Killer gave us a perfect code that told us where and when. But not why. In this way he made us focus on actions rather than the motive. Every hunter knows that if you want to see your prey in the dark, you mustn't focus on it directly, but beside it. It was when I stopped staring at facts that I heard it.'

'Heard it?'

'Yes. I could hear that these so-called serial killings were too perfect. They sounded right, but they didn't sound genuine. The killings followed the formula down to the last detail; they gave us an explanation that was as plausible as any lie, but seldom as plausible as the truth.'

'And you knew that?'

'No, but I stopped being so myopic and my vision cleared.'

The head of *Kripos* nodded while staring down into the bulbous beer glass which he kept rotating between his hands on the table. It sounded like a grindstone in the quiet, almost deserted bar.

He cleared his throat.

'I was wrong about Tom Waaler, Harry. And I apologise.'

Harry didn't answer.

'What I wanted to say to you is that I didn't sign your dismissal papers. I would like you to continue working. I want you to know that you have my confidence. My complete and unreserved confidence. And I hope, Harry . . .'

He raised his head and an opening – a kind of smile – appeared in the lower half of his face.

'. . . that I have yours.'

'I'll have to think about it,' Harry said.

The opening closed.

'About the job,' he added.

The head of *Kripos* smiled again. This time it also reached his eyes.

'Of course. Let me buy you a beer, Harry. They've closed but if I say.'

'I'm an alcoholic.'

The head of *Kripos* was caught off-balance for a moment. Then he chuckled.

'Apologies. Thoughtless of me. But one other thing, Harry. Have you . . .'

Harry waited as the glass completed another circuit.

'Have you thought about how you're going to present this case?'

'Present?'

'Yes. In the report. And to the press. They're going to want to talk to you. And they'll put the whole service under the magnifying glass if this arms smuggling of Waaler's comes out. For this reason it's vital that you don't say . . .'

Harry searched for his packet of cigarettes while the Chief Superintendent searched for words.

'. . . that you don't give them a version which leaves room for misinterpretation,' he said finally.

Harry stretched his lips in a thin smile and looked at his last cigarette.

The head of *Kripos* made up his mind, resolutely downed the last of his beer and dried his mouth with the back of his hand.

'Did he say anything?'

Harry raised an eyebrow. 'Are you thinking about Waaler?'

'Yes. Did he say anything before he died? Anything about who his partners were? Who else was involved?'

Harry decided to save the last cigarette. 'No, he didn't say anything. Not a thing.'

'Shame.' The head of *Kripos* observed him with a blank expression. 'What about these film recordings that were done? Do they reveal anything of that kind?'

Harry met the head of *Kripos*'s blue eyes. As far as Harry knew, the head of *Kripos* had been in the police force all his working life. His nose was as sharp as an axe blade, his mouth a straight line and surly, and his hands large and coarse. He was part of the bedrock of the Force: solid but secure granite.

'Who knows?' Harry answered. 'There's not much to worry about anyway. Since in this case it will be a version that leaves no room for . . .' Harry finally poked the dry crust of varnish free. '. . . misinterpretation.'

As if on cue, the lights in the bar began to flicker.

Harry stood up.

They looked at each other.

'Do you need a lift?' the head of *Kripos* asked.

Harry shook his head.

'I'll go for a stroll.'

The head of *Kripos* shook Harry's hand firmly and at length. Harry was going towards the door when he stopped and turned round.

'By the way, Waaler did say one thing.'

The head of *Kripos*'s white eyebrows fell.

'Oh?' he said cautiously.

'Yes. He asked for mercy.'

Harry took the shortcut through Our Saviour's Cemetery. The rain was dripping from the trees. The drops hit the leaves beneath with small sighs before they fell to the ground and the thirsty earth absorbed them. He walked on the path between the graves and heard the dead talking in mumbles. He stopped and listened. Gamle Aker church hall stood ahead of him, dark and dormant. There was the whispering sound of wet tongues and cheeks. He took the left fork and went out through the gate towards Telthus hill.

When Harry arrived in his flat he tore off his clothes, went into the shower and turned on the hot water. The steam ran down the walls and he stood there until his skin was red and sore. He went into the bedroom. The water evaporated and he lay on the bed without drying himself. He closed his eyes and waited. For sleep to come. Or images. Whichever came first.

Instead the mumbling came.

He listened.

What were they whispering about?

What plans were they making?

They were talking in codes.

He sat up. Rested his head against the wall and felt the carving of the devil's star against the back of his head.

He looked at his watch. It would soon be light outside.

He got up and went into the hall. He searched the pockets of his jacket and found his last cigarette. He ripped off the tip and lit it. He sat in the wing chair in the living room and waited for morning to come.

The light from the moon shone into the room.

He thought about Tom Waaler staring into eternity. And about the man he had talked to in Oslo Old Town after the conversation with Waaler outside the canteen on the roof terrace at Police HQ. It had been easy to find him, because he had kept his nickname and still worked in the family kiosk.

'Tom Brun?' the man behind the tiled counter had answered and had run a hand through his greasy hair. 'Yes, indeed I do remember him. Poor lad. Was beaten by his dad at home. His father was an unemployed brickie. Drank. Friend? No, I wasn't any pal of Tom Brun's. Yes, it was me who was called Solo. Inter-rail?'

The man had laughed.

'Furthest I've ever been by train is just down the coast, south of

Oslo. Don't think Tom Brun had that many pals in fact. I remember him as a nice lad, the kind of boy who would help old ladies cross the road, a bit like a Boy Scout. Strange guy though. There was something dodgy about his father's death. Very weird accident, that.'

Harry ran his ring finger over the smooth surface of the table. He felt small particles stick to his skin and knew it was the yellow dust from the chisel. The red light on his answerphone flashed. Journalists, presumably. It would start this morning. Harry put the tip of his finger on his tongue. It tasted bitter. Mortar. He remembered that it came from the wall over the door to room 406 where Wilhelm Barli had carved the devil's star. Harry made a smacking noise with his tongue. It must have been a strange mix the bricklayer had used because there was another taste in there somewhere. Sweet. No, metallic. It tasted of egg.

ALSO BY JO NESBØ

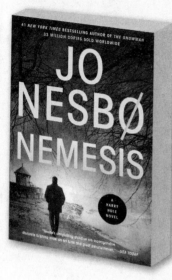

NEMESIS
A Harry Hole Novel, Vol. 4
Also available in Mass Market, Ebook, and Digital Audio

> "The high-intensity action is threaded through a series of Chinese boxes revealing one false solution after another before the brilliantly inventive final twist."

— *Kirkus Reviews* (starred review)

Jo Nesbø's extraordinary thriller *Nemesis* features Norwegian homicide detective Harry Hole, in a case as dark and chilling as an Oslo winter's night. The second Harry Hole novel to be released in America—following the critically acclaimed publication of *The Redbreast*—*Nemesis* is a superb and surprising nail-biter that places Jo Nesbø in the company of Lawrence Block, Ian Rankin, Michael Connelly, and other top masters of crime fiction.

THE REDBREAST
A Harry Hole Novel, Vol. 3
Also available in Mass Market and Ebook

> "An elegant and complex thriller.... Harrowingly beautiful."

— *New York Times Book Review*

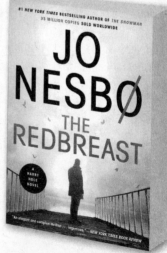

The Redbreast is a fabulous introduction to Nesbø's tough-as-nails series protagonist, Oslo police detective Harry Hole. A chilling tale of murder and betrayal that ranges from the battlefields of WWII to the streets of modern-day Oslo. Follow Hole as he races to stop a killer and disarm a ticking time-bomb from his nation's shadowy past.